THE WAG'S DIARY

Alison Kervin is an award-winning writer, biographer and journalist. Alison was formerly the Chief Sports Feature Writer of *The Times* where she wrote a weekly interview – The Kervin Interview – featuring stars ranging from Nick Faldo and Michael Owen to Prince Edward and Sean Connery. Before working as a newspaper and magazine interviewer, Alison was *The Times'* rugby editor, and prior to that she was editor of *Rugby World*. Alison also worked for the Rugby Football Union as the public relations manager of the England team, was the first woman presenter on *Rugby Special* and the first woman to referee at Twickenham. She holds coaching qualifications in ten sports and sits on numerous judging panels.

The Wag's Diary is Alison's debut novel. Her next novel, *A Wag Abroad*, will be published in July. For further information about Alison please visit the website at www.wagsdiary.com/traciemartin and visit www.AuthorTracker.co.uk for exclusive updates.

D1136263

By the same author:

A Wag Abroad

ALISON KERVIN

The Wag's Diary

AVON

For Mum and Dad and for George Kervin-Evans,
the beautiful little boy with the mischievous smile.

This edition produced exclusively for Glamour magazine by
AVON

A division of HarperCollins*Publishers*
77–85 Fulham Palace Road,
London W6 8JB

www.harpercollins.co.uk

Copyright © Alison Kervin 2008

Alison Kervin asserts the moral right to
be identified as the author of this work

A catalogue record for this book is
available from the British Library

ISBN 978-0-00782-615-5

Typeset in Minion by Palimpsest Book Production Limited,
Grangemouth, Stirlingshire

Printed and bound in Great Britain by
Clays Ltd, St Ives plc

Mixed Sources
Product group from well-managed
forests and other controlled sources
www.fsc.org Cert no. SW-COC-1806
© 1996 Forest Stewardship Council

Wednesday, 1 August
1.15 p.m.

It's quarter past one on a pleasant midsummer's day and I'm about to have a fight with a spotty teenager in a bashed-up Ford Fiesta. Quite how I get myself into these positions so frequently is an entire mystery to me.

I'm sitting in my gleaming, mud-free, furiously expensive Land Rover (exactly the same model as Victoria Beckham's . . . yeeeessss . . . took me ages to find it and it cost me more than a row of houses in most towns would, but it was worth every second and every penny). The Pussycat Dolls are blaring out, and the sun is shining down, bouncing off the windscreen and causing the sort of glare that makes every manoeuvre exciting for me and utterly hazardous for everyone else on the road. In short – I can't see a bloody thing! My leopard-skin headrests already prevent any use of the rear window, and now there's little point in looking through the front one either.

'Doncha!' I shout, clicking my fingers and tapping my feet. 'Whoops!' The pedals! The car lurches forward until it stalls terrifyingly close to an expensive-looking black and orange motorbike. The huge silver bumper on the side of my car is about an inch from its flame-painted engine.

It is at this point that I notice the ancient Fiesta directly in front of me, belching smoke and revving noisily. There's a spotty teenager driving it and he clearly wants me to reverse out of his way. Reverse? Me? That's *so* not going to happen!

'It's a one-way street,' shouts the boy, like I don't realise, and just for absolute clarity: 'You're going the wrong way down it.'

I smile alluringly, shrug innocently and pout seductively, but I don't move. I *can't* move. I can barely drive this thing forwards without crashing, let alone try to manoeuvre it backwards. Well, not without taking out all the bikes parked down the side of the road in the process, and if I did that I'd be even later for lunch than I'd planned to be.

We're staring at each other over our respective steering wheels (mine has a fleecy candyfloss-pink cover on it). I remove my sunglasses and smile at him, batting my luxuriously curled eyelashes; hoping to appear tempting yet vulnerable, and thus prompt him into action of a chivalrous nature. He's clearly not impressed. In fact, he's sneering and snarling like an angry bullmastiff as he growls and grimaces. He's not dribbling – yet – but a chin full of spittle is all that's separating him from the animal kingdom. I put my sunglasses back on. I'm sure they cost more than his car. I don't mean that in a bitchy way – I mean I genuinely think my glasses cost more than his car. They're VBD – from Posh's new range – and quality does not come cheap.

'Move your fucking car,' he mouths, his eyes narrowing and fists clenching in an alarmingly aggressive and not entirely gentlemanly fashion. I'd make a fist back, but my nail extensions don't allow for much movement at all in the finger department, so I just stare and smile, and leave the barbaric gestures to him. Neither of us is going to move. We might be here for the rest of our lives.

I would be more bothered by his aggression and male posturing if I weren't completely distracted by the sign at the end of the road, saying 'Capaliginni Piazza', venue for today's pre-season lunch – THE pre-season lunch, where you get to meet all the new girlfriends, see who's been dumped, put on weight, or had a nip 'n' tuck.

It's all women at today's lunch. ALL WOMEN. If you don't realise the implications of this then I should explain. An all-female lunch means but one thing to me and my fellow Wags – clothes! Not clothes to look pretty in, but clothes to compete in. There will be women at today's lunch who will be more dressed up than they were on their wedding day. Those who aren't will be outcasts – not spoken to and not invited anywhere for the rest of the season. If this sounds cruel then I'm sorry, but it's how things work in my world. One of the fundamental rules of being a Wag is the realisation that you're not dressing up for men – you're dressing up for other women. If this were all about looking good for a man would we need to have the very latest handbag? Or the precise shade of nail varnish that has sold out everywhere? Be honest, the average footballer wouldn't notice if you had fingernails at all, let alone whether they were coated in rouge noir or salmon pink. No, this is about becoming the Alpha Female – it's a very knowing attempt at one-upwagship, and it kicks off today at the pre-season lunch.

I'm all dressed up for the occasion, naturally, wearing a pink furry jacket with a sweet little hood and featuring pink and white pom-poms, like large marshmallows, that dangle prettily over my recently inflated breasts. It's cropped, so you can see my new tummy ring – it's in the shape of a 'D' with two little diamonds on it. My husband Dean bought it for me. Ahhh . . .

I'm wearing about £6,000 worth of clothes today, which may sound like a lot, but it is really expensive trying to look this cheap. So, while the jacket may appear as if I found it in Primark for a tenner, it actually cost £700 – that's *how* good it looks! In case there's any doubt – an item of clothing's merits should always be judged on price above all else. If you try on a £50 top and it looks great, then you see a £500 top that looks terrible, go for the £500 one every time. Remember – the designers know best. Who are you to argue with Donatella Versace if she's deemed that her top is worth ten times the price of another? You're not the international designer, she is, so trust her judgement. After all, she *always* looks fantastic, so she must be right.

So, back to me – I'm wearing a tight white Lycra miniskirt over my beautiful tanned thighs (£450! So when Mum said it made me look cheap she was sooo wrong), with a couple of heavy gold belts, hoop earrings and Chanel necklaces. Total jewellery cost: £2,500 – so there's no question about whether the jewellery looks good. I think, though, that it's the matching handbag and boots by Celine that set the whole thing off – well worth paying for quality, even if they cost a grand each, more than the cost of replacing all Dean's nan's windows last year.

Suddenly there's a clank of metal, the roaring sound of an engine that has not troubled a mechanic for years, and my would-be sparring partner is off backwards down the road – squealing tyres and rude words leaking through a cloud of charcoal-coloured smoke as he goes. The terrible language reminds me instantly of the words the fans were shouting at Dean when he got sent off at the end of last season. Mr Fiesta weaves frighteningly close to the pavement, much to the alarm of passing shoppers, because he's still staring at me – thin lips clamped into a snarl. I wave and smile, delighted by this unlikely turn of events, then I start up the engine, forgetting the car's in gear. The Land Rover pitches forward and smacks into the black and orange motorbike, forcing it backwards into the bike behind. Like dominoes they fall – four of them, one after the other – bang, thud, smack, crash.

Oh god, not again. I think there's something wrong with this car – it's always doing things like that.

1.35 p.m.

The restaurant is tantalisingly close, but the parking space is terrifyingly small. Indeed, it may well be that this parking spot is smaller than my car. I make a rather feeble attempt at getting into the space then think, sod it, I'm not going to try. I'm just wasting my time and I really don't need any more crashes today. As Dean is always saying to me: 'Tracie – one car accident a day is enough for anyone – even you.' So, with those words in mind, and with my car's substantial rear end poking out into the road, I climb out. I won't be long at the lunch, and I'm not going to drink so I'll be able to drive it home in a couple of hours' time. It'll be fine.

I clamber out to see everyone staring me. Ooooo . . . how lovely. I wonder if they know who I am? They're probably fans of my husband. Should I offer an autograph? Then a man starts singing, 'Ing-er-land, Ing-er-land, Ing-er-land', and I realise exactly what they're staring at. I always forget just how tiny this micro-skirt is. Now, everyone on Luton High Street has just had a clear view of the Cross of St George sitting proudly across the front of my knickers. Hmmph . . .

I stomp away on my white ten-inch platform boots, and swing open the door to the restaurant.

'Darlings,' I shriek. 'Let the party start. Tracie's here.'

I'm a good party animal because I like people – I like seeing other people and being seen by other people. I like football parties best of all because I LOVE being in the football world. Although I'd prefer to be in the England team's football world – with Victoria, Coleen, and the one who always wears crop tops – but until Dean gets his act together that's not going to happen.

I squeeze into a chair next to Michaela and Suzzi – the loveliest people in the world. I've known them for ages and they both always look great, with shiny white teeth and permanent tans. I always say you can tell things about someone's soul by how shiny and white their teeth are.

The waiter puts the menus down before us, and in one great synchronised move we all push them away quickly. The last thing you want to do is look at the menus, in case you see something really yummy on there.

There are twelve of us round the table – one girl has dark hair, all the others are blonde. The dark-haired girl is Michaela and she is not, strictly speaking, a Wag. All the blonde girls are. I'm not saying that for any other reason than to state the facts as they stand, but it does rather confirm my long-held belief that the real key to a footballer's heart is a head full of bleached hair. Mich has luxurious long dark hair that tumbles over her shoulders. It's glossy and healthy-looking and people stop her in the street to compliment her on it. Trouble is – it's not blonde. I've told her a million times to stop worrying about whether it will suit her or whether it will wreck her hair and just dye it – only then can she be sure of attracting a football-playing man.

While Mich has devoted her life – rather unsuccessfully, it has to be said – to attracting a footballer, and has gone through players from most clubs in the London region in the process, Suzzi is very much a one-man woman. She married her childhood sweetheart – Anton Chritchley. They've got three kids so far – Bobby and Jack (named after the Charleston brothers, who I assumed were a comedy duo but it turns out they were footballers) and Wayne. No need to tell you who the last one is named after!

Sometimes I'm envious of Suze. I've just got one daughter and I think I'd like to have had more. Then I go round to her house and see these boys crashing round the place and making a real mess and I think 'Wooooaahhhh . . . Trace – you got off lightly there.' I'm from a one-child family and so is Dean, and though I'd have loved to have brothers and sisters when I was growing up (and a father!), I've found myself repeating the pattern and only having one child myself. Odd, isn't it?

Still, I've got an extended family here at Luton Town, so I never feel lonely, and my daughter, Paskia Rose, loves watching the football (she does – seriously – she actually loves watching the football, whereas I only go to watch the other women and see what they're wearing, who they're talking to and what they're saying).

Some of the girls have gone to town today and, as predicted, they're really dressed up. I think the total cost of clothing around the table would pay off the debts of most third-world countries. Twenty-four eyes flicker around the room, taking in the assortment of clothing on display. The predominant colour is baby pink, of course, with white in second place. No change there then. We have a peculiar relationship with fashion, I guess, in that we have to be bang up-to-date on all the latest styles, but we still like to have them in the same shades of soft, girlish colours. So, in that latter respect, you could say we have our own distinctive take on fashion.

I recognise most of the outfits around the table.

'Mindy, you went for the Pucci swirls,' Suzzi says sarcastically. 'How brave of you. I saw that blouse but thought it looked just a little bit too much like Mum's shower curtain so decided against it.'

Ooooo . . . nice one, Suzzi. An early goal to us: 1–0.

Suzzi's pregnant at the moment but she manages to look great all the same, in a white Lycra sheath dress. The lovely thing about it is that it's so tight you can see her belly button through it where the Lycra's stretched over her bump at the front. Ahhhh . . . sweet! I'm so proud of her for continuing to look so great. You can tell just by looking at Suzzi that she's a Wag, and that's more than can be said for some of the girls I see on the terraces. Some would-be Wags last season didn't have a hope of bagging a footballer. One of them had trousers on with flat shoes. FLAT SHOES!!! At a football match!! I thought I'd die laughing when I saw her. Someone needs to do something to help these poor lost souls.

'Tracie, you've gone for pom-poms,' says Mindy. 'How last year!'

I smile, and they smile, and we all drink. 1–1. Shit.

Our group divides into the newer Wags (we call them the Slag Wags), and the more experienced Wags. Mindy is the leader of the Slag Wags in the same way as I would be considered leader of the Old Nag Wags – that is, the Wags over twenty-five. We're a bit outnumbered these days, to be honest. Most Wags are just out of their teens. It's only me, Mich, Suzzi and Loulou who are over twenty-five, and Loulou's husband is injured so she's off the scene at the moment.

There's a certain amount of bonding between all the Wags and a great deal of competing. I guess it's like the players themselves. During a game we're a close-knit group, but away from matches we're all jostling for position. We all want to be the number one in the team. The situation at Luton Town, though, is that I am the number one. My husband, Dean, is the captain. He's a former international player and the most experienced player in the side. That makes me the most experienced Wag, and I don't think there's a person round this table who would dispute that while I may not know much about Middle East politics or quantum physics, when it comes to matters of a Waggish nature I know all there is to know.

I'm pleased to see that no one round the table today is the colour of normal human skin. We're all shades of shoe polish – mainly orange tan, but with a few cherry browns from the girls who don't know when enough's enough at the spray tanner's.

'How's Nell?' asks Mich. 'Still crazy?'

Nell is Dean's nan and Mich thinks the world of her. I do, too – she's one of my favourite people in the world. I've no idea whether she was always so mad, or whether the ravaging effects of age actually cause *more* damage than wrinkles. Perhaps she was perfectly normal forty years ago? It's hard to believe.

Things have a tendency to go wrong around Nell. You know how some people are like that – they're always just three minutes away from the next crisis? (Luckily I'm not like that.) Nell went to have a gentle wave put in her hair a couple of weeks ago – she was after the sort of body that Elle Macpherson has but in her hair (like that was ever going to happen), but the hairdresser insisted on giving it a perm and now she looks more like Tammy Wynette.

'Nell's great,' I say. 'Mad as usual.' Then I tell them all about the hair. Mich and Suzzi are really upset about the perm until I explain that Nell's not bothered at all. The thing with Nell is that nothing really bothers her. She shrugged off World Wars and not seeing her husband for four years while he was away fighting the Germans, so I suppose a bad haircut's not going to affect her in the same way as it would cripple me. If I ever had a bad haircut it would be a drama of epic proportions, probably resulting in a suicide attempt and certainly ending in a flurry of threatening legal letters. Nell just pulls out the afro comb and gets on with life.

I can see some of the girls on the far side of the table making mock yawning signs. I ignore them. This is Nell we're talking about, she's not like other old ladies – she has the heart, if not the wardrobe, of a Wag. She's the life and soul of the nursing home she lives in. She used to be the social coordinator of the place until she invited a Barry Manilow look-alike to play there, and her best mate Gladys tried to get off with him. Barry's agent complained and Nell got an official warning. Then there was the time she was told off for chasing some old man down the corridor. 'Only having fun,' she said. But she nearly gave the poor guy a heart attack. She has a cat living in her flat, too, which is strictly against the regulations. Coleen (I named her) lives under the sink where no one can see her.

'I couldn't bear to spend so much time with an old lady, but I guess you're that much older than me,' Mindy says. 'And me,' say Debbie and Julie in harmony, before collapsing into fits of giggles.

'Not that much older,' I counter, smiling through the pain.

'Aw, come on,' says Mindy. 'How many of these lunches have you been to?'

A grin has spread across her pinched and painfully thin face. The others stare with open mouths. They're all rude, these Slag Wags, but even they can't believe the viciousness contained in the question I've just been asked. Their faces are registering utter disbelief. I can see they're dying to hear what I will say, and who can blame them – I'm dying to hear what I'll say, too. Right now, I have no idea. How can I answer a question like that – more loaded than the mini pizza starters we've just ordered but that no one will touch?

This is the Wag version of starting a brawl. It's like a footballer turning to a fellow player and asking him if he wants to go outside for a fight. No, it's worse than that – it's like one of the footballers punching another player in the ribs when he's not looking. I just stare back at Mindy. She knows what she's done and so do the others. Even though we are rival groups of Wags around this table, there is still a Wag bond, and she has just broken it. Certain topics are strictly off-limits. It's like the rule about not mentioning politics or religion at dinner parties. In Wag Land it's weight and age.

The thing is, we all lie about our ages all the time, so in order to answer questions likely to reveal your age, you first have to remember how old you said you were, and thus, with that age in mind, what the answer to the question might be. So, a simple 'How long have you been watching football?' demands the mathematical brain of a genius to work out the answer. I can't tell Mindy that I've been a Wag for exactly twelve years (it's my anniversary tomorrow!!!!), and that this is my eighth time at a Luton Town's pre-season ladies' lunch. I simply can't say that, because it's the truth, and the truth is outlawed. My world is a complex one . . . let me explain why:

Assuming Mindy can add up, which isn't guaranteed, me telling her that I've been married for twelve years will make it extremely unlikely that I am the twenty-six that I claim to be, unless it turns out that Dean's a bloody paedophile, or a podiatrist as Suzzi once said (as in: 'There's this child abuser in Luton advertising that he can get rid of veruccas!').

Still, she's asked the question, and I need to answer it. She fired a penalty at me when I was tying my shoelaces, and I have to work out whether I should leap up and defend it, or just let it go into the net and accept that we're 2–1 down against the Slags before the starters have even arrived.

Everyone's looking at me. There are glances and giggles, but I ignore them. I just offer a strained and unconvincing smile and down my Bacardi and Cherry Coke without answering. I've let the opposition score. Mindy had an open goal, and even if she did use dubious genital-grabbing tactics the fact remains that she scored. 2–1.

I call the waiter over and order myself a glass of champagne. I thought I could do this sober but, as ever, I can't. I also order a selection of fattening nibbles for the girls on the other side of the table. 'Deep-fried brie and tempura. Oh, and potato skins,' I say. 'Do they come with cheese and bacon? Do you have any deep-fried avocado?' I shove a twenty-pound note into his hand and whisper to him: 'If they don't eat the fried food, put dressings on their salads and sugar in their coffee.'

This is not an unusual state of affairs. This is what we do.

'You all right?' asks Suzzi.

I nod, but I'm not.

I'm the oldest person here and I don't want to be. I want to be like Mindy – a gorgeous twenty-two-year-old with the world of Wagdom at her pedicured feet and a beautiful striker from the Ivory Coast in her bed. I don't feel pretty and indestructible any more – I feel old. In a minute, and with one barbed comment, my world has come crashing down. This happens to me far too frequently these days – my grip on positivity becoming more tenuous as time passes and the wrinkles spread. I've gone from thinking my glass is half-full to being able to see, quite clearly, that it's almost empty.

I knock back my drink and try to think happy thoughts about my lovely daughter, Paskia Rose, and the great relationship I have with Nell. I try to think of Dean himself and how much I love him, but that makes it worse and it becomes a fight to stop the tears that threaten to spring forth and wreck my carefully and heavily applied eye make-up. The thought of my false eyelashes coming off in a torrent of tears makes me feel even more like crying. While I sit there, having a battle of wills with my tear ducts (do tear ducts have wills? Probably), the girls have moved on to talk about their holiday destinations. Mich went to the Seychelles with a guy she was seeing for a while. 'He had a yacht,' she announces, but she doesn't dwell on the subject because he wasn't a footballer so she really doesn't want people asking too many questions.

'We went to Spain,' announces Mindy, with a predictable, '*Olé!*' Then she climbs onto the table, much to the delight of the waiters who gather round to watch this drunk woman in a very short pink skirt negotiating the climb. '*Viva L'Espana*,' she shouts, while clicking her invisible castanets. She begins to undo the few buttons that are not already open and throws back her pink Pucci blouse to reveal a bikini full to the brim with fake breast.

'Good lord,' says Suzzi, as the Slag Wags cheer. They're all used to this behaviour on the youthful side of the table, except for Helen – the new girl in the group. To her credit, she is open-mouthed and looking very uncomfortable with the way the lunch party is developing. Mindy is simply unable to whisper discreetly, 'I've had my breasts done.' She has to put on a strip show at the ladies' lunch.

'Anyone for melon?' asks Mich.

'No, you mean anyone for football?' asks Suzzi, and they fall about laughing. Suze is so funny. Actually, though, in all honesty, each of Mindy's new breasts is roughly the size of a heavily inflated football.

My caesar salad comes, without croutons, cheese, anchovies or dressing, and I move the lettuce around the plate. Pudding arrives. I didn't order it. I haven't eaten pudding for years, certainly not since I started wearing a bra. The pudding is clearly part of the sabotage techniques of the Slag Wags, designed to test my willpower. I delicately smash up the creamy-white mound sitting in the centre of an icing-dusted plate and move it around without tasting it. I don't even know what it is, I just know that it's full of calories that I cannot possibly consume. I wonder whether Mindy has realised that I changed her order so she's drinking sweet white wine and normal lemonade! She doesn't seem to have noticed that it's not diet, not the way she's throwing it down her throat.

Julie's noticed, though. She's making funny faces as she drinks her cocktail. I guess it wasn't subtle to request it loaded with double cream. The sad thing is, though, that a few extra calories isn't going to make a difference to those girls – they're young, skinny and pretty . . . unlike me. I suddenly feel so obsessed by the thought of the passing years and the desperate, wrinkle-filled, grey-haired world towards which I'm clearly on a fast train, that I can't think properly, or take any joy from their sabotaged drinks.

In the end, I resort to testing myself by guessing the number of calories in every item on the menu. I work out all the various combinations. Christ, I can do calorie calculations in my sleep. I often think to myself that if they'd done sums at school in calories, I might be lecturing at Harvard now, instead of devoting my days to ensuring I look ten years younger than I am.

I'm so absorbed in the calorie-counting business that I don't see a burly man in a fluorescent jacket enter the restaurant and indulge in a heated exchange with one of the restaurant's waiting staff. The waiter walks over to the table, but I'm too busy wondering how much vanilla and caramel custard you're likely to get with the cinnamon whirl, and thus how many calories it's likely to be, to hear him ask,

'Does anyone have a four-by-four?'

Everyone at the table simultaneously says, 'Yes.'

'Is anyone's car parked illegally?' asks the waiter.

'Yes,' chorus the women.

He walks away, shaking his head, and tells the man in the fluorescent jacket that it's impossible to identify the driver.

'You're quiet,' Suzzi says to me, her voice full of concern. I'm normally the life and soul of these things.

'Sorry, just a bit tired,' I reply. 'Looking forward to the season, though.' I try, valiantly, to pull myself out of my morbid daydreams where the wrinkles and creases on my forehead are coming alive and starting to eat me up. 'I've got some fabulous new clothes. I went up to Liverpool for the weekend.'

'Oooooooooo,' they all coo, because they know what 'going up to Liverpool' means. All except Helen, our token newcomer – poor girl. She's sitting over with the Slag Wags, but she'd be better off over here with me so I could have a word with her about her clothing (her skirt's so long it's covering her knickers!!).

'What's in Liverpool?' she asks, her big blue line-free nineteen-year-old eyes twinkling like crazy.

'Cricket,' says Mich, leaning in to join the conversation. She's two years younger than I am, but everyone thinks she's four years older because she's been honest about her age. It's a shame because she could get away

10

with saying she was much younger. She's got these incredible pale green cat-like eyes. She's not as skinny as the rest of us (she's a size 8–10), but still manages to look great because she's very curvy and has these full, sensual lips that men seem to adore.

Helen is looking at Mich with such confusion on her face, you'd think Mich had just announced that she was planning a sex change.

'What – like bowling and batting and that?'

'Cricket's the ultimate Wag's shop,' Mich explains, delighting in the ignorance of a Slag Wag. It's clear that Helen is providing us with an open goal, and I can see Mich preparing for the kick. 'Fab clothes there. Have you really never heard of it?'

'No,' says Helen. 'To be honest, I really don't know anything much about this whole Wag thing.'

Not only does that make it 2–2, but the happy turn in the subject of the conversation means that I find myself on comfortable ground now and so I feel myself relax. There is nothing – NOTHING – that I don't know about being a Wag. It's my thing. I threw myself into the world as soon as I met Dean. When he played for Arsenal there was no one watching who was more tanned or more blonde.

'Yes, I got loads of new clothes at Cricket.' I'm peacocking now. 'I even got the Roland Mouret Moon Dress – you know, the limited-edition one that Posh wore when she and David arrived in Los Angeles.'

'No way,' says Julie, clearly impressed. Julie is wearing a tight leather corset dress in caramel, which is completely wrong for the time of year. As Suzzi said: 'She must be sweating like a pig.' She's wearing quite funky calf-length, shaggy-haired boots with it, and has a tan so orange it would put David Dickinson to shame, so she's redeemed herself in that department, but the dress itself is not at all Wagalicious. It certainly didn't come from Cricket, let's put it like that.

'If you've got a Moon Dress, why aren't you wearing it?' asks Mindy.

'It's being delivered,' I explain.

'Oh,' says Mindy, 'so you haven't actually *got* a Moon Dress then, you've just got one on order like everyone else.'

Bitch.

'And guess what?' I say quickly, pretending not to notice Mindy's spiteful comment. 'I had a red-carpet facial – you know, the one with the six-month waiting list and the oxygen injections.'

Helen's mouth has dropped wide open so I can see that she has absolutely no fillings – just beautiful neat pearly-white teeth. She has perfect alabaster skin and a little upturned nose. She looks like a young model, just about to take the world by storm. No surprise there, really, because a young model with the world at her feet is exactly what she is. I don't think I've ever hated anyone quite as much as I hate her right now.

'I've never heard of a red-carpet facial,' she says. 'Don't the injections hurt?'

Oh dear, I think. You have so much to learn, girlfriend. I want to say, 'Yes, they hurt. Of course they hurt, but it's my anniversary tomorrow and I HAVE to be line-free for it. Anyway, the injections don't hurt half as much as Botox, skin peels, breast lifts, liposuction, eyelid surgery, lip-plumping injections or collagen injections.' Of course, I don't say that. She's such an innocent and I don't want to scare her. 'They don't hurt too much,' I say. 'Anyway, the pain's worth it.' I think back to the time when I had fat removed from my bottom and injected into my lips. I'd thought it looked great until Dean said, 'Now you are, quite literally, talking out of your arse.'

Everyone's smiling in a half-drunk sort of way, and I can see they're pleased to have me back – their leader, the Queen Wag, the one who knows more about being a Wag than anyone. Even the Slag Wags look relieved. If there's one thing Wags don't like, it's change. Unless it's a change of clothes.

'Could you take me to Cricket one day?' Helen asks.

'One day,' I say, thinking how much fun it would be to help this poor girl – to take her under my wing and let all her Waggish beauty shine. I think of how lovely she will look once I've trowelled on her make-up, shortened her skirts, organised a boob job for her and covered her in jewellery. I order two bottles of champagne from the waiter. I'm in my element now – all thoughts of wrinkles and grey hair banished forever.

The sound of sobbing is coming from Suzzi's direction. She's been so emotional since she got pregnant.

'What's the matter?' I ask.

'I still can't believe Victoria's gone to LA,' she says. 'I'm going to miss her so much.'

'I know, I know,' I say, trying to comfort my dear friend. 'We'll all miss her, but we'll still have her in *Heat* and *Hello!*.'

Suzzi calms down a bit, then Tammie, one of the Slag Wags, starts to cry. Oh god, what now?

'Her hair. I still can't bear it,' says Tammie.

We were all upset when Victoria went for a short hairstyle, no one more than I, but you have to move on from these things. You have to let the pain go.

'Don't cry,' I say patiently. 'She didn't have all her hair cut off; she just had the extensions taken out. She can easily have them put in again.'

There's an audible sigh of relief from everyone present, and, not for the first time, I wonder whether I'm the only one who thinks these things through logically.

'You're amazing,' says Helen encouragingly. She wants to be my friend. I see Mindy sit back in her chair in disgust and I realise that young Helen has scored an own goal. 3–2 to us.

'Wags should have long hair and be done with it. 'Til death us do part. A Wag should be buried with her extensions attached. That's the way it should be – long nails, long hair, long legs . . .'

'And tans,' adds Julie.

'Of course,' I say dismissively. 'Of course, tans, and big handbags, and large accessories, and . . .' I could keep going for the rest of my life and they all know it. There's no one who understands Wags like me.

'You should write a book,' says Helen suddenly.

'A book?'

'Just for Wags. Telling people how they should dress and behave at matches . . . you know, a kind of Wags' Handbook.'

'Ooooo,' says Mindy sarcastically. 'That would be great. *Really* helpful.'

But so enthused are the others by the suggestion that Mindy's sarcastic tone is missed altogether, and they assume she's encouraging me. If I'm not mistaken that's the no-way-back victory goal to us.

I say nothing. They're all looking at me but I can't focus on any of them. In that minute, that second, I feel my life changing forever. I can sense my calling as I can sense a new trend in knitwear. This must be how Shakespeare felt when someone said to him, 'You should write a play, mate.' Perhaps it's how Churchill felt when someone said, 'You should be in charge of the country.' They would have known immediately, as I do now, that that was what they were born to do.

You see, I know the rules of Waggishness inside out and back to front. This is what I should do – use my age and experience to advantage instead of forever wishing I were younger and more innocent. It's my destiny.

I picture myself standing high on a mountain, addressing thousands of future Wags. I look down at my audience and am greeted by the sight of yellow hair extensions and black roots as far as the eye can see. It fills me with pride. Great pride. I raise my arm and the cheers ring out around the world. 'I have a dream . . .' I say, and the women fall silent, listening intently. 'I have a dream that one day all Wags will rise up and live out the true meaning of their creed.

'I have a dream that the tanning studios, hair-extension salons, beauty parlours and wine bars of Luton will be filled with desperately undernourished blonde women with large handbags, small poodles and long nails. I have a dream that Victoria Beckham will be put in charge of the world, with me and Coleen covered in expensive jewellery and working as her special envoys.

'I dream of colleges for Wags so they may learn about this art, and courses in spray-tanning and drinking obscene amounts of alcohol. I dream of every little girl being given my book for her birthday. I dream of a world in which sunglasses are compulsory, Cristal comes out of the taps and all shoes have colossal heels on them. I dream of orange legs, yellow hair, white teeth and heavy make-up. I dream of cat-fights, small rose tattoos and large lips. That, ladies, is my dream . . .'

'Yes,' I say, but my voice is barely a whisper as my mind is pre-occupied by my daydream, in which my followers chant my name on the mountainside, and cast off their flat shoes and smart trousers for platform wedges and micro-shorts. I'm so lost in thought that I don't see my car disappearing past the window on the back of a clamping truck.

'I will do it,' I say. 'Yes, I will do it.'

**Thursday, 2 August – our twelfth (ssshhh) wedding anniversary
9 a.m.**

When is it okay to wake him up? I've been coughing loudly and nudging him gently since 8 a.m. (practically the middle of the night for a Wag – before Paskia Rose was born, I would have just been leaving Chinawhite at this time of morning) in the hope that he'll open his eyes, realise what day it is, and leap like a gazelle from beneath the covers to retrieve the gift he's bought for me. I know what the present is, of course – mainly because I have spent most of the past year telling him about the adorable gold bangle I'd seen. When I didn't get the response I wanted, I told him about the gold bangle I'd seen that was sooooo beautiful and I would luuuuurvve more than anything in the world. Finally, finally, he came home last month with a bulge in his trouser pocket and I realised he'd bought it for me (I knew the bulge wouldn't be anything else – he gets so tired once pre-season training starts). Then he went through a ridiculously unsubtle performance of trying to hide the gift.

'Give me a minute,' he hollered through the house. 'Just busy doing something. Be out in a minute. Won't be long. Don't come in.'

Then he hid the present in such an utterly crap place that it took me approximately five seconds to find it. Why are men so hopeless at hiding things? Perhaps it's because to them everything is hidden to start with. 'I can't find my socks.' 'Anyone seen my shoes?' 'My grey trousers aren't here.' They always are, of course. Usually right in front of his eyes.

'Deeeaan,' I whisper gently, nudging him again. Maybe if I push him harder. 'Dean. Wake up.'

I'm really shaking him now, and there's no sign of life. How can anyone sleep this deeply? Perhaps he's dead. Could I still be a Wag if I were a widow? Hmmm . . .

I give him one almighty push and he rolls off the bed, smashing into the leopard-print bedside lamp on the way and landing with an almighty crash on the floor.

'Ow,' he says, rising to his feet, his hands clutching his head. 'Ow, ow, ow. What happened then?'

'You fell,' I say, in mock concern. 'Are you okay? Here, let me see.'

But even as I rub his head gently, all I can think is, Where's my bangle? Where's my bangle? Go get my bangle!

It's strange that I should be tending to an injury to Dean on our anniversary because that's how we first met. He was a twenty-year-old Arsenal player, knocking on a first-team place, when our paths crossed. I was an eighteen-year-old trainee hairdresser, living in a small flat above the salon, just down the road from where Dean's nan lived, hoping to become a model, and he was a local celebrity. He walked with a strut and wore oversized trousers with huge trainers that were always undone. When he shuffled into the hairdresser's where I was washing hair, I don't think I'd ever seen a more beautiful human being. I made to leave elderly Mrs Cooper at the sink, with shampoo dripping into her rheumy bloodshot eyes, and then I dropped the shower attachment, letting it bounce onto its back and hurl a heavy spray of water up into the air and all over the clients.

'Hi,' I said eagerly, ignoring the shrieks from the women at the basins, the agonised cries from Mrs Cooper and the angry shouts from Romeo, the salon owner. 'How can I help you?'

'I'd like my ears pierced, babe,' he said, winking at me.

'Certainly. Come in.'

While Mrs Cooper was being comforted in the corner with eye drops and a small glass of sweet sherry, I led Dean over to Sally, the only one of us qualified to pierce ears. Actually, when I say qualified, I mean brave. She was the only one brave enough to pierce ears. She was no more qualified than the rest of us, but she'd practised extensively with a hole punch and wasn't afraid of blood, so the task fell to her.

'Just sit down,' she said to Dean. 'I'll fetch some ice.'

Unfortunately, all the ice had gone into the gin and tonics that Romeo had been forced to provide for the soaking-wet clients at the basins, so Sally came back and told Dean it would be fine without ice. He just had to keep still.

There was a slight panic when she couldn't find the antiseptic wipes and we discovered the piercing gun hadn't been cleaned from the last time it was used, but in the end we carried on regardless. Sally pulled the trigger (making like she was John Wayne in the process, which further alarmed Dean). 'Click' went the machine. 'Bang' shouted Sally, as we both collapsed into fits of giggles. Then . . . 'Oh shit,' she said. The gun had clamped shut on Dean's ear and couldn't be removed.

Sally pushed, pulled, struggled and swore. She looked at me. I smiled at Dean, who was now exactly the same colour as the chipped magnolia paint on the walls. I pulled the gun too. No good.

'Oops,' Sally said, doing her best to dampen down the fear emanating from one of Arsenal's most promising footballers. 'Little problem, I'm afraid.'

Sally and I jiggled around with the gun, pulling and pushing it, trying to work it free from Dean's ear. Our every effort was accompanied by loud groans, cries and a considerable number of swear words from Dean. Then, he sighed loudly, made a grab for the arm of the chair and collapsed in a heap.

'Shit!' I said, jumping back. 'We've killed him!'

'No we haven't,' said Sally, showing herself to be infinitely more capable in a crisis. 'We just need to get the gun off his ear.'

Around us stood all the clients in the salon, sipping their complimentary beverages and watching closely. Even Mrs Cooper had joined them, but she stood watching with one eye – the other covered by a makeshift patch, constructed from a wad of cotton wool and a vast amount of masking tape.

Eventually, the gun came off and Sally and I both collapsed in a heap from the effort. Dean was still slumped exactly as he was before, but with a large hole in his earlobe where the gun had, until recently, resided.

I lost my job that day, but I gained a boyfriend and then, two years later, a husband. It was the happiest day of my life when Dean proposed to me, just eight months after we met. I'll never forget calling Mum and telling her:

'I've met someone and he wants to marry me.'

'Oh,' she said, with very little interest, more than a little resentment, and some comment about how old this was all going to make her look.

'His name's Dean Martin,' I said, and there was a silence on the end of the phone. Then:

'Dean . . . Martin? *The* Dean Martin?'

I was thrilled that Mum had heard about Arsenal's new sensation from all the way over there in Los Angeles.

'Yep, *the* Dean Martin,' I said, feeling very proud. '*The* Dean Martin is now *my* Dean Martin.'

'Where did you meet the great legend?'

'He came into the salon to get a piercing.'

'What? Was he with the other members of the Rat Pack?'

'No – he was on his own. The others had gone to get chips.'

'Chips? Two of the greatest swing singers in the history of Big Band music – gone to get chips?'

'No, Dean's mates . . . from Arsenal.'

'Hang on. So, who is this Dean Martin you're going to marry?'

'He plays for Arsenal.'

The line went dead. I asked a few people afterwards and they said that there was another Dean Martin in America who was seventy-odd at the time, and sang rubbish songs, so he must be the guy that Mum thought I was talking about. It turned out that the American Dean Martin died later that year . . . probably from a broken heart at being the wrong Dean Martin.

Meanwhile, back in London, the hole in my Dean's ear never properly healed (he wears three earrings in it now), but he says he forgives me. Sally left the salon at the same time as me. Last I heard, she'd retrained as a butcher, which seemed strangely appropriate.

Mum ended up coming round to the idea of the wedding when she realised how much money footballers earn. In fact, she came straight back over to live in England, giving up her sun-soaked LA life and throwing herself into the coordination of my wedding. It was great to have Mum back, although quite alarming to see how young she'd become in her time away. It turns out that three facelifts and buckets full of Botox and collagen fillers had done the trick, but heavens, she looked good. She looked exactly like Barbie. Only slightly less natural-looking.

Mum just adored Dean from the moment she met him. He really took a shine to her, too, giving her the money to buy a house and a car and some staff. She'd come round in tiny little shorts, poking her 32DD bra-less breasts at Dean, and he'd be like putty in her hands. Nothing's changed there, really.

'How's it feeling now?' I ask.

'Fine,' he says, still holding his head. 'Hey, I've got something for you.'

'Really?'

'Yes. I've just got to remember where I hid it.'

Sock drawer, I think. *Look in the sock drawer.*

'Gosh, I can't remember.'

'Well, put some socks on first, then try to remember,' I say.

'Don't be silly. I want to find your present for you, not put socks on. Now let me think.'

'I really think you'd be more comfortable with socks on,' I insist.

'No, I need to . . .'

'Put socks on.'

'But I . . .'

'SOCKS!!'

So off he goes, confused and agitated, still clinging on to his head. Off to put socks on because it's easier to do that than to keep opposing my absurd but heartfelt request. Bless him.

'Ah . . .' he says all of a sudden, the joy in his voice discernible through the wall of the dressing room. 'You won't believe what I just found in the sock drawer . . .'

Friday, 3 August
7.30 p.m.

'Deeeeeaaan . . .' I lean into my man, fluttering my eyelashes at him adoringly and thrusting my breasts at him provocatively as I attempt to wrestle the remote control from his grip. He's having none of it.

'What is it, doll?' he asks, expertly performing a quick manoeuvre to keep the remote firmly within his grasp. If only he were as adept at keeping the ball at his feet, he might have had a half-decent international career. As it is, he has a less than half-decent club career. If it weren't for me constantly pestering him to go training, get fit, eat healthily and wear bigger, golder jewellery, he'd barely be a footballer at all.

'I was just wondering,' I say, pouting my new, and let's be honest, terrifyingly plump lips at him to such an extent that he actually flinches in his seat and murmurs something about pink slugs. 'Why don't you contact David Beckham or Wayne Rooney or something? You know, make friends with them.'

'Eh?' he says, his eyes not leaving the television for the merest second, and his left hand not moving from between his legs, where he is attempting, by assuming some sort of absurd yoga pose, to adjust the crotch of his tight, shiny grey trousers that I bought him from Dolce & Gabbana. He lifts his pelvis right up into the air in an effort to disentangle himself further, and I notice how narrow his hips look in their BacoFoil-type coating. If I wore trousers like that I'd look the size of the *QE2*, whereas he looks as narrow as the ridiculous silver tiepin he was presented with by the club last year. Is that why he's not been selected for England for eight bloody years? Maybe if he were built like Frank Lampard instead of Frank Skinner he'd have had the call. Mmmm . . . Maybe I should do something to fatten him up. I'll buy loads of steak tomorrow, and chips and cakes and lard and stuff. I'll feed him till he explodes. It can be my new mission: OBUD – Operation Build Up Dean.

'You know – why don't you at least try to make friends with some England footballers? Some of them don't look too bright – I'm sure you could become their new best friend without them even noticing.

19

Then once the coaches see you out on the town with them, you might get selected to play for England again.'

'It doesn't work like that,' he says. 'It's not like school. They don't pick you because you're friends with the other players.'

'It can't hurt,' I try. I'd love him to play for England again. I don't think I've ever been prouder than I was when he won his cap for his country. It was against Cameroon. They're a really good side . . . I don't think they've won the World Cup, but they probably came second or something. Dean was outstanding in the match. It wasn't his fault that he only had four minutes to show how good he was. He got sent off, you see, then he was never picked again. No one knows why. I mean – it was only a little kick, and that guy deserved it. Ridiculous.

Anyway, I'm still proud of him. I display his cap in a large gold-rimmed frame. It's back-lit, like all that naff old stuff in museums is, and it looks fantastic. I've got the match programme framed too, and my ticket for the game. Oh, and all the cuttings about the game from every newspaper that covered it around the world (except for the one where they described Dean as a 'thug' – I threw that away). I've also got the precious squad list that the Football Association sent out with his name on it to confirm he was in the England squad. The annoying thing is that they've spelt his name wrong. Isn't that ridiculous? To spell your star player's name wrong! I rang them up at the time and screamed 'It's Dean Martin, not Martins', but the woman on reception just kept asking me what department I wanted, then threatened to hang up when I called her a crazy old bat. Still, I had the last laugh because the squad list is now hanging on a red velvet background in a magnificent golden frame.

The mementoes from Dean's international career cover an entire wall in the entrance hall. They're perfect, especially next to the large statue of Dean in his football kit. It's life-size. Actually, to be fair, parts of it are bigger than life-size. I don't know what Dean had down his shorts when the sculptor was assessing all the dimensions, but the statue is very impressive indeed. It looks wonderful, especially now we've put the spotlights directly above it. People said we didn't need spotlights, what with the three chandeliers lighting up the entrance hall, but I think it looks great.

I'd love Dean to have another chance to relive those four golden minutes and play for England once again. Above all, I'd like to be friends with Victoria, and go shopping and hang out with her and her Hollywood friends – and have a word with her about cutting her hair short.

Dean's gone back to watching television again, and fiddling with the crotch of his trousers. He can't hear a word I'm saying with the TV blaring out. I don't understand why he has to have it on so loud – he seems to nudge the volume up until everyone's shouting out at us from the large plasma screen on the far wall.

To be frank, I don't need this right now. I've had one hell of a day. A dismal, horrific day in which I made a complete fool of myself at the beautician's. Mallory normally tends to all my beauty needs – she's practically full-time, hovering over me with tweezers and emery board day and night. But, for reasons that with hindsight I can't begin to fathom, today I decided to pay a visit to the new salon in town for one of their oxygen facials. The beautician assigned to me was South African, which worried me from the start. I've only ever been to South Africa once and that was completely by accident. It was for our honeymoon and we ended up there after I told Dean that I really wanted to go to this fabulous club called *En Safari* in Ibiza. It never occurred to me that we'd go anywhere other than Ibiza for our honeymoon. I'm not sure I knew there were any other countries – just LA, where Mum had lived, England, where we lived, and Ibiza, where we went on holiday. Trouble was, Dean thought I'd said that I wanted to go 'on safari' so we ended up spending our entire honeymoon sleeping in a tent, covered in mosquitoes and watching a whole load of bloody animals. It was awful. I turned up on the first day wearing my specially chosen honeymoon outfit of little white hot-pants and fabulously high gold sandals with a gold halter-neck bikini top and a low-slung gold chain belt, and everyone was staring at me. They were all wearing plain, dull clothes. I had my gold-rimmed shades on and piles of bling that sparkled in the sunshine. I looked great and I knew it.

'Hey, man. You're gonna scare the animals,' said this man with a rifle. He was all dressed in khaki. 'And you need boots on your feet.'

I said the only boots I had were made of pink plastic and came up to the middle of my thigh, so he made me wear flat shoes belonging to some plain woman in our group. FLAT SHOES! – and they didn't match my outfit.

It was the honeymoon from hell. No shops, no nice wine bars, no fancy cocktails, just a whole bunch of rhinoceroses and lions and stuff, and all these people going, 'Aw, look – it's a baby elephant . . .' Don't they have televisions? There are bloody nature programmes on all the time. I can't get away from baby elephants when I'm flicking through to watch *Britain's Next Top Model*, and I have to say that I'd be perfectly happy if I never saw a jungle animal again – baby or otherwise.

We left the safari in the end. Or, more accurately, they asked us to leave. We went to some place called Cape Town for a couple of days. That was strange, too. I had this horrible moment when trying to find the shops. You see, they call their traffic lights 'robots' out there. I asked how to get to the shops and was told 'Turn left at the robots.'

'What?' I said. 'The robots? I want to go to the shops, not into the future.'

Anyway, that's why I was alarmed to have a South African beautician. Her name was Mandie.

'Lie on the bed and take off your knickers,' she said.

'Pardon?'

'I'll need you to lie on there without your knickers on.'

It seemed an odd request since I was only having my face massaged and plumped up with some oxygen-containing creams, but I did as I was told, lying on the bed entirely naked below the waist.

The beautician turned round from where she'd been mixing lotions and potions and jumped back when she saw me lying there smiling at her, completely knickerless. She looked at me in the same way you might regard a lunatic running down the street, clutching a large knife – backing away from me, eyes wide and looking more than a little fearful.

'What are you doing?' she eventually asked.

'I've taken off my knickers,' I said.

'No,' said Mandie, pointing to my neck. 'I said "Lie on the bed and take off your *necklace*".'

Fuck! I scrabbled back into my Luton Town thong and slipped off my choker. I'm sure she was laughing at me. The facial wasn't even that good anyway.

I rushed home afterwards to find Mum in the house – nothing odd about that, of course, she's always there, snooping around to see what I've bought and to try on all my new clothes. Today, though, I just couldn't handle talking to her and listening to all her criticisms of me.

'These shoes are horrible,' she said as soon as I walked in.

'Not now, Mum,' I said, walking right past her and going to look for Dean, hoping to have some sort of conversation with him. Now I've found him, though, he's just locked in his own little TV world. He's like a child when it comes to the goggle-box. He's kicked the zebra rug out of the way and shifted the sofa forwards, so he's practically nose-to-nose with the presenter. The only person I know who has the television on louder is Nell. She has it blaring out so much, you have to hold on to your ears in case your eardrums blow apart.

I once took Nell to the cinema and she complained all the way through the film about how loud it was. Eh? How does that work? I'll tell you what also confuses me about Nell is that she has the fire on, the central heating on *and* wears a coat, hat and gloves in August, then complains frequently of hot flushes. God help me if Dean ends up like her when he's older – I don't think I could cope.

'Can you turn it down, love,' I say for the third time, as if I'm asking him to make the ultimate sacrifice.

'It's celebrity darts,' he says, turning to face me. A wounded look had crept across his features. 'It's Syd Little against Ulrika Jonsson's sister's ex-boyfriend's uncle.'

'This is important,' I persist. 'Really important.'

Syd Little misses the dartboard completely and Dean spins round. 'And you think this isn't?'

'Paskia Rose's school report's here,' I say. 'I found it screwed up in her underwear drawer. It turns out she's really not doing very well at all.'

Dean shrugs and I feel like crying. For some reason I'm considerably more dismayed than I ever imagined I'd be at the sight of a bad school report – after all, it's not as if it's the first bad report I've ever seen. When I was at school I used to . . . never mind, that's not important now. The fact is that my baby has not excelled at her beautiful prep school. I feel as let down as I did when she refused to wear the ribbon-bedecked school boater.

Dean, though, looks entirely unmoved. He mutters to himself in a manner that suggests he's thinking, What the hell do you expect, you daft mare? We have neither a brain cell nor a qualification between us.

'Despite possessing a considerable intellect, quite precocious debating skills and having a remarkable grasp and understanding of women's liberation issues, Paskia Rose continues to let herself down in the core subjects,' reads Dean. 'Blimey, Trace. That's a brilliant report.'

'Women's liberation issues!' I say. 'By that they mean she knows all about the lezzers that chain themselves to gates and burn their bras.'

'Lezzers chaining each other to gates? What – you mean like in the videos they play on the team bus?'

'No, Dean. They mean different women. Ugly women.'

'Ah, that's a shame. I like them videos. But it says she's intelligent, love, and listen to this music report . . .' He coughs gently and prepares to read: 'Paskia Rose has managed to play her trumpet in time with the rest of the class on a couple of occasions this year. This is a great achievement for her, and a considerable relief for the rest of us.'

'Ah, that's nice,' I say.

'And there's more,' adds Dean. 'Paskia's footballing ability is staggering.' He tails off, smiling to himself. 'When it comes to football, she is the most talented pupil, of either sex, that I have ever had the pleasure of teaching.'

Dean screams with delight and tosses the report into the air in sheer joy. He's running around the room now, with his shirt over his head. 'Yeeeeesssss . . .' he is shouting. I, conversely, feel like crying. I'm not exaggerating. If you asked me to list the dreams, hopes and ambitions that I have for my only daughter, playing football would be right at the bottom; below drug-pushing and just above prostitution. However, Dean is now doing a highly embarrassing Peter Crouch-style robotic dance to mark his joy and delight at his daughter's prowess. 'Oh yes,' he is muttering. 'Oh yes.'

It's probably a combination of all the champagne at our anniversary dinner last night, the fact that I'm officially the oldest Wag who ever lived (well, not officially – but married for twelve years? I mean, that's like – old – whichever way you look at it), and discovering my daughter is set to turn into a football-playing lesbian with really short hair and earrings all up her earlobe, but I feel like weeping like a baby.

'Perhaps she'll be good at darts too,' Dean says optimistically, turning back to the television, adding a quick 'ooo' as Paul Gascoigne's hairdresser prepares to take on a guy who nearly made it onto *Big Brother*. 'The grand finale,' he says breathlessly.

We watch the finale, in which neither participant appears to get their darts even remotely close to the dartboard, me thinking constantly about Paskia Rose's problems. She's just finished the prep school and next term will start at Lady Arabella Georgia School for Girls, THE poshest school in Luton. What if she can't cope academically? Does it matter? I mean – does school have any bearing at all if you're going to become a Wag one day, which, obviously, I hope with all my heart that Pask will. In fact, isn't an education a disadvantage? Yeeesss! Now I feel like running around the room and doing strange mechanical dances myself. All that is happening here is that Paskia Rose is turning into a Wag! Perhaps when I write my Wags' Handbook (which I will definitely start tomorrow – it's been a busy day), I should have a section for young girls who hope someday to become Wags? Like career advice.

'Deeeaan,' I say, and he does that thing where he drops his head forward and closes his eyes, as if to say, 'Not now, woman.' Obviously, I completely ignore him. 'I'm going to write a handbook to help young Wags and make sure they know how to behave. What do you think?'

I'm asking him rhetorically – his views on this, as on most other things, are of no fundamental consequence. Even as I talk about it, I feel the pride bursting through my voice like a brilliant ray of sunshine.

He's looking at me as if I'm insane but doesn't answer the question in any way that could be described as helpful. 'My fucking balls are going to explode in these,' he says, standing up and walking towards the bedroom with the remote control still in his right hand and his left hand cupping himself in a rather obscene manner. 'I'm gonna stick some old trackies on.'

'Do you have to?' I am absolutely sure that Frank Lampard and Steven Gerrard never wander around the house in 'old trackies'. 'Why don't we go out somewhere special?'

'Nah,' he says.

'How about doing some training or something, then? Why don't I give you a lift to the gym?'

''S all right,' says Dean, quickly disappearing into the bedroom with a look that screams, *no way am I going to the gym and no way are you driving me.*

Good job really, because Doug, our driver, has gone home, and I've no idea where my car is. It had clean disappeared by the time I came out of the restaurant on Wednesday and I haven't had the time to look for it, contact the police, or do whatever else you're supposed to do when your car vanishes into thin air. God, life is so stressful sometimes. I bet Posh never has these sorts of problems.

Saturday, 4 August – first day of OBUD
2 p.m.

Bollocks. Where do they keep the cakes in these places? I'm pushing a shopping trolley with the sort of precision that I normally reserve for driving, crashing into the fruit section, then into the cans of soup, and then thundering into the bread products. Bread? Bread's fattening. I reach out for a couple of white loaves that look fat- and calorie-laden and hurl them into the trolley with unnecessary force. They land with a satisfying doughy thump at the bottom and sit there, looking up at me all misshapen and sad-looking. Then I spot something . . . something that looks all chocolatey and delicious . . . perfect for OBUD. Swiss roll. Outstanding! What a find! This shopping lark's not so difficult after all. Perhaps I should do it more often. I always do my shopping on the net. Or, rather, Alba, the Spanish au pair, does. She orders the same things every week – they're the only items that Magda – the housekeeper – can cook. I tried to get Magda to do the ordering herself, but she did something wrong, and that intimidating timebomb thing appeared on the screen. Then Alba threw herself on the floor, mumbling something about ETA, whatever that is, and sobbing all over the tiles. She refused to get up until Magda promised never to go near 'the violent machine' again.

It all got me so cross, especially since the only reason we employed Alba in the first place was because I wanted a Spanish member of staff. I kept thinking that Dean might be transferred to Real Madrid or something. You know – like Becks was.

For OBUD, though, I need to take full responsibility myself – no delegating the details to Barcelona's finest. So that's why I'm stumbling round Marks and Spencer's food section on a Saturday afternoon, instead of going to pilates with Gisella and Sophie – mums from Pask's school. Not that I'm bothered – bloody pilates bores me to tears – all that business with the stretching and breathing properly. I feel like shouting, 'I'm here because I want to be as thin as Posh, not to prepare for childbirth.' I read that Coleen does it – that's why I registered for the twelve-week course. This is week ten. I've only been once.

Oil. Perfect. I'm not sure quite how I'm going to get him to drink it, but I stick four large bottles into the supermarket trolley. Lard!!!

Eight blocks of it. Fairy cakes, chips, meat pies, jam, ice cream, chocolate, cream horns, rump steaks, filled potato skins, ready-made curries, pizzas, salami, cheese (six large blocks), twenty-four cans of beer . . . Out they all come onto the conveyor belt towards the cashier. I throw in handfuls of chocolate bars from the till point as I watch fruitcake, a block of marzipan, nuts, syrup, spotted dick, bread and butter pudding, pasties and sausage rolls trundling along . . .

'Tracie, Tracie? I thought it was you.'

Before me stands Mindy, clutching a wisp of silk in her dainty fingers as she watches the conveyor belt with undisguised horror. 'I'm just underwear shopping,' she says slowly, still observing the copious amounts of food being shoved into carrier bags.

'Do you want all this oil and lard together?' asks the assistant, holding up blocks of the stuff. 'There's a lot of it. Might break the bag.'

'Two bags, please,' I say, through gritted teeth, my eyes never leaving Mindy's as she tries to stop herself looking down at the beer, pizza, cakes and steamed puddings passing before her eyes.

'Well. You're obviously busy here. I'll leave you to it. Nice to see you. I'll see you for the first fat – I mean, first game.'

I smile and she's gone. She lets the silk underwear flutter onto a nearby clothes rack as she exits onto Luton High Street, and gets straight on her mobile phone, no doubt, to tell the world about my serious eating disorder . . .

Bugger, bugger, bugger.

5 p.m.

'Mum!' cries Paskia Rose in horror and amazement. 'What the hell are you doing in here?'

'Don't use words like "hell",' I instruct, as I take the swiss roll out of its packaging and lay it on a plate.

'But this is ridiculous,' she continues. 'You never, ever go in the kitchen. I've never seen you even touch food with your bare hands before. Why are you here? What's going on?'

'I've decided to cook something delicious for your father.'

'Right,' she says, picking a chocolate clump out of the top of the swiss roll and eating it. 'What are you going to cook with swiss roll?'

'I don't know,' I say, and that's the truth. I just figure that anything I cook with chocolate and fondant icing as its base will probably taste nice, so Dean will eat it, put on weight and be all muscly and manly come the start of the season. He'll then immediately capture the attention of the England selectors, who will probably make him England

27

captain, and I'll be on the cover of every magazine and be sent free shoes from every designer in the country. So Paskia Rose can scoff all she likes – there is method in my madness.

'Why don't you fetch an apron and help me?' I suggest. 'We could cook together – two little women in the kitchen, mother and daughter bonding over the cooker?'

'Yeah, right,' she replies. 'Or I could throw myself under an express train. Man, this is way too weird. Way weird.'

When I was a ten-year-old girl like Pask, I would have loved, adored, just worshipped the idea of cooking with my mum. Just being with Mum was wonderful. I couldn't get enough of it. Unfortunately, Mum never felt the same. Dad left when I was a few months old and she devoted the rest of her life to finding a replacement. My childhood memories are coloured by the images of men coming and going. Most of them were rich and much older than her. When there was a new man on the scene, she'd dance and sing and sweep me into her arms. I'd love those moments – moments when I'd feel warm and loved. Then she'd be dumped and take it all out on me. How could she ever find a man with a brat like me at home? The sound of her singing was replaced by the sound of her crying. And I knew – throughout my childhood – that I was causing all the pain. It was all my fault.

At the door to the kitchen, Pask, Alba, Marina (the live-in cleaner) and Magda are standing, hands over their mouths, as if they've just seen a flock of sheep cooking in the kitchen.

'And?' I say. 'Your problem is?'

'Oh, Mrs Martin, Mrs Martin. This is a kitchen – a kitchen,' says Marina, attempting to guide me out of the room with an arm around my shoulders, as if I am a little old lady who has just wandered into a gay bar. 'You shouldn't be in here. This place is not for you. Is dangerous. Come, come. Let me help.'

'No,' I say bravely, standing up straight and pushing her arm off. 'This is my kitchen and I *will* cook in it.'

I walk back to the swiss roll with my head held high, and reach into the cupboard to pull out the lard and the oil. I have no idea what to do with these, but I know they contain the necessary fat to build up Dean. There's a collective intake of breath from the doorway and the sound of three women and a girl muttering 'Lard?'

'I want to be alone,' I say to my spectators. 'I need peace and quiet.'

Okay, so it turns out that it's harder than I thought it would be. The swiss roll covered in lard looked terrible – as though it were preparing for a cross-Channel swim. Maybe I should have made it some teeny-weeny chocolate goggles and thrown it into the sea – it wasn't good for much else. In the end I decide to roast it in olive oil, so I squash it into a saucepan, pour olive oil over the whole lot and put it into the oven with the heat turned up as far as it will go. I don't know what temperature is right for pan-roasted swiss roll because there don't appear to be any recipes for it, but I'm guessing hottest is best – like with curling tongs. You're wasting your time on the half-heat settings, the curls fall out straightaway.

While my swiss roll is roasting in two bottles of olive oil (is that roasting or deep-fat frying? Must be roasting if it's in the oven), I decide to make custard to go with it. I have a sachet of powder, so I read down the instructions. Not fattening enough, so instead of using milk I decide to use melted cheese and I shove three blocks of cheese into the microwave.

Next thing to happen is the smell – kind of sickly and pungent, like car tyres, sort of rubbery. In the microwave nothing untoward is happening – just cheese melting everywhere. It strikes me that I probably should have put it on a plate or in a bowl first, but besides that everything is going according to plan. No, the smell is definitely coming from the oven.

I peel open the door and look inside. Shit. The handle of the saucepan has completely melted off and is dripping onto the bottom of the oven. Fuck. I slam the door shut and try to waft away the acrid smells with the skirt of Magda's apron, which thankfully I put on to protect my skinny jeans. I switch the whole thing off at the mains, indiscriminately pulling out plugs until the lights on the cooker go off.

Right. Breathe. Relax. Take a chill pill, as my mother's always saying. I take a deep breath and look across the kitchen at the utter devastation I've caused. It looks like a war zone – as if the paratroopers have just left. Thank god I've got plenty of staff to help me clear up.

'All right, Mum?' comes a voice from the doorway.

'I'm fine, darling,' I start to say. Then I see melted cheese running out from underneath the door of the microwave. Oh god. Oh no. Why do bad things always happen to me?

Midnight

We had a takeaway for supper in the end. I hate takeaways. I always think that someone will see the pizza man arriving, which would be awful (although after my experiences in M&S today, I think I'll have to redefine 'awful'), so I get him to pull up outside the house next door, then I give Magda the money and get her to go out and collect them. 'Do NOT let anyone see you,' I instruct.

Comparatively, pizza boxes are just mildly embarrassing. I hate the smell in the house (mind you, one of the happy consequences of the saucepan and the red-hot cooker incident earlier today was that it left a strong smell in the house that has disguised odour d'American Hot, odour de garlic bread and all the nasty side-order odours). I also hate the food itself, because I know that pizza is about 300 calories a mouthful, so I can't have any of it. Not one slice. Not so much as a sliver of pepperoni has passed my lips tonight.

Now I'm lying in bed feeling deflated and useless. I'm starving, of course, but nothing new there. I also feel like a complete failure. I've not been as utterly useless at anything since I took up ballet classes, aged twelve, to please Mum. I hated being in the limelight back then because I disliked the way I looked so much. I was terribly overweight – like a little Buddha with a big round tummy, chubby thighs and a fat face. Everyone took the mickey out of me, especially Mum. I had little round glasses and brown hair that bushed out at the ends. It just never hung properly like other girls' hair did. It had this awful frizz that lasted until I was around sixteen. I think the main reason I became a hairdresser was because I spent my youth experimenting with different ways to control my unruly hair. These were the days before hair straighteners and hair extensions! Can you imagine? What was the point in living?

The fact that I was so desperately shy and insecure meant that I hated dancing with anyone except my mother. It was lovely to be twirled round the kitchen by her. She smelled of Ma Griffe and was all soft and perfect-looking. Standing in a line at a bar with a dozen other girls, all much skinnier than me, and being made to bend, stretch, bend, stretch for an hour – that was no fun. But, still, I went to the classes to please Mum.

Then there were the performances. My abiding memory was of sitting on the number 11 bus on the way there, whacking my legs with my fist, hoping to break them into pieces so I wouldn't have to perform. I didn't manage to injure myself, of course, so I went on stage every time, looking out for Mum. But Mum didn't even turn up. She never came to watch me in anything.

When Mum went away to LA to live, I started to lose weight. It sounds odd, and no one understood it at the time, but Jean, my psycho woman, says that I was eating to cushion myself from all the abuse my mother was giving me. By the time Mum came back to live in England I was about to get married to Dean and felt settled and happy, so her comments didn't get to me in quite the same way. In fact, the only time she's managed to upset me since was in relation to the wedding.

I really wanted a pink coach pulled by Palomino horses with pink manes. I wanted Dean's nan, Nell, to give me away because she'd welcomed me into Dean's family like I'd never been welcomed anywhere before. I wanted all my old friends to be there. I wanted a big fairytale, I wanted the whole thing to be perfect.

Mum, however, was really keen for it all to be low-key. I remember that when I phoned her in Los Angeles to tell her about the wedding and that we were thinking of letting the magazines have pictures and making it a big occasion, she went nuts and got the first plane over here. She never went back. She was so keen to be involved in the wedding – and it was good, just more like Mum's wedding than mine. It was odd because it was really glitzy and we had loads of fab people there, but Mum made a real fuss about it not being in the paper under any circumstances and even stopped Arsenal from putting out a press release.

'Let's just keep this low-key,' she kept muttering, while flying in designers from Paris to measure her for her dress (which was way more spectacular than mine). Mum's been like that since she got back here – really keen for me never to be high-profile and always keep myself to myself. I suppose that's just the way she is. She's had a hard life, so I can't be too tough on her. My dad was a real monster – just the most evil person ever. He was horrible and he badly hurt Mum and would have nothing to do with us after I was born. I really, really hate him for the way he treated her. Thank god I found a diamond like Dean. Poor Mum.

IT HAS ARRIVED . . .
Saturday, 11 August – the season starts
10.30 a.m.

'Just try to relax,' says Mallory, examining the gleaming, silver-coloured butterflies glittering magnificently on my vibrant-pink acrylic fingernails and my matching pink toenails. She's been painting, filing and pushing back wayward cuticles for two hours. Now we're at the end of our morning of beautification. 'Just sit still for fifteen minutes while the paint dries. That's all you've got to do.'

I find myself nodding like a small child while Mallory packs away her things into what looks like a toolbox.

'Can't you find something prettier than that?' I ask, indicating the large metal container with a stretch of my new nail.

Mallory catches sight of the butterfly wings as they flit past. She draws a giant breath and clutches her hands to her chest.

'Be careful, Tracie,' she says. 'You don't want to smudge them.'

'But that box. It's not very ladylike, is it? It looks like the sort of thing that you keep nails, screws and chisels in.'

Mallory smiles to herself and continues to pack everything away, managing to stop herself commenting that, increasingly, nails and screws are exactly what are needed to keep Wags like me together. 'I'll look for something prettier,' she says. 'Same time next week?'

'Yes. I'll need some waxing this week, too, but I'll call you about that – my diary's hectic. Now, would you be a darling and see yourself out?' I offer her a heavily made-up cheek for a kiss. 'I would come with you, but I don't want to smudge these beautiful nails.'

'Sure.' Mallory smiles indulgently and heads for the door, stepping over the fluffy rug in the hallway that she says always reminds her of a dead lamb. 'Every time I step on it I expect it to start bleating imploringly,' she told me once, adding that when she wears her long cream coat she fears the rug might run after her, thinking she's its mother.

I know Mallory thinks the rug's a death trap on the shiny floor. Magda polishes the wood daily because I do like a tidy house, but I accept that it makes walking a bit tricky. I have lost count of the number of times that Mallory has put a foot on it only for it to fly away from underneath her, tipping her up and backwards and landing her on her back in a most unladylike fashion, with her legs in the air and the tools of her trade scattered liberally around the vast marble-pillared entrance hall.

I listen from the conservatory with my feet up on a cushion, cotton wool threaded through my toes and varnish still wet on my nails. No thud? Well done, Mallory! I feel like applauding. The silly girl has finally worked out that you have to step *round* the mat and not go galumphing over the top of it!

The door closes behind her and I know it's time to get going. I have so much to do. My make-up needs topping up, I have to get dressed, and Doug, the driver, is coming for me at midday. I must remember to collect the car from the clamping place next week. I got a letter telling me that it's at a vehicle recovery centre in Croydon.

It's the pre-match lunch at 12.30 p.m. and I really can't be late – not again. I must try to get there before pudding is served at least once this year. I ease myself off the chaise longue and place my feet carefully on the floor – walking like a duck with my toes curled up to stop them catching in the thick pile of the cream carpet.

I waddle towards the bedroom. My dressing table is neatly stacked with all the latest beauty products – lined up in descending order of size thanks to the organisational skills of my various European staff members. I attempt to push them to one side with the back of my hand, ensuring my nails don't smudge. Christ, being a Wag is so much more difficult than people realise.

Okay, so now I have some space. I just need to sit down in front of the mirror. I place my hands flat on the dressing table and lean my weight onto them, while I hook my foot round the dressing-table stool and push it backwards. Shit! I've bumped my big toenail against the carved leg of the stool. Shit, shit, shit. I hop to the bed, howling as if I've broken my toe rather than chipped my nail, and try to examine the damage without making things worse. I feel like crying – there's a mark right in the middle of my big toenail. There's no way on earth I can go to the first match of the season like this! I'm just not one of those Wags who can appear in public looking like a scruff. No one would ever speak to me again, and I couldn't bear that.

I reach for my mobile phone and dial Mallory's number. 'Turn round,' I beg, tears now coursing down my face, leaving greasy tracks in my orange foundation. 'Pleeeeease turn round straightaway. It's an emergency.'

Outside, Mallory opens the car door and crunches across the gravel towards the house. She hasn't left. She still has her toolbox in her hand.

She confesses later that she always sits in the car for twenty minutes after visiting me before she starts the engine, because every time in the five years she's been visiting me, I've called her back in near hysterics after spotting a smudge on some nail or other. 'Don't worry, I'm coming,' says Mallory, as if she were talking to a four-year-old. 'Mallory's coming.'

I collapse onto the bed in pure relief. My shocking-pink fingernails hit the snow-white duvet and stick immediately. 'Fuck, fuck, fuck, fuck, fuck.'

3.10 p.m. – the season has just started

'Why's he doing that?' asks Helen.

I don't have a clue.

'Why did the referee blow the whistle?' asks Helen seconds later.

I don't have a clue.

'Who's winning?'

I don't have a clue.

'Who's playing?'

I don't have a clue.

'How long did you say you'd been coming to these matches?'

Ladies and gentlemen, I have a confession to make – I know nothing about football. I've been coming to games since I got married a couple of years ago (*sshhh*) but I still don't know what they're all doing out there. I suspect that if I were to spend the rest of my life devoted to watching football I'd still be no more able to identify a goal-scoring opportunity than I could walk past Gucci without going in.

Someone called Trevor once tried to explain the offside rule to me by saying it was like shoe-shopping. Apparently, it's all got something to do with the fact that you're at the back of the shop with your husband and the shoes you want to buy are at the till. When you walk up to the counter to pay for them, if you forget to bring your bag, your husband has to bring it to you – he can't kick it to you or you'd be offside.

'I'd be offside? If he started kicking my handbag around, *he'd* be offside, out of the house, divorced, and paying an eye-watering amount of maintenance, thank you very much.'

'No, I'm just trying to explain,' Trevor had said. 'He couldn't kick your handbag.'

'No, he bloody couldn't!' I was starting to grasp why offside is so important. Kick my handbag? Who would ever do that? I'd rather he kicked me, to be honest.

'Anyway, Dean never goes shoe-shopping with me, Trev.'

'No, but if he did – that's how offside would work.'

'But Dean wouldn't come, and he'd never kick my handbag, so offside doesn't really apply to me.'

'But, say he did . . .'

'He wouldn't go shoe-shopping with me ever. End of story. End of offside rule.'

Trevor, in common with every other man I've met, never tried to explain anything about football to me again.

Helen leans over. 'I'm confused,' she says.

'I've been confused for over a decade,' I reply. Then I realise what I've confessed to. 'Since I was about ten,' I say quickly. 'Yes, I've been confused since I was at school.'

'Do you know what the offside rule is?' she asks, scared now.

'Yes,' I whisper. 'It's all about getting your boyfriend to go shoe-shopping with you. But I wouldn't if I were you.'

5.30 p.m. – the season has just got off to the worst start imaginable

'Three–nil,' says Suzzi, shaking her head. 'Three–nil to them. I can't believe it.'

'No, it can't be three–nil to them,' says Helen, who has been very quiet and wearing a rather bemused expression since the offside conversation. 'Dean scored twice, so I know we got some goals.'

I just smile and back away so I don't have to explain. There's very, very little that I know about football, but I do know that you have to get the ball in the right net.

'Oh,' I hear Helen say, when my husband's double faux pas are explained to her by a gleeful Mindy. 'Is that why he decided not to come out and play any more after the interval?'

'No,' says Mindy, her voice rising so she can be sure that I can hear her. 'That's because he was subbed off. You see, he wasn't very good today. Captains *never* get subbed off.'

'Oh,' I hear Helen say as she looks around for me. She walks over. 'Are you all right?' she asks me.

I nod and tell her that I'm fine. Dean had an 'off match' but he'll be fine soon and back on song.

'Oh good,' says Helen. 'Look – I've got a massive favour to ask you. When are you going to write your handbook? You know – the one you said you'd write. I've been asked to be a promotions girl at a posh race course – you know, with horses and that. I just don't know how I should behave there as a Wag. I don't want to get it wrong and let my man down. I've also been asked to be a topless waitress at a stag party that's being held in a private room at the opera. I've never been to such posh places before, Tracie. You have to help me.'

'The first thing is not to worry,' I tell her. Then I promise to think about this difficult dilemma and let her have my thoughts. 'One thing I want you to remember, though, is that you can take a Wag out of a football club, but you can't take the football club out of a Wag. Not a true Wag. You need to be clear about who you are, Helen, even if you're surrounded by posh people.'

'That's great advice, Trace,' she says. 'I'll try to remember that.'

'Yes, always remember that,' I declare, and I promise that I'll have a proper think about her tricky situation. 'Now, I must find my husband.'

7 p.m.

Dean has never looked sadder or more dejected than he does this evening. We're sitting in the players' bar with all the guys and their Wags, but my Deany is too distressed to get involved with anyone. His head has dropped right forward and his chin is resting on his chest, while his big blue eyes are shutting, trying to block out the pain and misery . . . the sheer horror of what happened today. His hands lay over his heart and I watch his shoulders start to heave forwards gently. He's silently sobbing inside. I drop to my knees next to him, appalled that this strong man is crumbling before me.

I'm devastated that this should happen to him – my beautiful, talented husband. I see his hands rubbing his chest, as if trying to mend his broken heart. Then his shoulders heave again. He's obviously going to start crying. I don't think I can bear it.

He throws his head back and, just as I think he might start wailing in pain and misery, he emits the loudest, most disgusting belch I've ever heard.

'Oooo, that's better,' he declares, sitting up properly and smiling at me. 'Way too much lager.'

Sunday, 12 August
10 a.m.

Helen's dilemma has been on my mind all night. We have an early-season party at the club this afternoon, and I know Helen will be eager to have answers to her questions. Her turning to me for advice in this way has made me realise more keenly than ever just how valuable, how essential, my Wags' Handbook will be. I will write out an answer to Helen's question and it will be the start of my book. This afternoon, when I hand the piece of paper over to Helen, I will tell her that she is making history by being the first person to see a piece of advice that will one day change the Wag world.

'Paskia,' I shout, walking up to my daughter's bedroom and knocking on her door. I ease it open and peer in. She lifts her head off the pillow and squints at me. Her short brown hair is all messed up. (I know, I know – it's such a giveaway. Children should be born with hair the colour that you've dyed your own, not the colour your own hair is naturally.) I switch on the light and she throws her head under the pillow rather dramatically.

'I need you to show me how to use the computer,' I say, while looking around at the football posters all over the wall. It's heartbreaking. She should have pictures of pop stars on her wall by now and have a comprehensive plan in place for becoming a groupie. She's never going to be in a position to sleep with one, sell her story and pose topless for a national newspaper if she doesn't start to identify some potential targets now. From what I can gather, becoming famous through kissing and telling is a sure-fire route to a night with a footballer. It's unconventional but it works. It's all any mother could want for her daughter.

Paskia lifts her head up. She such a big girl, with her large shoulders and chunky thighs, but she's pretty . . . in her own way. She has so many freckles on her face that they're almost touching each other. It's a shame that they don't – then she'd look permanently spray-tanned. I've thought about sneaking into her room one night while she's sleeping and joining them all up. Perhaps if she was a nice colour it would distract from the big metal braces running across the front of her teeth.

'Pask, I need you to show me how to work the computer thing.'

She crawls out of bed, very unwillingly, and shuffles towards the computer. Her Luton Town pyjamas are too tight. She's obviously putting on weight again. I'm desperately hoping that she won't develop issues with food like the ones I had when I was younger.

Pask presses a series of buttons and the whole screen lights up. 'Whoooaahhh . . .' I say, jumping back from it. 'What's it doing?'

'It's just coming on, Mum. Relax.'

Finally, the machine is running and Pask 'opens Word' – whatever that means.

'There. Just type,' she says. 'Next time, use Dad's laptop instead of waking me up.'

'I'm not using your father as a lapdog,' I retort. She's getting so cheeky.

Right. Here we go.

My advice for Helen, by Tracie Martin.

I can't work out how to do a little heart above the 'i' in Tracie, so I'll have to write that on by hand afterwards.

Rules for a Wag forced to endure events that are not really very Wag-friendly. Specificalorie – the opera and the horse racing.

Opera can be a trial for any human being to endure, let alone a Wag who will find herself feeling particularly uncomfortable at the sight of very overweight women screaming at each other in Italian. Once the bunch of fat tarts have finished their screeching, with a bit of luck you'll get a half-tasty bloke on to sing, but nine times out of ten he'll be fat too, and probably sweat a lot <u>and</u> have a beard. In fact, I think there is really only one male opera singer and he's called Perverted-hottie, or something like that, and he's not very good because he just sings the song that he nicked from Italia '90 when Gazza cried. It's called 'Nests on Dormouse', which is clearly nonsense.

If you are forced to go to the opera, obviously make sure it's being performed in a theatre. This may sound like rather an obvious thing to say, but it is important to remember that some people go to watch opera in parks and fields. Fields?! You should avoid fields at the best of times in case you get foot and mouth disease, and I'm sure it goes without saying that you should particularly avoid them when there are fat people singing in them.

Now, as well as opera, another posh social event is horse racing. The nice thing about this is that it does have quite a 'chavvy' edge to it – what with the links with gambling and drinking – so it's not quite as 'otherworldly' as opera is, and there's no reason why a properly dressed Wag should not fit in perfectly. So – how to dress. Obviously, having a ridiculous hat with loads of feathers poking out of it so you look like a bleedin' budgie is a good start, as is making sure that you've got your hemlines exactly right. I think that, because it's quite a posh occasion, you should have your dress covering your knickers, but only just! A little flash of gusset is always nice (if you're going to adopt this style of dress, remember not to wear crotchless knickers!).

Obviously, when it comes to choosing colours, baby pink is always nice. Making sure the outfit is expensive is vital, and in manmade fibres where possible. If you can find a top for £500 made entirely of nylon – snap it up. They're hard to come by. If you don't fancy pink (and if you don't, you need to ask yourself why not?) then just go for colours unknown to Nature.

Picking the right size for your outfit is crucial. You know how it is when you see someone in clothes that fit properly – they look so dull and plain. Always dress at least a size too small, making sure as much flesh as possible is on display. This strategy works particularly well with bigger girls.

You need to make sure your skin has been heavily spray-tanned (again – the colour you're aiming for is one that can safely be described as 'unknown to Nature'). If you haven't had a spray tan (and, again, if not WHY NOT), then make sure your skin has been turned bright lobster-pink by the sun. Certainly, you don't want white flesh on display. That would be like having natural hair or small sunglasses or a small handbag – no, no, no, no. If you have a small dog, take him in a silly little basket and put a ribbon round his neck to match your outfit.

There. That's good. That should really help Helen.

2 p.m.

'Oh my god,' shrieks Helen. 'You are a complete genius.'

I've just handed her the sheet of paper with my advice for Wags in compromising (i.e. posh) social situations on it, and she is delighting in the words as if they were made of diamonds.

'Thank you, thank you, thank you,' she says, while I stand back, a little embarrassed at how loudly she's speaking, and a little frustrated that there's no one near enough to hear it all. Half of me wants to say,

'Oh please, Helen, do be quiet', while the other half wants to say, 'Speak up, love, Mindy can't hear you.'

Dean really didn't want to come to this party today. 'They're always crap and there are three old episodes of *Minder* on UK Gold this afternoon,' he said. But I know it's because he's embarrassed about yesterday, and doesn't want to face everyone. I asked him but he said, 'No, it's just *Minder*, sweetheart. I love it. It really cracks me up.' Admittedly, he does love his *Minder*, so perhaps it's a combination of the two things. I managed to get him here by promising that we wouldn't stay long, but now he's here he seems to be really enjoying himself. That's the thing with my Dean – he's a bit like a seven-year-old. Once you get him away from the television he has a really good time, but while he's watching the box, peeling him away from it is almost impossible – like peeling the skin from a potato with your teeth.

'Awright, babes,' he says, coming up to me. 'What was that bird saying?'

I tell him about the help I've given Helen and how grateful she was and Dean gives me a big hug. 'You're a doll,' he says.

Dean's looking great today. He's got his mirror shades on and low-slung jeans with a white T-shirt and loads of bling. He's got all his rings on together, which I think looks really cool. He's carrying his jacket over his shoulder. I was trying to show him how to carry it with just one finger, but after the incident when someone pulled the jacket and almost broke his finger he clenches it in the palm of his hand these days.

'I'm gonna get a lager,' he says, turning and walking towards the bar in a manner that reminds me of *Happy Days* and that bloke called The Fonz. It was on the telly when I was really little and they keep re-showing it on UK Gold. I think Dean's watching too much of that channel. As he gets to the bar, he moves to run both hands through his mousy brown hair, forgetting that he's got his jacket in one of them. He almost takes out the Luton Town directors as his jacket swings wildly. I can see him apologising, mopping up drinks and throwing his jacket down on a nearby table. Bless him. He's so cool is my Dean.

He saunters back over and I find myself becoming obsessed with the miracle that his trousers are staying on at all. They are so low-slung that his Ralph Lauren pants are showing (he finds the Calvin Klein ones too loose). How does he do that? They're barely over his hips yet they manage to stay there.

'Mich is over there,' he says, pointing towards the other side of the bar.

We're in the Luton clubhouse and it stinks of alcohol from last night.

I preferred it when people smoked in here, at least it hid the smell of sick and beer. The other side of the bar smells worse than this side, but it's where most of the single players are, so I can see why Mich would be over there.

On this side it's all coupley. I wave over at Suze as she waddles in wearing great multicoloured hot-pants and matching high-heeled shoes.

'Wow!' I say. 'Are they Pucci?'

'Yes,' she answers, pulling out a cigarette and reaching for her lighter. She's so heavily pregnant now that her stomach gets in the way when she bends down, so she has to sort of crouch with her legs open, allowing her enormous stomach to drop between her knees. It's at this point that I'm reminded of an important lesson: never open your legs really wide while wearing hot-pants and being heavily pregnant if you have not had a bikini wax.

'You shouldn't be smoking that, should you?' asks Mindy, striding in behind her. Mindy looks like a goddess. She's wearing a tight satin basque and . . . well, that's all she's wearing, really. She's done that thing that Sienna Miller did, and come out in her knickers. Luckily, Mindy – like Sienna – has the body for it.

'I'll smoke if I want to. Just because I'm pregnant doesn't mean you can tell me what to do.'

'No – I don't mean because you're up the duff, I mean because of the no-smoking laws. I know it's fine to smoke when you're pregnant. Christ – I'd take it up if I got pregnant, even though I don't normally touch cigarettes – it keeps the baby small.'

Sunday, 19 August
Midday

'Darling, darling, darling. It's Angie here,' says Mum. She's talking into the answer-phone because I can't face picking up. 'I've heard the news . . . I've been trying to call all morning. I was going to pop round, but I've been in your house every day this week and I simply couldn't bear to come round again. How's Dean? Tell him to call me if he needs anything. Maybe I should bring him some of my tea made from mud taken from the claws of African spider monkeys. Or there are some tablets containing the resin from the Umbaka tree. It's collected by tribesmen who keep it in their nose for ten days before it's dried in the sun.'

Luton Town lost again. Dean was subbed off again. Two weeks, two defeats. No own goals for Dean yesterday, which obviously made a pleasant change, but he was, in the words of the fans that I followed out of the stadium, 'fucking crap'.

I reach for the handset. 'I'm here, Mum,' I say, adding, 'Dean will be fine' with more conviction than I feel.

'How many times do I have to say don't call me "Mum"', she huffs. 'Call me Angie.'

Dean is sure that she wants me to call her Angie instead of Mum because she is labouring under the misapprehension that if I do, no one will realise how old she is. I spent years thinking she didn't want me to call her Mum because she didn't like me very much and didn't want to be associated with me. I suspect that the real reason is an unflattering mixture of the two.

'That's three matches in a row that he's been subbed off. Darling, you have to do something,' Mum implores. 'You could try giving him vienow juice.'

'What's that?' I ask, but I'm not sure I really want to know.

'It comes from the berries of the vienow tree . . .'

'Oh.' How nice. A simple, straightforward answer.

'. . . and they collect it by sucking the juice through large vine leaves that have been soaked in the Nile.'

'Of course they do.'

'Three matches. It's looking like the end, darling.'

'Well, it's two actually, and what can I do? Run on there and kick the ball for him? Take out the goalkeeper when he's about to score?'

'Humour is entirely overrated as a communication tool,' she says sniffily. 'And I don't think it should be used at all when you're talking about something as serious as your husband's career . . . your entire lifestyle depends on him playing kick-ball well. It's really not a laughing matter. Now – is he eating properly? Does he take enough supplements? Wild yam cream? Maybe he should be taking human growth hormones. A lot of these athletes do.'

'Yes, and then they are banned for life,' I say.

'Such negativity,' she replies, spitting out the word 'negativity' at me. I know she's rubbing her temples as she says it, and lifting her chin to the skies. 'Breathe deeply, through the nostrils,' she is saying. 'Take three drops of mimosa flower extract every hour. Think happy thoughts . . . always.'

The trouble with Mum is that she lived in Los Angeles for ten years. Once I was old enough to look after myself, she headed for the bright lights, convinced that she could make it as a film star. The major movie career never materialised, but she returned with the face of a thirty-year-old, the breasts of a sixteen-year-old and a nauseatingly positive attitude. Now it's the gym every morning, pilates every afternoon, and 257 different supplements in between. She's painfully thin and looks permanently surprised. Her hair is the colour of corn and her eyes have gone from hazel to sapphire. She took some getting used to – especially the body shape, with the tiny, tiny waist and the enormous breasts. I kept thinking she was going to fall over. I've had my breasts done recently, but they're nothing like as large, full or youthful as my fifty-three-year-old mother's are.

'Darling, I need to know the gossip while I'm on the phone – is that delectable Andre Howchenski going out with that dope Michaela? Did I hear that correctly?'

'Well, I'm hoping so. She met him after the game yesterday and really likes him. I think they'd make a lovely couple.'

'He's too good for her,' she says. 'It won't last.'

I don't want to debate this with my mother because I want so much for it to work out for my lovely friend that I can't bear to consider that it might not. I can hear bells ringing in the background on the phone. 'Where are you, Mum?'

'At church,' she replies in her singsong voice. 'Praying for Dean. Praying for both of you. Praying that this phase will pass and that I won't be the mother of a woman who's married to the *bad* player from

43

Luton. I'm praying for you, too. Marrying a footballer's the only decent thing you've ever done. Let's hope it doesn't end. You do understand how bad this is, don't you?'

'Yes,' I reply, because I do know how bad it is. I'm no Bobby Charleston but I know that the captain's supposed to stay on the pitch and, ideally, contribute to the match in some way other than scoring own goals.

Dean realises it too. 'They'll probably sell me,' he said last night, as if he were an old car or an unwanted sofa. 'Free transfer to some god-forsaken place.' It had made me shudder. What if the new place was somewhere dreadful like Sunderland?

'I don't think prayers are what he needs right now,' I say, slightly unkindly, but I hate the way she insists on making a huge drama out of everything. 'Anyway, I didn't know you were religious.'

'I'm not, silly. I'm not here to pray, though I did light a candle for poor, poor Dean. No, I'm here because there's a woman who comes to church who I want to befriend because she runs the best pilates classes in the area and is booked up for twelve months. I thought I would bump into her and become her best friend.'

'What? You went to church to befriend some woman?'

'Not *some* woman – the pilates teacher to end all pilates teachers. If you want to befriend someone, you just follow him or her and start talking to them. I learned that in LA. She went to church, and so did I.'

If you want to befriend someone, you just follow him or her . . . I find myself thinking. *Just follow them.*

'Oh,' I say, my mind ticking over with thoughts, plans, an idea of how I might be able to help my husband. 'And did you make friends with her?'

'Of course,' says Mum breezily. 'We're off for organic grass and dandelion-stalk tea now. It's easy. Honestly, you Brits are so funny – everyone else has put their names down on Leaf's pilates list and they are all just waiting patiently for a gap to open up. They don't stand a chance. If you want to be friends with someone just go and "bump" into them. It's not rocket science. Right, must go – need to balance my chakras and chant my *Buddhabhivadana*.'

'Chant your what?'

'Salutation to the Buddha, silly girl. Don't you know anything?'

Saturday, 25 August
10 a.m.

Oh dear. Very difficult situation. Very, very difficult situation. It's 8 a.m. on Saturday morning and I'm pacing around the bedroom in a state of considerable distress. Today it's not even the prospect of Dean scoring eighteen own goals and getting booed off the pitch that's distressing me ... though I have to say life would be altogether more pleasant if he just went out there and kicked it into the right net like the others manage to do. No, the real problem today is that I think I might have to sack Mallory. Can you imagine it? The thing is – I can't see any way round it. She's committed a cardinal sin and it would be unforgivable of me not to punish her in some way. I feel like Sir Alan Sugar as I spin on my heels and point at the mirror. 'You're fired,' I growl, with all the seriousness that a woman with her hair in Carmen rollers can muster. 'You, Mallory. You're fired.'

Okay, let me think about how I can word this as I explain to you what happened. Mallory came round at 6 a.m., as she usually does on match days, but she forgot to bring her fake-tan spray with her!! Can you imagine? A beautician, going to see a Wag before a match and forgetting the fake tan! It would have been less disastrous to me if she'd forgotten to bring her head.

This is how the whole sorry scene played itself out. Sensitive readers may choose to look away at this point.

'Mallory, darling, how lovely to see you,' I said in my best, most welcoming voice. 'In you come. Have you got everything there?'

Note, please, how I managed to spot immediately that she was less encumbered than usual. Note, please, also, that she did not notice at all that she was carrying significantly less gear than is usual or, as it turns out, desirable.

'Yes, everything I need is here,' said Mallory. Or, should I say, 'lied Mallory', because that's what it was – a damned lie.

'Can I do the fake tan first?' I asked, peeling off my top and kicking my Jimmy Choos to one side.

'Sure,' said Mallory (lying). Then began the fumble through all her bags as she searched in vain for her fake-tanning stuff.

'I'm sure it's here somewhere,' she muttered, throwing things out of her enormous shopper as she did. 'Mmmmmm . . . that's strange.'

More instruments of the beautification process were hurled outwards and upwards as Mallory scoured her bag. A small pot of wax rolled across the carpet. Tea-tree oil, tweezers and nail files tumbled out. Facepacks, toner, moisturiser, creme bleach, a pumice stone, hot stones for massage . . . no fake-tan sprayer though. No sign of a spray-tan machine anywhere.

'Oh Tracie,' said Mallory, clutching her hands around her face in horror. 'Tracie, I'm so sorry.'

I squawked. I know it was a squawk and I know it was extremely loud, because a horrible grimace descended onto Mallory's face – the same look she'd had when she'd stepped back and put her stiletto heel through my cashmere cushion. For one horrible moment she thought she'd skewered the cat.

'How could you possibly forget it?' I asked.

'I'm sorry,' she said for the twenty-fifth time. 'I'm really sorry.'

The trouble is, 'really sorry' isn't going to make me the colour of a rusty nail by 3 p.m., is it?

I got Mallory to do all the other essential treatments. My fingernails were long and blunt at the end and painted with white tips. Nail extensions had been applied to my toenails and not a stray hair remained anywhere. My body was soft, my nails were tough and my hair was long and thick. But my skin? White.

'I'll drop you at the tanning shop on Luton High Street if you want,' says Mallory, and not for the first time I wondered whether she'd forgotten the spray tan on purpose. I know she doesn't like doing the spray business. She's been a bit funny with the whole thing since the unfortunate incident with another Wag and a white Chihuahua. No amount of pleading would convince the woman that her dog looked fine the colour of a ginger-nut biscuit.

I think the fundamental problem that Mallory and other women like her face in a spray-tan sense when working with Wags, is that most Wags have entirely white furniture in their homes, which means that there's every chance of a major disaster happening.

'I'll wait outside,' says Mallory, as I walk into the salon and request a double spray tan. It goes well to start with. Once I'd got over being told to wear paper knickers, which were entirely unflattering in every respect.

'Okay, turn round,' says Debbie, the tanning lady. 'And back again . . . Great . . . Nearly done. Just need to spray your face now. Breathe in when I say, then hold your breath until I've finished spraying. Okay?'

Breathe in. How hard can that be? Normally breathing comes to me as easily as applying mascara, driving and drinking a cappuccino at the same time, but suddenly I don't know how to hold my breath. And just as Debbie sprays a fine mist of cocoa-coloured skin dye, I take a massive gulp in.

'Great – that'll be my lungs nicely tanned then.' I'm choking and straining and feeling like I'm about to be sick.

'I'll get you a drink of water,' says Debbie, swinging open the door leading directly to the reception area, and thus to the main door to the salon, where around a dozen people got an eyeful of a choking Luton Town Wag in paper knickers and a fetching shower cap. I was a lovely shade of mahogany though.

Tuesday, 28 August
8 p.m.

My mother and Dean are staring at me, utter confusion registering on their familiar faces. I'm not really listening to them any more. I'm peeling off the small rose tattoos that Mallory fixed onto my fingernails on Saturday morning as an apology for not having her tanning system with her. God, Saturday seems like a long time ago – before I was arrested for causing criminal damage . . .

'Are you listening?' Mum says. 'I asked you what on earth you thought you were doing?'

Mum had turned up at the house as soon as she heard the news. She was dressed in a cream Lanvin dress that she'd had specially altered for the occasion. It was so short I could see that she'd had her bikini line specially done for the occasion, too. She wore the dress with sky-high Christian Louboutin shoes and looked fantastic, with her make-up professionally applied and her hair styled like Farrah Fawcett Majors'. She'd obviously feared there would be photographers camped out in the driveway. Luckily she was wrong. When I came home in the taxi at lunchtime the place was deserted and I had just Mum and Dean to contend with. Neither can quite believe the turn of events.

'I mean, what possessed you?' Mum is asking.

'I was trying to help,' I say.

'Help?' says Dean. 'Help? Tell me how causing over two thousand pounds' worth of damage in Faux Fur in Bishop's Stortford helped anyone.'

Mum puts her arm round Dean's shoulder and hugs him into her massive bosoms. 'What possessed you today?' she asks, turning to face me aggressively, while stroking his thinning hair affectionately.

'Nothing possessed me,' I answer, and I feel like screaming. You see, it was all her fault. It was Mum telling me that you should just go and bump into someone if you want to befriend them that started me off on all this in the first place.

It was after the call with Mum that I started to think about the ways in which I could help Dean, and I became convinced that if he were to become friends with some of the England players, he'd be more likely to get a good transfer deal. I knew Dean would never go and knock on Beckham's door so I thought, I know, I'll befriend Victoria. She'll understand after all she went through when Becks kicked that bloke in the Argentina game, and the *Daily Mirror* did a David Beckham dartboard in the paper the next day; she'll know what it's like to live life as a piranha, or was that a pariah?

I knew she was in England because I'd seen her in the *Daily Mail* yesterday, and I knew where she lived because when they had their World Cup party there were pictures of the house (which I cut out and kept in a scrapbook) and it said that the house was in Sawbridgeshire. So I woke up at 7 a.m. this morning, dressed, and left the house to head for Beckingham Palace . . .

Flashback to 9 a.m.

Shit. The gates are opening. Fuck. What do I do? Perhaps I should have thought this through a bit more carefully first. I'm sitting in a tiny orange car in the middle of Essex, outside an enormous mansion belonging to David and Victoria Beckham, wondering what to do next. I should be at home, looking after my daughter and my husband, and preparing for a morning at the hairdresser's with Mich. She's agreed to have just a few blonde highlights weaved in at the front of her hair because we're now ten days into the season and she still hasn't bagged a footballer. Andre's shown some interest but there's no real sign of commitment. It must be her hair. It's just so . . . dark. I feel awful for abandoning her to face the bleach alone, but I think she'll be able to cope. She knows it's the right thing to do. She knows that blonde hair is the key to unlocking the heart of a footballer.

I'm paranoid that someone's going to see me and realise I'm hanging around, so I drop myself down in the driver's seat and peer up over the windscreen – all that can be seen of me now is the black headscarf wound tightly around my head and the top half-moon of my massive sunglasses. To be honest, I'd look far less suspicious if I just sat there, smiling, but I'm so determined not to be seen that I opt for this ridiculous semi-reclining position that just screams 'Stalker!'. I hear the gates start to close behind me and I ease myself up a little, just as a fabulous car glides out and sweeps majestically onto the road in front of me. There are two women sitting in the back. I am absolutely *sure* that one of them is Victoria Beckham. My heart starts pounding and my hands are shaking a little, sweating inside the leather driving gloves that I am wearing so as not to leave fingerprints anywhere.

I start up the engine and drive up behind them, still reclining a little but able – just – to see over the steering wheel. I'm in a rented car (I'm having horrific problems getting my car back. I went to the Croydon place on Sunday and was told it was shut. Great! So it's fine for them to come and steal my car off the road but they can't be bothered to stay open on Sundays for me to pick it up. It's almost enough to make me want to park properly in future. I could see the car through the railings on Sunday. It was like I was visiting it in jail. As I walked away I swear I heard it sobbing). Anyway, I went for the plainest rental car I could find – just so I wouldn't be easily spotted by Vic. This fabulous yellow Lamborghini was screaming at me in the showroom last night, but even I realised some muscle-head driver, bouncer or security guard would notice if a banana-coloured sports car tailed him for more than a couple of minutes. I don't think I realised, at the time, just how orange this car is, though. It looks like a little tangerine rolling down the road after them.

Victoria's car is moving at a nice gentle pace, so obviously they don't realise they're being followed. Great. The fact that the Mercedes is not going very fast means that I can keep up with it in my little Fiat Punto. I'm better at this stalking lark than I thought I'd be.

The car is heading towards Bishop's Stortford. I know this not because of any prior knowledge of the backstreets of Hertfordshire, but because there are great big road signs everywhere. Eventually, the driver pulls over and out he gets – fucking brilliant! – it's Victoria, and – double fucking brilliant! – she's with Geri Halliwell, who is clutching an extraordinary-looking basket containing two tiny poodles. This is *sooo* much better than I thought it would be.

I dump the car on the side of the road and jump out, crossing over to where V & G are, so that I'm in the slipstream of the two most famous Spice Girls. They stop and peer into a window. I do, too. They continue. I follow. On we go, down the road in procession, until Geri suddenly spins round with a terribly aggressive look on her face.

Is she looking at me? I'm not sure. I immediately dive into the nearest shop, just in case . . . It's a butcher's . . . fuck, what the hell am I supposed to do in a butcher's shop? I can hardly browse through the chops.

'Tracie?'

Oh god, please tell me it's not Mindy. I couldn't bear it if she saw me out stalking. Bad enough that she should see me buying baskets full of lard, but this is a whole different level of madness.

'Tracie Smegglesworth?' repeats the voice, louder this time.

Shit. Who on earth would know my embarrassing maiden name?

'It's me.'

The face is vaguely familiar – a plump blonde girl with messy hair.

'Sally. Don't you remember . . . we worked together at the hair-dresser's on the High Street years ago. You used to live above it.' She takes off her glasses and I find myself momentarily transported back in time to a simpler world – when brushing hair and sneaking out for a cigarette were the only things that concerned me.

'You look fantastic,' says Sally, and I suddenly realise that this chubby, unremarkable woman is how I would look without Dean's money and the wisdom of Wagdom on my side. She's roughly the same height as me, but I'm wearing four-inch heels so look considerably taller. She's a good three stone heavier, her hair's all over the place and she doesn't have a scrap of make-up on.

'Don't you get cold in that skirt, though?' She's pointing at my thighs as she speaks.

'It's a tulip skirt,' I say stupidly. 'Dolce and Gabbana.'

She smiles. 'Must get cold, though.'

'Not really.' I'm wondering what cold's got to do with anything when you're wearing £500 of the very latest clothing to come off the catwalks of Milan.

Sally is wearing jeans beneath her blood-splattered white coat and she has on these clumpy trainers that remind me of Cornish pasties. Still, she looks happy.

'It all turned out all right for you, didn't it?' she says, eyes wide. She looks genuinely pleased to see me, which is quite touching. 'Yes – you landed right on your feet, didn't you? You know – after that trouble at Romeo's – marrying Dean Martin. Great! I followed it all in the maga-zines and papers. It was so grand – the wedding and that. I was so pleased for you, mate. So pleased and proud. I was telling everyone that I knew you.'

I hadn't invited Sally to the wedding, just as I hadn't invited any of my old friends. I had brand-new, gleaming, exciting, beautiful friends by then. Mum told me who to invite. She said it had to be a new start for me, and a whole load of wedding designers, lifestyle coaches and style advisers descended on me to make sure everything was done with the necessary Wag-like aplomb. Dean told me to invite my old mates and have some fun, but I was so obsessed with becoming a great Wag that I just did what Mum and the design team advised. I never saw Sally again from the moment I'd walked out of the hairdresser's that day.

'What are you doing round here?' she asks, and I mumble some-thing about seeing friends. I can't meet her eye because I keep thinking of all the fun we had together and how I just never called her again, never checked she was okay. I'm worried that she thinks I can't meet

51

her eye because I'm embarrassed about knowing a common butcher, but I don't know what to say to make it all right. She's desperate for me to say something friendly and I'm desperate not to say anything offensive.

I keep thinking of all the stupid things we used to get up to, like when we did highlights for the first time – using a plastic cap. We pulled the hair through the tiny holes with those little crochet needles, lathered on the bleach and left the lady for twenty minutes. Trouble is, we forgot all about her. The two of us had gone out to the pub for a lunch of crisps and cider when Romeo's daft assistant from Czechoslovakia came galloping in.

'Quick!' he cried. 'Mrs Johnstone agony is in.'

'Who's Mrs Johnstone?' we asked.

'Lady bleach head. Funny hat wear.'

'Oh shit!' We raced back over the road to be greeted by the sight of a lady parading round the salon with a scalp the colour of sun-dried tomatoes. Patches of beetroot-coloured skin were appearing on the top of her forehead and the sides of her face where the bleach had leaked through the cap. She was in considerable distress, and it wasn't hard to see why. Sally pulled off the cap with an almighty tug and half the bleached hair came off with it. We had to tell Mrs Johnstone that she only had three blonde highlights and considerably less hair than when she had come into the salon because she'd made us take the cap off too soon.

'Can I have some bacon, please, Sally?' I finally ask.

'Sure. How much?'

Sally starts slicing and I stop her when there's a small pile. She wraps it all up, I pay her, tell her how nice it was to see her again and leave. I'm out on the street before I realise that I never once asked her how she was, where she lives or who with. I didn't make any effort to try to see her again, take her number or leave mine. Shit. Shit. I run back into the butcher's, throw my carefully crafted card at her and say, 'Stay in touch, Sal.'

Sally strokes the lipstick-pink embossed writing and looks at me as if I've just given her my kidney. 'I will,' she whispers.

I run out of the shop and look around. There they are – V & G ... wandering down the street arm-in-arm giggling and chatting like teenagers. Right, concentrate – back in pursuit again.

My targets have wandered into a shop calling itself Faux Fur. It looks predominantly like a fur shop, fake of course, but there are bags, shoes, jewellery and all sorts of other stuff in there. It looks gorgeous through the window. I'll wait until their backs are turned before I go in.

There are gales of laughter as four assistants descend on V & G and I find myself bursting with envy – how can it take four assistants to help them? Three of the assistants appear to be just standing around laughing at their jokes, while the other is pulling clothes off the rails and hanging them up in a small changing room. Once V & G wander into the changing room (together – in the same small changing room – bizarre. I'm making a note of all this über-Wag behaviour. It takes going to the toilets at the same time to a whole new level . . .), I enter the shop, help myself to a couple of items (note – there are no assistants to help me!) and push my way through the heavy curtain into the changing room next to theirs.

There's something really strange about coming so close to your role model. I find myself wanting to know all about her: what bag is she carrying (Chloé), what shoes is she wearing (Gucci), what size is she? She looks tiny, but it's hard to guess whether she's a size zero, or whether she's made it down to that all-important double zero. On the floor of her changing room lies a camisole top. If I could just look at the label on it, I'd know what size she is. On hands and knees, I lean under the thick curtain that separates us and stretch out as far as I can. It's no good, I can't reach it. What can I use? The only thing I have with me is a large packet of streaky bacon. With the pig produce in my hand I can just about touch it, so I push the bacon out as far as I can, then drag it back along the floor towards me, pulling the camisole top with it. Things are going perfectly – the top is just within grasp, then – quite suddenly – there's an almighty yapping sound and one of Geri's dogs leaps from its basket and charges towards me, biting into the meat with his silly little gnashers. I realise, in that moment, how much I dislike Geri Halliwell – I think her solo songs are hopeless and her dress sense ridiculous. Now her dog's attacking me just when I was about to see what size Posh Spice is. I yank the bacon back before anyone realises what's going on, but I don't realise just how attached the dog is and I pull the stupid, curly-haired pooch, too. He comes zooming under the curtain, attached to the bacon, causing me to stagger back, go tumbling out of the changing cubicle and straight into an elaborate display of clothes, shoes and bags. There's a loud crunching sound beneath me.

'Vic,' screeches Geri. 'Look who it is! It's that woman who was following us earlier. I think she's killed my dog.'

'Right,' says the manageress, locking the door. 'I'm calling the police.'

Wednesday, 29 August
11 a.m.

Mum and Dean must have such sore necks. They haven't stopped shaking their heads for almost twenty-four hours now. Mum's the worst, though. 'Bacon?' she says. 'Why did you even have a packet of bacon on you?' So I go through the whole sorry tale again.

'Faux Fur?' she replies. 'I don't understand why you would have been in a shop called Faux Fur.'

So I tell her that bit again too. It's like being interviewed by Jeremy Paxman. I feel like I've run through the whole sorry saga more times than is of any use to anyone. Now we're awaiting the arrival of Magick PR – specialist celebrity PR agency to the stars – and I know I'll have to go through the whole thing again . . . and again . . . Bringing in a PR firm was Nell's idea (I ended up calling her last night when I tired of watching the nodding dogs failing to come up with any ideas of remote value or help to anyone).

It was such a relief to talk to Nell because, unlike anyone else I'd spoken to that day, she found the whole thing funny. *Funny!* Imagine how refreshing that was, after all the 'Why does everything have to end up in such a total fiasco with you?' comments. Take this as an example: Mum said, 'You are shameful. You have embarrassed your man. There are times when I dislike you intensely.'

I know she doesn't really mean it quite as nastily as it sounds. She's always saying things like that – like she used to when I was little. All this 'children should be seen and not heard' has now become 'a footballer's wife should be seen and not heard'.

Nell, though, just collapsed into laughter when I'd finished telling her. 'I love you, you great banana. That's the funniest thing I've ever heard. Tell me about the bit with the dog and the bacon again.'

I told Nell everything about ten times, and it never once felt like she was judging me.

'Look, sweetheart,' she said. 'Just don't worry about it. Things like that happen all the time.'

Perhaps they do in Sunnyside Sheltered Accommodation, but they certainly don't in most people's worlds.

'You should have seen us in the war . . .' continues Nell. 'We used to have such a laugh. Did I tell you about the time we bricked up the air-raid shelter and five families nearly died?'

If you have a grandmother like Dean's, you'll know that any mention of the war, air-raid shelters or having a laugh is the beginning of a very heavily romanticised trip down Memory Lane that goes on for about three days. It's a trip that involves Nell laughing in a high-pitched and quite hysterical fashion at some frankly very unamusing things like near-death experiences and the day that old Mr Simpson was bombed as he sat on the loo in the shed at the bottom of the garden on Christmas morning.

'You know what you should do, don't you?' asks Nell, pulling herself back into the same century as the rest of us with unaccustomed speed. 'Ring one of those glossy magazines and tell your side of the story to them. Get some good publicity for you and Dean and everything will be fine, don't you worry.'

So that's exactly what we did.

There's the distinctive sound of the bell (it plays the theme tune from *Match of the Day*) and the equally distinctive sound of footsteps padding down the hall to answer the door. 'Ccccchello,' says Alba. 'Ccccchhow can I 'elp you?'

When Alba first came to work with us, with her beautiful Spanish accent, we spent all the time trying to get her to say words beginning with 'h' because her pronunciation of them was out of this world. That deep guttural *ccccc* sound that preceded every 'h' was great.

'Can you do that?' I'd say, pointing at the hoover.

'Ccccccchoover?' Alba would reply, and Pask and I would roar with laughter. Mum thought it was all very juvenile, and that I was setting a bad example, but we did it in a nice way, we weren't being nasty.

While Alba leads the guys from Magick PR into the house, Mum doesn't move at all – in fact she's still too busy shaking her head and muttering some sort of Buddhist chant. If she's not careful there's every chance that her head will come off altogether.

'I really don't think you should be doing this,' she says, once she's returned from her brief meditation to rejoin the world the rest of us are living in. 'You should remain silent and dignified and just keep yourself out of the papers. You certainly should not be doing something that is going to get more publicity than ever – it's absurd, utterly absurd.'

When the PR people walk into the room, though, Mum is straight to her feet and introducing herself to everyone. She's air-kissing and explaining that she used to be a public relations executive in Los

Angeles. Even Dean manages to look baffled by this sudden announcement. Up until this point he's been like a little puppy dog next to her, nodding along with her and grinning inanely at her every suggestion. He's always been like that around Mum. She does seem to have this peculiar hold over him. Indeed, she has a peculiar hold over all men. Dean says he just makes an effort with her because he knows how important she is to me, but it's more than that, I'm sure of it. Not in a bad way – just that she has this kind of allure, this lustre, that men find irresistible. Perhaps it's the macrobiotic diet that she's always bleating on about, or the eighty-six supplements that she seems to take every day, but men are drawn to her like moths to a flame in some subconscious, deeply primitive fashion. They seem to want to be liked by her.

'Were you really in PR?' he asks, and Mum smiles in an unnecessarily flirty way and says yes she was, adding that there is much about Mum that Dean does not yet know. To his credit, at this point he does look rather scared.

11.04 a.m.

In they come, and all my worst fears are confirmed in an instant. 'Dahhhling, how are you?' they ask in their absurdly plummy voices. I smile and say 'Hey, these things happen', as if swinging Geri Halliwell's dog around attached to a packet of bacon in a fake fur shop is something that happens daily – to everyone.

'Now,' says the man in the group, though 'man' is a very generous description of him. He weighs about the same as I do and has thinner thighs. Not good. 'Let me introduce everyone.' With a dramatic flourish, he says: 'This is Arabella, this is Philonella and this is Marinella.' Presumably, Salmonella was off sick. 'We're Magick!' he announces, and the girls all giggle like helpless schoolgirls.

The level of my dislike for them has risen to quite staggering heights, considering that a) I've never met them before, and b) they've done absolutely nothing wrong. The thing is, they're young, they're pretty and they're sensibly dressed. They all have flat shoes on – in my house! One of them is wearing a string of pearls. Can you imagine? The only pearls I own are attached to a rather sexy little g-string, and there was this one time when Dean licked every pearl before . . . no, sorry, I shouldn't really go into that here. Anyway, the girl with the pearl – Arabella or Rubella or something – well, she does not look like the sort of woman who runs about town dressed in a sexy thong, and perhaps that's why I dislike her. Or it could be the combination of the gratingly upper-class voice and the fact that she's young. Bitch.

It turns out the guy is called Rupert Sebastian. Rupert Sebastian!

'Ya,' Rupert Sebastian is saying, for no good reason, as he reaches into one of those laptop computer bag things that are basically just handbags for men. He pulls out a slim cream file then unwinds the scarf from round his neck. He looks even thinner without it. 'Right.' He opens the file and scans a page of notes inside. 'Tell us, Tracie, in your own words, exactly what happened yesterday and what the issues are that we need to address here today in our media planning and campaign strategising.'

So, once again, to much head-shaking and muttering, I run through the whole sorry tale.

'Then, the manageress locked the door and said they were going to call the police.'

'Did the police come?' asks Philonella in a high-pitched squeal that all the dogs in the neighbourhood can no doubt hear.

'No, they changed their minds and said that if I kept away from Vic then they wouldn't call the police. I think Posh's PR person said it was a bad idea to get the police involved and thus subject us all to massive press interest.'

'Ya,' says Rupert Sebastian. 'So you're saying that this has all been kept out of the press?'

'I think so,' I reply. 'But the manageress's daughter apparently works for *Luton Today* so there's every chance that the story will emerge at some time.'

'Ya,' says Rupert Sebastian, pushing his thumb and index finger into his temples. 'Ya.'

'So we wondered whether we should pre-empt that in some way by doing something . . . you know, an exclusive 'at home with' type of feature to show we're all normal and nice. Then, if the paper does run something, at least people will know I'm not a complete nutter before it appears. If you know what I mean.'

'I think it's utterly ludicrous,' says Mum. 'Just let it go. Keep out of the papers. Why do you want to be in the papers?'

'I don't,' I reply. 'I'm just trying to think of ways of making the situation all right again.'

'I'll tell you how you do that, shall I?' says Mum. 'You don't get into such a fucking mess in the first place. You don't whirl dogs around and cause menace and mayhem. That, my dear, is how you make situations all right.'

With that, she stands up, wiggles past Rupert Sebastian, blowing him a kiss (waste of time if you ask me, Rupert Sebastian is clearly more interested in Dean), and leaves the room.

Dean backs me the minute Mum leaves, which is interesting. He stands up, walks over to Rupert Sebastian and asks whether a photo-shoot with a paper can be arranged. Rupert Sebastian grabs his note-book with a flourish and starts scribbling and hurling out instructions to the girls. There's lots of 'oh yahs' and a certain number of 'fascin-ating, yas' and a decent number of 'you can rely on me, Rupert Sebastians' and off they all trot.

There does seem to be an astonishing amount of flapping, calling, texting and waving of Blackcurrants, or whatever those things that you get your emails on are called. All they have to do is make one phone call to a magazine about whether they want to do a photo-shoot with us. Why do they have to make everything so unnecessarily complicated? Is that what PR is? The process of over-doing the things that we'd all do naturally anyway? It wounds me to say this, but perhaps I'm not cut out to be Posh's best friend after all. She must have to put up with this sort of thing all the time, and I just don't think that I could.

Thursday, 30 August
10 a.m.

The journalist's name is Simon.

'Hi, *Hello! Luton*,' he says when Alba answers the door, and I spend most of the interview thinking 'Hella Luttyne? What sort of cruel joke is that for parents to play on their offspring?' Later he explains that he is called Simon and his magazine is *Hello! Luton*, which makes considerably more sense.

'So, what's it like being a footballer's wife?' he asks, and I tell him all about the hair extensions and fake tans and the importance of short skirts and tight tops. He says something about not understanding why all Wags dress like that, which throws me for a while. What's not to understand? Still, Simon's a man, so perhaps he doesn't quite get it. I explain all the rules of being a Wag and, slowly, he starts to laugh – which is an unexpected response, to put it mildly.

'Something funny?' I ask.

'Yes, you are.'

'Oh.'

'You're really witty. Your rules for being a Wag are great.'

He's genuinely laughing, which is nice, so I tell him that I'd really like to write a handbook for Wags but I'm worried that I won't be able to. I tell him that I had this idea while we were in the Italian place a few weeks ago, but haven't done anything about it except give Helen some basic advice. I start to tell him a few more of the rules of being a Wag. Things like my advice to Wags on ageing gracefully or disgracefully. Neither is the answer. My advice is not to do it at all.

'Simon,' I say. 'When it comes to getting older, don't do it! Get Botox, facelifts, fillers, plumpers, dye your hair, moisturise, fill out your lips, replace your teeth, have a cheek lift, chin enhancement, boob job, tummy tuck. Get veneers, permanent make-up and a range of light-reflecting clothing and make-up, but do not, in any circumstances, allow yourself to age.

'Ageing is pointless. Really, it has nothing to commend it. Forget all this bollocks about wisdom coming with age. Think of all the old people you've ever met. Are they wise? I bet they're not. All the ones I know are completely barking mad. No, I really don't see any point at all in getting old – don't do it.

'It annoys me immensely that there are all these scientists messing around trying to get cures for cancer, AIDS and other horrible, dirty old illnesses that no one I know ever has, while everyone, *everyone*, is ageing all the time, and these boffins just don't seem to be able to do anything to stop it. Imagine how happy the scientists could make everyone, and how much money they could make for themselves . . . If only they could see it like I can see it – that avoiding ageing, or all the signs of ageing, is the key to long-term happiness. Until that day, though, I think we all need to do our bit to look after ourselves and avoid all those things that will lead us to leathery skin, wrinkly eyes and greying hair. I'm not suggesting that you give up burgers, alcohol, chips or cigarettes, but I am suggesting that you get a good surgeon who will slice and fold and stitch and repair until your skin is so taut you can bounce table-tennis balls off it.'

Simon's in hysterics. It's hard to think why he's laughing so much but I find myself strangely flattered. It's nice to make people laugh, isn't it?

'You should write these things down,' he says with a huge smile. 'They're really funny.'

'But I can't write,' I explain.

'Of course you can,' says Simon. 'It's easy. Listen, I'm running a writing course in September. Why don't you come along? You might pick up some hints or even just get the confidence to write your handbook.'

'Mmmmm . . .' I mutter.

'I do think you should come, I do,' Simon is repeating. He goes on and on about the bloody course so much that I end up promising him that I'll go on it just to please him. I'm always like this – trying to please people, to make sure they like me, appreciate me and want me around. I guess it's from growing up without my dad – I'm forever chasing male approval. I even give Simon a cheque to pay for the bloody course, a gesture that delights him.

'Thank you, thank you!' he exclaims, as if I've given him the key to heaven, not a cheque for thirty pounds.

'Now then, back to the interview,' he says, and once again he's asking me a whole pile of questions that I answer as honestly and thoroughly as I can.

'You're incredible,' Simon says. 'So honest and straightforward. Such simple elegance of thought beneath that complicated, cluttered exterior. Who'd have thought?'

'Writers – they're all nuts!' I think to myself, trying to remember whether it was a writer or a painter who cut off his ear. Then I remember. 'Oh my god – I'm going to be a writer, too.' I worry, fleetingly, about whether my ascent into the literary world will involve me slicing off body parts, but decide it probably won't. Well, not unless a cosmetic surgeon advises it.

'You really are the most honest person I've ever met. Are you sure you're happy with everything you've said?' Simon checks as he finishes asking me questions.

'Yes,' I say.

'Even the stuff about the slave trade? Most people will think badly of you for saying that.'

'Let them,' I say. 'I have been true to myself and that is the most important thing in the world.'

'Okay. See you on the course,' he says.

Saturday, 1 September – match day and the day that _Hello! Luton_ magazine comes out
8 a.m.

I don't need an alarm clock this morning, nor the sounds of birds tweeting gently at my window. Mum's scream up the stairs and the sound of phones ringing and people dashing about alert me to the fact that morning has broken.

I get up and hunt around for my short, candyfloss-pink, marabou-trimmed dressing gown. I've got my extensions tied up in a bun . . . what's left of them. I really need to get them redone soon. I let them down and watch as the highlighted locks imported from somewhere in Russia, bleached and then heat-sealed to the roots of my own hair, cascade down and fall across my shoulders. I give them a bit of a ruffle and apply lipstick and powder. Then, in my marabou-fringed sandals, I descend the stairs. Blimey. Rupert Sebastian, Arabella and co. are standing around at the bottom of the stairs, all nervously looking at _Hello! Luton_ magazine. They see me coming and stare with their mouths open. I look down to make sure that my dressing gown hasn't swung open to reveal my marabou-fringed g-string (there's a bit of a marabou-fringe theme going on this morning). The other 'Ellas', whose names escape me, are frantically phoning and scribbling notes. It's like mission control. They all look so serious.

'Morning,' I chirrup, and they all look at me as if I've pulled out an AK47.

'You silly, silly girl,' screams Mum, flouncing in from the kitchen. 'What have you done?'

'I've just woken up,' I say in all innocence, amazed that my appearance has caused this level of consternation.

'Oh dear, this is terrible,' wails Mum. She waves _Hello! Luton_ magazine at me, and I start to scan the first page of the feature.

'"_Grace Kelly was lovely and all that, but let's be honest she was no Jordan_,"' I read out. 'What's wrong with that?'

I read on. '"I'd be Jodie Marsh over Lauren Bacall any day." Is there a problem here? It's just basic common sense. It's just my views and thoughts on the important issues of the day.'

'No,' says Mum. 'This is the problem.' She turns over the page with an almighty swish of her diamond-encrusted fingers, and there it is – in all its technicolour and deadly glory. It's horrific. A picture of me with my hair looking just awful. Awful. My extensions *seriously* need redoing. They look bushy on the ends – like Worzel Gummidge. 'Shit!' I declare, swinging my hands to the sides of my head in utter dismay. I've never been so humiliated. 'This is why you called Rupert Sebastian and the Ellas, isn't it?'

They all nod.

'Don't worry,' says the Ella with really dark hair who looks about sixteen. 'We can help you sort all this out. We can crisis-manage this. We're all firefighters at Magick.'

'You're what? Where's the fire?'

'Not literally,' says Rupert Sebastian in a very condescending way.

'But what can be done?' I ask, ignoring the rather confusing fire mention. 'Millions of people have seen this. What can possibly be done now?'

'Well, it's not millions for starters,' says Rupert Sebastian. 'It's only *Hello! Luton*. I doubt very many people have seen it at all. Us six reading it in this room have probably doubled their readership.'

'Why did we do an interview with *Hello! Luton* then?'

'We couldn't get you into any of the nationals. The *Daily Mail* said "Who?" and the guy on the *Express* just laughed.'

'Right,' I say. 'But it's still not good for a Wag to be seen with her hair looking like that.'

'Your hair?' says Rupert Sebastian.

'I knew you shouldn't have done this,' says Mum. 'Didn't I say this was a bad idea? You're a liability. What were you thinking of? And why are you now bleating on about your hair?'

'My hair looks terrible. That's the crisis, yes?'

'NO!' they all chorus.

It turns out the crisis is the few tiny comments I made that, in Rupert Sebastian lingo, 'could be construed as being racist'. Duh! All I was doing was talking about the various shades of spray tans that you can get and what they make you look like. Perhaps I should have been more careful with the language I used but I didn't mean it in an offensive way at all. I'm not racist. I think Beyoncé is great.

'Is it really such a problem?' I ask.

'YES!' they all chorus.

Rupert Sebastian starts reading, and I suppose, if I'm honest, I do kind of see what he means. Saying 'foreign players are selected because their dark skins look better in the team strip than the English players' skins do' probably isn't the done thing, even if that's how all the players joke after the games. And I guess calling all female players lesbians was unwise, not to say untrue. Shit! The worse thing, though, is my hair. It looks a sort of honey colour. HONEY!!! Since when was honey an appropriate colour for a Wag's hair? It should be platinum – think Marilyn, Diana Dors and woolly sheep.

'I've made a list of the issues we need to address,' says Rupert Sebastian, reading from his posh-looking notebook. 'There's racism, sexism, more sexism, more racism, talk of drugs, alcoholics, over-spending, and the stuff about the worst thing about life in a wheelchair must be the fact that you can't wiggle your way down the street in the latest platform-heeled wedges. You have a dig at disabled footballers, blind people, deaf people and single mothers. That's on page one. On page two there's . . .'

'STOP!' cries Mum. 'We all know what she's done. It's a full house. She's offended everyone in the world. The question is – what do we do about it?'

Rupert Sebastian and the Ellas continue to make notes and not offer an ounce of help. They just nod and say 'Mmmm' from time to time. I decide to sneak away and talk to Nell, she'll know what to do.

'I'm going to the bathroom,' I announce, and I stomp back upstairs. A quick phone call and I'm back down again.

'I've had an idea,' I say, knowing that if I tell Mum that it's Nell's idea she'll just dismiss it out of hand. 'We should just leave it. The article might not be read by many people, it may not get picked up by the nationals. I should just forget it rather than risk making things worse.'

The collection of PR geniuses scribble harder on their notebooks and Rupert Sebastian makes about three phone calls and starts frantic-ally issuing instructions to the others. They all nod and say 'ya' a lot and agree that would be a good media strategy moving forwards. They leave, saying they'll put their bill in the post, and I smile to myself at the thought that an eighty-four-year-old woman in a nursing home just outside Luton is the real coordinator of our 'media strategy moving forwards'.

'Well done, Nell,' I say under my breath, promising that I'll buy her a Black Russian next time I see her.

Sunday, 2 September
7.40 p.m.

'I'm back,' says Dean, slamming the door behind him so violently that all the chandeliers shake. He shuffles through the entrance hall and stops momentarily before the statue of himself. He glances over at the tributes to his international career and drops his head.

'It's over,' he says.

I immediately assume he must be talking about *Midsomer Murders*. 'No it's not,' I say. 'It doesn't start for twenty minutes.'

'No, I mean me . . . football . . . Luton Town . . . It's over. They've taken the captaincy off me.'

'Oh no,' I say. 'No, they can't have, Dean. That's awful.'

I lean onto the edge of the sofa, my head spinning, trying to take in the news. I am no longer the captain's wife, so no longer the Queen of all the Wags by right. I feel let down and humiliated.

'How could they?' I ask, plaintively. 'How could Luton do this to us?'

This is the trouble with football managers – they're selfish. All they think about is their bloody team. They never stop to think about the poor Wags.

'What about me?' I feel like screaming. 'Doesn't anyone at that place ever think about me?'

I glance at the pictures of Dean, covering the wall next to us, and at the pictures of the two of us on the day he was first made captain. I'm positively glowing, and it's not just because of the eight coats of glossy foundation. It's real pride shining through. Dean looks proud too. It's hard to tell from his face because he's got a gob full of chewing gum, but just from his posture you can sense that this is a man bursting with pride. What could have gone wrong? Why would they snatch the treasured captaincy position from him in this cruel and heartless fashion?

'Why, Dean?' I repeat, close to tears. 'Why would they do this to us? It's nothing to do with me and what I said in *Luton Life*, is it?'

'No, love,' he replies. 'It's 'cos I'm crap.'

Monday, 3 September
2 p.m.

I look like a mermaid! Like Lady Godiva! And oh how I love it! It's the greatest feeling in the world when my outer Wag is restored. I've gone a bit longer on this visit to the hairdresser – actually, a lot longer, which may defy all the basic rules of hair-cutting when you think about it, but that's what I've done. I can actually sit on my hair – isn't that amazing?! I just need to remember that small fact every time I go to the loo and all will be fine.

It was the sight of myself in the photo spread in *Hello! Luton* that propelled me in the direction of Mario's Manes. Then, once I got there, as with everywhere I ever go, I got completely carried away. You see, when you go to have extensions in your hair, they put them in very long to start with ('*ludo-crossly* long', as Mario is fond of saying in his fake Italian accent – I don't think he's been out of Luton, myself. I'm sure he learned all his Italian from gangster movies). Once the *ludo-crossly* long hair is in place, they cut it to the length and style you want. Today, I was sitting in the hairdresser's, looking at my reflection in the mirror as platinum hair cascaded down to my waist. Mario was standing behind me, poised, with the scissors in his hand, when I remembered how much Dean liked it last time I went really long. He liked it a lot. I'd been in the house about five minutes before he tore all my clothes off and – well, you know, did what a footballer does to his Wag. Admittedly, it was about ten years ago, but the memory of that afternoon flashed quite suddenly before my eyes as I sat there, and I don't know whether it was the free Asti Spumante they gave me or the sight of Mario's younger brother bending over the perming solutions in his tight Italian trousers, but I found myself suddenly wanting Dean to feel that way about me again.

'Leave it long. Very long, Mario,' I cry. 'Don't cut anything off it. I'll wear it long today.'

'Okay,' says Mario. 'You are sure, though? If it is this long, everyone will know you have had extensions. Your secret of beautiful hair will be known to the world.'

It was kind of him to say that but I'm sure the fact that I leave clumps of matted hair wherever I go and have little knots of glue dotted across the top of my head give it away anyway.

'Leave it long, long, long,' I said. '*Ludo-crossly* long.' And he did.

Now, here I am, striding down the street with my hair flapping around my hips. It's beautiful and sunny – one of those days on which you long to swish your long blonde hair from side to side and feel it land softly and settle elegantly across your shoulders. Or, in my case, land in something of a lump, because I've gone for artificial hair this time and it does weigh a hell of a lot more than human hair. I'm going to swing it with such ferocity one of these days that it'll fly back in my face and I'll end up knocking myself out, or breaking a shop window or something.

I walk into a fabulous lingerie shop and decide to buy something sophisticated and elegant to wow Dean with.

'Do you have anything crotchless?' I ask, glancing across the racks of uplift bras and lacy teddies. The lady looks me up and down and hands me a bright red lacy teddy – crotchless *and* nippleless!

'Wrap it up,' I say with something of a growl. 'Wrap it up.'

'But would madam like to try it on?'

'No, don't worry. I don't plan to be wearing it for long,' I say, winking and handing over my gold card.

'Taxi!' I shout. I have no driver today. I've given Doug the day off. The plan was that I would walk home in order to get some exercise. I read an article about French women and why they always look so glamorous and gorgeous – it said they always build exercise into their daily lives – walking everywhere, upstairs, to do the shopping, everywhere. But now it's come to it I've remembered that these shoes, and possibly every other pair of shoes I've ever owned or ever will own, were not, and will not be, made for walking. Besides, I'm not French – I'm an English Wag and proud of it.

A young and rather dishy-looking taxi driver pulls up, and I slide in, trying to look like Samantha from *Sex and the City*. Though not as old.

'Hi,' I say breathily. 'My name's Tracie.'

He looks at me and begins driving off, very slowly, while looking in the mirror quizzically. Oh no, I think. He's obviously recognised me from the article. Hopefully he didn't notice how awful my extensions were in the picture. He's probably thinking right now, 'My god, she looks just like the woman in the article, only this lady has much nicer hair.' I smile at the mirror as he's looking at me – his face looks ever more quizzical. Should I put him out of his misery? He really should keep his eyes on the road a bit more instead of trying to catch my eye.

'You're wondering where you know me from, aren't you?' I say.

'No, love,' he growls back. 'I'm just wondering where the hell you want to go.'

Oh shit, I haven't told him where I live.

I give him the address, but his unchivalrous outburst has rather ruined my mood, so I sit back and don't attempt to make any small talk or give him any tidbits about Luton Town to share with his mates in the pub. We arrive at the large gates and I can see he likes the look of the house. 'Wooooaaahhh,' he says with a whistle. 'Nice pad, love.'

I don't even dignify his comment with a reply. Instead I swing back my hair in dramatic fashion and slam the car door shut in an almighty huff, preparing to go into the house. As I say, that's what I was *preparing* to do. Unfortunately, in the process of flinging my hair back – hair that, I should add, is much longer than I am used to – and slamming the taxi door shut, I manage to trap my newly applied locks in the door. The taxi driver eases away slowly, with me half-running, half-skipping beside the taxi, knocking gently then more violently on the window in the hope of attracting his attention. He starts to speed up and I run faster to keep up with him. The door to the taxi is locked because they do, don't they? The bloody things lock as soon as the taxi is in motion. We're quite a sight now. He's reaching the end of our drive and I'm praying with every bone in my body that he will slow to a stop before turning right. If he doesn't I'm not sure what will become of me and, more importantly, my lovely brand-new sleek and silky hair extensions. He slows down and I hammer on the window. The road ahead is clear. Oh god, oh no. With an almighty whoosh he spins the wheel and takes the car onto the road at a roaring speed. 'Woooooaaahahhhhhhhhaaaahhhhhhhh . . .'

The car zooms up the road with about £550 of hair extensions hanging out of the rear passenger-side window. I clutch my head in horror as the taxi driver continues on his journey, oblivious to his newly acquired wig of hair.

Slowly, I stagger back down the drive to where I dropped my handbag and lacy undergarments. Only then do I realise that I've left the carrier bag in the back of the car. Blimey, the taxi driver has my entire seduction outfit at his disposal. If he shaves his chest he'll be in with Dean tonight. I certainly won't be.

Saturday, 8 September
6 p.m.

Another match, another embarrassing afternoon in which no one wanted to talk to me, sit next to me, or have anything to do with me. I'm sitting here with a jaunty little beret perched on one side of my head (I think you know why, but don't tell the girls). Suzzi and Michaela are the only Wags I have anything to do with down here now. The others walk past me as if they haven't seen me. I don't know why. Presumably they don't like to talk to me because Dean is not in the side. I know that sounds odd, but it's the only thing I can think of. I say 'Hi' to Mindy and the others, but they just keep clip-clopping past, heads in the air, fake-tanned shoulders back, and Dior handbags swinging magnificently by their sides.

'Helen,' I shout. 'Is there a problem?'

I thought that Helen and I would be friends forever when I gave her the advice on behaving like a Wag.

She gives the 'whatever' sign with her fingers and continues past me, looking thinner, younger, blonder and more orange than ever. Bitch! That upset me more than her rude hand signs ever could. Helen's great pals with Deb 'n' Jules now – the inseparable, unbearable nineteen-year-old Slag Wags with perfect nails, perfect extensions and immaculate, heavily-made-up skin. There's a core of five of them who dominate the Luton Wags scene. There's no question that Suze, Mich and I have been pushed aside. It's thoughtless and heartless of them, but I guess it comes to us all eventually.

I know that I'm being ostrich-sized because Dean's not playing well, just as I'm loved and adored when he's scoring goals and making tactical decisions that make some sort of sense. It's hard being a Wag sometimes, with no personal control over how people treat you and respond to you.

Thank god for Suze and Mich – they tell me not to worry about 'those losers' and they'll stick by me. They are girls I've known forever. You know what it's like when you have friends like that. You might not see them for ages, then when you do see them it's as if you see them every day. They're probably a bit like me. You know – we like the same clothes and stuff, we have the same hairstyles and scream with delight at the arrival of the new lipstick lines. We're fundamentally the same. We have a deep intellectual connection; an attraction on a spiritual and emotional level.

Suze and I first met when her husband Anton played at Arsenal with Dean, so we go back years. It was completely fab when Anton signed for Luton Town last season.

Michaela's the third member of the gang. She's lovely – especially now she's got blonde highlights at the front of her hair. She's been on a big search to find a footballer now that she's blonde – you know, dating everything that moves. Not that there's anything wrong with that – as far as I'm concerned you become a Wag by whatever means possible, you can't just hold out for the right man to come along. If you look around a bar and there are three rich, successful, handsome and emotionally mature men there drinking pints of bitter in a manly fashion, and one ne'er-do-well at the end of the bar getting pissed on Bacardi Breezers, and if all three said men turns towards you and wink seductively . . . which one are you going home with? You know what the answer is? The one who's a footballer. None of that other stuff matters – all that emotional maturity twaddle; all that being hand-some and well-dressed – it's all complete baloney, and so is all this rich-beyond-your-wildest-dreams nonsense. It's all about finding the right footballer, not finding the right man. If, like me, you find the perfect man and he happens to be a great footballer then you're sorted. I feel truly blessed, and I mean that genuinely and truly. As true at the Versace 'sparkle 'n' glo' plastered carelessly across my shiny face.

So, back to Michaela. She's had a few problems in the man depart-ment, bless her. I don't know why, because her extensions always look lovely, you'd think any footballer worth the laces in his boots would be honoured to be seen with her. Her problems started when Jamie Muller broke his leg and couldn't play any more, so obviously she dumped him immediately despite being massively in love with him, and went out with another player. Then, when that relationship broke up it was all looking really awful because for one terrible moment it seemed that she'd have to go out with a commoner (a non-footballer). Then, just two weeks ago, something magical happened. Andre Howchenski, the Luton Town goalkeeper, actually returned her call after the two of them spent the night together. He didn't move house, pretend to be dead or change his phone number – he answered her call and asked her on a date. Imagine that! Mich was thrilled. They've been seeing each other for a couple of weeks now so it's really serious.

Andre took Mich out to dinner at this lovely French restaurant on their first date, and all was looking good. They seemed to like each other. She went a deeper shade of orange, which is always a sure sign of a Wag-on-the-pull, and he had a certain swagger about him that I hadn't seen in a long time (not since before Dean started scoring own goals against him, to be honest). The two of them kept smiling and giggling at hidden secrets. But I haven't asked her about him recently because I just haven't seen that much of her.

She seems happy, though, snuggled up in her lime-green fleecy dress with bare legs and white high-heeled boots. As I glance at her hair, I notice something really odd.

'What's up with your extensions?' I ask in horror. It looks like they're all starting to come apart. Not a good look at all, and not very Mich.

'It's not the extensions,' she says, turning from deep orange to deep red, traffic-light style. 'It's wax.'

'Wax?' reply Suze and I in harmony. 'How have you managed to get wax into your hair?'

Okay, so it turns out that Mich's second date with Andre was last night, and she wasn't quite as well-behaved as she was on the first date.

'We were going to a friend of his for supper,' says Mich, a look of horror creeping across her face as she recalls the events of the night before.

'Oh,' say Suze and I, moving in closer to hear the gossip more clearly. 'Do tell.'

'It was just awful. We went to this guy Martin's flat in Wandsworth. It was a beautiful place, right on the river, and I didn't know anyone else there – except Andre, of course – so I was trying my hardest to make them like me, you know how you do. I had my toenail pierced for the occasion and I remember throwing my leg onto the table to show them and knocking three glasses off in the process. I guess I'm not as flexible as I thought I was. They looked a bit alarmed – with my foot appearing on the table at the same time as the scallops and pancetta starters – but I showed them anyway.'

Suzzi and I must look a bit shocked by this time, because Mich gets all defensive. 'I couldn't help it,' she says. 'I'd drunk about six cocktails, four Bacardi and cokes and been necking tequila slammers all night.'

'Okay,' we say sympathetically. 'Carry on with the story.'

'Well, I kind of had a disaster, and there are three reasons for that. First, I got drunker and drunker as the evening progressed. Second, I had really high shoes on – obviously. Third, I decided I needed to put more lip-gloss on, so I leapt to my feet to go to the bathroom.'

'Oooooooo,' we both say at the thought of drunk women in high heels leaping anywhere. 'Where did you end up?'

'Well, there were these candles all lined up at the side of the room . . .'

'Oooooooo,' we both say.

'Yep,' says Mich, nodding as we grimace in sympathy. 'I went careering into them. There was wax everywhere – wax on the walls, splattered across the floor, the table, the chairs and across all the guests. Two of the women yelped in pain as hot wax burned them.'

'Oh god,' we both mutter, then I say, 'You were lucky not to be burned.'

'I wish I had been,' says Mich. 'I wish I'd just been burned to death, there and then, because what happened next was even worse.'

'Worse than throwing yourself head first into the candles in a strange man's luxury Wandsworth flat on a second date?'

'Yes,' says Mich. 'Much worse than that. You see, the wax was all in my hair and getting tangled in my extensions, so I instinctively swung my head away from the candles and ended up splattering wax into Andre's lap. The wax burned straight through his really tight, shiny grey trousers and . . . how can I say this . . . Well, I kind of gave him a rather major bikini wax.'

'Ewwwwwww,' we both cry, knowing, as we do, all about major bikini waxes and how dreadfully inappropriate they would be for a handsome goalkeeper from Luton Town.

'You know, in that minute, all my dreams popped like bubbles in front of me . . . all my plans for a beautiful little cottage and three kids called Roons, Becks and Lampy . . . all gone. I thought he'd hate me forever. I thought all chances of a relationship would be gone.'

'Ohhhhhhhhh,' we both utter sympathetically. We desperately want Mich's relationship to work out so she's fully back in the Wag-race.

'How's Andre now?' I ask, out of sympathy for him and interest in my friend's social life, but also out of sheer panic because without him in goal to stop Dean's mad own-goal scoring, Luton might as well not take to the pitch. Dean will simply run riot and Luton will lose every game about 25–0 – all scored by their former captain.

'He's okay,' says Mich. 'The doctors say it's second-degree burns, but it won't require a skin graft or anything. Thank god!'

'Do you think you'll see him again?' asks Suzzi, knowing how much Mich likes this guy but equally aware that embarrassing a guy in front of all his mates then giving him second-degree burns isn't necessarily ideal second-date behaviour. It's not in *The Rules*, let's put it that way.

'Yes,' says Mich, delight all over her face. 'We're meeting next week. I'm going to wear sensible shoes and I'm not going to drink.'

'Sensible shoes?'

'Only joking,' she says with an unfeminine snort. 'I'm going to get completely off my tits and wear my skyscraper heels. He might as well know what he's dealing with here. There's no point in kidding him. I'm a Wag and proud of it, and he should realise that.'

'Aaaahhh,' we both say in relief, and I think we're both thinking that Andre and Mich might well be perfectly suited to one another.

Sunday, 9 September
10 a.m.

I've had the now weekly phone call from Mum in which she announces her intense displeasure at me for one thing or another. It's quite peculiar that she comes to my house all the time when I'm out, but on Sundays – when she knows I'm in – she phones instead. Recently it has been Dean's performance on the pitch that she's complaining about in her calls – and this is something I struggle to accept as my problem even though I'm usually inclined to take everyone's problems on board as my own. Why is it my problem if he's now complete rubbish, a shadow of his former self, and an embarrassment to the team? They've taken the captaincy off him, they've pretty much taken his place away from him. Now it's only a matter of time before they take his boots off him altogether. Most matches he sits on the bench, looking up into the crowd and trying to spot me. I wave madly, much to the shame of Paskia when she's with me. He smiles and jumps around when he sees me. It's all nice. Trouble is, though he's as great a bloke as ever, and Suze and Mich keep calling him the perfect man, he's really not as great a footballer as ever. I'm not saying he was ever George Best but he could at least locate the right goal mouth and kick the ball when it came to him, instead of tripping over it like a toddler. I mean – he was an international. He wore the three lions proudly on his chest. But now it feels as if that part of his life has gone forever – drifted away from us on a sea of rubbish footwork and on waves of stupid decision-making. Yes, there are days, I must be honest, when I think his career has drowned altogether.

Dean's started to question himself as a footballer, too. He even talked about whether he should leave the club altogether. You know – try his hand at something else. Aaaaarghhhh . . . him not being a footballer is a hugely terrifying prospect. What happens to me? How can I be a Wag if my man isn't a footballer? I know in my heart of hearts that I'll always be a Wag because I'm such a natural at it. I don't think it would be possible to walk past me without thinking, *She's a Wag*, but I suppose that while being a Wag is very much about a state of mind and having the right wardrobe, it's also about having a husband or boyfriend who plays football . . . and mine doesn't. Oh god. What am I going to do?

Mum had a go at me today for not being nice to the other Wags yesterday. She says I am rude and that sitting in the corner giggling and laughing with Mich and Suze is no way to behave. She says the other Wags knew I was laughing about them. *Hello?* I try to explain that I was laughing about Mich's date with the goalkeeper who ended up having a bikini wax after Mich had ended up head-first in the candles . . . but no good.

'It was clear that you were laughing at us,' says Mum.

'Us?'

'Yes, us,' says Mum.

'So, you're a Luton Town Wag now, Mum?' I say jokingly, trying to get her into a happier mood, but my attempt fails miserably.

'There's so much negativity in your voice. I'm going to light some candles,' she says. 'They're made from lemongrass, ginger and crushed soya beans taken from the hooves of mountain goats. You should try to embrace the light of the world and move out of the darkness. Why don't you try blessing your inner woman with the sprig of lavender that I gave you? Dance a little, chant and praise the forces of nature for all they have given you. Have you still got that tambourine?'

'Er . . . yes,' I say, which, strictly speaking, is true. It's in a box in the loft with all the other loony things she presents us with. The box is marked 'Mad Angie'.

Monday, 10 September
7 p.m.

I've really gone off Luton Town. There's a girl here, hanging around the Bobbers Stand (that's where all us Wags sit) wearing a fitted navy-blue jumper that looks as if it's made from lambs' wool or some other such rubbish fabric. She has flat leather shoes and tailored trousers. She looks like bloody Princess Diana. Subtle, expensive-looking jewellery, a simple, elegant handbag and a Hermes scarf. I'm almost choking with laughter. It's the funniest thing I've ever seen. I'm laughing so much, in fact, that my g-string has got all tangled. Happily my skirt's so short I can untangle it easily enough. In fact it was Mich who noticed it was tangled in the first place. 'Oy, love, you've got your knickers in a right old twist there,' she said, and we howled with laughter.

The woman keeps looking round. She's got one of those faces that looks like she's just drunk sour milk. At least, every time she looks over at me she pulls this awful face. I've never seen anyone who is more in need of my help. I can't help thinking how great she would look if we sorted out her make-up, gave her some false tits and put her in hotpants. I really must write that handbook. There are women here screaming out for help. I bet the country's terraces are full of women like this – clueless individuals in their comfy knitwear thinking that they can turn up and bag a man simply by having a nice personality and a passable face. It's much, much more complicated than that, but with a few simple rules they could be well on their way to a night of passion with a footie man.

It's just so hard to find the time to write anything when I'm so busy. I went to Croydon again last night to collect the car. They wouldn't let me take it because I didn't have my driving licence with me. How absurd is that? I mean – really – who carries their licence round with them? Not me! 'Back we go,' I said to Doug. 'We'll have to come back again next week.'

It's me, Mich and Suze sitting here together again for this Monday night game. Mich looks fab. She's had more blonde put in the front of her hair and they have to put so much bleach on to make her dark hair blonde that it's really starting to take its toll on the condition. It's gone from being thick and glossy to quite coarse and unruly, which is ideal!

'I don't look like a beaver, do I?' she asks.

'Not at all,' I say, but actually she does a bit. I think she probably needs more blonde to lose the stripe effect. The great thing is that she's looking more Waggish all the time. No wonder it's going so well with Andre.

'I think I'm in love,' she says, and Suzzi and I start mentally planning the wedding. We're bound to be bridesmaids.

The other Wags are sitting a few rows away from us. They're all cuddled up with their bare arms wrapped round one another to keep warm. I notice Mum's there again. I wonder why she didn't tell me she was coming.

'Come and sit next to us,' I shout over in my friendliest voice.

'I'm happy here,' she shouts back. There's a lot of giggling from the Slag Wags either side of her.

'She's a Wag now,' they say.

'She's the mother of a Wag,' Michaela corrects.

'No, I'm a Wag,' says Mum, standing up so that everyone in the stand can see what a fifty-three-year-old woman with enormous fake breasts looks like in a lurid green, skin-tight crop top and matching hot-pants. I think blue-jumper woman just fainted. Mum's also wearing cowboy boots with really high heels! They're gorgeous. I didn't know you could get high heels like that on cowboy boots.

'I'm seeing Ludo,' she says proudly. 'I am a Wag.'

'Ludo,' I laugh. Mum's being silly. Ludonio Svetcarior is about nineteen years old.

'Yes, Ludo,' she says. 'We're in love.'

'Right,' I reply, waiting for a punch-line that never comes. 'Ludo, huh?'

So, Mum's a Luton Town Wag. She's going out with a Croatian who's barely started shaving. Great. She's part of the clique of Wags at Luton Town and I'm on the fringes. It seems obscene. No, what am I saying – it *is* obscene. Things just can't get any worse.

Tuesday, 11 September
6 a.m.

Today is the first day of the rest of my life. The day on which I will become a literary genius like Jackie Collins, Jordan and . . . what's his name? The bloke who wrote all the crap that we had to learn at school. What was his name? Can't remember. Anyway, I have to be honest, I'm looking forward to this so much that I can't help myself from squealing out loud at the thought of it. It's great to be doing something to improve myself that doesn't involve any physical pain . . . I haven't ever done that. To be honest, I didn't know that it could be done! I'm also really looking forward to seeing Simon again. He called a few times after the interview appeared, just to check everything was okay with it.

'Of course!' I said. 'You wrote it beautifully.'

'And you were happy with how you came over?' he asked, sounding concerned.

I said that I was, and he said he was pleased. I seem to have a real connection with him. I don't know what it is about Simon but he's not like other men I know – like the guys down the football club who I always feel slightly on edge with. He's so comforting and just – well – nice. He makes me feel like I'm a good person. How can someone make you feel like that just by talking to you? I don't know really . . . but he does.

He said that he's moving from *Hello! Luton* to work at the *Guardian*, so he's done really well for himself. Well, I don't know whether he has really. I think *Hello! Luton* is a good read and the *Guardian*'s crap, but Simon seems to be very pleased with the decision to go from a publication full of glamorous pictures to a newspaper where there are basically no pictures, except of boy soldiers armed to the teeth in Africa, and po-faced politicians with bad hair, and skinny environmentalists with no charisma or style.

It's now 6 a.m. and I have to be there for 9 a.m. The driver's picking me up at 8.50 a.m. (I don't trust taxis any more – not since the extensions disaster. I had to go back to Mario's and have the whole lot redone). So, there's no time to waste. There's so much to be done. I've bought a fabulous white crocodile-skin briefcase, a Montblanc pen, which I had specially made in rose-pink with Dean 'n' Trace engraved down the side, and a Smythson notebook because I read that Alex Curran was carrying one. I look a bit like Alex Curran, and Dean looks a bit like Steven Gerrard, and we used to copy them and dress like them. I don't do that now, though – not since she hit that girl outside the Chinese restaurant. I decided she wasn't a great role model, so I packed away the flouncy tunic tops and told Dean to get his hair spiked again.

Anyway, she's no role model for me now, is she? What with me all set to become a literally type. I should take my inspiration from J.K. Rowling instead. Mmmm . . . maybe not. Her hair's too short. Anyway, whoever I decide to honour by calling them my role model, it's obvious that they will be someone lovely and sophisticated, but obviously with a massive wardrobe. That's really important for a writer. Don't think for one minute that Zadie Smith sat down in a scruffy old pair of trackies and bashed out *White Teeth*. Not that I read it. I picked it up thinking it was a guide to getting white veneers fitted by a cosmetic dentist. What a letdown.

Anyway, I bet Zadie doesn't work like that. You need to present yourself properly and creatively in order for the creative feelings to flow through your mind like a gently babbling brook (Do they babble gently? I don't know).

I've been through my wardrobe about twenty times and have settled for something that I believe to be suave and sophisticated, and given it a sharp Waggy edge by more make-up than you've ever seen in your life before . . . more, perhaps, than is seen on an entire Girls Aloud tour. I've piled the fake tan on, too, so at least I look healthy!

Clothing-wise, it's the really high platform-soled shoes in white with the ties that go up to my calf. They're twelve centimetres high, so walking is a problem, but I'm not going to walk, I'm going to write, so I figure they're fine. I've also gone for a really, really short denim miniskirt. When I bend over you can see my knickers, so I've taken them off. On top, I've got a Juicy Couture boob tube and a white leather jacket with heavy fringing, loads of studs and a kind of stand-up collar. Dean bursts into Elvis songs every time he sees me wearing it, which is so NOT funny. When he does, I tell him his singing's worse than his football. He soon stops.

With all the jewellery and a flower in my hair, it looks perfect! Just perfect for a writing course. I stagger out to the car, hoping once again that I won't have to do any standing or walking around, because if there's one thing these shoes definitely aren't designed for, it's any sort of contact with the floor.

Doug smiles at me, and I smile back and tell him I'm going on a course and I'm worried because it's all about punctuation.

'Oh, don't worry about that,' he says, revving the engine and moving at quite a speed down our long drive. 'I'll get you there on time.'

'Blimey,' says Simon when I stagger into his scruffy little classroom. 'Are you off out somewhere afterwards?'

'No,' I say, a little baffled. 'I'd have worn underwear if I was.'

Simon drops his notebook and I offer to pick it up for him. 'Noooooooooo,' he cries as I begin to bend over. 'Just take a seat.'

I've ended up arriving really early because Doug raced here like a lunatic, telling me all the way not to worry about punctuation. What's interesting is how the others are early, too. I'm used to arriving everywhere late but this is quite fun, being on time.

What's not fun, though, is looking at what everyone's wearing. *Hello!!!!!* This is a writing course! It's like Jackie Collins never existed. We need a new, stronger word for dowdy. These people are appallingly badly dressed. Really – it's just staggering. There are women here in flat shoes and no make-up! There's a woman with cropped brown hair and these kind of Doc Marten style boots! How does she think she's going to make it as a writer dressed like that? I begin to hope she never saw Simon's article in which I said all women with short hair are lesbians and that all lesbians should be jailed for wearing dungarees.

'Okay,' says Simon. 'Everyone take a seat.'

I perch on the end of the chair at the far side of the room and proudly pull out my pink pen. The others seem to have brought stubby old pencils or terrible inky Bic biros. Nasty! One by one we go round and say why we're here. Most of them say they did English at university and feel like there's a writer in them trying to get out.

When a fat girl says there's a writer inside her trying to get out, all I can think is, There's more than one! Is that nasty of me? Am I being fattist? When Simon gets to me, my mind goes completely blank. Why am I here? It's because I want help writing my Wags' Handbook, but it all feels too complicated and difficult to explain.

'Tracie?' says Simon again. 'Why are you here?'

'Because some Wags are awful!' I announce. 'They have no idea how to dress, and their hair is terrible and they sometimes don't drink on nights out. I saw one girl in jeans. Jeans! Not denim shorts or a denim skirt, but jeans . . . like a man! There are women with nowhere near enough make-up. It's just awful, and they need me to guide the way. Like the star of Bethlehem . . . but instead I come to show womankind the right way to live, and how to conduct themselves.'

There are sniggers from the corner of the room, but I notice that those who are sniggering are ugly, so I just laugh back at them.

'Do you have Ugg boots?' I ask.

'Er, no,' says the woman in a big jumper and glasses.

'Then I rest my case.'

Simon looks at me as if he doesn't quite know whether to call the police or an ambulance. 'But what's that got to do with writing?' he encourages. 'I asked you why you came on the course.'

'I want to write a handbook – the greatest-ever guide to being a Wag – knowing what to say, do, and most, most, most importantly – knowing what to wear.'

'Thank you,' says Simon, looking relieved. 'Well, we've got a mixture of people here today – some of you with a feeling that you were put on this earth to write, and others, like Tracie, with a very real project in mind. How do you think we should start?' He turns to a small Indian man who has been hastily scribbling down everything Simon has said. 'How do *you* think we should start?' he repeats.

The man shrugs. He looks quite terrified and I feel enormously sorry for him, and desperate to put him out of his misery.

'I think we should just all start writing,' I say. 'Simon, you can't teach us to become writers, it has to come from within us. You can just offer guidelines and helpful hints. Perhaps if we just got going, and started writing, then you could look at what we've done and start from there?'

What a load of bollocks I'm spouting, but Simon seems happy enough. He's smiling, which I guess is a good thing, and when he mouths 'thank you' I feel my cheeks go red.

Actually, in the end the course isn't much fun. Simon seems to be inordinately pleased with me, though – praising me, thanking me for my contributions and generally being very nice. The nicer he is, the more I want to contribute, and in the end it is very much the Trace 'n' Simon show.

But, in the moments when I'm not contributing, god, I am bored. Bored, bored, bored. What makes it worse is that every time I get my nail file out, Simon tells me to stop. 'Concentrate, Tracie. Think, Tracie.' He talks about Dickens and that Shaky bloke. Shakin' Stevens, is it? Or is that someone else? And those ugly birds – the ones who always wore such dull, plain dresses – Plain Jane Austen and Emily dull-as-death Brontë.

'Can we talk about writers that aren't dead?' I ask.

Simon shakes his head and says we're talking about the *best* writers. I pull a facepack out and start putting it on, but apparently that isn't allowed either. Blimey, for someone who likes to think of himself as being creative and alternative and bohemian Simon doesn't half have a lot of rules.

At lunchtime people sit and eat sandwiches in a circle and talk about French writers and some Russian bloke who once turned into a big fly or something. I've had enough. Clip clop clip I go – off to the wine bar for half a bottle of something fizzy and pink, a quick look in the shops and a quick clip clop click back again. How am I supposed to know they are halfway through the next exercise?

'You've been three hours!' exclaims Simon.

'I know. I only had half a bottle and there weren't many shops,' I say with the self-righteous pride of the truly abstemious.

'Well, you'll just have to catch up here. We can't start it all again. There's twenty minutes of the exercise left. Everyone is drafting the first five hundred words of a novel, screenplay or drama that they'd like to write. It can be fiction or non-fiction, real or imagined. I just want to get everyone writing. We'll break for coffee and biscuits after that, and I'll look through all the work and feedback my thoughts to you in a group environment and we'll all learn from each other.'

Oh god, it's all so hippie-like. Then we'll all put flowers in our hair (luckily I already have one), pass round a pipe and sing 'Kumbaya'. Christ. I'm off back to the wine bar.

But Simon hands me some paper and a terrible little pencil and points at the clock. He says that we have to be finished by 4 p.m. 'Thanks,' I mutter, taking the paper and pencil and sitting back down. I know what I will do, and I am fairly sure that Simon and the others will mock me, but that certainly isn't going to stop me. I will begin to write my handbook.

'Tracie,' says Simon somewhat later, making me jump and paint a stripe of liquid ruby nail polish all over my feet.

Oh god, I'm in trouble again. All I did was paint the little toenail on my right foot where it rubbed off against the inside of my shoe. The lezzers are all staring at me as if they think it better to go through the day with scruffy toenails than to poison the air with the fumes from my nail-varnish bottle.

'Sorry,' I say, swinging my foot onto the desk to dry the toe as quickly as possible, before remembering that I have no knickers on and quickly swinging the foot back down again.

Simon almost drops the papers he is holding, composes himself and stares straight back at me. 'Tracie,' he repeats. 'This is fantastic. It's amazing. It's funny and clever. It's well-observed. It shows understanding of the specific sub-culture you're addressing while retaining enough crucial objectivity to be critical. I think your handbook is brilliant. I think it has real potential, and if you come and talk to me after the class I'll run through exactly what you should do to finish this book and how you might get it published.'

'Published?'

'Yes, Tracie, you have talent, despite your best efforts to mask it. We should probably think about setting it up as a blog.'

Setting me up in a bog? Who does he think I am? Shrek or something?

Friday, 14 September
11 a.m.

I suppose it's predictable really, but it turns out that Simon was just being kind. I'm not really any good at writing at all. Mum says my writing is rubbish. She is doing her facial exercises in the mirror while telling me what she thinks. It is confusing to understand her at first, but I soon get the gist of it. 'Utter crap' are the exact words she utters, in between making faces like a fish. I just showed her the work I did on the course and she laughed out loud. At first I thought that was a good thing because Simon had said it was very funny. Mum's laugh was different, though – it was a kind of 'my-god-you're-rubbish' cackle rather than a hearty laugh and a pat on the back.

'I can't wait to tell the other Wags,' says Mum, flouncing off towards the kitchen, still laughing. 'You were never any good at anything. Some things never change.'

More and more frequently I find that the only way I can cheer myself up when Mum says something hurtful to me is to go and see Nell. As Mum flees out into the garden, to moan, no doubt, about how much colder it is here than in Malibu, her harsh words hang like a poisonous cloud in the air. I can't stay here and subject myself to more abuse. I decide to take my notes and head for Sunnyside Sheltered Accommodation for the Elderly. Even if Nell doesn't think my writing is very good, at least she'll have a nicer way of telling me, and she's intelligent and perceptive enough to give me an indication of why it's no good. Mum's reasoning seems to be that it is no good because I'm no good, which seems rather harsh.

Here we are! I seem to have got here in record time. I'm a bit like that with my driving – I either get places in three minutes flat (mainly because I never take any notice of speed limits ... or red lights ... or oncoming traffic ... or give way at roundabouts) or it takes me bloody ages to get anywhere, because while I ignore all traffic-controlling devices, I also ignore all maps and instructions, so spend most of my time driving round at high speed, totally lost!

Still, I make it in good time today, and even manage to squeeze in a little detour round Marks and Spencer's, which is great. It's not an unpleasant-looking place is Sunnyside Sheltered Accommodation. It looks a little bit like where students live when they go away to university. Dean had to go to a university for some fitness tests once and I went with him. Funny places, aren't they? Full of dull people in bad clothes reading books. What's all that about?

There are loads of trees and ponds everywhere at Sunnyside with little ducks waddling about. I pull into the car park, dumping the hire car across three parking bays, next to the sign saying 'Strictly no parking – reserved for ambulances'. I went back to get my car last night and it turns out you can't pay by credit card. 'Madam, it has to be a debit card or cash,' said the bloke who looked like a gone-to-seed bouncer (I quite fancied him, in a way. He had lovely tattoos). Doug says his car knows the way to Croydon all by itself now, which is of limited value, I would imagine, but I didn't tell him that.

I've brought Nell some flowers and a couple of huge bags of shopping because she seems to get alarmingly excited at the prospect of groceries. Must be something to do with the shortages during the war, but confronted with the choice between a designer bag and a bag of potatoes, I know she'd take the spuds every time.

'Hello, love,' she says, eyeing the white Marks and Spencer's carrier bags in my hands and almost salivating. 'How nice of you. I'll ring the girls now.'

The 'girls' are Ethel and Gladys. Ethel is a rather mad eighty-three-year-old neighbour who, in common with everyone else in the building, loves bingo and can't hear anything unless her hearing aid is turned right up. Gladys is Nell's ninety-two-year-old best friend. Nell is very, very old, but Gladys looks like Nell's mother – she's older than time itself. She's lived through the World Wars, a whole pile of kings, queens and prime ministers, and the Ark. Whenever I take food to Nell's, the 'girls' come round and they all divide the food up. Nell tips it onto the counter. 'Oooo, Ethel, you like mushrooms, don't you? Well, you can have those and I'll have three extra sprouts.'

They go through both bags in this bizarre fashion, exclaiming, 'You brought three chickens, three steaks and three loaves . . . isn't that lucky! We can have one each.'

We've been doing this ridiculous activity for years. I may not be Alfred Einstein but I'm certainly able to recognise that if I buy three of everything it makes their lives much easier. When Nell first got to the home I brought over a bag of food, but it contained just one chicken. The complicated way in which these little old ladies divided up the poor bird – with blunt knives, broken rulers and sharp words – has scarred me for life.

We stand around in Nell's small but spotless kitchen, eyeing the produce on the counters in three piles. There's lettuce, broccoli, spinach and cabbage all piled up, threatening to overflow and tumble to the ground. 'Ooo – that reminds me!' says Nell, still staring at the array of greenery. 'I've got something for you.' She winks at me and rushes away while Gladys and Ethel wipe the spotless work surfaces and the sink, scrubbing at imaginary dirt, unable to stop cleaning or stop looking after one another. They've all brought up families in the toughest conditions imaginable. They've devoted their lives to looking after people, and I guess that's something they'll always do.

I often think about the lives these women have had and realise how lucky I am. Poor old Nell brought up her own family (six children!), then when her only daughter died (Dean's mum – Sandra) she brought Dean up on her own as well. Nell's husband died fifteen years ago, but he was always away when the children were growing up, so she's effectively brought seven kids up by herself, working full-time to support them, coping with everything on her own. I think she's amazing. I'd love her to come and live with us – I'd just love her around the house, and I'd love knowing that she was safe and being properly cared for. But she's too independent. Perhaps in a few years when she's senile and thus a little bit more malleable.

'Da-da,' says Nell, walking into the kitchen and holding up something utterly disgusting. All the nice thoughts I've been having about her fade away to nothing as she unveils her gift to me – the most vile green-coloured mock-velour tracksuit. It's kind of pea-coloured and the seams are coming apart. There's nothing to commend the garment at all. It's made from that terrible rough material that catches your nails when you touch it.

Nell puts it on along with a matching and equally disgusting jacket, and shows me how 'good' they look by running around her compact kitchen and dancing like a loon. 'I got it free – from the bingo,' she says, as if that's a surprise; as if I could ever have imagined in a million years that anyone would have paid for such a hellish outfit.

'Oooo, Nell,' says Gladys as Dean's gran wiggles about in her old-lady way. She looks not unlike Shrek. 'It does look expensive.'

The reality, of course, is that nothing has ever looked cheaper.

'Nell, you look so good in it – why don't you keep it?' I suggest.

It turns out that Nell already has one. In fact, Nell has about a dozen. She swings open her hall-cupboard door and I can see them lined up – every one of them the colour of Kermit the Frog.

'You don't have to have it if you don't want it,' says Nell, looking more than a little upset.

'No, Nell – I'd love it,' I lie. 'I'd really love it. Thank you.'

All of them are looking at me as we stand around in the kitchen. I can feel their beady little eyes. It's as if they are waiting for me to say something earth-shattering, which simply isn't going to happen. When I don't speak, they immediately assume that there is something wrong with me.

'You seem a bit low today, love, are you sure you're all right?' asks Gladys. 'Not your usual bright and breezy self.'

I decide not to say that the sight of the lurid green costume has made me feel quite queasy. Instead, I tell them all about the course and how Simon thought I was a good writer, but then Mum said I wasn't and that I should abandon all my plans in that direction straightaway. At the mention of Mum I see Nell's lip curl. The two of them have never got on at all, which has made it quite difficult for Dean over the years. Mum clearly thinks Nell is common, and Nell clearly thinks that Mum is a blood-thirsty locust who's hell-bent on sucking us dry. I know this because Nell used those exact words when Dean bought Mum a house, a car and a wardrobe full of clothes. She repeated them when Mum announced that she wanted a key to our house and started treating it as her own. Nell would never behave like that – she has too much pride. She'd much rather be in the silly old home with her crazy friends than think, for one second, that she was imposing on anyone.

'Let's see it then,' says Nell, and I hand over the work I did on the course. She, Ethel and Gladys reach over at exactly the same time and put their glasses on the ends of their noses, squinting through them and looking in such pain in the process that you wonder what on earth good the glasses are doing. There's a silence, then some laughter, then Nell looks up. 'This is brilliant. You didn't write this!'

'I did,' I say, feeling all happy and alive again. 'I wrote it in twenty minutes.'

There are lots of 'Ooooooos' and 'Aaahhhhhs' from the old ladies, and Nell is saying things like 'Well, I never' and 'To be honest, I'm not surprised, I always thought there was something special about you', and as Nell fills the kettle with water I feel about as happy as a human being can feel . . . possibly happier than when I had all my extensions redone after the incident with the runaway taxi. Or possibly not. But nearly. In fact, odd as it may seem, I want to stay in this moment forever – Nell in her bright green tracksuit with the pockets that have been sewn on the wrong way, and the two old ladies with their curly perms and wrinkly old skin. They're lovely, proper people. It would have been nice to grow up with a woman like Nell. It makes me realise why Dean's such a great person. I love Mum to death, but there's something a bit funny about her . . .

'They want me to do a blog,' I say, knowing that the old ladies will look at each other in alarm and gasp in amazement when I explain what it is and exclaim 'You don't know you're born', and tell me that they were down the coal-mines when they were fourteen years old, never mind sitting and writing blogs. What's the world coming to? And all that . . . But no! Much to my surprise . . .

'I think a blog's a really good idea,' says Nell, tipping boiling water into the ancient teapot. 'Ethel's got one, haven't you, dear?'

'Ethel?' I say. 'Ethel has a blog? Are you sure?'

'What's that, love?' Ethel fiddles around with her hearing aid until it emits a loud shrieking sound and presumably dogs in the neighbour-hood wrap their paws around their ears while whales and dolphins make their way up the Thames. 'Blog? Yes, love. I've got a blog.'

I should point out that until I went on the writing course I'd never heard of a blog. How can Ethel have one?

'She tells all her stories about the war on the computer, don't you, love?' says Nell. 'Her blog's called "War Babe" and apparently lots of people hit on her – whatever that means. Now, come on, let's have a sit down in the best room and a nice cup of tea and we'll discuss your new handbook, love. It's freezing in here.'

Nell opens the ludicrously large fire doors to the sitting room, or 'best room' as she calls it – as if she has a host of sitting rooms in her flat, and this is the best one. The truth is that it's the only one. As we walk into it, a wall of sound and warmth hits me. Going through the doorway is like crossing the equator. It turns out Nell's best room is in the Sahara Desert. I've never walked into a hotter room in my entire life. The tele-vision is blaring out in the corner so loudly that I actually wince in pain. There's a sudden and rather undignified rush for the seats nearest to the fire, as Nell reaches over and raises the temperature a couple of notches.

'That's as high as it goes,' she says, and the other two sigh. 'You can't get any heat out of them, can you?' says Ethel. 'It's a mystery why they don't make them hotter.'

No, I think. The only mystery is why the furniture isn't melting into pools on the floor. It's quite impossible to believe that a room can get this hot. I can feel myself gasping for air, and the physical feeling I have of my make-up sliding off down my face is quite terrifying. Still, my elderly companions appear to remain cold, as they rub their rickety fingers together and the click-clacking sound reverberates around the tiny self-contained flat. They all fiddle with their hearing aids constantly, looking around and smiling in an almost dream-like way, as if they've had eight sweet sherries with their breakfast. Perhaps they have. It might explain the strange smells.

Nell puts weak, sugary tea and horrible stale-looking biscuits down in front of us. I notice that she isn't sharing the luxurious Belgian chocolate biscuits that I bought.

'The nith thin th-about it ith tha it woul wor thor thay or th'evening,' says Ethel in a very gummy fashion. She is still obsessing about the vile green suit Nell is sporting. She gives us all a broad smile, which reveals that she has taken her teeth out for no good reason, somewhere between the kitchen and the sitting room.

'The only thing is – it does make you look a bit like a sprout,' says Gladys, before nudging Ethel with more vigour than she had planned, almost breaking poor Ethel's dodgy hips as the octogenarian flies across the sofa towards the door.

'Whoooaaahh,' mumbles Ethel, rubbing herself miserably.

Gladys points to Ethel's missing teeth in what is clearly meant to be a subtle move, but Ethel doesn't pick up on it at all. So, rather disconcertingly, Gladys starts click-clacking her own teeth in her mouth as some sort of hint, but she performs the action rather too vigorously and her teeth clatter out onto the carpet where they lie, looking up at us like we're suddenly in some hideous French farce, 'Oops, there go my dentures'. With mounting alarm I realise that there is no bending in old-lady land, and there is only one person in the room who can possibly retrieve the runaway teeth. 'Be a dear and pick them up for me, would you,' she gums, in a barely intelligible fashion. 'You are a love.'

So it was that I found myself on my hands and knees that afternoon crawling on thinning, patterned carpet picking up dentures for a ninety-two-year-old widow whose husband was killed in the D-Day landings.

'Give 'em a rinse out, would you?'

Oh god, this is all just too terrible for words. The sickly heat, the pungent aroma rising from the dentures . . . it's all making me feel quite ill. I pick up the teeth and carry them to the kitchen, trying not to breathe in as I go. The others are watching and commenting on how nice I'd look in the damn forest-green tracksuit. Will they ever stop talking about it? In the kitchen I see Ethel's teeth sitting on the side of the sink. I decide to rinse those, too, and take them back into the sauna-like sitting room. I assume that Ethel will be delighted by the return of her teeth. I would have thought that losing your teeth was a fairly major incident and liable to wholly ruin your day. But no – Ethel barely looks up at me when I hand them back to her. She just plonks them down so close to her teacup that for one horrible minute I think she's going to drop them into it.

Gladys clanks hers into place, and there's a small clatter as she adjusts them in her mouth. A look of horror passes across her face before she emits a sound not dissimilar to that offered by a dying cat. She hurriedly removes them and declares that her tongue was trapped. For about ten minutes, the sound of Gladys click-clattering her teeth as she tries to fit them back in properly provides a constant soundtrack.

'I'm sure these are the wrong ones,' she says suddenly. No one says anything. I, to be frank, don't know what the appropriate response is to a comment like that. The prospect of her being right and wearing the wrong ones is too awful to contemplate. 'Either that, or my mouth's just got bigger,' she rationalises.

'Aw wour teef wav wot schmaller,' says Ethel helpfully. Why doesn't she just put *her* teeth back in?

Then the two women look at each other.

'These might be yours,' said Gladys, removing them. Then, without flinching, and in what must be considered the most gross act ever performed by any human being, ever, she hands over the teeth and Ethel clicks them in.

'Perfect,' she says, handing hers to Gladys.

'That's better,' says Gladys, and I must say that I feel enormously grateful that the Denturegate crisis is over.

'Time for me to go,' I say, standing and moving to kiss three powdery-soft cheeks.

'Oooo, don't forget this,' says Nell, hanging me a white carrier bag. Even through its thick plastic I can see the green glaring out at me.

'Thanks,' I say.

'And remember to do that blog, love,' she adds. 'I mean it. I think it's a great idea.'

Tuesday, 2 October
5 p.m.

Coleen is up on the screen in all her lovely, youthful glory. The picture is so heavily backlit and her face so porcelain clear (a mixture of good genes and great airbrushing) that she looks not unlike the Virgin Mary – glowing innocently and beaming down upon computer users around the world. It's like she's looking straight at me. Can she see me? I hope not – I'm not exactly wearing my best clothes.

'Click here', it says, at the bottom, 'if you want a blog of your own.'

Here goes. I click the button and am directed to a blank page on which I'm instructed to produce a title for my blog. 'The Wags' Handbook,' I type carefully. Then, I can't do it. It's no good. What if she can see me? I drop to the floor and crawl across the carpet towards the bedroom.

'Mum, what are you doing?' Paskia Rose is looking at me as if I'm mad. 'Why are you crawling around like a dog?'

'Oh, Pask,' I say. 'You know that little computer in there.'

'The laptop?'

'Yes – the lap-dancing computer. Well, if someone's on the screen, and you can see them, can they see you?'

'What?'

'Can Coleen see me? She's on the screen.'

'No, of course she can't,' says Pask, rubbing her nose furiously with the back of her hand in a really annoying way. It makes her nose go red, which is terribly unattractive. 'Of course she can't see you. Why would she be able to?'

'Well, Ethel at the old people's home has got a blog and Nell said that people keep hitting her. If they're hitting her, they can obviously see her. Now Coleen's on the screen and I haven't got any make-up on and . . .'

'Mum, you have loads of make-up on. What are you talking about?'

'Yes, but I don't have the *right* make-up on for a meeting with Coleen. I've got some make-up, jewellery and clothes that I bought specially in case I ever meet them – the Queen Wags. And what about poor Ethel getting hit on the lap-dancing machine when she was doing her blog?'

'Mum, a hit means that someone has gone onto your site. It means that lots of people have been going onto Ethel's blog. That's all.'

'And can they see her?'

'NO!! For crying out loud, Mum – of course they can't.'

'Well, I think I'll just put some make-up on anyway – in case.'

So, back at the screen, coated in vast quantities of thick brown paint. The big question now is – what the hell am I going to write about for my first blog? My mind's gone completely blank. Should I just put online what I wrote on the course? That seemed to go down well with Simon. I try to think about the advice he gave us.

'Write about what you know,' Simon had said.

What do I know? What do I know? It's all right for Simon – he's so clever. What if you don't actually know anything? What do you write about then?

I look around the room. There's nothing here to guide me. 'Relax, be yourself,' Simon had said. I breathe deeply and think through the things that concern me most . . . Global warming? No, not really, I'd love the whole planet to warm up to boiling point if I'm honest. Then I wouldn't have to spend half a million quid a year on spray-tanning and risk major lung infection. No, there must be something. The trouble is that important subjects pass me by. They just don't hold any interest for me. What really fascinates me is looking good, and the way twenty-four coats of high-density make-up can transform the skin's texture. I also love the way in which it's possible to have fake breasts, fake tan, fake hair, fake nails, fake eyelashes and fake lips and still look like a genuine Wag. I'm in love with the process of transformation from mere mortal to Wag. I'm in love, more than anything, with make-up. Make-up . . .

Okay – make-up. I'll write all about make-up and how to best apply it. Then I'll write about drinking – yes, that's a good idea, because I really like drinking, too.

Okay . . . how to start? Gosh, I bet this is the hardest bit of any writing project, the beginning . . . and the end – I bet that's hard too. Oh, and the sticky bit in the middle that's neither the beginning nor the end. Right, here goes . . . okay . . .

MY WAGS' HANDBOOK
TRACIE MARTIN

Hello everyone, and welcome to my Wags' Handbook, designed to teach you all the tricks of the trade and show you all the rules and regulations that you must follow if you want to become a Wag, like

*me. My name is Tracie Martin, and I'm Queen Wag at Luton Town
Football Club where my husband Dean who used to play for England
and Arsenal plays. He's the team's highest goal-scorer this season!
Below you'll see that I have looked today at two crucial questions
that Wags need to address: getting your make-up absolutely right
and making sure that you have exactly the right approach to alcohol.*

There. That's good. Blimey, it took me ages to do – these false nails cover
two keys at the same time, making it a very complicated procedure. It
reads well, though. Has all the important points in it. Mentions me. It's
frustrating that I can't get the computer to do a heart over the 'i' in
Tracie, because that would complete the look of the thing, but at least
it mentions all about Dean and his great history in football. I think it's
important to include his England career so people know I'm a serious
Wag and not just some bleach-blonde bimbo with nothing to do all day
except paint her nails pink and fret about whether I've spent enough
money on handbags that morning. No need to mention that Dean only
played for his country once and was sent off after four minutes for
getting into a fight. Everyone knows the fight wasn't his fault. That
Cameroon player was asking for it. Dean said the bloke was looking at
him when they were singing the anthems (looking at him! He should
know better than to be looking at my man. Dean doesn't like being dis-
respected). Dean also said the player half-smiled at him when Dean
posed for the cameras and tripped over his laces. Dean says that's asking
for a punch. So, anyway, as I say, no need to include that. Nor any need
to explain the 'highest goal-scorer' remark. To be honest, the fact that
he's the highest scorer because he scores tons of own goals is just a detail,
and if you include too much detail early on you kill the narrative flow.
That's what Simon says. Now then – on to the first part of the book.

MAKE-UP FOR WAGS

*First we're going to look at the tricky world of Wag make-up. Get
it right, and your look will scream 'I'M A WAG!!! LOOK AT ME
– IT'S SO OBVIOUS THAT MY BOYFRIEND PLAYS FOOT-
BALL'. Get it wrong, and your look won't scream anything. It'll
whisper, whimper and apologise for itself on the terraces. Horrible
thought. Pale and interesting may be okay if you want to marry a
milkman and spend your life making cakes and growing flowers,
but if you're seriously contemplating aiming for the highest goal
open to a woman – marriage to a footballer – then you really need
to get the basics right, and make-up is fundamental in that. If you*

have the wrong make-up on it's like a scientist trying to crack the meaning of the universe without wearing a white coat and glasses. It's so not going to happen, is it? So, how do you get it right?

The first thing to realise is that you should ALWAYS wear make-up. In fact, it would be more accurate to say that the make-up should wear you – every Wag should be so heavily made up that her colossally mascara-ed, false eyelashes enter the room up to five minutes before the rest of her.

The key to achieving the right look lies in the quantity and manner of application. First, the foundation: you'll need a big pot of it so no scrimping and saving and buying anything small enough to lift – a great big huge bucket of the stuff is what's needed. Open the foundation and breathe in its gloopy, artificial, cloying aroma. Mmmmm . . . Who needs cocaine when you can have Guerlain?

Apply the make-up thickly onto heavily moisturised skin – that way you will achieve the lovely, shiny, glossy Wag look. Your foundation is a mask – plaster it on – it should look as if you are about to step onto the stage or perform as a clown in the Billy Smart circus. Good judges of well-applied Wag make-up are small children. Their reaction tells you everything – if they gasp in alarm and back away, you've cracked it! If they're not crying and asking for their mothers when they see you, you need more make-up. It would be useful to keep a small child in your make-up bag for this purpose.

A quick note here about spots: you will get them from time to time, given that you'll be covering your face in all manner of crap twenty-four hours a day, but – and this is great Wag news – it doesn't matter because no one will be able to see them beneath the four and a half inches of make-up that Wags legally have to wear. So, the only time to worry is when the spot protrudes beyond your make-up (i.e. reaches a peak of over five inches above skin level). If it does that, seek medical advice immediately – the way you look is the least of your problems.

The colour of the foundation is obviously crucial – it must be an orangey/American tan colour to be properly Waggish. This is not hard to achieve if you have enough fake tan on first. In fact, all but the most foolish of Wags should struggle to turn their faces a desirable shade of tangerine, which makes them look as if they've been living unhealthily close to a nuclear plant, drinking too much Tango, or eating too many cheesy Wotsits.

Now – on to the blusher: this should be liberally applied, of course, taking care to make sure it forms an unnatural diagonal line across your face. Cream blusher is good for achieving that silky look we all covet (i.e. makes your face look like it's covered in lard). Colour-wise, go for either a browny-orange colour to further develop the tan, or try a sugary-pink shade that makes it look as if you have a ridge of glittery candyfloss lying across your cheek.

Almost there now – just eyes and lips to go. With eye make-up you should stop just short of looking as if you've been punched in the face by Mike Tyson. Pile on loads of dark eye make-up for day, and paint on shimmering shades that sparkle for evening. It must all be finished off with eyelashes of such magnificent proportions that they look like spiders have lain down to sleep underneath and above your eyes. In short – if you think Panda Bear for the eye make-up and Daddy Long Legs for the lashes, you'll be there!

So, to the piece de la raisins – the lips. They should be as plump as pillows, as wet as wine; they should be pouting, glossy and pink. Either sugary Barbie pink (in which case lined with a brown lip-liner that does not match at all) or a bold, bright pink, verging on purple – the sort of colour that does not exist anywhere in nature. It must stop traffic, demand a double glance and have doctors heading for their textbooks . . . What illness could have caused such a violent colour burst? Obviously, lip-gloss over the top until the stuff is literally dripping off you. Now, my love, you are ready to head for a tacky nightclub in search of your prey.

DRINKING FOR WAGS

The question is, can you drink if you're a Wag? The answer is, most definitely, YES: 99.4 per cent of your nutrition should come from champagne or Bacardi Breezers. Drinking is vitally important if you are a Wag, as is getting drunk. The key skill to learn is to be able to continue to walk in eight-inch heels while on the wrong side of a crate of vodka. No collapsing into the gutter or trying to get off with the doorman. You're a Wag now . . . Hold your head up – throw your hair extensions back and walk towards the car without being sick all over the paparazzi.

Drinks are also great because you can eat the ice if you're really hungry, but if you're a non-eating Wag then don't touch the glacé cherries, instead you should skewer them out of the drink on a cock-tail stick and put them in the ash tray. If you touch them, some of the sugar might enter your bloodstream by osmosis or something, and you'll wake up three stone heavier (i.e. twice the weight you are now).

Champagne is always a good Wag choice of drink, but there are important things to remember when ordering champagne. If you're in a restaurant there are a few things that you should bear in mind. First, there's the simple matter of etiquette: lady, you should not be choosing, ordering or buying champagne in restaurants. That is your first mistake. What have you married a footballer for? He should be doing all that, and if you haven't bagged yourself a footballer yet, and are a single girl, then I would point out that if you're buying your own champagne in restaurants then you're doing something wrong appearance-wise, and you probably need to go back through my previous columns to rectify this. At a guess, I would say that you haven't got enough of your underwear on show – but that's just a guess.

Now, assuming you have a footballer with you who's paying the bill, which champagne should you choose? Mmmmm . . . tricky. No, not really – just choose Cristal – it's the most expensive. Next question?

Wednesday, 3 October
11 a.m.

Oh my god! The weirdest thing has happened. When I put a log on my computer this morning (not literally, of course, I'm not stupid! After I did that once and got bark and small brittle leaves stuck between the keys, I realised my mistake and didn't do it again) . . . anyway, I have sixty emails replying to my blog thing yesterday! Sixty! And what's really funny is that the emails are obviously about my blog, because they mention the stuff that I wrote about, but at the same time they are obviously not about my blog at all because they say really odd things. Listen to this:

Tracie Martin – you are sooooo funny. I loved your blog about make-up. I was crying with laughter! It was the funniest thing ever! Please put some more blogs on. I'm going to tell all my friends. You are the funniest blogger in the world.

And this:

Hello Tracie Martin, I just wanted to say how funny I thought your blog was. It made me laugh all day – I had to let you know how funny you are. That line tickled me – 'It would be useful to keep a small child in your make-up bag for this purpose' – that really made me laugh.

Er. Hello? Funny? I am seriously not being funny. I am deadly serious when I talk about make-up. Why would people read my make-up piece and think it's funny? I am pleased they like it, of course. I'm pleased they want me to write more. But funny?

There were three emails on there signed 'anonymous', which, it turns out, means that they're sent from people who don't want you to know their names. I think I can guess though . . .

Hello Tracie Martin. I think you are a great blogger. Your make-up entry was very good, but I think you should definitely have written that it is important to wear green when doing your make-up. Green tracksuits are the only way to dress.

And:

Tracie, your blog was good but not as good as Ethel's blog called War Babe, which is very great. PS You should wear a green suit at all times.

And:

Lovely article, dear. Are you wearing a green tracksuit?

I'm not entirely sure whether I should reply to everyone who's written to me. If I do, should I ask them why they think the blog is funny and why they don't think I'm being deadly serious? God, this is difficult. Luckily, I know a man who'll help.

'Simon, it's Tracie. I'm worried about my blogging. They all think I'm being funny.'

Simon laughs, which serves to further confuse me. What is with everyone suddenly thinking I'm so funny? One minute I'm wandering around the place without a care in the world beyond whether my eye make-up is sparkly enough, then – boom – suddenly I'm Dawn French. How did that happen? How did I suddenly become a stand-up comic?

'I don't understand why you're laughing at me,' I say.

'I'm not laughing at you, Tracie,' he says in that sweet, kind and gentle way of his. 'I'm really not laughing at you at all. I'm laughing because you have no idea how incredibly funny and engaging you are. You have talent, Tracie. I have told you that many times, now everyone is agreeing with me and it's time for you to start believing it yourself. I want you to make sure you put a blog entry up every day. Okay?'

'Okay,' I reply meekly, because I've spent most of my life not really understanding things so it seems churlish to make a fuss about it now. 'I'll put a serious blog up about how to be a good Wag and everyone will laugh and I won't know why, or they'll say I'm some sort of genius writer and I won't know why either . . . but that's fine. I can cope with that.'

Okay, here goes.

Hi, Tracie here again. Can I just say, first of all, thank you so much for all your lovely emails and notes about my blog. I hope you enjoy this as much. It's an important note about Wags and shoes. You MUST get the shoe situation sorted if you are going to make a proper fist of being a Wag. Here's my heartfelt advice:

Goodness me! You walk into a shoe shop, look up, and what do you see? There are simply hundreds of shoes, boots and sandals covering the walls and shelves all around you. So, where do you start in trying to work out which ones you ought to buy? What are the rules? Obviously, the first thing to remember is to reach for the shoes that wouldn't look out of place on a lap-dancer. Perspex platforms are clearly ideal. White is great. Expensive patent white leather is perfect, especially the stuff that sits tightly on the skin and combines being both extraordinarily expensive and looking violently cheap. Bling is good too – the more the better . . . pile it on and watch it sparkle and shine. Look for quantity above quality, obviously. The more bling, the better. You really don't need to be looking too closely at shoes to see if they have bling on them – it should be staring you in the eyes and practically blinding you with its glare. The same goes for any leather you buy – make sure it's as plastic-looking as possible. You want to be able to see your face in its sheen.

One final point on shoes: obviously anything that shrieks 'designer' in an entirely unsubtle manner is good. Certainly, Christian Louboutin –a respected designer brand – is a good choice because of the red soles, which scream 'designer'. This is as discreet as you ever want to get with shoes. Clearly Ugg boots and the fantastic Burberry prints are perfect because they are plainly designer and immediately mark you out as a certain 'sort of person', which is, more than anything, what you are after. Matching shoes and handbags can be a good look, but only if they're obviously matching. Again, avoid subtlety. Take your lead in this respect, as in so many respects when it comes to Wag dressing, from the likes of former soap stars and singers like Jennifer Ellison, Kerry Katona and Daniella Westbrook. In fact, you could do worse than to pin pictures of Daniella Westbrook, taken on that fateful day when she wore an entire outfit of Burberry checks, to the inside of your wardrobe door, and refer to it at regular times through the day. You may recall that she had the hat, scarf, umbrella, coat, shoes, bag and baby – all coordinated. Perfect! That, my dear Blog-readers, is style!

Friday, 5 October
9 a.m.

My mobile phone bursts into life. (My ring-tone is fantastic – I've got Pussycat Dolls downloaded onto it. Paskia did it for me. I had one of Posh Spice's songs on there before, but after the dog incident I took it off – it was crap anyway, let's be brutal. She's skinny and has loads of nice shoes but her voice is worse than mine.) Dean catches a few chords of 'Doncha!' blaring out from my tiny pink phone and emits that strange grunting sound that means he's unimpressed and wants the noise to go away.

'Sorry, Dean,' I say, as I lever myself out of bed and remove my pale-pink eye mask, careful not to let the glitter fall off the mask and land in my eyes like it did before. God, that was painful! I couldn't see anything for an hour. 'I'm going blind, I'm going blind,' I'd shrieked as I ran around the room, the heels of my hands pushed into my eye sockets. Dean had pulled my hands away from my eyes on that occasion and announced that it actually looked quite bad – my eyes were coated in pink dots. I'd shrieked while he held my face tenderly and told me he'd love me whatever, and I'd cried soft, gentle tears, wondering how I would cope being blind. What would be the point of that? My world is a very visual one. Without worrying about how I look, how I plan to look, how I wished I looked, and how everyone else looked, what would be the point in being? Was there a point in being beyond looking and being looked at? My very consciousness was tied up with all the fears, delights, frustrations and envy that arise from an obsession with appearance. So the moment I nearly went blind was a deeply philosophical one in many ways. It was a time when I contemplated what it was to be me, and whether I was as fulfilled a human being as I might be. Then a miraculous thing had happened – all the tears I'd cried over my fast-fading sight started to wash the glitter out of my eyes and the pain had disappeared.

'The pink spots have gone,' Dean had said in a crazy 'Eureka!' moment as he stared into the whites of my eyes.

'I can see! I can see!' I'd shouted, falling to my knees to thank the Lord for his mercy.

It had been such a stressful morning – what with the near-blindness,

Dean's announcement of unconditional devotion and the philosophical re-evaluation of my life – that I'd simply had to get out and spend a shed-load of money. I'd never told Dean that it was glitter in my eyes. I'd told him that his love had cured me from certain blindness. He'd liked that, and we went out and celebrated wildly, which involved more collisions than usual between his credit card and some terrifyingly expensive shoes, handbags and oversized sunglasses.

Anyway . . . where was I? Oh yes – the phone call. I removed the eye shade without causing myself too much distress, and grabbed the mobile quickly while Dean closed his eyes and went back to snuffling and snorting in that annoying way of his, sounding like a baby pig searching for its mother.

'Hi, it's Simon,' said the voice on the other end. There's something about Simon's voice – it's all warm and comforting. Whenever I talk to him I think that this is what people who have fathers must think when they talk to them. It would be nice to have a father. Sadly, mine never wanted anything to do with me. I used to write so many letters to him when I was younger, and Mum sent them off to the last address she had for him. None of them were even replied to. Mum tried so hard to get him involved with us, but he didn't want to know. He left us both high and dry.

'I've been looking at your blog,' Simon continues. 'It's great.'

'Thanks,' I say. 'Though I don't know why you have to call so early in the morning to let me know.'

'It's nine a.m.,' says Simon in a way that is supposed to imply that 9 a.m. isn't early. Doh! It was only soon after I gave birth to Pask that I realised there was a nine o'clock in the morning. I thought nine o'clock was at night. What sort of life does that man lead, for god's sake?

'I've been in the office for two hours thinking about this,' he says. 'And I think you could be huge.'

There is not a Wag in all the world who wants to be told, 'I think you could be huge.'

'Sorry?' I say. Though I do feel that it's him who should be apologising.

'I'm going to call David Blackmore on the *Daily Mail* – have you heard of him?'

Of course I haven't. If he's in *Hello!*, I'll have heard of him, and if he plays football Dean will have heard of him, but beside that, no. All these *Panoranorama* types are not really on my radar.

'He commissions all new talent. I think you could have a column in the *Daily Mail* – you'd be read by millions. This could be huge. You could be huge.'

'Stop saying that,' I say.

'Don't be modest,' says Simon. 'You will be a major talent.'

'No – I don't mind you saying that, I just don't like it when you say that I could be huge. I don't want to be huge. The thought terrifies me. The fear of putting on half a pound keeps me awake at night and leads to nightmares. I wake sometimes shaking and shivering at the thought of it, and I know that if I do that – if I end up not sleeping properly – then I'll be tired in the day, and when I'm tired I end up wanting to eat sugar, and if I eat sugar I'll put on weight, and so when I wake up screaming at the thought of putting on weight what I'm actually doing is creating a situation that is most likely to lead to me putting on weight. Faced with the thought of that, I end up really hating myself, and that makes the whole thing worse – so, you see, don't keep saying that I'm going to be huge.'

There's a silence, then an 'okay' from Simon and I realise that I can see the look on his face as he's saying it. I can sense the smile in his voice and it makes me feel like everything's going to be okay. 'Just put three blogs on today if you can, and I'll call David tonight and get him to take a look.'

'Okay,' I say, and it's my turn to smile to myself as I tuck the phone back into my bag and curl up on the other side of the bed towards my husband.

'What are you smiling like that for?' asks Dean. 'I've never seen you smile like that before.'

'Oh, nothing,' I say. 'Just this blog thing I've been doing – people seem to think it's quite good.'

'Hummmph,' says Dean. 'More likely they're trying to get into your knickers.'

'I'm not wearing any,' I say, because I'm not. And his look changes then; he slides over to me and starts trying to lift the covers off me. 'Come on, baby,' he says. And all the time I'm thinking about my blog and what I should write in it. 'Come over here, baby.'

I lay back and look up at our ceiling painted with scenes from Dean's international career. It's just like the Cistern Chapel.

'You're gorgeous, babes,' Dean is saying as he releases the satin ties on my baby-doll nightie.

'Mmmm . . .' I reply, feeling his hands wander all over my body, across my concave stomach and up onto my 34D breasts. As he starts rubbing my nipples and pushing himself into my side with growing urgency, all I can think is that I hope there's not going to be too much friction between my hair and the pillow because I really don't want my hair extensions to get dislodged. I wonder how Posh manages? Perhaps that's why she had the extensions taken out – so she could have sex with David. For a considerable amount of time – while Dean is groping me madly and telling me how perfect I am – I'm completely lost in this fascinating conundrum: Would I be willing to take out my hair extensions for sex with David Beckham? Blimey. That's a tough one.

'Oooooooh,' says Dean.

I wonder whether Posh will read my articles in the *Daily Mail*. Perhaps I should put a copy of the newspaper through her letterbox every week? That would be a good idea.

'I wonder whether I'll be given a column,' I say. 'Because if I am, I've got this great idea.'

'Not now,' says Dean, and I realise that he's actually inside me. He emits a host of animal noises then collapses into a sweaty heap and rolls off me.

'Can I talk to you now?' I ask, but it's too late. All that is left of my man is a snoring lump on the other side of the bed.

2 p.m.

Half the day is gone and I've only just got to my computer. I promised Simon that I would send in three blogs and I haven't started writing even the first one. Pressure . . . stress . . . this must be what it's like to be a senior executive at a major investment bank or a high-flying human-rights lawyer or something. I haven't stopped today. I got out of bed at 9.30 a.m. and got dressed and made-up so quickly that by 11 a.m. I was sitting downstairs having a cup of coffee and eating Jelly Tots by the handful. I love Jelly Tots. I think they're fantastic! I refuse to believe that you can get fat eating little sweeties – how could you when they're all small and all pretty and look like little jewels?

The last few hours have flown past. I seemed to spend most of the time looking for things I can't find. Some of my jewellery has gone walkabout and my two favourite dresses are nowhere to be seen. It's odd, to say the least. I'm normally so organised with my clothes and accessories – whereas everything else in my house is in chaos. If it weren't for the staff I'd never find a thing. Where my clothes are concerned, though, I know exactly where everything is. Or should I say 'knew', because things have just vanished into thin air. Weird!

Still, at least I have about fifty thousand necklaces and two million dresses in my ever-expanding, now ludicrously over-stuffed walk-in wardrobe, so it's not like I don't have anything else to wear – it just seems that way sometimes. Most times. When I look at my cupboard with more clothes in it than the average department store, I don't think 'there are no clothes in there'. That would be plainly absurd. I think 'there are no clothes in there that I can put on and feel like a million dollars and be guaranteed to look the best in the room tonight'. What I mean, as every woman means when she moans about having nothing to wear, is that in the wardrobe there is not the answer to all dreams, there is not the outfit to transform me. There is not a piece of clothing in there that is absolutely right for this particular event. And such is the power of advertising that when I buy clothes or even see clothes in shop windows, I do believe in some small part of me that they will do that – they will make me feel perfect.

Okay, I am now nicely dressed and not feeling at all bad. I've gone for my 'uniform', if you like! It's the cowboy boots with big chunky heels, a tiny-weeny tight white miniskirt and a crop top in pink that shows off my boob job magnificently. It says, 'I'm a Wag, talk slowly' on it. How funny is that? Okay. Time to get going. The system is almost clogged up with emails from people, including the three mad witches from Sunnyside who have written to say that they like my blog and that I really would be better at blogging if I wore a green tracksuit. I have called Nell three times to tell her that I know it's her and that, while I appreciate her support and encouragement, there's no need to keep sending emails because I'm getting loads of them. Still, she keeps sending them. And still, she keeps mentioning the fact that I should be in a lurid pea-coloured outfit. There are nearly one hundred emails today, all telling their own stories about shoe shopping. At the bottom there's an email from someone called Mindy. 'You are rubbish, you old cow. Everyone is laughing at you.'

Are they? It takes me two hours to stop crying. Is everyone laughing at me?

Hi. Tracie here again. Today we're going to look at two of the most crucial areas of Wags' appearance – tans and hair extensions. Then I'll look at the dreadful situation that can happen if you don't look after yourself properly – that's right, I'll take a look at the awful, barely thinkable situation when a Wag is dumped by her footballer.

SUNTANS

The question I'm sure you're asking is, should Wags have suntans? Mmmmm . . . this is an interesting debate. The answer is – yes and no. You should certainly look tanned, but the preferred method of tanning is not to lie in the sun all day, wasting crucial shopping time. Instead, opt for making liberal applications of fake tan – wasting marginally less shopping time and managing to spend money in the process. The added bonus is that fake tans will turn you a ludicrous shade of amber in the process. Remember the Wag mantra: Wags can be orange, they can be caramel, but they CANNOT be white. If you feel your skin colour is heading towards white, or even cream or vanilla, it is important to get yourself spray-tanned as a matter of urgency. A wise Wag always knows where the nearest spray-tanning salon is, wherever she is in the world. If you find yourself looking white outside of tanning-salon hours (why oh why oh why aren't they twenty-four-hour?) then your only choice is to apply tanning cream yourself. The principal fact associated with self-application of tanning cream, and something that you simply have to accept, is that you are going to end up looking odd. You won't look tanned, you'll look as if someone has made a patch-work quilt of different skin colours and draped it over you. Whatever precautions you take, your palms will be orange, as will the gaps between your fingers and toes. Around your knees and ankles there will be streaks and probably patches of brightest tangerine. There will be little patches where you've missed skin and little patches where you can't reach. One ear will be tanned and the other one won't be and you'll probably end up with orange streaks in your hair. But at least you won't be white!

HAIR EXTENSIONS

All Wags should have them. I can't even begin to tell you how important it is to have majorly extended hair. Even if you have lovely glossy long hair to start with, you should put extensions in to make your hair even longer. It can never be too long. The extensions, with their brittle texture, will help you to achieve that crucial Wag look where your hair has a feeling more commonly associated with wire brushes than with youthful, feminine hair. If your hair is short, head to the nearest extensions salon IMMEDIATELY. You should have the longest, thickest hair that money can buy. Big hair, big sunglasses, small body, small skirt. It's not rocket science. Just because Posh has gone and had her hair chopped doesn't mean you should. At least she has dyed her hair the brightest blonde. When she went through that transition stage of having it short and dark I nearly killed myself. What was that about? Short and dark? Did she want to become a pottery teacher or something?

'Babe, it's started,' shouts Dean, just as I'm about to write my final blog. If I'm honest, I'm a bit cross because I need to concentrate for this next entry. I'm going to tackle the subject of how a Wag should cope when she's dumped, and I need to write this as sensitively and intelligently as possible. I shouldn't be distracted. It's an important piece and could influence so many people. But when I look up, Dean's standing by the door dressed in some sort of ridiculous, and strangely familiar, green trousers and a football shirt. He looks terrible. No wonder he's not doing very well in the team. How could he with clothes like that on? I mean, how could he possibly put up an exhibition of sublime skills and reveal his gloriously clever tactics while showing legs like Kermit the frog? Hang on a minute . . .

'Dean, where are those trousers from?' I ask.

'Nan gave them to me,' he says. 'Apparently she got them free from the bingo or something. Nice, aren't they?'

'No, they're not,' I retort. 'They're not at all nice. Why would you wear them?'

'Because she wanted me to,' says Dean, as if it's the most natural thing in the world to go around making people happy. 'I knew it would please her, so I just said I'd wear them. She likes looking after people and giving them things but she doesn't have much money – and you know she doesn't like handouts – so I thought I should take the trousers and wear them with good grace to make her happy. Why?'

'Nothing,' I say, wondering, not for the first time, how my husband got to be so nice, and how on earth I got to be so selfish. Images of Mum and Nell flash into my mind before I can stop them and I shudder. 'I'll be with you in a minute. I've just got to write another blog. Nearly finished.'

'No, Trace – you've been doing that blogging thing all afternoon and *Midsomer Murders* is about to start. You know what you're like – if you miss the beginning of the show you'll never be able to catch up and you'll never work out who the murderer is . . . especially in this one. If you miss the clues when the vicar walks through the church and looks towards the vestry, you won't know it's him. Oh no! Shit! I've gone and given it away. Oh, Trace, I'm sorry. Come and watch it, though, babes. I've seen this episode about five times, and it's great even when you know the vicar strangled them with the cord from the vestry curtains.'

'Okay, Dean,' I say, but I really want to get this next blog done. I don't want to let Simon down, and it surprises me how much I don't want to do that. I'm not really bothered about whether this journalist from the *Daily Mail* sees them or not, but I would like Simon to think that I'm not a complete flake. I'd like him to know that I appreciate his attention . . .

'Trace. The church cleaner is in the vestry and trying to work out how the curtains hang back . . . Trace . . . Come on, doll . . . the cleaner's realised that the cord's missing. Oh Trace . . . come and see this. She's looking for the cord. "IT'S BEHIND THE PULPIT. " Shit, Trace. Come on, love. You know how scared I get in these shows. Come and give me a cuddle.'

Nightmare. I feel like Nicola Horlicks or one of those serious corporate women with families at home that they need to look after at night while they try to run a major business empire by day. It's so hard to be a modern woman. I have the demands of my newly discovered literary career to attend to, while there's all this pressure on me to be the perfect wife and mother.

'TRACE!!!!!!!!' comes a piercing cry from the sitting room. 'Come QUICK. The cleaner's just found the blood-soaked cord and is heading off to find Detective Barnaby. Quick, Trace.'

I close the laptop and rush to my terrified husband. He's holding up a leopard-skin patterned silk cushion in front of his eyes and squinting at the TV – trying hard not to look but totally hooked so that he can't look away.

'Tracie's here,' I say, as I cuddle up next to him on the sofa. 'Don't worry – Tracie's here.' And all the time I'm thinking about the blog and hoping that I can write it kindly enough to dispense wisdom and sympathy in equal measure.

'HE'S BEHIND YOU!!!!!' shrieks Dean. 'WATCH OUT FOR THE VICAR!'

6 p.m.

Readers, sorry about the delay in finishing my blog, but here is the final instalment of the day . . . I was delayed in sending it because I was attending to an important Wag task – no, not my nails or my hair, but my husband!! How funny is that? You see, the role of a Wag is more than just looking as good as possible. It has struck me a few times, as I've been putting this together over the past week, that there's more to being a Wag than that. You have to actually get on with the person to whom you're married. Dean wanted me to watch a TV programme with him so I thought I should. In that moment, it seemed to me that looking after him should take priority over everything else. But what if you look after him, get your nails done regularly, always have nice hair, and things still don't go well? What then? How do you survive?

Oh dear, how I hate even having to contemplate the pain you must be going through if you are asking this question – it's just too much for me to bear. Obviously, you have to sit down, take a deep breath, think about all the good times you had together – the real special times – then screw him for every penny he's got, embarrass him, expose him, bring him down. Let nothing stand in the way of ruining his life. If he's found another girlfriend – ruin her life, too (especially if she's younger than you are). Stop at nothing. Call the papers, smash his car up, lie about him, humiliate him, keep all the jewellery, sell all your keepsakes, do a revenge book. There, that's enough ideas for now. Call me personally if you need any more . . . I keep an ideas file for emergencies. Note that the proper terminology for a jilted wife of a footballer indulging in this sort of behaviour is 'having a Wag-lash'.

It's important for every Wag to be prepared for this eventuality in the same way that she prepares to cope with a fire in the home. Just because you buy a smoke alarm or a fire extinguisher does not mean you expect a fire. I have a Dean Dump Ideas File even though I know that Dean would never, ever finish our relationship because it's so special and perfect. He's a diamond is my Dean – a wonderful man. I'm very lucky, I feel very secure about our life together, but I'm also very prepared to screw him if he tries to back out of our lovely, glorious, romantic future.

Saturday, 13 October
3 p.m.

Freezing cold. So freezing cold, in fact, that I'm sitting here wishing I hadn't worn such a short skirt – that's how cold it is! And it's not just the temperature that is causing the great freeze, it's the icy stares from the other girls who are sitting around Mum and clutching on to her arm as though they're distressed toddlers who don't want to be left alone at a birthday party. I feel like charging over there and telling them what it's really like to be a distressed toddler left alone . . . but I don't, of course. I find myself sitting still while desperately trying to hear what they're all saying. Phrases like 'She's not even a Wag . . . he's never in the team' filter across on the cold afternoon air. 'You should be doing that internet blog thing, not her,' one of them spits out. 'Why does she think she's so special?'

'I don't,' I feel like crying out. 'I don't feel special at all.'

When they sense that I'm listening to them, they put their hands up to guard their mouths and whisper behind them like teenage girls. I decide to try and ignore them . . . something that would be infinitely easier if Mum weren't there. It's hard knowing that she's talking about me. As tough as it is knowing that her boyfriend is almost half the age of my husband. Thank god for Mich and Suzzi. With them I can sit, relax and hear all their gossip, as well as learning about Mich's continuing fight to snare a footballer permanently.

'It's easy to get a football player into your bed. It's not so easy to get a footie player into your life, though,' she is saying wisely. She can be deeply philosophical at times, can Mich. 'They just don't seem to want to commit.'

The whole of the front of Mich's hair is now the brightest blonde imaginable, so it's hard to see why they wouldn't.

'Perhaps you're spending too much time with your back to them?' I venture. Her hair's very dark behind her head. I wonder whether that's the root of the problem.

However, it turns out Andre went a bit weird after the hot-wax incident, and suggested they go to the theatre.

'Eugghhhh,' says Mich at the memory of his words. 'That's so posh. Why would I do that?'

Andre had relented when he saw her reaction, and they ended up going to the Biggin Hill Airshow instead.

'Eeeeugghhh,' says Suze, making exactly the same noise as Mich had made at the thought of them going to the theatre. I have to say, I agree with her. It's all very 'eeeeugghhh'.

'There's nothing nice to buy there and no nice men. Why would you go there?' asks Suze.

'Precisely the question I asked,' Mich replies. 'He answered that he thought it might be a fun thing to do – something different!'

'My god,' says Suze. 'What on earth do you want to be doing something different for? What's wrong with just shopping, getting pissed and shagging? What did you say?'

'I told him he was sick.'

While the girls are chatting on, I take a moment to look around at some of the newer Wags on the scene. It's a frightening sight, to be honest. It's like they simply don't know the protocol. One of the girls isn't drinking any alcohol and three of them have trousers on. T-r-o-u-s-e-r-s! At a football match! Clueless. Honestly! I look down at my own legs – mottled and turning a gentle shade of blue beneath the orange veneer left by the spray-tanner's – and I can't help but think how much the trouser-clad girls are missing out on, and how awful it must be for their men when they look up into the crowds and see that their Wags are in trousers. I'm sure Dean would hit the roof! He's always saying daft things like he'd love me no matter what I wore, but that's clearly ridiculous . . . and he only says it when he wants sex.

One of the girls is blonde and her extensions are really nasty and half falling out, and I find myself smiling at her. She has jeans on – not good – but they are designer label – good – and very low cut – excellent. When she bends over to pick up her Bacardi Breezer (happily she is drinking, unlike her dodgy mate), I get an almighty flash of zebra-print g-string with candyfloss-pink lace across the top. The jeans are so low that I actually see most of her bum as well. Hoorah, at least she is Wagtastic beneath her trousers, which reassures me a little.

Jeans girl has enormous boobs – the sort that you can only get with a boob job – and fake nipples in her bra. I think I may befriend her later. When I first saw her, she looked young and pert and I could see that most of the men in the bar were simply unable to take their eyes off her chest. Now I notice that one of the fake nipples has slipped down a little, making her look highly disfigured. Obviously, no one's going to tell her, but I've noticed that the male gazes reek more of concern than lust now. At least she is making an effort, though. At least

110

she understands the look for which she is striving, even if, to be honest, she's some way off achieving it. Her friends are far worse. They need tons of help. They seem lost, helpless, drowning in a sea of fashion-related decision-making.

Should I tell these girls about my blog and advise them to read it? It would certainly benefit them to study its contents because it's written with women like them in mind – women who have no f***ing clue when it comes to appropriate Wag dress and conduct (ex-squeeze my language). Obviously, I've told Suze and Mich all about my blog, and they've been reading it and telling me what they think (they love it!). Mum thinks it's appalling but I kind of think that Mum would be appalled at anything I did – even if I found a cure for cancer or solved third-world poverty. I'd be collecting the Nobel Prize for Peace and she'd still be muttering out loud about the time I failed my final ballet exam and had to go back and redo it so she missed her hairdressing appointment.

I glance over at Mum and see her laughing loudly with her new friends as she studiously ignores me. It's the cold-shoulder treatment – but I've survived before, I'll survive again. Presumably I'm getting it this time for two reasons – first, because Dean isn't in the team any more so I'm *persona non grazia*, and second, because my Wags' Handbook means I'm raising my head above the parapet, so I'm there to be shot down. It's ironic really – I'm writing the Handbook in order to help other Wags fit in and become part of the Wag world again, but in the process of writing it I find that I have unwittingly alienated myself from the same world and don't fit in any more.

It would have been nice if Mum could have just said 'hello' back when I spoke to her, instead of laughing like a pre-pubescent teenager. I know she hates the blog because she told Dean that if I didn't stop it I'd bring shame on him and the entire family – i.e. her. Dean said he didn't want to stop me because I seemed so happy writing it (which is nice!) but he did suggest that I talk to Mum about it, and run things past her to make her feel more involved. He's such a sweetie is Dean – I'm so lucky to have found him. I'll probably ignore his advice though.

I can see my lovely man from here – he's on the bench . . . again. He hasn't started a match for so long now that he thinks he's probably forgotten how to play. He says it's so boring on the bench that he's thinking of taking up knitting or something. Poor love. I think it's the coach's fault – he doesn't seem to understand Dean's game plan. Admittedly no one else does either – least of all Dean – but the coach in particular seems confused. 'What the hell were you doing out there?' he asks of Dean. 'Were you concentrating at all?'

'Hey, guess what?' I say brightly. However, Mich and Suze are distracted by an aeroplane flying overhead so they go straight back into the story about Biggin Hill.

'Bloody wing-walkers!' Mich is saying. 'Wing-walkers? Wing-walkers? What's that all about?'

'What is it, love?' asks Suze, addressing herself to me.

'I have some fab news,' I say, but I'm not sure whether it is fab news or not – I can't work it out. 'You know that blog I've been writing – well, a guy from the *Daily Mail* wants to see me. They're thinking of making it into a column . . . in the newspaper. I'd write one every week and they even said I might start the whole thing off by doing a makeover piece.'

I had the call from David Blackmore yesterday but I haven't told anyone till now because nothing's guaranteed. I've got to go in for a meeting with them in a couple of weeks and I don't know what they'll think of me . . . they probably won't be very impressed and so won't go along with the column idea . . . we'll see!

'Oh-my-god!!!' shrieks Suze. Mich's hands have flown to her mouth. They look at me with undisguised awe.

'You're amazing,' says Suze. 'Really amazing.'

'Do you think I should do it?' I ask. 'I'm not sure, because Mum said I was rubbish and Mindy sent an email saying I was rubbish. Perhaps I am rubbish.'

'You HAVE to do it!!!!' they chorus.

'Ignore those bitches,' says Suzzi, suddenly clutching her stomach and squealing like a small pig.

Then they both smile at me and we sip our Bacardi Breezers, me thinking about how I don't want to be a star, and the other two gassing about what Mindy and the Slag Wags will say when they hear.

'Ha!' says Suzzi.

'Double ha!' says Mich. 'They'll be sooo pissed off when you're in the *Daily Mail*.'

'Oooooo,' says Suzzi, clutching herself again. 'I think I'm going into labour.'

'Oh god,' I say. Michaela is looking to me for advice, and Suzzi looks like she's in the most astonishing pain. 'Don't you have a caesarean booked?'

'Yes,' she replies through gritted teeth. 'It's next week.'

Shit.

'You've had a baby,' says Mich, looking at me. 'What's the first thing she should do?'

'Um – put her cigarette out?' I venture.

Suzzi takes one last enormous drag before we take it off her. 'Aaahhhhhhh . . .' she cries, so I give it back to her while Mich goes running off to get help.

Monday, 15 October
7.30 p.m.

Ahhhh . . . babies are so small, aren't they? We're at Anton and Suzzi's place to 'wet the baby's head'. Dean and Anton are completely trollied. I've had two bottles of champagne and Suzzi's on her ninth Bacardi Breezer. It's turning into quite a party.

'You okay now?' I ask Suze.

'Yeah,' she says. 'Feeling much better. Still can't get into my hot-pants though.'

'Give it another week,' I say. 'You can't rush these things.'

I don't mind admitting that it took me three weeks to lose weight after having Pask. I did it by not eating very much when I was pregnant and not eating anything at all for three weeks after she was born. The weight came off, though. I'd recommend it as a diet plan.

'When are you seeing the *Daily Mail* people?' asks Suze, pouring herself another drink.

'Next week,' I reply. 'Not sure whether I'll go, though.'

'What do you mean? Why wouldn't you go?'

'I've had so many emails on my blog – all saying how rubbish I am. I don't think I can face it. I know it's Mindy, Julie and Debs sending them, but, well, what if they're right and I am rubbish?'

'Stop this right away,' says Suzzi, running her hands through her long blonde hair and flashing me a steely look with her large brown eyes. She's got the most amazing eyes has Suze. Sometimes they're green, sometimes they're hazel, and at other times they look so dark brown they're almost black. Right now, they're deep chocolate.

'You are fantastic, your blog is brilliant. Don't listen to those Slag Wags, they're just jealous.'

'But Mum thinks I'm rubbish, too.'

'No, she doesn't. You know what your mum's like – she just wants you to keep a low profile. She hates you being in the papers – she always has. Your blog is brilliant, and the *Daily Mail* are going to love you. You go, girl.'

Wednesday, 24 October
10 a.m.

Don't panic! Nobody panic! I'm an expert at this. I know all about how to look perfect for every occasion – so why, right now, does it feel as if I simply don't know what on earth I'm doing? I feel as if I've never dressed properly for anything in my life ever before. I've got my meeting at the *Daily Mail* and I'm looking at the rails and rails of clothes containing garments from just about every Wagalicious designer who ever lived, and yet nothing seems quite right. Everything seems wrong. Not one top seems right. Not one skirt seems appropriate. Not one jacket or boob tube or pair of hot-pants seems to work. My shoes seem silly and clumpy. I keep thinking of how sophisticated other writers must look, and then there's me. Perhaps I'm not cut out to be a writer. Perhaps my lack of any literary credentials will show itself in my appearance.

It's just two hours before I am due to head off to a meeting at a major national newspaper. Little me! My goodness. It's hard to believe! I don't even read newspapers. I just look at the pictures, then pass them to Dean so he can read the sports reports and shout about how rubbish they all are. Dean's hovering around, trying to offer advice, which seems to involve sober black suits and flat shoes. In other words, he's hanging around offering really crap advice.

'No, Dean,' I keep saying. 'A black suit with big baggy trousers is soooo not going to happen. It really won't work at all. I'll look like bloody Charlie Chaplin.'

'Oh,' he says, walking away. 'I'm just trying to help.'

The truth is that there's only one person who can help. There's always only one person I can turn to at the first sign of any trouble – always just the one person who instinctively knows what to do. I pick up the phone and ring Nell's number.

'I've gotta get ready. I have to . . . but can't . . . don't know . . . What am I going to do and what should I wear? And it's . . . ? And I . . . ? When should I . . . ? Oh god, Nell. What should I do?'

'Morning, Trace,' says Nell all calmly, as if this is not the trickiest predicament she's ever faced.

'Nell,' I scream. 'I don't know what to wear. I've *never* not known what to wear. What to wear has always been second nature to me. What's going wrong with me today?'

In the background I can see the shadowy spectre of Dean, as he goes through the wardrobe looking for the sort of shapeless suits that he has spent all morning describing. I know with absolute certainty that he will not find such a garment in my wardrobe, so I leave him to his search in the knowledge that he will be unsuccessful.

I see him pull out leopard-skin tops, skirts and jackets, and discard them quickly. I watch him holding up white patent-leather hot-pants and long white boots and drop them again.

'It seems easy to me,' says Nell.

'I'm not wearing a green tracksuit,' I say quickly. She may have conned Dean into wearing one, but I'm so not going to a meeting with the Features Executives at the *Daily Mail* dressed like the Incredible Hulk when he's angry. It just ain't happening.

'I'm not suggesting that you wear a green tracksuit,' says Nell. 'All I was going to say was that you should take the advice you've been dispensing – why don't you look at the advice you're planning to give to Wags, and copy that? You need to be a living, walking, breathing advert for your columns. I think you need to be true to yourself.'

I'm clutching the phone so tight that my hand hurts She's right – again. She always is. She's got the whole thing sussed . . . this whole life thing. Whenever I think there are no benefits at all to getting older, I think of Nell and how great she is, and realise that there are some things that improve with age, and I think you do start to 'get it' as you get older.

'Thanks, Nell . . . Be true to myself,' I repeat as I drop the phone and rush to my wardrobe, newly enthused about the task before me. I pull out the long, white boots that Dean had dropped to the floor, and team them with the leopard-skin patterned leather skirt that barely covers my bum. I slip on leopard-skin knickers because I'm bound to go flashing them at some stage, and I feel, instinctively, that it would be better not to flash my bits and pieces when in a rather formal meeting with the senior bods at the *Daily Mail*.

1 p.m.

'And you,' says a man sporting an old-looking T-shirt with a band I've never heard of on it. '*You* must be Tracie Martin.'

'Yes,' I reply.

'You look exactly the way I thought you'd look.'

'Okay. You don't,' I reply. It's true. He doesn't. Neither do any of the people slouching around the place in their tatty sweatshirts and trainers. I thought there would be writers gliding down the corridors dressed in velvet smoking jackets and cravats. I thought they'd look like David Niven as they waved neatly manicured fingers in the air and quoted Oscar Wilde. Instead, most of the people here look as if they should be hanging around shopping malls or in parks, drinking cider and scrawling graffiti over the roundabout for the children to read in the morning. The man who's come to collect me from reception, walk me through the glass atrium and up the long escalators is called Paul. He has these bits of leather tied around his wrists.

'Friendship bracelets,' he explains when I ask. 'I picked them up in Thailand.'

'It's Tie Rack,' I correct. There's nothing about shopping that I don't know.

We go into 'editorial' where he promises that I will meet 'the team'. They are, he insists, 'The best bunch of guys on the planet.' They may well be, but their offices aren't up to much. It turns out that newspaper offices are nowhere near as glamorous as you'd think they'd be. There are no celebrities knocking around, no nice clothes – just a bunch of people and rows upon rows of computers. It looks more like a call centre in Scunthorpe than a leading newspaper office in one of the more fashionable parts of London.

'Come in, come in,' says the features-editor lady when we reach her office – a tiny little room off the main floor. Either she's just moved into it or she doesn't go in for interior décor much, because the room is dismal. Nothing on the walls except a couple of pull-outs from the paper, and a very dull-looking calendar with dates circled and notes scribbled. On her desk there's a photo of a plain-looking child in a purple school uniform and just piles and piles of books and notes. There are no scatter cushions, pot plants or little feminine touches that make a room come alive. I feel like rushing out onto Kensington High Street and buying leopard-print lamps with tassels, and huge, dramatic, sweeping white curtains, drapes, cushions and rugs to make the room look more homely. Perhaps when I know her a bit better.

'Come in,' she repeats in a rather sergeant-majorly fashion, rising from her chair and shaking my hand with unnecessary firmness. She has the whiff of the lesbian about her and I immediately take against her. 'I see you're dressed the part.'

'Thank you,' I say, assuming the comment is meant as a compliment, but not feeling entirely sure. She's such a big woman. Very hefty, with a large backside that takes me right back to those baby elephants we were looking at on our honeymoon. Her shapeless navy skirt, navy court shoes and white blouse all look as if they were bought from a supermarket. When stretched over her matronly bosom I can see through her shirt and notice she's wearing a very substantial and plain bra that looks as if it has come from the 1950s. No pretty colours or fancy frills for her. She'd have one hell of a shock if she saw my underwear drawer.

'Take a seat,' she barks, indicating the chairs at her large plastic grey table. Then she turns away to take a call.

I adjust my micro-skirt and sit down, smiling at three other people in the room – two men who look very arty and ever so slightly effeminate and a girl so young she looks as if she's on work experience. They don't introduce themselves, so we all just smile at one another in an embarrassed fashion. Just as the whole smiling thing's beginning to feel a bit odd, a smart but stressed-looking man enters the room. He has a commanding presence and I feel instantly at ease, as if there's finally someone in charge.

'David Blackmore,' he says, offering his hand. 'I loved your blog. You're very talented, very funny.'

The others are mumbling their agreement, so I think I ought to correct them. 'It's not meant to be funny,' I say. 'It's meant to be serious.'

'Ha, ha, ha, ha ... Love it. You're funny.' The laughter ricochets around the room, bouncing off the dull grey walls and skidding across the large Formica table. There are white plastic cups on the table, half-filled with brown sludgy stuff that I guess passes for coffee round here. Paul offered me a cup but it's yet to arrive. Looking at these, it would be far better for my health if it stayed that way.

'If you can keep up the high standard you've set in these first blogs, we'd love to offer you the chance to write them regularly for us,' says David. 'Do you think you can?'

'Yes,' I say, because I feel it would be both inadvisable and self-defeating to say otherwise.

'And the humour? Can you maintain that?'

'Oh yes – Tracie Martin's always humorous.'

They laugh again and smile at me like I'm a slightly backward child who's delighting them all with my piano-playing.

'We'd like a column of about three hundred words every Monday. We have lots of writers here who can help you with it, if you get stuck.'

'No, that's fine,' I say, thinking that I may have to work closely with Ms All-dressed-in-navy-I'm-a-lesbian-but-don't-tell-anyone Features Editor (She did tell me her name but she said it so quickly and aggressively that it sounded like 'Saucepan Head' and I didn't have the nerve to ask her to repeat it, so I have the choice of going through the whole meeting without referring to her by name or calling her 'Saucepan Head' – I have opted for the former).

'And we thought about starting it all off with a makeover piece, where you pick three ordinary members of the public and make them over like Wags, then write about the process of transformation.'

'That's fine,' I say. I just want to go home now. This meeting's nowhere near as exciting as I thought it would be.

'Again, we can organise a writer to work with you and help you put the piece together.'

'No, it's fine.'

'And a stylist to help with the transformations.'

I think of what Saucepan Head is wearing. 'No, no, no. Honestly – I'll be fine. I'm good at that.'

'Excellent. Well, it's lovely that you're so confident. I'm sure this is going to work out splendidly,' says David. 'Just the business matters to discuss. Now, we pay six hundred pounds for a column. How does that sound?'

'Great,' I say. I hadn't expected to be paid. To be honest, six hundred pounds is not exactly a fortune, but it's a new bag every week, so not to be sniffed at.

'And we'll pay you seven hundred and fifty for the transformation piece.'

New boots.

'Do you have any questions?'

'Oh, there is one thing,' I say. 'Can the money be paid directly into my account at Cricket?'

'Ha, ha, ha, ha, ha!' they all laugh, looking at me as if I've solved the mysteries of the universe. 'Very good,' says David. 'Really – very good.'

He sees me to the door, where Paul jumps up and escorts me out of the building. I walk out into the bitter cold afternoon, pleased with how the meeting went, but a little baffled by the scenes at the end. What were they laughing at? And why didn't they answer my question? I'm still entirely clueless as to whether they can or can't pay the money direct to Cricket. It just seems so silly not to. The performance of paying it into my account first means that I then have to transfer it, which I find very hard to do, and which usually causes me no end of grief. One of the other bonuses of the money going straight to Cricket is that Dean will have no idea how much money I spend in that shop. Not that I think he would mind. Just that it's altogether better if he simply doesn't know.

Monday, 29 October
6 a.m.

I can't sleep. It's all too scary. I keep having nightmares about the articles going in the paper and everyone at the football club laughing hysterically at me. God. What am I going to do? My first piece is due in today. I promised them that I would 'makeover' three members of the public as Wags and write an introduction to myself and the columns I will be doing for the paper. I said that I would write about the whole idea of what it is to be a Wag, and 'No, I don't need any help. I'll be fine.' What was I thinking of? I have no idea what to write. Every time I sit at the desk, my mind drifts off to thoughts of new boots (they've got the high-heeled short furry ones coming in to Cricket next week – the ones that Cheryl Cole was wearing – god knows how she got them before they have even appeared in the shops. I mean, I know when things are coming *into* the shops. But Cheryl can clearly get things before they even *arrive* in the shops. That's genius).

8 a.m.

Nightmare. What am I going to do? How will I ever get this article written when I don't have a clue where to start? Mum was right – I've been ridiculous to even think I could do this. Bloody hell, what a lemon.

'Debate the concept,' the features editor had said. Debate the concept? Bloody hell.

I have sent a text to Simon asking for his help but he hasn't responded yet. I sent it two hours ago . . . when I first woke up. Two hours! What's keeping him? I really need him to come round and help me make some sort of sense of all this. My head's jumbled and I have to get the article written by midday because I have a nail appointment at 1 p.m. that I can't possibly miss because my nails are in a real state. I also have a jewellery adviser coming at 3 p.m. to have a look at my collection for me and make some suggestions as last night I realised that most of the women in *Hello!* were wearing silver and platinum and my jewellery collection is mainly gold. Aaarghh . . . One of her ideas might be to put a lock on the door, I suspect, because I'm sure half of it has gone missing again.

9.30 a.m.

The phone finally rings. 'Hi,' says Simon, and I almost burst into tears.

'I-have-about-three-hours-to-write-an-article-and-I-can't-do-it-and-I-don't-know-where-to-start-and-I . . .'

'Calm down,' he says, in quite a manly way considering that, if we're honest about this, he's not very manly at all. I mean – he'd never make a footballer, there's something incredibly delicate about him. He's got long, elegant hands like you'd imagine a violinist would have, with tiny wrists and neat, manicured fingernails that I know I should approve of but I just don't. Not on a man. 'Put the kettle on and I'll be there as soon as I can. This is not hard. You can do this. Have you got the pictures of the women that you dressed up as Wags?'

'Yes,' I say. 'They're here.'

I look over at the ridiculous before-and-after pictures and I wince a little. Was it really such a great idea to use Nell, Ethel and Gladys? In the before picture they're proudly sporting their ridiculous Shrek suits. Ethel has a little face powder on and so much lipstick that it looks as if she's been eating strawberry ice cream, but the others are bare-faced. Nell looks like a convict as she stares at the camera. It makes me laugh every time I look at it.

Next to these lie the 'after' pictures. I do feel immense pride when I glance at them. Ethel looks spectacular, with her grey curls tucked under a wig of long blonde hair. Her eyes are made up magnificently with luscious false eyelashes. She looks like Brigitte Bardot (but after she spent too much time in the sun and got all obsessed with saving animals, not when she was an adorable teenage sex kitten). The veins in her legs are sticking out through the fake tan, which isn't ideal. She wanted to wear support stockings but – honestly – however would that have looked like a Wag? Gladys, I have to confess, looks plain ridiculous. I'm good at this Wag stuff but it struck me earlier today that some people, however desperately sad this sounds, are simply not cut out to be Wags! Can you believe that? Perhaps sixty years ago she'd have made a better fist of it, but right now, the more I make Gladys look like a Wag, the more she looks like a man. The scowl at the camera isn't helping, neither is the fact that her ancient-looking support-bra thing is showing under the basque. Her arms look like they're made of days-old uncooked dough, and the make-up I've applied to her face with a large brush is sitting on the hills and ravines of her tired old skin like snow on the side of a mountain. She looks like Denis Healey in drag. It's not turned out the way I intended at all.

So to my favourite – Nell. She doesn't look like a man. Heavens no. She doesn't look like a Wag either – she looks, let's be fair here, like a hooker. Like a very old hooker. Instead of scowling like her elderly friends, she's smiling in such a lascivious way that if I didn't know her better I'd think Cary Grant had his hand on her bum. I can see now that I've used way too much lip-liner because it's given her an absurd pout. Her lips are several inches in front of the rest of her face, which isn't how I planned it. I was thinking of Marilyn Monroe but even I can see she looks like a duck. I also think the long boots were a mistake, because she can't stand up in them so is leaning forwards and sticking her bum out, which is only exacerbating the duck-ness of the situation.

9.50 a.m.

'*She* looks like a cross between a hooker and a duck, while *she* looks like a transvestite and *she* looks like a mental patient,' says Simon as he sips his coffee and laughs heartily at my efforts. 'Didn't they send a stylist?'

'Yes,' I reply defensively. 'They sent a stylist but I told her that I knew what I was doing and to keep out of the way.'

'Right,' says Simon. 'So she didn't help at all?'

I just look at him.

'What did the stylist say about the way you dressed Nell?' he asks. He kind of knows what's coming next.

'Okay,' I volunteer. 'The stylist said "Oh no – you don't want to do it like that. You've made the woman look like a duck."'

Simon laughs so much I think he's never going to stop, and I can feel tears welling in my eyes.

'Hey, come here,' he says, wrapping his arms around me in a moment of warm good humour and, as it will transpire, exceptionally bad timing. Simon's a good hugger, it turns out, he just needs to work out when to do it.

'What's going on?' says Dean, walking through the door with his tracksuit trousers rolled up to his knees, no shirt and a mess of tattoos scattered across his hairless chest.

Simon leaps back and sends coffee splattering all across the pictures on the desk in front of us. 'Nothing,' he says, looking quite terrified.

The two men look at each other and shake hands. Simon explains that he's come to help me write my piece.

'Whhhaaaaaattttt?' says Dean.

'I'm just going to help her with the writing,' explains Simon, quite taken aback by my husband's response.

'No, not that,' says Dean. 'THAT!' He points at the pictures and I notice how pale he looks. 'It's my nan,' he's muttering.

Shit. I sort of forget she's his nan, I think of her as my special little mate. I probably should have mentioned this to Dean first, shouldn't I?

'She wanted to do it,' I lie. 'She begged me.'

Dean is talking to the ceiling as if addressing his grandfather in heaven. He's muttering apologies, and saying things like 'you went through a war . . . and this is what we've done with your wife . . .'

'DEAN!' I shout, rather louder than I expected to. 'We have work to do. Your granddad would be proud of Nell. Now, go and put some clothes on.'

'Okay,' he says meekly, leaving the room.

I've never seen a man look more terrified than Simon does in this minute.

Midday

It's done. Somehow. I don't have any idea how. Well, I do – to be fair – I know exactly how it got done . . . Simon did it. I called and made hair appointments, sorted out the personal training sessions I need to do, and arranged for my dry-cleaning to be delivered. While I fussed about with matters of a minor domestic nature, Simon wrote the piece. God, he's good. I'm so impressed with how he managed to just write it instead of fussing over it and distracting himself and finding other, less important things to do. Simon sat there, bashing on the computer like a raving loony. I thought steam and smoke were going to start pouring out of the front of it.

The nice thing about Simon is that he didn't make me feel bad. He kept asking me questions, and slotted my answers into the article. Then he said afterwards that I wrote it because I provided all the information, even though I didn't. He also asked me to jot a few pieces of advice down. Okay . . . umm . . .

CHOOSING WINE IN A RESTAURANT

It can look a bit daunting when the wine list arrives in a restaurant. All these meaningless foreign names jumbled together with ridiculous descriptions like 'essence of juniper berry' and 'hint of wild elderflower'. Bollocks to all that. There are two basic rules to follow; two things to look for when you're selecting wine.

First, look at the price: always go for the most expensive. Then once the waiter has brought you your Chateaux Du-pe-du-pe-du at £500 a bottle, slug in some cheap, sweet lemonade, and a slice of lemon and ice. Perfect. This, actually, is a general rule of drinking . . . if the drink is expensive, add a particularly sickly fizzy drink to it. So, if someone offers you brandy at £100 a shot, throw in half a can of Diet Coke and you're away.

Second, get the one called 'chardonnay'.

Once I'd written this down, Simon went on and on about how funny my 'advice pieces' were, which I didn't quite understand. People seem to have a strange way of interpreting my heartfelt and much-cherished advice as being funny.

'The trouble is,' he said to me at one point. 'You don't believe you're funny.'

Er . . . hello? No! I don't.

'But you are, and you're a good writer,' he reiterated.

I explained that this simply wasn't true, and the evidence was in front of us: i.e. Simon was writing the piece instead of me. I even told him about the time that I went to the Complementary Health Clinic, thinking it would all be free. I thought this would show him how dopey I can be at times, but instead he just laughed to himself and shook his head at me in that smiley, lovely, familiar way.

'I just feel a bit bad that you've ended up writing it all,' I said.

'Stop being so silly,' Simon replied. 'I'm a writer – that's what I do. I'm also a friend, and more than happy to help get you started. I'm sure you'll be fine with everything now because your skills are in chatting away about being a Wag and writing that funny stuff – like you showed me when you were on the course. You're a diarist, Tracie, that's what you are. They shouldn't have asked you to write this feature piece on your own. They should have sent a journalist to interview you and he could have written it.'

'I think that was my fault,' I reply. 'I told them that I didn't need any help. I told them I'd be fine on my own. I just felt silly, asking for help with the first piece. Just like with the stylist, I suppose.'

Simon smiles at me and says he thinks everything will be fine now. 'Just send this in, then you go off and get your nails done or whatever.'

'I will,' I reply. 'I'm the Jam Bank of the Wag world, remember?'

Simon smiles – thrilled, no doubt, that I've remembered what he once called me. 'Anne Frank,' he says, suddenly, for no good reason.

Wednesday, 31 October
Midday

After the 'utter success and brilliance' (their words, not mine) of the article I 'wrote' for the *Daily Mail*, they have been 'plugging' – see how much new lingo I've learned since starting this writing nonsense – even the word 'lingo' to be fair. I know about by-lines, pic credits, snappers, scribblers and subs – anyway, they have been 'plugging' my new column solidly for the past few days. It's going in on Monday, so I have to try and send it in today . . . aahh . . . shit!

The fact it's being plugged constantly means:

a) I have to write it. I had thought of inventing some bizarre excuse for not doing it . . . like my hands have fallen off, or I've been injured in a dreadful crash and have lost all my memory, so I no longer know what hair extensions are, nor do I have any clue what sort of tan I should be opting for, or what sort of make-up looks good! As if!

b) There's no chance of Mum and the Slag Wags not noticing it, so now I'm seriously out of the loop. Mum won't return any of my calls, emails or texts (the latter is understandable, her fingernails are so long these days that texting of any kind is a thing of the past for her).

c) The article needs to be good in order to justify all the effort they've put in to promoting it, or I'll look really silly.

Blimey . . . the pressure!

One thing they kept going on about last time was how much they liked my one-liners – what 'fun' they thought they were! 'Fun', it turns out, is quite an abstract concept. Certainly, it defies all explanation or description. It's extremely odd.

In the light of all this, and because I simply don't know how else to go about things, I'm going to just speak from my heart and give common-sense, logical advice and see how it all works out – if that constitutes 'fun' in their book, then so be it. Perhaps they all just need to get out a bit more . . . okay?

Hello, my name is Tracie Martin and I will be writing a regular article giving you helpful advice on how to be a Wag. Today I'm going to start with two things that sound as if they should be very easy – eating and going out – but, remember, there is a right way to do everything. There's even a right way to breathe, smile and blink. When I say a 'right way', I mean a 'Wag way', because the Waggier the better as far as I'm concerned. Food is important for living, but if consumed properly it also provides ways in which you can exhibit the core traits of a Wag.

So, first of all, the question is: **What should I eat, as a Wag?**

I would point out that Wags divide into two clear groups on the subject of food. There are the chips 'n' lager girls and the f-word girls. The former tend to be younger and love a kebab to soak up the vodka and Red Bulls. The latter group are impossibly and quite frighteningly thin, and can't say the f-word without feeling so trau-matised that they have to rush out and buy eight pairs of Jimmy Choos (think Posh). Most genuine f-word girls haven't had a decent meal since they left kindergarten.

The easiest way to work out which camp you fall into is to measure your waist. If the number you come up with is smaller than twenty you're an f-word girl. If it's between twenty and twenty-three you have f-word leanings, and bigger than that and you're a chips 'n' lager girl. There can be movement between the two groups – for example, a young Wag may be a c&l girl then find god (Good Old-fashioned Determination), lose weight and become an f-word girl.

The two sub-sections are entirely opposite and there is no happy medium when it comes to Wags and food. You simply can't be the sort of girl who just eats healthily whenever she can and has the occasional binge. You've got to have a heavily complex relationship with food to be considered a 'proper' Wag. For example, I just avoid it altogether until I'm about to faint, then I'll eat enough to keep me going for a while, and afterwards feel enormously guilty at what I've done – imagining myself fat again, like I used to be when I was a child, until I adopted starvation as a lifestyle choice. Once my stomach's empty I feel happier again until those fainting feel-ings come on. See – a complex relationship with food – every Wag needs that.

Then there's the whole issue of special days out. The burning question is:

How should I conduct myself when going to a wedding?

I'll give you one piece of advice that will serve you well when going to weddings: upstage the bride. That's your aim, and if you achieve that you are truly a Wag. Think of Liz Hurley (not a Wag in the true sense of the word because she didn't marry a footballer, but a Wag in the spirit of the word because she's got where she is by being someone's girlfriend and flashing her knickers and her cleavage at every given opportunity). When Liz attended the wedding of her friend Henry Dent Brocklehurst she wore a thigh-flashing red dress that revealed leopard-skin print knickers. Her breasts were falling out of her dress and her face had as much make-up on as it is possible for the face to carry. It looked weighed down by camouflage paint, light-reflecting particles and lipstick. That's before we even get onto the eyes, which looked like they'd been stolen from a sleeping panda bear. It was an astonishing achievement – covering the three key points in Wag wedding dressing:

1. The heaviest of make-up – always!

2. Try to show your knickers and your cleavage – if you can't manage both then you must ensure that you display one. If you can't find a dress that displays at least one of these key body parts then don't go to the wedding.

3. The dress should be an unacceptable wedding colour. Forget muted shades. You could go for white (a great choice in achieving the fundamental aim of wedding-going), or you could wear black (if you do this, to avoid looking boring, make it very short and make sure your breasts are hanging out of the front of it), or you could go for bold red and leopard-skin – perfect Wag-wear. Hurley, we salute you!

So, to summarise, the fundamental aim of a Wag at a wedding is to upstage the bride. If you do this you are bound to enjoy the day.

Tuesday, 6 November
10 a.m.

Oh my god!!!! Saucepan Head, the features-editor woman (except it turns out her name is Susan Sped) has just called to say that she has never seen anything like it! Apparently the *Daily Mail*'s whole email system almost went down overnight with the weight of responses to my article.

'Was it because it was so terrible?' I asked.

'Er, no!' she responded. 'Not at all. Your article was funny and silly and everyone adored it.'

Here we go, I thought – it's all about the other f-word again.

'Did you really think it was funny?' I ask. 'I mean, didn't you think it was useful and helpful and good advice?'

Susan laughs so loudly I think she's having some sort of breakdown. 'I adore you,' she shrieks at me. 'I fucking adore you.'

Her exclamation seems both unwarranted and inappropriate, so I just stand there, looking at the mouthpiece, waiting for her to calm down. 'Fucking marvellous. Must go,' she squeals, and the line goes dead.

Simon emails to say he thought the piece was good – '*very funny*' he concludes.

'*Why?*' I email back to him. '*I'm not trying to be funny. I'm just trying to help people understand about the life of a Wag.*'

'*You rock,*' he replies.

Is that any sort of reply? Christ, it's not even a sentence. Simon's only connection with Paris Hilton, perhaps – neither of them can finish a sentence.

Wednesday, 7 November
9 a.m.

There's been a mixed bag of reaction to my article in the *Daily Mail*. When I say 'mixed bag', what I mean is that everyone in the entire universe thought it was great – except Mum who thinks I'm the devil himself for even considering getting involved in writing for a newspaper. 'Why don't you keep a low profile and keep some dignity?' she says. Her request lost some impact because she was wearing a skirt so short that it barely covered her gusset. She simply wasn't appropriately dressed for giving lectures on dignity.

It's a shame she feels like that because everyone on the newspaper seems to think the column is great, Nell thinks I'm the latest literary sensation since Bridget Jones, whoever she is, and the Wags I talk to – not all that many, to be honest – when I say 'Wags I talk to' you can read 'Suzzi and Mich' – anyway, they think my advice is sound (they're the only ones who don't say my pieces are 'funny'. I guess they 'get' them more than other people). The 'senior management' on the *Daily Mail* have been full of praise. Then there's been the response from readers. God, that's been unreal. The editor of the *Daily Mail* phoned me last night and said that in the newspaper's entire history they haven't had a response to an article like that which they received after my advice piece appeared on Monday. He said they had loved the piece and were delighted with the way readers responded to me. 'You're going to be a star,' he said, which made me giggle a bit. Then he went in for the kill: 'Can you do another piece for Friday's paper? I know we said every Monday, but can we do an extra one now the ball's rolling?'

Aaaarghhhhh . . . I'm so busy this week. I have to get three of my eyelashes lengthened, I need nail extensions on my toes, plus I have to buy a new belly-button ring and find a feng shui guy to come and sort out Paskia's bedroom – I'm convinced she's into all this football nonsense because she's not harmonious with her environment. At least that's what Mum told Dean, and while I do think Mum can be a little bonkers, it sounds like it's worth a try. Although quite where you find a Chinese man specialising in the ancient art of placement and design is a mystery. Certainly haven't seen any strolling down Luton High Street. Then I need to buy the cracked black pepper, clay, vine leaf and ginger bath oils that Coleen says she uses when she's stressed, and to get some Adukini Mingo Bingo beans because they helped Darren Bent's girl-friend lose three pounds. How am I supposed to fit all this in?

'Yes, okay,' I say meekly, because I hate upsetting people. I'm like that at the hairdresser's – I come over all wimpy and unassertive when they ask me whether the water's too hot when they're washing my hair. Even though the temperature is boiling hot and I can feel the bones in my skull melting under the intensity of it, I still say 'no, that's fine' when they ask.

So I've agreed to do another piece this week and, in return, the editor will 'sell it hard', whatever that might mean. 'Big front-page puff,' he said. I thought he was talking about Michael Barrymore at first, but turns out that a 'puff' is when they promote the fact that your piece will be in the paper – so, much like a 'plug', as it turns out. At the end of the conversation I've agreed to write a piece that I simply don't have time to do, and he's agreed to write about me all over the front of the *Daily Mail* – something I don't really want him to do. I think, in short, the conversation could represent my mother's worst nightmare.

As it turns out, it might also be Paskia's worst nightmare. We had a long chat about it this morning, and she doesn't like the fact that I talk about being a Wag all the time.

'Why don't I teach you about football and you could write about that?' she says, reaching for one of her books. She's being helpful but she's totally missing the point of the column.

'I can't write about football,' I say. 'The column's about how to be a Wag.'

With that, she just tutted, turned on her heels (flat heels!) and left.

It's funny the way people have reacted to this column. There's me taking my role seriously and dispensing advice that I believe to be both helpful and crucial, then there's the majority of the world who are inter-preting this as being somehow funny. And then there's Paskia Rose with her bizarre view that it's 'demeaning to women'. That's what she said. 'Demeaning to women.' How bizarre is that? I'm writing a column with the express intention of helping women, and she thinks I'm doing some sort of damage. Honestly – kids today!

Friday, 9 November
9 a.m.

Now, the great thing is that it's all getting easier. Honestly! I did the piece that went into this morning's paper so much more quickly than I did the first piece that I feel like I'm a proper writer. I've just looked at it and BLOODY HELL!!!! Did they 'puff' me or what? My little face is all over the front page, there's a big line across the top of the paper saying *'Exclusive!!! The funniest Wag in the world tells you all about her life. See page five.'*

Funny? This morning I did a subject that not even the nutters on the *Daily Mail* could describe as being 'funny' – I wrote about smoking and gardening, so I really don't know what all this description of my 'funny' stuff is about. It's just mad. Crazy! This is what I wrote:

SMOKING

Smoking is not considered terribly Waggish behaviour because of the effect on the skin and the fact that it looks unladylike (unlike falling out of taxis at midnight with your knickers showing, or singing 'Who let the dogs out?' when rival Wags enter the room, which are both considered entirely appropriate and acceptably feminine). However, if you must smoke then Marlboro Lights are the cigarettes of choice. They should always be held out at arm's length and you should swing them animatedly around when talking, as if conducting an invisible orchestra. People should be ducking and bowing as they go past you. A minimum of thirty-three people should have ash or cigarette burns on their clothes by the time you leave.

GARDENING

Clearly the whole point of a garden is the gardener. It goes without saying that you won't do any weeding, planting or fertilising your-self. You can get away with watering the garden, but only if you do it Desperate Housewives*-style, dressed to the nines, in killer heels.*

131

Whatever you do, avoid looking like Felicity Kendall in The Good
Life *– nice bum and all that, but those clothes were truly atrocious.*

*So, if you're not doing any gardening yourself then who are you
going to employ? Someone male, for starters – you don't want some
old bag wandering up and down, cutting the buds off your
hydrangeas, and you certainly don't want someone feminine, young
and pretty. Go for a younger, stronger and more handsome man
than your husband and there'll be daily eye-candy in the garden,
especially if you can get him to work without his shirt on. Mmmm
. . . the thought is making me feel quite hot and bothered.*

Midday

Already the day has descended into madness. I've been trying to get
hold of Mum on an almost hourly basis for days. Now she's finally on
the phone and is howling at me to keep a lower profile and get myself
off the bloody front pages.

'It's not my fault,' I say. 'They just like my articles so want to puff
them.'

'Puff them?' she replies in a mocking voice. 'What are they? Articles
or cigarettes?'

I explain all about front-page puffs but I am wasting my time. She
isn't interested. She keeps saying 'Ya, ya, ya, whatever, whatever, whatever' while I am talking, which is very rude, and not unlike a fourteen-
year-old schoolgirl. I'm quite fed up of it all. She seems obsessed with
me writing for the newspapers, wanting me to keep a low profile and
certainly not to write any more articles. She seems desperate for me to
be quietly locked away in the house, not talking to anyone, while she
behaves like a schoolgirl – wearing tiny skirts and dating teenage football sensations whose balls have barely dropped. I suppose the two
things are linked. She wants to act like a young woman and doesn't
want me all over the papers proving that she isn't.

Still, it does feel odd. She always used to go on at me to get out
more, make more friends and be more sociable, and now she doesn't
seem happy if I'm out anywhere. It seems that she always wants me
to do what I'm not doing, almost as if I can't ever do anything right.
Oh dear. Perhaps I'm just tired. I really shouldn't talk about Mum like
that.

I put the phone down and go into the kitchen to get something to
eat, berating myself with every step and trying to remember the words
of my psychologist. 'Food is not the answer, food is not the answer . . .'
Well, I'm sorry, but right now, it is.

I've taken a huge bite of the chocolate biscuit when the phone rings again.

'Hi Tracie, it's Mindy.'

'Sorry?'

'Mindy . . . from Luton Town.'

'Oh,' I say. 'Nice of you to call.'

'I just wondered whether you wanted to come round tonight – I'm having a girls' night with some fab women. A couple of them mentioned seeing your articles, so I thought you might like to come.'

'Um . . . I can't tonight,' I say. 'But I'll see you at the match tomorrow.'

'Uh . . . yeah,' says Mindy. 'Umm . . . don't mention to anyone that I called, will you? I mean, don't mention it to any of the other Wags – especially your mum.'

What a cow! For some reason, though, I don't say this. I'm not brave enough without my fellow Wag-mates by my side. We're very much pack animals when it comes to fighting, us Wags. So I just lay the receiver back down, move away from the phone and throw a pile of cushions at the wall.

Straight after Mindy's call, after the seventh cushion has been chucked, there's a call from *Marie-Claire*. The features editor there wants to interview me for a 'my individual style' feature. There's also a call from . . . wait for it . . . *GMTV*!! Whoaaaahhh! It's like a dream come true – I *always* watch *GMTV* to keep up with current affairs, i.e. what other Wags are doing. I think Lorraine is just fab, and suddenly here I am – little old me, being asked to go on there, and all just because of a little article I wrote in the paper! Can you believe it? They want me to go on Monday's programme – and it's Friday today – and I don't have a thing to wear – and Monday's also the day that my next article is to be in the newspaper, so I've really got to sort myself out, and get writing, and shopping, and dressing, and . . . Oh shit! What will Mum say? Should I tell her? Should I do it . . . ?

Better ring Nell.

Sunday, 11 November
9 a.m.

There are times when it feels as if Mum is all around us – crawling over us like some terrible, unstoppable rash. I long, I have to be honest, for her to go and leave us in our familial bliss. There are times when the sound of her voice, the sight of her moving things around, tutting and complaining, makes me want to attack walls, throw things about and beat-up innocent passers-by. And then there are days like today, when I really need to get hold of her, want to have a proper talk to her, but just can't find her anywhere and have no idea where she can possibly be. It seems to me that where Mum is concerned it's very much a case of all or nothing. She's either straightening out my g-strings and asking me what contraception I take, or she's on the moon – or somewhere totally unreachable.

Today I want to talk to Mum. I want to sit her down and ask her why she has such a problem with me doing my articles – it's what Nell suggested I should do, so it must be right. I want to know what it is about me writing little pieces for newspapers about life as a Wag that has led her to withdraw from me so dramatically. But can I get hold of her? Can I just have five minutes on the phone with my mother? No. It's utterly hopeless. I've been ringing her mobile since 7 a.m. I need to talk to her before my *Daily Mail* piece goes in tomorrow, and before I pop up on *GMTV*. I really don't want her getting angrier with me. I can't stand it when she has a reason to be cross with me. I can put up with her anger when it has no justification, I can do 'mad, angry Angie' because I've coped with mad, angry Angie since I was a child, but what I find incredibly difficult is when I think any of it is justified. I suppose it's that 'only child of a single mother' thing – you feel like, when it comes to it, you have no one else, so if that solitary parent turns on you it feels like everything is over, as if there's no way forward. It's at times like these that I really wish my father was in my life.

It's not that I feel I've missed having a father, but I do feel there's a void. I have a tendency towards panic and over-excitement that may have been avoided if the early days of my life had been filled with one solid man who I could have called father, instead of several dozen good-looking, sweet-smelling, short-staying men who smiled, gave Mum flowers, made her dazzlingly happy, then left – making her dazzlingly sad. More than anything, I wish my father had been around when I was younger just to give Mum support – financial, obviously, but also moral support. It must be hard bringing up a child on your own. Since I've had Paskia I've realised how hard it is to bring up children, and I realise that without Dean's support, his comforting arm around me and the backing he gives me at every turn – not least financial – I'd find it so difficult. When I think back to my childhood, I'm so grateful to Mum for providing the lifestyle we had – I don't know how she did it. We always had food, clothes and a nice place to live. Mum always had great nights out, lovely jewellery and the best shoes and handbags in town. She did some modelling and some beauty therapy, though I don't think she's in any way qualified. She also advised people on interior design. I just don't know how she did it. I don't know how she made enough money to keep us afloat.

I pick up the phone to try her again. Finally, someone answers.

'Hello?' I say.

There's nothing on the other end. I can hear the sea, or the river, or something – a vague and gentle sound of water.

'Hello?'

I can also hear someone moving around and I get the distinct impression that the person holding the phone isn't Mum, and that it's Mum wandering around in the background. I get the feeling that the person holding the phone is a man. I don't know why . . . it's just a feeling I get.

'Hello Ludo,' I say again, then the phone goes dead.

Minutes later, the phone rings and it's Mum.

'Hi,' I say. 'I've just been trying to call you.'

'Yes, dear,' she says. 'I think I got cut off.'

'I've been trying to call all morning. Where are you?'

'Just with a friend,' she says. 'Nothing to fret about. Now, what are you trying so desperately to talk to me for?'

'Just wanted to talk to you about all these articles,' I say, waiting for the barrage of abuse. 'I know you said you weren't happy, and I'm worried. Perhaps I should show you the articles first? Or you could help me write the pieces? Would you prefer that?'

'Everything's fine, dear, don't worry about me,' says Mum. 'Honestly, sweetie, I'm fine. I'm not worried at all.'

I know instinctively that there is someone in the background, and that Mum doesn't want to be rude in front of whoever it is who is padding around barefoot, presumably in a towel and ruffling his shower-wet hair like a model in an advertisement for healthy breakfast cereal.

'I'm on *GMTV* tomorrow,' I say.

'Lovely, dear.'

This is too weird.

'And my next piece goes into the *Daily Mail* tomorrow.'

'What a thrill!'

Even weirder. This is now truly odd. She's acting like a normal mother. At the match yesterday she'd called me 'worthless, pointless and embarrassing'. She had said that I was a disgrace to the family name with my articles and told me to stop it at once. Even when I'd adopted a very assertive approach (like my counsellor told me to), and said 'Look, I'm here to watch Dean play football, let's talk about this later', she still managed to turn it all on me, and screamed, 'Watch Dean play football? You wish!' With her glossy red fingernail she'd traced down the team list to the bottom, where Dean's name sat below the reserves. 'There'll have to be about twenty-five injuries before you get to watch Dean play football,' she'd said, laughing uproariously. 'I think they'll call *me* before *him*.'

The Slag Wags had all collapsed with laughter, smiling, giggling and choking on their own hilarity.

'See you later,' I'd said, leaving the ground. 'I have things to do.'

The things I had to do, of course, involved lying on my bed and crying. Dean's career was collapsing; my mother hated me; I had been humiliated in front of the Wags. Not the best day I'd ever had.

'Talk very soon, darling,' she says now. 'I really have to go.'

'Of course,' I say. 'Talk soon.'

Possibly the only thing more disconcerting and troubling than Mum being nasty to me is Mum being nice. It feels most peculiar.

Midday

Oh dear. The day's getting worse with every hour. First Mum's acting all out of character and now poor Mich has arrived on the doorstep in floods of tears. It turns out she's not a Wag any more. It's the most dreadful news imaginable. Poor old Mich, it must be like losing a limb. I really thought she'd found true love with Andre, but this time the most awful, heartbreaking thing has happened. I can hardly contain my anger and frustration.

Mich falls through the door telling me how well it had all been going with Andre. She says he'd seemed to like her, too, as he wrapped his signet-ring-bedecked hand around hers. He's even had the tattoo with the name of his ex-girlfriend removed from his lower arm! When she told me that I said, 'Honestly, Mich, that's *true* love.' I thought it was all really, really romantic. They seemed so happy . . . once they'd got over the incident with the air display and the wax. Now, though – well, you won't believe what happened.

They went out to dinner at Nobu last night after the match and had more bottles of wine than a young goalkeeper should be having mid-season, and then went back to his flat. They went in and 'crashed out' (I think what Mich means is that they went to bed and did unspeakable things to one another). Then Mich heard her phone bleep with a message. Her Mum's not well so Mich always worries when she gets a message. When the phone bleeped, she leapt from the bed, donning, I'm sure, some fetching pink fluffy mules and shuffling off to find her phone. There it is, and you won't believe it – a rude text message telling her that her boyfriend's been unfaithful. *'Oy, slut,'* it says. *'Don't think you're the only woman in his life.'*

Mich had dropped her pretty, heavily tanned face into her orange palms. She'd felt her heart beating beneath her thin voile baby-doll nightie. This was a nightmare. Worse than when she went on that internet date with a guy who said he was a footballer and turned out not to be. He was married with three kids, a drug pusher, a former convict and wanted for tax evasion, too, but what had really broken Mich's heart was that he wasn't a footballer. Such betrayal.

The text was obviously sent by a crazed woman who was after her man, but when Mich tried to call the number back, the phone had been disconnected. Mich told Andre straightaway and he swore that there was no one else.

'Thank god,' said Mich, delighted and relieved. But if my dear friend thought that was the worst thing that was to happen she was completely mistaken. This morning she got up and left Andre's fabulous riverfront apartment. She got home, got her false eyelashes done (they look great, actually, even through the tears) and had her legs waxed. By the time she got out of the salon she had a frantic message from Andre's home number saying that his mobile phone had been stolen, and following it were twelve messages, all sent from Andre's stolen mobile. They were clearly messages that he had been sending to other women.

'The bloody thief has forwarded the messages from his phone to me,' squealed Mich. 'It turns out he has been having phone sex with all these complete tarts!'

'What tarts?' I ask.

'I don't know, look . . .' she says, pointing to the screen.

She shows me the phone and I have to say that the case for the defence of Andre Howchenski is falling apart. The inbox is full of the evidence of Andre's infidelity. '*Hi big boy, enjoyed it 2. 3 x in 1 nite is enuf 4 any1. Looking 4wood 2 2morrow. M xxxxxxx*', and '*You on top, me underneath. Mmmm . . . xxxx M*'. Hard to see how a jury would acquit based on this sort of evidence.

'But why would a thief start sending messages from a stolen phone's inbox? It doesn't make any sense,' I say.

She shrugs. 'Perhaps he thought he'd have a bit of fun with his stolen phone. I don't know. Does it matter? What matters is that Andre is a complete shit, and I really thought he was more mature than this.'

'I did too,' I agree. 'He wears Gucci shoes, for heaven's sake. You just don't expect this sort of behaviour from a man shod in Gucci.'

'I thought I was going out with a man, but it turns out I've been dating a schoolboy,' says Mich.

As we are sitting there, her phone bleeps again, and more texts arrive. This time they're more abusive. They call her all these names and tell her she's vile. And fat! The horror! I can see that Mich is very upset by this whole thing. I feel like grabbing Andre by his big, fat, ugly neck and strangling him.

She hands the phone to me. Blimey, the phone thief is having a field day. Pictures of naked women playing with themselves appear along with more copies of texts that he's been sending to all these slappers. It's like the secret world of a fourteen-year-old boy laid bare.

'This is so awful,' Mich says, her big green eyes filling with tears. The eyelashes seem to be holding up, though, which is something. 'So awful. Why did he turn out to be such an idiot? Why are all these horrible texts being sent to me? Why me?'

'Because you're his girlfriend,' I offer, but I have to say I'm slightly confused by the whole thing. Who could be sending these texts? Who would want Mich to know that Andre's cheating on her?

'I think you need to phone him. You two need to talk this through. Tell him to come round and talk to you.'

'I can't call him,' she howled back. 'His phone's been nicked.'

Mich stayed for three hours as more texts poured in. Poor girl. She left messages on Andre's landline then we sat there, hoping he'd call soon. Quite what he'll say, though, is impossible to work out. He's obviously been texting every woman in Luton. It'll take some explaining. The women can't be all that bright, or terribly discerning, to allow him to text them like that. Why do they put up with it? The photographs indicated that one of the women, at least, is not the most attractive on earth. They are obviously just old tarts he's picked up along the way. They look cheap and tacky – not one of them worthy of the title Wag, that's for sure, and not one of them in the same league as Michaela.

The texts begin to get quite abusive. The thief has moved from forwarding texts from Andre's sent box to sending texts of their own. Poor Mich looks as if she's been in a coach crash or a major World War or something.

'I thought it was all going well once we got over the Biggin Hill thing,' she says, her voice strained and the pain leaping through the syllables like a salmon through water. The anguish drips from her tongue, her voice is empty, hollow but still full of pain. She looks over at me and I know she is going to say something momentous. 'Perhaps I'll never be a Wag.'

That's when my tears began to fall. It's a lovely moment. Two Wags bonding over the broken remains of a once-promising relationship.

'Maybe it will be all okay,' I say, offering hope. 'Maybe those texts can be explained?'

'Mmmmmm . . .' mutters Michaela, looking down and reading through the texts. 'How?'

She has a point. The texts are all about who will be going on top next time they get together, and what they'll do with one another given half a chance.

Mich and I are just about coping with the situation, thanks to two cheeky early-afternoon glasses of champagne, and by eating our joint body weights in small savoury snacks, when her phone rings.

We both peer down at it. It's Andre's home number. Thank god for that. At last she can talk it all through with him and establish why, how and when the texts have been sent, or even whether they are from his mobile phone at all. I still can't believe he'd do that to her.

'Hi,' she says, and I wander out of the room, leaving them alone for him to explain, and for her to decide whether to accept his explanations and his apologies.

Then there's an almighty shriek. I run back into the kitchen where she's sitting, ashen-faced, staring at the wall in front of her. 'He's accused me –' she mumbles, her voice barely audible beneath the thick layer of pain and confusion. 'He's accused me of stealing his phone and sending these texts to myself!'

We look at each other for a while in the way that two people might look at one another if a large hamster made entirely from green jelly walked into the kitchen.

'He, I, you, who . . . WHAT?' I ask – okay so not the most articulated of expressions but what do you expect? 'He thinks you stole his phone and proceeded to text yourself with a whole load of abuse?'

'No – I don't know,' says Mich. She is all folded in on herself and fidgeting in a horrible, uncomfortable way. 'I don't think he believes that I received those messages. He thinks I pinched his phone and lied about receiving them.'

The big green jelly hamster is giving birth before us.

'This is the maddest thing I've ever heard,' I say. 'Truly. It's utterly insane. It's mad. Madder than when I left that cucumber facepack in the fridge and Mum came round and ate it on crackers. What are you talking about?'

'He says his friend had a girlfriend once who stole his phone and deleted all his numbers, so I must have stolen his.'

'Yeah, okay,' I say. 'But I just saw a whole load of texts coming through. You definitely received them. You couldn't have sent them to yourself. This is insane. Let me call him.'

Mich's shriek can be heard the other side of the M25. 'Nooooo,' she says. 'He already thinks I'm mad. It'll just prove I'm mad if you call him.'

'But I can tell him that you can't possibly have sent those texts to yourself. You have to let me call him.'

And so it was that I lifted the phone and talked to Andre's brother, given that Andre himself had no mobile phone for me to call and did not have the wit or presence of mind to answer the landline in his riverside apartment. 'Kulshav,' I said. 'May I speak with Andre?'

'Noooo,' said Kulshav. 'You not Andre. You have lady voice.'

'That's right. I'm not Andre. CAN I SPEAK TO HIM?'

I won't bore you with the number of times the man misunderstood me, the number of times we had to go back over the same bit of conversation, the number of times I felt like crawling through the phone and boxing him in the ear. Eventually, he put me on to Andre.

'Hey, how are you doing?' said Serbia's number-one goalkeeping sensation in his deep, manly voice, like some sort of James Bond villain. Usually when I hear him talk it makes me think of Dean and how unassertive his voice is. Today I just think 'tosser'.

'Listen,' I say. 'Mich is here, and she's very upset. What on earth is going on? Why are you accusing her of stealing your phone? What is *wrong* with you?'

There is silence on the other end of the phone as this man who I'd thought so much of mumbles something about having to go training but thanks me for calling. I'm quite big on gut instinct, and my gut instinct is that the man knows something about the stolen phone that he is not letting on. He has decided to make the accusation that Mich stole it to divert attention from the fact that he has a load of inappropriate texts on it, and to divert attention from the fact that he's had it nicked. Something is going on here . . . I'm just not sure what.

Mich walks back into the kitchen. She's far less upset about the fact that her relationship has hit the wall than she is about the fact that she's got this random accusation against her, which I take as being a good thing, and rare, too. I would have thought that Mich's overwhelming concern would be for her social life and Wag-standing, not for her honour. It suddenly makes me think that she might not be cut out to be a Wag after all.

'It's probably for the best,' I say, in a way that is utterly annoying and really quite old-ladyish. I prepare to explain myself when Mich blurts out: 'Have you ever been accused of something you haven't done? Because it's the worst feeling in the whole world.'

'Blimey, yes,' I say. 'I grew up with Mum, remember. Not a day went by when I wasn't accused of doing something terrible. The truth was that I never did anything wrong. Just got accused of being responsible for everything in the world that went wrong.'

'Oh,' says Mich. And then there's silence . . . I accept that my outburst might easily be categorised as a conversation-stopper, so it's probably not too surprising.

'Listen,' I say, cutting through the heavy silence. 'I'm going to have to head out to old-lady land in a minute. Do you want to come?'

'Old-lady land?' she asks, and I explain that it's the anniversary of Nell's husband's death, and that I always take her to the crematorium.

'You're asking me if I want to come and look at where dead people are buried with a bunch of old ladies?'

'That pretty much summarises the offer,' I reply.

'Okay,' she says. 'But I'll have to fix my make-up first.'

'Er . . . yes,' I say. As if we've *ever* left the house without fixing our make-up! She's obviously even more upset than I thought . . .

4 p.m.

They're genuinely thrilled to be here. That's the most bizarre thing. They are all dressed up in their ridiculous green tracksuits over jumpers, fleeces, scarves and boots. As they sit in the back of the car, driving towards the crematorium, it's like a meeting of the Jolly Green Giants. They seem to have forgotten or blatantly ignored all my fashion and grooming advice. None of them looks any more like a Wag than they did before I laid my hands on them.

'Was I wasting my time?' I ask to no one in particular.

'Yes, dear,' they all say, with the patronising tone that seems to come so easily to the elderly.

As we pull into the crematorium car park there is great excitement.

141

Gladys spots it first. 'Ooooooo,' she says, gazing up at the smoke as it billows out of the chimneys. 'Look . . . there's a crem taking place.'

The others are so excited – craning their necks to look out of the window and gasping in awe and wonder – you'd think they'd just seen Marilyn Monroe and Elvis Presley dancing on the lawns. There are gasps, smiles and nudges as the three elderly ladies in green can't quite believe their tremendous luck. A real live crematorium taking place before their eyes! 'Ahhh . . . god love 'em,' says Nell, but her momentary sensitivity doesn't seem to stop her gawping.

'Wonder who it is . . .' says Ethel, squinting to focus, as if the clue to the identity of the deceased may be hidden in the smoke trailing through the sky. 'It's hard to tell,' she concedes, though the others seem more confident.

'We'll work it out,' Nell is saying, and I realise that she really does think it's something that can be worked out from the back seat of my hire car (note, please, that those idiots in Croydon still haven't given me my car. I went back there with the cash and they said it wasn't enough. I have to pay £270 extra because my car's been there for months).

Every time I come here with Nell it strikes me how comfortable she is in this environment, with its close proximity to death. I'd rather go through my life believing that I'm not going to die, believing that I alone will be blessed with eternal life and live on in a magical castle somewhere, brushing my hair extensions and fussing with my eye make-up into my fifth century. Death is the oddest thing because you just can't understand it. Yet here we are with three women for whom it might be just around the corner. They're all ancient, though so lively and exuberant and damn silly that I can't honestly believe that any of them are ever going to die. How could someone like Gladys be snatched away? She might be ninety-two, but here she is, desperately pressing buttons on the car door to open the window (clearly we now have to smell the smoke as well as see it). I've put the child-lock on, and she can't work out why the window won't open. The average five-year-old would have worked out that the child-lock is on by now, but not Gladys. She just shrugs her bony little shoulders and sits back with a soppy smile on her face.

'Mourners!' shrieks Nell, and the three of them jump bolt upright like Marines on parade. These same old women who shuffle along, barely able to get through the routine of the day because they're so old and decrepit, are now displaying the speed and flexibility of greyhounds.

'They might invite us back to the party afterwards,' says Nell. 'I love a good wake. They're always such good parties.'

'It's not a party,' I say, mildly concerned with their thrill at the prospect of a free sweet sherry.

'Okay, here we are,' I say, having parked so badly in the car park that not a single car can get out without scraping past me. I'm basically obstructing the narrow driveway out of the car park. That doesn't bother me, though – I'm more concerned in dropping these old ladies near the entrance so they don't get freezing cold or slip on the ice and break a hip or something terrible. I'm also so colossally bad at parking that I know that, however hard I try, I won't be able to park well, so it makes sense to save time and effort and park badly in the first place.

Once I've helped the women out of the car, checked my lipstick in the mirror, reapplied it, added glitter to my temples, and looked around furtively to check that no one's watching, it's time to unload the bags. Now, I love a big bag but they have brought with them a quite insane amount of luggage for a trip to a crematorium. I'm half-thinking that they're planning to stay for a few nights. All three have brought those absurd shopping trolleys on wheels that old ladies cling to as surely as their late husbands clung to their war memories.

The room containing the *Book of Memories* is where the day starts for Nell and her mates. I remember when Pask was younger and various nannies would take her to Legoland. They'd report back that she always liked to start with the Billy Bunter Magic Flying Hat. Well, this is Legoland for the ancient, and they always start with 'the book'. The trouble is, the book is in a very small room – actually, 'room' is an overly generous description of its location, it's really a cupboard – and around the book there are loads of old people, all of whom look the same. They smell the same and they are wearing the same sort of clothes as one another. I'm not convinced they haven't all been cloned from one old person, then each wrapped in dull shades of brown from Marks and Spencer and sent out into the world to moan and complain and talk about how much better life was when there were Germans trying to blow them up at every turn. I can almost see, watching these odd little creatures, why Nell wants to wear her absurd and offensive green tracksuit everywhere. At least she stands out. It would be fair to say that people are staring at her. She seems to love it, which I figure is okay really. I love being looked at too. The only daft thing is that Nell's posse are dressed identically, so they look like they're on a nursing-home day out and so, like children on school trips, are wearing distinctive colours so they can be easily found before they wander off too far.

They open the book on today's date. Because it's the anniversary of Tom's death, his name is in the book. I don't know why this should be so reassuring and such an incredibly pleasant thing for them to do. I don't understand the proud smile that settles on Nell's face when she sees his name. It's as if she's able to reach out and touch him, as if the anniversary of his death is less a time to mourn him and more a gateway through which she might be reunited with him. I watch her looking at the book and I think of how I'd feel if Dean died. The thought is so wounding, I feel tears running down my face and a real pain in my chest. It's as if I've been shot. I can't imagine anything more terrifying, awful or painful than losing him or Pask. I know people think I'm a lemon sometimes, and I know I spend too much time on my appearance, but Pask and Dean mean the world to me.

I give Nell a big hug and she reaches out to wipe away my tears.

'Wish you could have known him,' she says, still smiling like a schoolgirl with a crush. 'He was a lovely, lovely man. He'd have thought you were great.'

There are times in life when you suddenly feel as if everything's going to be okay. There are times when you feel truly blessed and happy. This is one of them. I just stand there, thinking that I'm so lucky. I'm so lucky that life has turned out the way it has. I look at Nell and her barmy friends – the three musketeers – and feel a warm rush through me, washing away that anxious, painful feeling that was squeezing me inside when I thought about something bad happening to my husband. Dean, Pask, Nell – they're my life.

Behind me I hear the strangled sobs of a woman in deep distress, and I turn to see Mich desperately trying to stop herself crying and not wanting to draw attention to herself, but, in the process of trying to muffle her own sobs, actually making far too much noise and bringing far more attention to herself than she would have if she'd just got on with it and had a little cry.

'Mich,' I say, wrapping my arms around her. But the warm embrace I envisaged turns ugly when I discover that she's left about twenty pounds' worth of mascara, a false eyelash and a great smear of foundation all over my lovely cream furry Versace top. 'Mich,' I say, jumping back and almost knocking over some old guy. I don't want to be unfriendly in Mich's hour of need, but I'd rather not do the female bonding thing if it's going to involve me looking a mess at the end of it. 'Let's go outside.'

We stand there. It's one of those bitter, bitter November days when the temperature feels as if it's stabbing you mercilessly and there's no escape from it. As you rub your hands together, your feet feel as if they might freeze to the pavement. Then, as you stamp your feet on the ground, hoping to lift the pain of the icy cold, your ears are so cold it feels as if they will freeze entirely and you'll never be able to hear anything again. We're standing there, Mich sobbing, me trying not to look at the smoke or to consider what it represents in case I start crying again, and also attempting not to look at the three mad frogs, reading aloud to one another the inscriptions on cards on the flowers in the room, in order to try to discover the identity of the deceased.

'How you feeling?' I ask Mich, a bit like Sally Gunnell always used to ask the athletes when they finished last, having broken their ankle en route.

'I feel so low. I'm so fed up about this Andre thing. You know what I think happened? I think he had a girl round there after I left this morning. He was acting odd, so I bet he did, and I bet she found his phone down the back of a sofa, nicked it, and decided to disrespect me with all those texts.'

'No, sweetheart, I'm sure he didn't,' I say. Though I'm not sure at all. I thought Andre was a nice guy, but the texts he was sending to other women indicate otherwise.

'He must have. He says the phone was in the flat last night then it wasn't there this morning. I was the only one there last night, so either he's stolen it from himself, or I stole it and I'm somehow texting myself all this crap.'

'But I know you can't have stolen it because I saw those texts arrive. And he knows you didn't because I just explained to him that I saw all those texts arrive. Listen, people get phones nicked all the time. It's unfortunate that his was nicked by a nutter, but the fact that the nutter had such great ammunition to fire is entirely his fault for having such awful texts on there in the first place. He's just blaming you because he feels guilty about having behaved like a creep. I think you're well out of it. He may be a footballer, but he's no gentleman.'

'I know what you're saying,' says Mich, chewing the cuffs of her skin-tight tiger-print dress. I want to beg her to stop – it cost seven hundred pounds! But I know she is traumatised. 'The thing is, I am really upset at being accused of something I haven't done. I need to work out what happened to that phone so I can prove my innocence.'

Gosh, Mich is getting all serious on me.

'I just want you to tell me how the phone could have got out of his flat if there wasn't anyone in there besides him and me.'

I admit I'm stuck, but I need to attend to Nell because not only is this a very stressful day for her, but a loud cheer and a thumbs-up have just been seen and heard, which means two things: First, that the deceased is female so there's every chance that Nell will know the woman and so feel even more a part of the day's events, and thus bag herself one of those elusive wake invitations. Second, that by flower-card deduction it's possible to establish that the late woman's husband is still alive. Or, as Gladys puts it, 'Ding, dong, the witch is dead.' I know, not nice, but these are the laws of the jungle. If you think how hard it is meeting

145

a man when you're over forty, imagine what it's like meeting a man over eighty, especially when half of them were killed in the war.

The pressure of knowing that I need to get away and look after Nell combines with a sudden rush of affection for Mich. 'Look,' I say, taking her orange face in my hands, all worries about foundation carnage instantly vanishing. 'I promise you that we will get to the bottom of this. I will not rest until I find out what happened to that phone and why Andre is behaving like such a plonker over it, okay?'

'Thank you, thank you,' cries Mich, and I realise I've committed myself to spending the next week analysing every bloody move they made that night in minute detail in an effort to make her feel better about the fact that Andre is a loser. Bloody hell. Who does she think I am – Shirley Holmes?

'Right, now, come on, let's go and find the wrinklies . . .'

Mich says that she'll go and sort her make-up out first, which isn't a bad decision since most of it is busy sinking into, and ruining, my ludicrously expensive top. I totter off in the direction of the three old ladies and their shopping trolleys. When I get to them they're clearly having something of a crisis meeting.

'Tom first, then clockwise,' says Nell.

'Okay,' says Ethel. 'As long as we don't miss out the girls I used to work in the kitchens with.'

'We won't miss anyone,' says Nell, and Gladys gives her a big smile.

As smoke flumes out through the air and the bitter winter's day tortures every pore of our skin and every fibre of our muscles, the four of us walk round the crematorium, following the pre-prescribed route, laying flowers for every one of their fallen friends and relatives. The shopping trolleys, it turns out, are full of flowers for this purpose.

'I wish I knew as many people alive as I know dead,' said Ethel, without a hint of sadness.

'Well, at least you know them dead,' replies Nell, without a hint of humour. And I realise she means she's glad they knew these people, she's glad their lives were touched by the love and friendship of the people they're now honouring with flowers. I realise that she means *Tom* more than anything, and I have to steel myself against the tears that threaten to fall again. I realise that, despite the sadness, heartache and loneliness she's experienced since his death, Nell's glad she had him when she did and she's glad of the memories and the life they shared.

I don't think anyone has ever looked more beautiful to me than Nell in this minute. Posh Spice looked amazing on her wedding day but Nell looks radiant, and I realise that while I want Posh's wardrobe,

Cheryl Cole's pretty face and Jordan's boobs, I want Nell's heart and soul.

'Nell, will you come and spend Christmas with us this year?' I ask, rather dramatically, and totally out of the blue. She looks up, away from the carnations she's laying across the place where a lady called Chrissie is buried. 'Did you hear that, love?' she says to the rose bush, though clearly it's meant for Chrissie. 'Christmas with my lovely granddaughter.'

She smiles at 'Chrissie', tells her late friend that she hopes they have lots of cakes in heaven because she knows how much she likes cakes, and then she walks towards me and gives me a hug. I notice the other two have tears in their eyes.

'It's the nicest thing that could ever happen to me,' says Nell, and I realise that, judging by the faces of the others, spending Christmas at Sunnyside is not something that one does willingly if one has any sort of alternative. I feel immediately grief-stricken for never having invited Nell before, but I know, deep down, that she feels a responsibility to Ethel and Gladys and wouldn't want to leave them behind.

'Why don't all three of you come?' I ask.

It's been an emotional day, but nothing prepares me for the utter delight and amazement of the women, as they smile, laugh, hug and dance across the grass, trampling graves and flowers as they do so. Oh well, they can't feel it.

'Thank you,' they say. 'Thank you so much.'

I can't remember when anything ever made me feel better. Not even when I came back from Ibiza thinking I'd put on forty-three stone while I'd been away, then realised that the scales out there were in kilos, not stone. 'I'm fifty-one kilograms, not fifty-one stone,' I'd told Dean ecstatically.

7 p.m.

It's now dark, and they're about to close the gates, but still these loony mad women keep on going – shuffling around the place, handing out flowers and smiling at patches of ground where they are convinced the ashes of their dead friends are buried. They've scattered so many flowers between them, all with such love and tenderness on the hard ground.

'Come on,' I say gently, guiding them back to the car as they pull their empty trolleys along behind them. We head for where I left the car, but when we reach the car park I can see straightaway that it's gone. Damn. Presumably towed away. This is getting silly.

'What will we do now?' asks Nell, as I reach for my mobile and dial Dean's number.

'I'm calling my saviour,' I say, as Dean's voice barks in my ear.

'You wan' me ta wot?' he howls, as I make my unusual request for him to pick up me and three old ladies and a rather tipsy Mich from the crematorium (I had no idea she'd brought Bacardi Breezers with her, but I'm glad she did). 'I can't do it, I'm in me kegs, watching *Celebrity Boxing*, and I've given Dougie Drives the night off.'

This is not the response one would dream of getting from one's hero, but I know that Dean can be persuaded. 'Stick some trakkie bums on and get Doug back,' I urge. 'Come on, it's freezing.'

We stand in the room containing the *Book of Memories*, sipping the dregs of the Bacardi Breezers and talking about the fun we're going to have at Christmas.

'You lot don't know you're born,' says Nell with a laugh, hiccupping softly. 'You really don't know you're born. You know, when I was young we didn't really have Christmas at all ... all we had was an orange between us, and we had to put it back in the fruit bowl afterwards.'

I know Nell had a tough life, like most working-class people of her generation. I know that she craves the finer things while not really understanding what the point of them is, or appreciating them at all. She declared once that she wanted a Black Russian. 'I'd love one,' she said. Dean thought she was talking about a dark-skinned man from the Soviet Union at first, and got quite shirty with her, saying she was disrespecting his grandfather, but it turned out she wanted a cocktail – she'd obviously heard them mentioned on some Hollywood film and had decided she'd like to try one. Dean had rushed to the bar and come back with it. 'Mmmmmm ...' she'd cried with every sip. Then, when she'd put the glass down, we took the fruit and the umbrella out of the top and put them into Pask's coke to see whether Nell would notice the difference. She had reached for Pask's glass and sipped. 'Mmmmm ...' she said. 'I looove Black Russians.'

Yeah, right, we all thought, and since then we've bought her just a glass of coke with fruit and an umbrella in it. She drinks the coke, gets riotously drunk because she thinks it's a Black Russian, and tells everyone some more stories about life during the war, and how they had to use gravy browning on their legs because they couldn't get stockings. I have to say that I did stop and think at that point – if we put gravy into the spray-tanning machine would that give a better overall colour?

Monday, 12 November
4 a.m.

These might be classed as the most ridiculous days of my life. After spending the whole of Sunday trailing round a crematorium after three wayward pensioners, and being pursued by a Bacardi-sipping, depressed and angry former Wag who's hell-bent on finding out the truth behind a missing phone, now – a matter of hours later – I'm sitting in a car on the way to the studios of *GMTV*!!!!!! Clutching a copy of the *Daily Mail* in which my most recent article is featured! Just a month ago, I wouldn't have believed any of this was possible.

We're stopping en route to pick up Mallory and I'm going to take her with me because I'm just not convinced that these TV make-up artists really know what they're doing with their 'less is more' approach. I'm much more a 'more is not enough' sort of a girl. 'Slap it on,' I say to Mallory. 'You can never have too much make-up, too many handbags or too much champagne. Equally, your hair, nails and eyelashes can never be too long. Your heels can never be too high, and your skirt and shorts can never be too short.' I must remember all this for later – when Lorraine and I are having a chat. She'll want to hear all these handy little tips and tidbits, I'm sure. I also think she might ask me about my article, so I pull open the paper and start to read through it.

HOW TO BEHAVE LIKE A WAG WHEN YOU'RE VISITING A HEALTH FARM

Mmmmm, lovely – all those treatments . . . And the great thing is that they often have groups of footballers arriving at places like Champneys because the coaches take them there for rest, relaxation and wheatgrass and smoothies and stuff. So, what's the Wagalicious way to behave? An interesting question. Okay, first thing: ditch the absurd old-lady towelling robe and take your own far more fetching, stand-out-in-a-crowd number. Obviously, marabou-fringed is my own personal choice, but as long as what you wear is arresting and interesting, to be honest, anything goes! Leopard-skin, baby pink, sequins . . . any, any, anything!

Obviously, make sure you don't wear those terrible white towelling slippers either! Euch – horrible! Go for mules that make a nice clickerty clackerty sound as you walk down the corridor.

Now, one of the downsides of health farms is obviously the need to remove your make-up to have facials and other treatments. Proceed with caution if you opt for such treatments. Certainly, go into the treatment with a full face of make-up and have it removed in there. Some therapists obviously used to be in the Gestapo, and they ask you not to put make-up back on again immediately afterwards. Really. They do. They mutter on about letting your skin breathe and stuff. No, no, no, no, no! Breathing is overrated. Pile the slap back on and redo your false eyelashes (actually, get the beautician to do them – arrange this when you book the appointment, if you remember). There are other, less personal treatments that you can have at a health farm – or 'spa', as they tend to be called now – like bikini waxes. You should be having one of these a week anyway so use the chance of being at the health farm to have every last hair pulled out of you by means of hot wax. Then there are spray-tanning booths, manicures, pedicures and other delicious options. How about a body scrub or wrap? Apparently they have gyms at health farms, too, so you could go and have a look at the men working out in them by peeping through the window, but don't venture inside yourself – they're nasty places. Or you could try one of those absurd newfangled classes where a load of women sit around (and one bloke who either thought he'd try it just this once and will never go again, is gay, or walked in by mistake while following the rather pert bottoms of the women heading for the class), usually called yoga, pilates or the 'something' method. Like the Putshfgnkshuhshnsh Method. Don't worry about what the class is called – they do the same thing in all of them, just touching their toes and putting their feet behind their ears. If you hear loads of moaning sounds just put on some headphones, or even bring in an iPod with your favourite tracks downloaded onto it. The moaning can get a bit repetitive. (They call it chanting but it reminds me of the sound that commoners make when they're going into labour – and by commoners I mean non-elective caesarean women . . . Ooooooooo, natural childbirth – why would anyone do that to themselves?) Don't worry about it, though. Just download the Pussycat Dolls or that lovely song by Paris Hilton onto a music system and take that with you, and you'll be just fine.

When we pick up Mallory she is white with fear and shaking slightly. 'I've never, ever been in a TV studio before,' she says, with a look of alarm spreading all over her little face. 'I'm a bit worried.'

I explain that she won't have to go anywhere near the cameras and that all she has to do is to do my make-up in the same way that she does my make-up every time I go anywhere of note.

'Mmmm . . .' she says, but she doesn't look entirely convinced. It doesn't seem as if she's listening to me. Her teeth are still chattering and her hands are still shaking. Her eyes have wandered to the building we've pulled up next to. It says 'TELEVISION STUDIOS' on the outside.

'Oh dear, perhaps you should go in on your own. This really isn't my thing.'

Now the truth is that it's not my thing either. I never asked to be on *GMTV*, I never wanted to be turned into a superstar. I just wrote a little column telling the world how to be a Wag, and all this happened. My column was supposed to be a public information service, but everyone has told me I'm funny, clever and post-ironic, and now here we are heading for national fame and glory.

'Tracie Martin for *GMTV*,' I say proudly when I reach the reception desk. 'I think Fiona Phillips is probably expecting me.'

A tough-looking security guard looks down at his notepad and spots my name. 'We weren't expecting you till seven,' he says. 'I don't think you're on air until nine.'

'No,' I say. 'But I wanted to get here in plenty of time so I could get my make-up done and make sure my hair's right. This is Mallory, she's my make-up artist.'

The guard looks at my heavily made-up face, then looks around for Mallory. I follow his gaze to the large floor to ceiling windows through which we can see Mallory, bent over a small rose bush, being sick. 'Oh dear. It's the stress,' I say. 'Why don't you just show me to my dressing room?'

'I'll get someone to take you to the green room,' says the security guard, and suddenly I think of Nell, Ethel and Gladys again. Could they have called up in advance and requested a green room, in the hope that I'd be wearing the green tracksuit? Presumably not.

'Well, I'd prefer pink, but a green room will be just fine,' I say graciously. 'Thank you very much.'

8.50 a.m.

Gosh, Lorraine Kelly's small. And Fiona Phillips – is she skinny enough?! I can't believe it. I haven't eaten carbs for six years, I don't touch sugar or dairy products and I limit myself to five hundred calories a day, and Phillips, who I note had a croissant during one of the ad breaks, is thinner than me! I'm just so, so, so, so grateful that it's not her who is interviewing me. Lorraine Kelly is thin, too, but not as thin as me – phew!

I'm still recovering from the green-room nightmare. I won't bore you with all the details but we got up there and the room *wasn't* green, so I made a fuss and they went off to investigate while I had a wander round and found a room perfectly green in every way, so settled myself in. Unbeknown to me it was the room they were keeping for Tom Jones, who was singing his latest hit on TV at the time. Mallory set up the straighteners, curlers, crimpers and blowers, she unpacked creams, lotions, potions, varnishes and make-up. We moved the furniture around so she could set up the fake-tanning machine and, just as we were all ready to go, in came Mr Snake Hips himself.

I recognised him straightaway and thought he'd popped in to say hello, and thus that my popularity was even more widespread than I thought!

'My, my, my, Tom Jones,' I belted out, in the tune of his very own 'Delilah'.

He just looked at me, in my marabou-fringed gown, with my hair in all manner of curlers and my face covered in a light green moss and crushed acorn facemask that promised to make my skin look plumped, youthful and relaxed. Underneath the mask I had a lifting and energising oil that Mum gave me for my birthday. It's made from torn bird feathers, the untreated milk from a cow living in peace and harmony on a dairy farm in southern Spain, and the oil from the hair of a monk called Pievetery who lives in a monastery near Pompeii.

'What are you doing in my dressing room?' he asked in that deep, dulcet baritone voice of his.

'It's *my* dressing room, Tom,' I said, attempting to bat my eyelashes, then realising I wasn't wearing them. Really, it was not good to be caught in this state of undress by a major singing sensation who was once a close friend of Elvis Presley's, but what could I do?

Tom, less gentlemanly than one might have predicted for a sex god, shouted for a security guard, and I've never seen grown men run so quickly since that time when a three-year-old Paskia fell off the side of a boat and into the Thames. In fact, these guys were quicker – so I think perhaps the distress caused to Tom Jones by the sight of a green-skinned woman in his dressing room at 7 a.m. may be considered greater than that being suffered by a drowning baby. We were moved out of there and into a large, airy room containing a table of food, many guests and no privacy. Mallory had to finish the beautification process in the ladies' toilets – crammed between a tampon machine and a hand-dryer that kept going off and drying out my extensions even more than they already are – which was far from ideal.

10 a.m.

God, how weird. After the frightful performance before getting on air, the show itself has gone really, really well. Can you believe it? Everything Lorraine is asking me I am answering sensibly. I don't feel nervous at all, and she is so lovely.

'I love it,' she says in her gentle Scottish accent. 'You're just one of the funniest people I've ever met.'

'Thank you,' I reply, a little confused, but less so these days since my ability to be funny while answering simple, straightforward questions is now clear to me.

People say, 'What colour should Wags be?' I answer, 'Wags can be orange, they can be caramel, but they CANNOT be white', and everybody laughs. I'm a comedy genius without ever saying anything funny. This morning, Lorraine is hugging me and begging me to come on the show again soon. 'Is it true you were here at seven?' she asks.

I tell her that I was actually in the building at more like 4.15 a.m., and she smiles and says 'Ahhhh . . .' while clutching her chest as if I were a four-year-old cancer patient who has just said she loves her mummy and daddy very much.

'I came early to do my hair and make-up,' I explain, and she gets me to talk through the whole morning and everyone's in stitches. They even cut to pictures of me arriving that morning – obviously with loads of make-up on.

'That's my arrival make-up,' I explain. 'I didn't want to come without any on – that would be like arriving here naked.'

I then tell her all about the Tom Jones situation and she's crying with laughter. The humour of being booted out of a nice dressing room by an ageing Welsh rock god and being made to get changed in the ladies' toilets is a little beyond me. I tell her this, and she's laughing even more – asking me how I keep a straight face. Is she asking whether I have Botox? Well, I'm proud of it!

'I wish we could talk all morning,' she says, dabbing away at the tears in the corners of her eyes. 'I've not laughed so much in ages. Thank you, thank you, thank you – the talented and gorgeous Tracie Martin.'

She goes to give me a kiss and I say 'Woooahhhh . . . watch the extensions, they're new.' Of course, that's just a cue for more hysteria from her and her crew. It's like I'm living in some sort of alternative and surreal world where I've turned into Peter Kay overnight without even realising it. It's like *The Truman Show* for Wags.

I switch on my phone and there are eight messages from Michaela, asking me about the show, and whether I have had any further thoughts on the Andre situation. She's been receiving vulgar texts overnight and this morning, and she's not sure what to do. I call her and suggest she calls the police – it's the only thing I can think of.

'You will help me sort this out, Trace, won't you?' she says. 'You did promise.'

'I did, and I will,' I say. She has been a great friend to me. I need to be there for her, but what can I do? It turns out that Andre has the brain of a flea and the morals of a sewer rat. She's better off without him but clearly she doesn't see it that way. I never thought I'd see the day when I'd tell a fellow Wag to ditch her footballer . . .

'Listen, call me any time,' I say to Michaela. 'And why don't you come round on Wednesday morning and we'll have another chat about what you can do? I'll put my thinking cap on and I'll have a word with Dean. There must be something we can do to get this relationship back on track. There must be something that we can do to assist you in your re-Wagification.'

Tuesday, 13 November
10.30 a.m.

When I woke up this morning I realised what's wrong. It's like I'm in some dramatic production where the main characters have been switched. I am no longer the rather silly, useless and aimless blonde with a pretty, pouty smile and unfeasibly large breasts . . . now, I am a superstar!

There have been several crucial happenings that have led me to this conclusion – first, my mother hasn't called back and shouted at me after being nice to me on the phone. Second, I appear to be wanted by every television producer and every magazine editor in the land. They all think I'm 'sooo funny'. This accusation was never levelled at me in my pb days (pre-blog) – it's an entirely new phenomenon. Now, to cap it all – my former mentor; the quite brilliant writer whose skills helped me, strengthened me and made me what I am, is sitting before me as my secretary.

You see, Simon is in my kitchen with a notebook, pen, diary and mobile phone.

'This is the list,' I say to him, handing over a long, handwritten list of phone numbers, with names – most of them barely legible – scrawled next to them.

'Blimey,' he says, his little eyes wide. 'All these people have phoned? These are some of the most important people around!'

The phone has been bleeping away nonstop since I left the *GMTV* studios. I'm wanted on every television programme from serious news programmes that are seeking to dissect and analyse the culture of Wags, to *Loose Women* and *Richard and Judy*, where they just want me on as a fun guest to liven up the show.

'It's so much pressure,' I say, rather dramatically, and without really meaning it at all. I just want to distract from the fact that Simon looks so impressed with me and I'm not impressive at all. *He's* the impressive one, *he's* the one with all the talent. I'm not quite sure why this has happened, but I think it's unfair that something like this hasn't happened to Simon.

'Why don't you come on with me?' I say. 'We could be a partnership!

Like Posh and Becks! Except not married and without the matching perfumes.'

'Don't be daft,' he says. 'Why the hell would anyone want me on their show? You're the superstar.'

'But you wrote that first piece,' I say. 'You were the one who saved me from making a complete and utter fool of myself. If you hadn't written that, I wouldn't be a writer . . .' Clearly that makes no sense at all.

'If I hadn't written that, someone else would have helped you, and ghosted it for you. Just because you don't write everything doesn't mean you're not a writer – look along the bookshelves and count the number of people who have never actually put pen to paper. Writing is not about writing, it's about selling books and newspapers. And anyway – you *do* write! So in the current climate that makes you a quite brilliant writer . . . compared to people who have reputations as writers but who don't actually write a thing.' Simon trails off at this point, because he knows he is on dodgy ground, and probably thinks that if he tails off I won't notice what nonsense he's talking.

'So, *Richard and Judy* – they're a must!' he declares, looking down at the notepad. 'They suggest next week – can you do that?'

'Mmmmm . . .' I say, indicating the diary. 'I think so.'

'The producer left a message saying you have an astonishingly well-developed sense of irony. They say you're refreshing and unusual and they'd adore having you on the show . . .'

'Sure,' I say. 'I like Judy a lot and I know Mum fancies Richard, so let's do it.'

'Now then,' says Simon, placing a big red tick against *R&J*. 'There's a publishing company here, interested in you writing a book – how does that grab you?'

'How does it grab me? A book. Mmmmmm . . . No – I couldn't write a book if my life depended on it. I've not even read one. Like Posh,' I add proudly.

'Of course you could,' says Simon, looking alarmed. 'The book would just be a collection of all your diary entries – that's all you'd have to do. Come on – isn't this how it all started? With you wanting to write a book?'

'But why would anyone want to read it?' I ask, genuinely fearing that this is all getting completely out of hand. 'Why would anyone in their right mind want to buy a book full of my silly diary entries that they have already read in the newspaper? Why would anyone want to do that?'

'For god's sake, Tracie, you're becoming a national treasure. Not everyone reads the *Daily Mail* for starters, and even people who have seen your articles might like you enough to buy the book, to read more about you. People love what you've got to say – they think you're wonderful and, I have to say, I think they're right. You may not understand this whole thing but I have a feeling it's going to get bigger and bigger.'

'Do it with me,' I say, and I've never seen a man look more alarmed and simultaneously thrilled with anything.'

'You want me to do it with you?' he asks, rubbing his long fingers across his small, thin lips.

'Yes,' I say. 'We can split the money fifty-fifty, and we'll just write it together. I can keep doing the diary entries like I have for the *Daily Mail*, and you can help me get it all into a book.'

'Ohhhhh,' says Simon, as if I'd previously suggested something else entirely.

'Well, will you? I really don't want to do it on my own.'

'You really don't need me.'

'Do.'

'No, you . . .'

'Do.'

'Tracie, you don't . . .'

'Do, do, do, do, do . . . I'm not doing the book unless you help me.'

'Fine,' says Simon, and he picks up the phone. 'I'll arrange for us to go in and talk to them as soon as possible.'

A minute later he puts the phone down. 'Bloody hell!' he exclaims. 'They want us to go in there tomorrow!'

8 p.m.

Dean comes back from footie training about an hour after he's left and slumps onto the sofa.

'You're early,' I say. He's normally gone for about three hours on training nights.

'What?' he replies.

I have a vicious peel-off facemask on and it's at that stage where I can't open my mouth more than a millimetre, so my speech sounds much like Ethel's did that time she lost her teeth. Instead, I point vigorously at my wrist.

'Yeah,' he responds with a sigh, and by kicking off his trainers. They cost around two hundred pounds, they're gold, and he's kicking them off without undoing the laces. It's most unlike him. I mean – he's a bloke and all that, but he does normally look after his trainers properly. In fact, if I so much as step within an inch of his bloody shoes, I'm glared at and screamed at. It's like, 'you can disrespect me, you can disrespect my family and disrespect my religion, but do not EVER disrespect my trainers'.

So when he kicks them off all willy-nilly I know that trouble is brewing.

'What's up, love?' I mumble.

'Nothing,' he says with a coy turn of his head, and a rather effeminate shrug of his shoulders.

'Something's wrong,' I insist.

'Mmmmm . . .' comes the reply.

Bloody hell. Suddenly I have three youngsters in my life. I don't mind that one of them is my daughter, but I do mind that another of them is my mother, and I *really* mind that the other is my husband.

'I'm fed up,' he says eventually. 'You know – going down there and just watching, joining in occasionally, but knowing I won't be playing on Saturday.'

'It must be tough,' I concede. I'm trying hard to be the proper, doting wife, but inside I'm screaming, 'Why the f**k don't you score in the right f**king net, then none of this would be happening, you great big idiot. Though I say, 'I'll love you all the same . . . whatever happens.'

'Thanks, love,' says Dean, and he seems to mean it. 'I'm glad you said that, because there's something I want to talk to you about.'

I can sense danger here in the same way I can sense danger when someone's going for the boots in Cricket that I am desperate to have. When I see a woman walking in roughly the direction of the shoes I somehow know with every fibre in my being that she's heading towards the short white furry boots in size five. There have been times when I've sprinted like Ben Johnson across the shop, eyes bulging and determination leaking from every pore, and tackled the boots rugby-style just before the filthy Wag gets her nail-extended fingers anywhere near them.

Here, I'm feeling the same sense of self-preservation. 'Hey, everything's going to be just fine!' I hear myself yell through the mask, with more ferociousness and intensity than I ever intended. The volume of my voice is quite a surprise to me. I realise how much I don't want him to announce that he is going to give up football. I realise just how difficult it will be if I find myself de-Wagged by his actions.

'You know what I'd really like to do,' says Dean, and I brace myself. 'I'd like to give up being a player, maybe do a bit of coaching.'

Coach's wife? Now I could do *that*. Maybe Dean could be the new England coach and I'd be like Nancy, a new mentor for all the Wags. Maybe she could give me some tips?

'I was thinking I could concentrate on helping Paskia Rose with her football career. You know – become coach of her team.'

'You will do no such thing!!!' I holler, like some sort of wartime fishwife. 'Paskia will not be taking her football seriously. It's ludocross. And you will certainly not be wasting your time coaching them.'

'Oh,' says Dean. 'I thought you might say that.'

I'm pleased that in some small part of his brain he realised that I would object to his absurd proposal.

'So I thought I might think about buying a pub and opening that instead.'

Alarming images of Peggy Mitchell swim around my head. Does he think I'm going to become some sort of brassy landlady overnight? 'No you won't,' I say.

'But I'd like that – not some trendy wine-bar place, but a proper pub where locals can come with their dogs on Sundays and sit with a pint and have a nice Sunday roast.'

'Right. And who the hell's cooking the roast dinner? Me and Mum?'

'No, love, I wouldn't expect you to get involved. It would be nice if you helped out sometimes, though – you know, pulling pints and that.'

'Are you mad?' I ask.

'Probably,' he says forlornly. 'I guess it's just a dream I have. Never mind. I guess I'll just cling on at the club for as long as I can and hope they don't sell me to some tiny little village somewhere.'

Oh god. The thought of that happening fills me with almost as much dread as Dean becoming Paskia's football coach. Imagine it – transferred to a club in a town with no nice shops! What would I do? Where would I go? What would become of me? It's too awful that Dean should suddenly announce his intense displeasure with football, today of all days, when tomorrow I am preparing to go into the publishers' and discuss my life as a Wag and how my thoughts, feelings and advice on the subject can be transferred into a book for all future generations of Wags to read. Imagine the mockery, the laughter and the stares if I write my book about being the perfect Wag, then it is revealed to the world that I am, in fact, not a Wag at all. The humiliation!

'Yes, good idea,' I say to Dean, mainly because I can't think what else to say. 'Goodnight.'

But as I walk into our large white bedroom with its murals on the ceiling and lovely pink hot-tub in the middle, with 'Dean & Trace' in gold across its base, I'm thinking, not in a million years am I going to let his career slip away from him. I'll do all I can to make sure the guys at Luton Town keep him on.

I collapse onto the bed. All the dreams I had for myself as the wife of the man suddenly called back into the England football team appear around me like they are contained in the soapy bubbles blown by children. The respect, the admiration . . . then – pop, pop, pop – they're all gone.

'You all right?' asks Dean, walking into the room.

I smile at him. I don't want to say 'yes' because that would be a lie. Dean has been speaking about de-Wagging me. I'd be less upset if he'd been talking about punching me. At least the bruises would fade one day. I don't think I'll ever get over it if I have to stop being a Wag.

'I'm not talking about giving up football yet, you know,' he says. 'I'm just trying to, like, think forward to the end of the season and make plans for then.'

I breathe a sigh of relief. That means I've got about nine months to get the book written before potential de-Wagulation.

Wednesday, 14 November
8.30 a.m.

Today is the day. The moment when I, a simple slip of a girl with a head for advising would-be Wags, become an author – a literary sensation – a writer of worldwide renown and kudos . . . like Jordan, Kerry Katona and Posh Spice. I can't believe it's happening really. I've done three coats of fake tan to reflect my overwhelming excitement, and though I look like Dale Winton I still think it's a good look. I did it myself, which was a big mistake, but since the *GMTV* fiasco, when Tom Jones shouted at us and sent us running from his dressing room, Mallory hasn't come round so much, and claims always to be busy when I need her. I called and spoke at length to her answering-machine about how I was going to be the new Jodi Trollope, and got nothing back from her bar a garbled message saying.

'I am not a trollop, and you feel like that about me, you should find someone else to spray-paint you orange.'

Frankly, it's her loss, especially since it turns out I'm quite good with the old spray-tanning machine. The only problem is, it costs me twice as much to get the house cleaned afterwards than it ever would just going down to the salon. But this is not about saving money – nothing in my life ever is. I did it myself because I like the tan so much darker than they ever do it, and even when I tell them this, they always mutter on about my skin being naturally pale . . . blah, blah . . . and this all means that I shouldn't have skin the colour of an antique pine dresser.

However, the point is that I *want* to be the colour of a beef Madras curry, and the nice thing about doing it yourself is that you can choose the colour you want to go. I am now my chosen colour. The bathroom is also the same chosen colour, which is infinitely less attractive, and there's a rather funny outline of me against the back wall – like some police crime scene in negative – as I stand there against the expensive white tiles while the tanning spray douses me from head to foot. I madly squirted bathroom cleaner at it, but I didn't want to ruin my tan, so in the end I left Magda to deal with it.

My task now is to dry the fake tan so I can do my make-up. To aid this process as much as possible I am sitting at my dressing table with a hairdryer trained on my face. Clearly, this approach has got disaster written all over it. I'm terrified of scorching my nose or burning the small, fine blonde hairs of my face. Going in to the publishing meeting with third-degree burns wouldn't be ideal.

Once the colour appears to be dry (though my face is now bright red as a result of the heat from the dryer, but that can't be helped), I rub Vaseline into my skin – I want to be gorgeously Wag-glossy for today's meeting. My face is gleaming, shining and brown. I look like a conker newly taken from its casing. Onto this desirable surface I paint foundation, glossing lotion, high-gloss blusher and a sparkly powder. Then I go for a purple eye-shadow and lashings of mascara. I put on some sugar-pink, long platform boots, a short sugar-pink dress, matching sugar-pink knickers, and the biggest chandelier earrings that I can find. The dress is way too tight, so it rides up constantly, but I figure that once I'm sitting down it will be just fine.

My judgement of how Wagtastic I look when in Simon's company has come to be based entirely on the man's reaction when he catches sight of me. If I'm looking great, Simon takes a slight gasp and says something like 'I hardly recognised you.' Or he says something hysterical like 'You look so much better without make-up.' Ha! Nutter. As if any female, ever, in the history of the universe, looked better without make-up. What is all that about?

This morning he nearly chokes on the mouthful of black coffee he's just taken from a polystyrene cup in the back of the car. He manages to swallow, just about, and leans forward to kiss me on the cheek. I sit down next to him and laugh a little at the fact that he now has pink glitter in his beard. I decide not to tell him because I think that he should be Wagtastic too, and this might just be the first stage in the Wagtastification of Simon, serious writer, lecturer and all-round proper good guy.

1 p.m.

We're back in the car after a fantastic meeting. The glitter may have faded from Simon's beard, but his eyes are glittering like mad, his mouth is smiling and we're now sipping champagne instead of that terrible instant coffee. Simon and I are, unlikely as this seems, on the fast-track to literary stardom.

'We should probably get an agent,' he says, and I shrug.

'Why? They've offered us a huge deal. Why don't we just take it? What do we need an agent for?'

'I don't know,' says Simon, refilling his glass. 'Just thought it's something we should consider. Don't we need to get someone to check the contracts and make sure we're not signing our lives away? What about international sales? Film rights? TV rights? What about all the business and financial stuff? Shouldn't we have someone on board who knows what they're talking about? It's just not my area of expertise. Everyone I know who's written books has had someone to do the business stuff for them. Shouldn't we?'

He's finished his champagne, so he fills his glass again. I'm astonished by how much he can put away. He's almost caught up with me.

'I could get Dean's agent to look at it.'

'Okay,' says Simon. 'What's his name?'

'It's Barry, I think. Barry Button or something.'

'Barry Button – he sounds like a children's entertainer.'

'Okay, perhaps it's not Barry Button. I don't know – something like that. I'll find out.'

'Great news though, eh?' says Simon, raising his glass. 'Sod it, shall we just take it? I mean, it seems a bit pointless to bring in some guy called Barry Button when they've offered us about four times what we thought they would.'

I like this reckless side to Simon. He's got no more clue about business than I do, so together we're deciding, after half a bottle of champagne each, to take no advice, consult no one and sign a major deal without understanding in any way, shape or form what we're doing.

'Yes!' I declare irresponsibly. 'Let's just sign. In any case, Barry Button is the most despicable man on the planet.' I took a dislike to him after he pooh-poohed my idea about getting Dean to star in the Gillette ads with Becks.

'Let's just sign,' agrees Simon. 'They're a big company, I'm sure it'll be a standard contract. I'm sure they won't try to stitch us up.' He pulls his mobile phone from one of the hundreds of pockets on his army-style jacket, and dials the publisher. I can hear the cackle of the publisher's high-pitched posh voice slicing through the sound of the engine purring as we drive out of London. I can hear her voice but not what she's saying. 'Yes, of course,' says Simon. 'By the end of the week. Of course, no problem.' He moves the phone so I can hear it too.

'Dahling, that's marvellous,' howls our publisher. 'What wonderful news.' The contract, she explains, will be put in the post, but we have a gentleman's agreement (?) and as far as she's concerned it's binding and the deal is done. We're going to be writers and they're going to be our publishers.

'It's brill,' I chirrup, feeling quite light-headed with the daytime champagne-drinking, as I always do. 'Completely brill.'

The truth is that I'm terrified out of my mind. How can we have been offered a £450,000 two-book deal when neither of us has written a book before?

Simon was outstanding in the meeting. I'm so glad he was there or I would have crumbled under the heavy questioning. Christ, that publisher was like Jeremy Paxman. How long will it take you? How long do you envisage it being? Would you be willing to promote it? Who are your articles geared towards? Where do you get your inspiration from? Blimey, it was hard work. I didn't know the answer to any of the questions, but Simon did. Imagine that! How would Simon know where I get my inspiration from? When I asked him he said, 'Just answer them, don't worry about what you say, just give them an answer they want to hear so you get the book deal!' Happily, Simon seemed to know what answers they wanted, and with every answer he gave, their enthusiasm grew, along with their commitment to me, excitement about me, and the amount of money they were prepared to invest in me.

'Okay,' they said at the end of the meeting. 'We would like to offer you £450K, but that would be for two books. Do you think you can do that?'

'Of course she can,' piped up Simon. 'She'd be delighted to.'

The publishers ran through in detail the sort of book they are after – clearly they had known long before we arrived at the meeting what they were looking for, and just wanted to ensure that I could deliver. They want the book to be all my cuttings and other 'new' diary entries, and they want to call the book *The Wags' Handbook*, but they also want a section in the book called 'The Making of a Wag', and for that I have to include all sorts of information about my childhood, and when I first started watching football. (I did explain, of course, that when I go to football matches the very last thing on my mind is watching the football. They just laughed.)

'It is important to us that you include autobiographical detail,' the publishers said. 'The deal we're offering is based on your ability to do that. We'd welcome information from all sources – your mother particularly – but anyone from your background. We think it's vital that the readers connect with you on a human level.'

They want me to include all sorts of 'important' details in the piece – like when I first remember wanting to be a Wag. When did I realise that it was a lifestyle choice? Not sure how I'm going to do that, but they are desperately keen for all sorts of information about my childhood to go in there. This fills me with dread, but Simon says it's great 'padding', adding that to write over one hundred thousand words of diary entries and advice to would-be Wags would be incredibly difficult, even with my immense knowledge, and the chance to use biographical information makes it much easier.

'But I don't know where I'll get it from,' I say to Simon. I don't remember much about school at all except that I was ugly and overweight and everyone hated me. 'I'm not really in touch with anyone from my past. There was this girl called Sally who I worked with when I was a hairdresser. She was lovely. I bumped into her not long ago. I could talk to her . . .'

'And you could ask your mum,' he says, and the way he says 'your mum' as if it's the most natural thing in the world makes me feel quite sad, because I know Mum won't remember anything about my childhood. It would be the most unnatural thing for me to ask her to do.

'Not Mum,' I say.

'We're going to have to talk to your mum,' he persists, deadly serious. 'They just said that they need a basic outline of the autobiographical section by the end of the week. The only way we're going to get information for it is through your mum – she must have old schoolbooks, remember names of old teachers . . . things like that.'

'Mmmmm . . .' I reply. Talking to Mum about my childhood would be about number 9999 on my list of 'things I really want to do today'. But Simon insists that we have no choice. 'You heard what they said in the meeting,' he reminds me. 'If we can get them good clean copy on your childhood by Friday, then the pressure will be off us for a while and we can get on with writing the book. If we don't get something through to them, the pressure's going to be on, and we'll have them hanging over us and watching every word we write.'

I do remember them saying that in the meeting. I remember very clearly that they said they wanted 'clean' copy. I raised my eyebrows at Simon at that point (actually, that's not true, my eyebrows don't go anywhere these days – but I made all the motions of a woman who was in the process of raising her eyebrows). 'I'll explain,' he had whispered to me when he saw the confusion on my face. The nice thing about Simon is that when he says this he always does explain. It's not like Dean, who says 'I'll explain later, doll-face', then when I talk to him afterwards it turns out that he can't explain at all, as he really didn't know what was going on either but had to act all manly and pretend he did. With Simon, the man who knows everything, that's never an issue.

'Clean copy', he says, 'is writing that doesn't need much work doing to it – it doesn't need editors working on it for weeks after it's been sent in, so they can move forward quickly with the book. Can you go and see your Mum straightaway? I'll be able to relax once we've got this autobiog breakdown to them. I don't want us to do anything to jeopardise the deal.'

Simon jumps out of the car in the rough part of town. 'You're welcome to come in for a coffee,' he says, and I must admit I'm really tempted. Real life stands still when I'm with Simon. I stop worrying about the way I look, I stop worrying about the way people are judging me. I manage to 'be'. I manage to enjoy every minute as it's happening, instead of worrying intensely about the future and what horrors may be lurking in as yet unseen shadows. But I decline coffee and tell Simon that I'm going straight round to Mum's to talk to her and set up a meeting for the three of us.

'Great!' says Simon, looking flushed and excited. Either it's the champagne or he's as genuinely excited about this book as I am. I'm seriously hoping it's the latter.

I take another couple of large gulps of champagne and lay my head back on the plush leather seats, smiling vacantly at Doug the Driver. The man's been with us for so many years now. He gets fed up at times – what with the many trips to Croydon in search of my car, and the fact that Dean can't drive at all so needs to be taken everywhere – but he's a good bloke, really. All my staff are – I'm incredibly lucky.

Doug smiles back and I feel myself drifting off into a deep and lovely sleep. I dream of the book I'm going to write, and the many ways in which it's going to help people. I picture young girls who just can't get themselves a footballer reading my sage advice and suddenly finding themselves surrounded by footballers – shaking them off, kicking them out of bed and unloading them from the boot. It's such a thrill to me that this book could really help people. I feel like Mother Teresa or Princess Di. Imagine that? People being genuinely helped by me. I drift deeper into sleep . . . I am sitting atop a soft bouncy cloud as it floats on a light summer breeze. I'm wearing a diaphanous white silk dress (which is open at the front to reveal a knockout tan and my lilac zebra-print Agent Provocateur undies). My nails and hair extensions are perfect. I have no fine lines anywhere, and my eyes are bright, youthful and gorgeous – rimmed with perfect eye make-up and the longest fake eyelashes ever created. Around me float happy and contented footballers and their Wags, all with tiny babies – the baby girls have soft hair extensions and bright orange skin, and the little boys have tattoos across their arms and most of their torsos. Everyone is happy . . . everything is perfect and serene . . . The footballers and their Wags are off to buy multi-million-pound houses and to transform them through sheer good taste into visions of beauty. In my mind I can picture a pale-pink grand piano – one of those ones that plays itself. I can see the names of the lovebirds written in gold italic writing across black sunken baths, at the bottom of pools and above the heart-shaped beds. I made this happen. It was me with my handbook. I changed the world and made it into a version of heaven, but one with diamanté gates instead of pearly ones, and in which St Peter is clean-shaven and dressed head to toe in D&G. He's wearing a £600K watch and half a million pounds' worth of bling. In his hand is a clipboard. 'If your name ain't on the list, you ain't comin' in,' he growls. But all the Wags get in, along with all their big-ring-wearing, large-chain-wearing, much-pierced boyfriends. 'Thank you, Tracie. Thank you,' all the Wags are saying. 'Thank you, thank you, thank . . .'

'Tracie, Tracie . . .' calls Doug. 'We're here. Time to wake up, love.'

I open my eyes and I know instantly that I have been dribbling. The pattern from the leather car seats is imprinted on the side of my face, and my contact lenses are all dirty and stuck to my eyes and I can hardly see beyond my hand. Despite this, I manage to notice that two long blonde extensions have fallen out and are lying on my naked thighs, where my skirt has ridden up to somewhere near my pierced navel. When I blink and adjust my lenses in my eyes, I can see that there are clumps of mascara on the pale leather interior of the car, which means my eye make-up's all smudged and I probably look like a panda bear on one side – the same side with the pattern of the seats on my face. Perfect.

'All right?' asks Doug. He's been watching me in the rear-view mirror as I've been squinting and scowling at the seats.

'Yes,' I say.

'You had a deep sleep,' he tells me.

'Mmm . . .' I respond, looking out of the window. I feel terrible but it's odd that I don't recognise where I am at all. I have no sense of this place. I can't see my drive at all. 'Where are we?' I ask.

'At your mum's place,' says Doug. 'You said to that man earlier that you wanted to go to your mum's house.'

So I did. But I didn't mean it.

'Don't you want to go in?' he asks.

'Well, she'll probably be out,' I say.

'I'll try, shall I?' he asks, moving to open the car door. Funny how men are always so keen to talk to Mum.

'Sure,' I reply, mentally weighing up the awfulness of seeing Mum when I look like this with just how impressed Simon will be if I manage to go back to him with a load of information for the book, or at least a possible date for us all to get together to discuss it further.

Doug goes running off through driving sleet, towards the front door, his big bulky bottom bouncing along behind him. He looks like Roo bounding off after Tigger, with all of his weight in his giant bottom. Doug has the look of a man who does not exert himself often, and suddenly, for no good reason, I get a terrifying image of him in bed with his wife. She's very small and pinched-looking. I guess she was probably terribly dainty a few years ago but now she just looks like a bird of some description. Not a beautiful, multicoloured, song-singing one, but a scrawny old vulture that's had her best days and is just scavenging for food and trying to put off the inevitable death by starvation.

I think women look best when they're painfully thin, but looking at Doug's wife reminds me that this law of female beauty applies only to those under forty. After then, it's all a lot more complicated, and women do have to consider that they will look utterly haggard in the face department if they continue to aspire for a skeletal look in the figure department. Something I don't have to worry about for a decade, but life's a cruel and heartless bitch.

I move to pull out my make-up mirror as Doug's large hindquarters disappear from view. The only way to hide the lines etched into the side of my face by the car seats (the fact said lines are still there and not fading away from my plump skin being, of course, a sure indicator of a less-than-youthful complexion, which is distressing in itself) is to pile make-up on in such quantities as to cover the unsightly ridges. This is exactly what I attempt to do. The trouble is that the compact I put into my handbag this morning is the only one in the world without a mirror on it. There's a sponge one side and the make-up the other side. I can see Doug at the door. I don't have long, and if Mum sees me looking like this she'll have a complete fit, so I literally coat one side of my face with thick foundation, and leave it to settle without rubbing it in. I don't want to end up rubbing it out of the grooves in my skin, so I just leave it there – sitting on top of my skin. I then grab a lip-gloss and whiz it round and round on my lips, and quickly curl my eyelashes. By the time Doug walks back to the car I'm ready. He opens the door, looks at me with utter alarm, thus lifting my confidence in my appearance, and smiles inanely as I walk towards Mum's gorgeous mock-Georgian house. We bought, furnished and pay the bills on this place. It's the least I could do after she brought me up single-handedly. Having said that, despite our financial investment in the place, I never really come here. Probably because Mum spends so much time at ours. In fact, I've never just turned up like this before – out of the blue, unexpected and uninvited.

This place is fabulous. It cost more than our house, but is smaller. All the money is in the incredibly intricate detail, like the great pool in the cellar with water cascading down from the ceiling into cupped gold hands before falling into the water. It's just perfect. There's a silhouette of Mum drawn on the base of the pool in black, and there are flat-screen TVs in there – with underwater sound. The house is so stylish. Even outside, the pink Doric columns and gold-embossed fountain in the front garden tell you straightaway that the owner is just oozing charm and sophistication. It's all so perfect, like Mum herself I suppose.

'What on earth do you look like?' she asks, appearing in the hallway dressed in a fabulous black kaftan covered with tiny turquoise sparkles. The brightly coloured stones bring out the blue of her amazing eyes. She's astonishingly attractive this morning. Has she had surgery of some kind? She looks as if she has. Her eyes are wider, more alert and more youthful.

'Did you hear me?' she says.

'Yes, Angie – I fell asleep in the car and have grooves all over my face. Can you believe it? How ridiculous!' I laugh nervously.

'You don't have grooves across your face, you have an absurd amount of make-up coating one side of your face. I've never seen you look so stupid and that's *really* saying something.'

I have this ability to weed out the nastier of her comments and hear only blah, blah, blah . . . so I am able to smile rather stupidly, even as she's calling me some rather choice names.

'And what have you done to your lips?'

I touch them instinctively, and quite defensively, and look at her questioningly.

'LOOK!' she screams, spinning me around and pointing me towards the full-length mirror where a clown looks back at me. It turns out that in my half-asleep state I pulled a bright red lip-gloss, not a clear one, from my make-up bag, and waved it madly around my face. From just underneath my nose to the middle of my chin is scarlet. I have to admit that my make-up looks as if it's been applied by a deranged child.

'Okay, so I did it without a mirror,' I reply, sounding just like the petulant child I always feel inside whenever she starts having a go at me. 'I'll sort it out now.' Then, reaching for something to distract from my wayward attempts at make-up application, I dig out the biggest diversion in the western world.

'Oh, Nell's coming to ours for Christmas,' I say.

'She's not.'

'What do you mean, she's not. I've invited her.'

'Where does that leave me?' asks Mum, looking – I have to say – somewhat distraught.

'You can come too,' I offer.

'What? And end up sitting all day talking to some smelly old lady who wants to witter incessantly about the war?'

'She's not smelly, and you won't have to talk to her because Ethel will be there to keep her company.'

'Ethel?'

'And Gladys.'

'You've invited three old women to come for Christmas? Are you completely mad? Why are you doing this to me?'

Mum has tears in her eyes. She looks devastated. She staggers back clutching her hand to her head like they do on those American daytime TV shows – only Mum's not acting, this is genuine, heartfelt distress I'm witnessing here, and I really wasn't expecting it at all.

'I beg of you, cancel them,' says Mum. 'Please, I beg of you, cancel straightaway.'

With that, she falls to the ground, saying she can't stand it, she feels rejected by the only person in her life who ever cared. 'Why don't you love me? Why don't you love me?' she says, while I stand there, eyes wide with amazement. 'Your father left us high and dry and now you're deserting me too.'

On the floor, Mum is clutching her knees to her chest, swaying and crying. She's in a terrible state. I've never seen anything like it.

'We always had such lovely Christmases together, you and me. Didn't we? Didn't we?'

'Yes,' I say, but all I can really think of is the time I woke up on Christmas morning to no presents and no Mum. She'd gone out the night before and met a man. When she finally appeared, at around 11 a.m., she said she'd get me some presents later, she hadn't had time to get them before. I was only ten. That's when I realised Father Christmas didn't exist.

'When your father left, I did my best. Didn't I? Didn't I, Tracie? Was there more I could have done?'

'No,' I mumble. 'Mu-Angie, you did brilliantly.'

'Then please, I beg of you, have the decency to treat me like a daughter should. Please show me some love and tenderness . . . after all we've been through together.'

'Okay,' I say. 'I'll tell Nell she can't come. I'll call her this afternoon.'

Mum rises to her feet, tears cascading down her face, and I realise for the first time how vulnerable, lost and isolated she must feel. I must make more effort. I must involve her in my articles; maybe I should ask her now to help me with the book? Perhaps she thinks my sudden success is driving a wedge between us? We are both in tears, hugging each other and saying that nothing will come between us, and I repeat that I'll cancel Nell straightaway.

'Will you?' she asks, the tears cascading down her pretty face. 'Will you really?'

'Oh yes, Angie,' I say. 'Of course I will.'

That's when the oddest thing happens. She stands bolt upright, wipes her eyes, and her voice is normal all of a sudden.

'Do it immediately,' she instructs.

'I will,' I say. 'And there's something I want to tell you. I've been asked to write a book – you know, based on my columns.' I wait for the exclamations of pride and joy but they don't come. 'I have to include some stuff in it about my childhood and what I was like when I was growing up, and that sort of thing, and I wondered . . .'

'Are you serious?' shrieks Mum. 'You can't be. No, no, no, no, no . . . I will not have you raking up old tales from the past and trying to make me look silly.'

'I don't want to make you look silly. I just want to find out if you've got any old photographs or diaries, or anything like that to help us put it together.'

'You're being absurd,' she says. 'Who would want to read a book by you in any case? You can't write. I don't know what all this nonsense is about, really I don't. Now, I have an appointment. I'll be back later. Use the phone in the hall to call Nell, then let yourself out. I'm much too busy for all this nonsense, I really am.'

And with that, she's gone. The tears have dried in an instant and the moment of emotional instability and insecurity has passed. She's Angie again – full of pizzazz. She's confident and putting me in my place. I'm twelve years old again – vulnerable, stupid Tracie, hanging off her every word, eager to do what she wants in the hope that she'll find it within herself to love me. So, in the name of love, I'm standing at the phone in the hall as instructed, preparing to break the heart of an elderly lady who never did a thing to hurt anyone. An elderly lady who, let's be honest, loves me more than Mum ever will. Whoever said blood was thicker than water was right. Thicker, messier and more cloying.

10 minutes later

Who do you ring for comfort when you've just desperately upset the person to whom you always turn for comfort? If I had to make a call like the one I just made to Nell to anyone else on earth, I'd have picked up the phone to Nell straight afterwards and sobbed my heart out . . .

My phone's bleeping like mad in my bag. I know it won't be Nell calling back because she doesn't believe in mobile phones. She thinks there's something rather sinister and devil-worshipy about them. To be honest, after all the trouble Mich is having at the moment, all because of a missing phone, I think she may have a point.

It's Simon.

'Hi, how are you?' I say.

'I'm okay. You sound terrible. What's the matter?'

'Nothing. I'm absolutely fine. No, I'm not, I feel awful. I can't believe it. Mum made me . . . and I . . . and it's awful . . . and Nell sounded so . . . it was just . . .'

'Okay, okay, okay,' he says. 'You're not making any sense at all. Now, where are you?'

'I'm at Mum's house. She's gone out.'

'Shall I come there?'

'You don't know where it is,' I say, hoping to god that he doesn't. I couldn't bear to discover that lovely Simon has been having a major affair with my mother.

'No, you'd have to tell me,' he says.

Before I've thought things through properly, I've given Simon my mother's address, and he's gone to get his bicycle. I told him that I could send Doug, but he seemed to think that was a crazy idea. 'I'll be there in less than twenty minutes,' he said. 'I'll be on my bike. It's good for the environment, good for the spirit and good for the soul.'

Shit, is he still pissed or something?

20 minutes later

He's here. He comes sauntering into the house with his bicycle clips still around his trousers and with his beard and hair all messed up. His face is bright red. I'll wager that no man has ever walked into this house looking so scruffy. Not ever.

'Whooah . . . champagne and cycling,' he comments. 'Not good. I nearly fell off!'

I let him in and we pace around each other for a while like two male tigers sizing each other up.

'What's the matter?' he says eventually, and I explain what I've done. He looks a bit embarrassed, shrugs and says, 'She's a funny one, your mum, isn't she? Still, I'm sure Dean's nan will be fine with it. Perhaps she could come next year?' Ever the one for the understatement, ever the diplomat.

I nod my agreement and there doesn't seem to be too much else to say on the subject, so Simon changes the conversation rather dramatically. 'While we're here, we should look for some photo albums, diaries, anything to help us with the book,' he says. 'Did you mention it to your mum?'

172

'I did,' I say, and I explain that Mum was about as unhelpful as it's possible for a woman to be.

'Then do you think she'd mind if we just took a quick look ourselves?' he asks.

Er, yes, she'd mind a lot, I think to myself, but I can see from Simon's face that it's important for us to get some information together about my childhood, so I say, 'I'm sure that wouldn't be a problem.'

The fact remains, though, that I am slightly unsure about randomly going through Mum's stuff while she's out. When she goes through my things (which she does ALL THE TIME), I get really upset. I'm also really concerned (and I did hint this to Simon in the car, but he brushed my concerns aside) that Mum won't actually have any pictures, mementoes or diaries that relate to me in any way. Simon thinks the suggestion's absurd.

'Look,' he says. 'You have a great chance to do a fabulous book. All we need is information about your childhood. Now there must be something here – some old photos we can use to help us summon up the past. I don't believe that any mother has no mementoes from the past. I bet she's got an old diary or something. We just need to look.'

'Okay,' I say meekly, still musing on the fact that Simon has come all this way on his bike and is still enthusiastic. Last time I went anywhere on a bike was when I was ten . . .

'Oh, I've had a thought,' I say. 'I've just had a really vivid memory of when I was younger. I remember being out on a bike – it was borrowed from a neighbour, and I was cycling down the road and this hand came out in front of me and knocked me completely off it.'

'What?' asks Simon with a laugh. 'Someone hailing a taxi and didn't see you?'

'That's what I thought, then when I stood up I realised it was Mum. She was so cross about me cycling along that she decided to knock me off with her umbrella.'

'But you could have been seriously hurt, or fallen into the traffic or something . . .'

'I guess. But it was all okay.'

'Mmmm . . .' says Simon, but I can see from the look on his face that he thinks Mum is poisonous.

'All happy families are alike; each unhappy family is unhappy in its own way,' he muses.

'Is it?' I say.

'According to Leo Tolstoy it is.'

'Leo who?' I ask, but he doesn't reply, so I'm left thinking through the Leos I know, and concluding that Simon has dug the sentence from a Leo Sayer track.

' "When I Need You?" or "You make Me Feel Like Dancing"?' I ask. Silence and a look of confusion.

'Let's get searching,' he says. But while Simon hunts for some sort of evidence that I am more to Mum than a complete pain in the arse, I just sit down and watch him.

'We'll find something, angel – don't you worry,' he says, gently flicking through the notes, salon appointments and meetings with cosmetic surgeons scheduled for the coming weeks. He hunts, and I sit quietly. He offers placatory words. 'She's probably put them some-where special!' But the kindness of his words and the tenderness of his feelings towards me just seem to clash alarmingly with the lack of any sort of feeling from my mother. I am now convinced that he won't find a thing, and watching him in his fruitless mission is becoming boring, so I walk over to the big tea chest and start to look through it. There's nothing in here of any significance, I'm sure of it, but there's something quite fascinating about looking through the things of someone you know well and realising that you really don't know them at all.

There's an old phone that I pull out.

'Switch it on and look at the messages,' says Simon wickedly.

I switch it on, but I don't think there's any real point. 'It's not her phone, she has one of those blackcherry phones that gives you all your emails, and she'll have that with her. This is just an old one.'

'If it's an old phone, it may yield something of value, or give us some names and numbers from the past,' he says, tapping his nose. My funny little mate is turning into Inspector Cluedo.

'Thank you, Inspector,' I say. 'I think it was Mrs Peacock in the library with the lead piping.'

'Nice to see your sense of humour hasn't deserted you,' he says, smiling at me before returning to his task. I decide to return to mine, but when I attempt to switch on the phone there's no response from it at all – it's completely dead.

'Nothing,' I say to Simon. 'I think it's probably a really old phone.'

'It doesn't look it,' he says, coming over and taking it from my hands. He pushes a button on the left side that I'd not even seen and hands it back to me. 'There you go, Miss Technical,' he says. 'Turns out you have to press the "on" button first.'

The phone's screen lights up in my hand, and a picture of a foot-baller bursts into view. It's not Dean. It's not the ridiculous teenage Ludo either. I recognise him though.

'Holy fucking Christ!' I whisper to myself. 'It's Andre!'

But what is Andre's phone doing at Mum's house?

'Anything interesting?' asks Simon. He's turning Mum's computer on as he speaks.

'No,' I lie. 'Just some old phone with nothing on it. I don't think there's even one of those slim cards in it.'

While Simon navigates his way through the security system on Mum's computer (password – Angie), I take a closer look at the phone. The message outbox is full of messages to Michaela. Whoever stole the phone from Andre must have then planted it in Mum's house. I look through the inbox and the outbox. The messages that were sent to Mich are all there, and her aggressive messages back are all there. But why would it be in Mum's house? I mean – why would whoever stole the phone from Andre leave it here? Unless it was . . . Oh god, no. Surely not. Mum stole Andre's phone? No, not Mum. How could she have? And why would she have stolen it? Why would she steal a man's phone and start abusing my friend with it? It's not like anything was happening between Mum and Andre.

I sit down on the floor. Andre's phone goes missing sometime Saturday night or Sunday morning. Mich is the only one there on Saturday night, so Andre starts to think that she stole it. But what if . . . what if there was someone round there on the Sunday morning who saw the phone lying there? What if that person was already dead set on breaking up Mich and Andre because they'd sent an anonymous text the night before the phone was stolen? What if that someone was Mum? It has to be. It's suddenly completely clear to me – as if someone's just posted the answer through my ear straight into my brain.

I can't believe it. Mum stole Andre's phone and has been doing all she can to wreck Mich's relationship because she's been having an affair with him. Oh god.

I tuck it into my back pocket before returning to the tea chest. There is an odd assortment of things in this chest that seem very out of character for Mum. Everything else in her house is extraordinarily well organised – very different to the drawers in my house where things are just thrown in – but this chest is a mixture of things. There's a spangly clutch bag that I open to see match boxes, theatre tickets and compliments slips from hotels. They don't seem to relate to anything in particular – just bits and pieces that Mum's keeping. Then there's a bright red carrier bag from an expensive-looking Italian stationer's. I peer inside to see lots of letters all folded up. The writing on them looks very childlike and for a second I think they may be from my childhood. I pull out the first one and glance down it.

Andre! The letter is from Andre. It's dated two months ago. Two months! They've obviously been having a fling for a while. Christ, this is awful.

What about Ludo? I thought Mum was madly in love with *him*? Has she been seeing both of them?

For god's sake, it's bad enough that Mum wants to have affairs with men half her age, but worse still that she's picking ones belonging to my friends. Among the letters there's also a SIM card.

'Okay there?' asks Simon.

'Yep. Nothing here,' I say, sliding the handful of letters and the SIM into my bag. 'Just old junk – bits and pieces that aren't any help at all.' My heart's beating and my hands are trembling. Mum's having an affair with Mich's boyfriend. This is fucking awful.

'Just going to see if Doug is okay,' I say to Simon, who is frantically flicking through notes with one hand while staring at the screen and typing with the other – all indicative of a man who is finding things of some value. 'I'll be back in just a second.'

'Sure,' he says, 'but take a look at this first.'

He hands me a copy of Mum's birth certificate. It turns out she's fifty-eight!! And there's a bundle of photographs taken before she went for her facelift. There are 'before' pictures then pictures illustrating her recovery from the operation in which she looks like she's been beaten up, and then the photographs taken a couple of months on where she looks fifteen years younger.

'Thanks,' I say, then I run outside, jotting Mich's address on a piece of paper, and hand it to Doug along with the phone and a letter to her. In the note, I ask Mich to check what the SIM card number is, and to see whether it's the same number that was used to text her from on that fateful Saturday night.

'Can you take this urgently to this address?' I say. 'Then come back here. I'll need you to go back and collect it later. It's not far.'

'No problem,' says Doug as he takes the loot and starts the engine. I text Mich and tell her I've found Andre's phone and to call me the minute the package turns up.

Then it's back into the sitting room to witness the moment when life slips into another dimension.

Simon says, 'Ah, here we are . . . lots of letters, notes and stuff – all about you. Perfect!' He has plonked himself down on the furry cream rug and tipped the contents of the file he's found onto the floor in front of him. 'Mmmm . . .' he mutters. 'Oh. Oh my god. Oh, Tracie. Shit. Oh my god. Oh, Tracie.'

As I look up and smile, I have no idea that all life as I knew it has now changed. Like those American students who come bounding over to England with a picture of what the place will look like built entirely from their reading of Charles Dickens, I had got everything about my life wrong. The American teenagers expect to be greeted by ladies in big dresses and magnificent flouncy hats saying 'How do you do?' and are alarmed to stumble instead upon drunk girls in ripped jeans drinking snakebite, swearing loudly and shouting 'fuck off'. My feelings about the world, and my feelings about the past, have been built on the same shaky foundations.

30 minutes later, still trembling

It turns out that 'Dad' – this fictitious monster from the past who I'd been taught to hate and despise despite not knowing his name or anything at all about him – is a kind man who is very keen to meet me, eager to find out all about me and not at all 'evil personified'. Simon and I scan down the letters, wide-eyed and shocked, like children who have stumbled upon their parents having sex.

'I can't believe it,' I mutter, as we read that Dad has been sending Mum an absolute fortune every month since my birth, and gave her a lump sum of £100K when I was born.

'He must have been seriously loaded. Imagine what one hundred grand could buy all that time ago,' says Simon.

'Not that long ago!' I correct.

'That must be how she bought this house. I bet she's got no mortgage,' he says.

'No – we bought this house for her,' I say. 'She always said she had no money and would have to get a council house. We bought her this, and Dean gives her money all the time.'

'Fuck!' says Simon.

The deception over Mum's financial situation is nothing like as awful as the deception over my father's eagerness to see me, though. I can barely speak. I clutch my stomach, trying to hold myself together.

'This can't be happening,' I hear myself muttering. 'How can this be happening? God, how can this be happening?'

I keep thinking of the stories that Pask used to read when she was younger, about dinosaurs who ate stones that sat in their stomachs, grinding up the food they ate to make it digestible. I feel like I've got those stones in my stomach – heavy inside me, and grinding away, pulling down on my insides.

Simon's on auto-pilot. Instead of hugging me and comforting me and telling me everything will be okay, he's going through files, writing things down, making notes, and shaking his head in alarm. He pulls out his mobile phone.

'Who are you calling? Don't call the police,' I say in my semi-alert state. 'I don't want to get her into trouble.'

'God bless you,' he says with real feeling. 'Trace, everything's going to be okay, you know. I'm not calling anyone. I'm just going to photograph these documents so we've got proof.' He carries on scribbling, looking at dates on letters and date stamps on envelopes. I realise he's being a journalist – pulling together his story – but this is the story of my life. He's clicked and clacked, he's written and noted, and he's jotted down thoughts, ideas and investigations he intends to do. He's even tapping away on his phone's calculator.

'It comes to over a million,' he says. 'And that's just the money we know about! Presumably there was other stuff – birthday presents and Christmas presents that he's sent. He's referring to them in the letters.'

And that's when I break down completely. Sobbing, howling and screaming in pain as I think about just how happy I would have been, in any given year, to receive just one card, present or phone call from my father. The hatred that I thought he felt towards me – always so keenly exaggerated by my mother – coloured my childhood. His distance from me and her coldness towards me confirmed what I always suspected – I was worthless, why would anyone bother with me? I could quite see why my father didn't hang around.

It wasn't until I met Dean that I had some salvation, and felt lovable and worth something. When I became a Wag I felt like I *truly* belonged. I know that probably sounds daft, but if you've not had much of a family and grew up in a world without rules, deadlines, boundaries or love, then the simplicity of a life with rules is enormously appealing – I know that's why I've thrown myself hook, line and sinker into it. I know that's why my articles are such an enormous success and why I'm suddenly on this bizarre media treadmill . . .

Because when it comes to being a Wag, it really matters to me, and people pick up on that – they sense my genuine love for it, and that's what seems to be enthralling them in such numbers. Whenever I talk to Simon about why this whole thing is taking off, he says the same thing. 'Integrity, love . . . that's the key. Once you can fake that, you've got it made.'

He means it as a joke – he means that you can't fake integrity, that's the very point. Basically, integrity means not faking it, it means really meaning it. I looked it up in the dictionary and everything – once I worked out how to spell it. The publisher said the same, she said that readers can see through what you write if you dash something off without thinking, and they can see straight through someone who's writing something to get great sales and doesn't have a passion for their subject. I bet that's why people laugh at what I'm doing – I genuinely believe in it all, I have integrity, but what I'm writing about might seem silly and trivial to those who know no better, so it makes people laugh that I take it seriously.

But being a Wag isn't silly and trivial for me. Being a Wag is about being part of a group, supporting my husband, making him proud, and showing the world that I belong, at last, to *something* and to *someone*.

'I'm going to make this book great,' I declare to Simon. 'We'll do all about being a Wag and how important it is to look good, but we'll also do all about my background, and that'll help explain why being a Wag is so important to me. The philosophy of being a Wag,' I say proudly. Perhaps they'll offer a degree in Wag Studies and I can be a professor! I can just see it now – although there's no way I'm wearing a long gown and one of those silly mortal board hats.

'But what about your mother?'

'What about her?' I ask, with a toss of my hair extensions. 'Why should I care what she thinks?'

'Are you going to tell her what we found?'

I don't know, is the honest answer.

'What do you think?' I ask Simon, as if he can possibly know what I should do.

'Well, I don't think that the first time she knows that you know should be when she reads about it in your book – that would be kind of sinking to her level. I think you should confront her before then, but you don't have to do it straightaway. Also, have you thought about whether you'll contact your dad?'

'Oh god.' I give an involuntary groan. I really haven't thought about that. 'Contact my dad?' I repeat. 'Shit. Should I?'

'Tracie, you should think about it. Don't do anything immediately. I think it might be worth talking to a counsellor or something.'

'Okay,' I say. 'Yes, I will. I'll call Jean, my psycho woman, and see what she says.'

'I'll take all this away,' Simon says, indicating the notes he's made and the pictures he's taken, 'and I'll do some searches on your mum and dad and I'll help you pull all this together. Then and only then will we decide whether any of it goes in the book. Okay? You're under no pressure to put any of it in there.'

It's so nice having a man like Simon around at a time like this – he's being incredibly helpful, kind and thoughtful – but there's a part of me forever burning brightly, no matter how bad I'm feeling, that wants to sort out his physical appearance for him. For example, I really think that he should shave his long and unkempt beard into a goatie – that way he'll look more ageing pop-star than follower of Jesus. When I suggest this to him he gives me a rather sinister look and advises me that goaties look good on no one, not even goats. I refrain, despite all my better judgements, from saying, 'Er, yeah, and the full ZZ Top beard looks good, does it, matey?'

'I think we should go,' he says, as I clamber to my feet, displaying my knickers and acres of spray-tanned thigh to him. I see him glance and look away, and wonder what he's thinking. I never feel any sexual tension with Simon – none of the stuff I feel with other men when I'm left alone with them. I don't feel this need for him to adore me physically, because I feel that he adores me anyway – in a kind of matey and nice sort of way. Like two friends in the playground enjoying each other's company – playing marbles or conkers or hopscotch. Then someone points out that you're a boy and a girl and the two of you look at each other and the spell is broken. An Adam and Eve moment has happened and all the innocence has evaporated. I hope that Simon and I will always stay friends. I've never had a male friend before.

'Shall we go for a drink?' he asks, all his notes collected in his ridiculous knapsack.

'Sure,' I reply. I watch him put his bicycle clips on. 'Do you have to put those on? I mean, can't we just jump in the car, go to a nice wine bar for a drink without looking like we're hikers?'

'Okay,' says Simon.

'I'll just go and brush my hair.'

When I look in the mirror, I can't believe it. I look ridiculous. Why didn't he say anything? It's like he doesn't care at all about how I look. It's like he doesn't even notice. Bizarre!

The red lip-gloss is still all around my chin and lips, my eye make-up is all over my face where I've been crying, and smudged into my cheeks and nose. Basically, half my face is black, and the other half is red. I don't think it would be possible for me to look any more strange. The feeling of utter despair that has been crunching in the bottom of my stomach suddenly overwhelms me. I feel weak and faint and throw up in the sink. Then the oddest thing happens – I start to laugh. I look at my face and I squeal with laughter, falling to the floor in mild hysteria, rolling around, clutching my sides and laughing like I'll never stop. I'm crying, laughing, squealing and screaming when Simon finds me. There's black and red make-up all over Mum's cream carpet and the sink is full of sick.

Next day

Woke up, felt awful, went back to bed.

Day after that

Woke up, hoping I'd feel much better – didn't. Wondered why all the women in books and films wake up two days after any sort of drama or trauma feeling strong and glorious and able to change the world, whereas I feel like a punch-bag. Mum rang. Didn't return the call. Simon's been ringing every hour, on the hour. I think he must be sitting there with his mobile phone and just hitting the redial button. My phone is switched off and every time I turn it on again it announces that I have loads of missed calls – all from Simon's number. I also have eight voice-mail messages but I can't be arsed to play them. Just want to stay in bed and re-create my childhood in a fantastical way – with Mum and Dad skipping beside me and telling me how much they love me. Every time the dream takes over my mind, though, more real and damaging memories come marching along and wipe away the happy thoughts. I'm alone, I'm scared, she doesn't like me. 'No wonder your father wants nothing to do with you – what man would?' comes her angry voice over and over again.

Day after that – Saturday, 17 November
10 a.m.

Dean left for the match today, asking me whether I was okay to be left alone. I haven't told him anything about the discovery in Mum's house. He thinks I'm in bed suffering from 'women's problems'. I've told him that because, like most men, the mere mention of women's problems has him going, 'Yeah, fine, whatever,' and leaving the room as quickly as humanly possible. He asked whether I was okay to be left alone in the hope that I'd say 'no' and he could pull out of the match (or pull out of being ninety-seventh reserve). He's so fed up with football and with Luton Town that he'd rather sit at the end of the bed and talk 'lady problems' than go down there and be humiliated as sixteen-year-olds take his place, but I insisted that he go.

I feel as if my grip on Wagdom is weakening with every Saturday that passes. Pask came to tell me that Simon has been calling me three times an hour and is absolutely desperate to talk to me. The *Daily Mail* want to speak to me about Monday's column and getting a new picture of me, and a book publisher wants to speak to me about a book I'm writing.

'Like, yeah,' says Pask. 'I told them they must be completely mad, and hung up.'

She's become so unladylike has Paskia. I'm sure it's all that football she's been playing – it's not right for a girl of her age. She's just started senior school, she should be rolling her skirt up so high that her knickers are on show, shoving handkerchiefs down her bra and practising blow-jobs on carrots. That's what I was doing at her age, anyway. Not wearing long navy-blue socks to hide the bruises all over her shins, and wanting to talk endlessly about the tactics and the 3–9–2 formation or whatever it is.

'I'm in, you know,' Pask is saying. 'I got through the trials.'

'Trials for what?'

'The school team. I'm the only first year in it. Dad reckons I've got real talent. I mean *real* talent. He says I'm better than any boys he's seen of my age. He thinks I could play for England one day.'

Oh god. As if things aren't tough enough. Not only has she no interest in her appearance, she's now definitely a lesbian.

'I should take you to Cricket!' I tell her.

'I prefer football,' she responds. 'I'd like to play cricket in the summer, though.'

'No, not the stupid game that goes on for days with the bat and ball and the horrible woolly jumpers. The shop. Cricket . . . where all the beautiful clothes are. It's full of lovely things and beautiful people and you nearly always see a really famous Wag in there.'

'Sounds like hell,' mutters Pask.

'I should get you a subscription to *Heat* magazine,' I offer kindly. 'Then you'll be able to find out all about what the Wags are up to, and you'll learn about Cricket.'

'I'd rather have *FourFourTwo*,' says Paskia.

I have no idea what my daughter's talking about. 'What's that? Some sort of new dance?'

'It's a football magazine, Mum,' she says, with that air of utter disbelief that kids manage to summon up with far too much regularity. 'It's, like, all about football.'

'Where did I fail you?' I ask, and I mean it. What did I do to let her down like this? What did I do to push her away from me and into this masculine world of tactics and tackling? Did I inherit such bad parental skills that I've messed everything up? I've tried to engage my daughter in important and meaningful activities but she just wants to talk to Dean about corners, defensive formations and the great Liverpool teams of the 1970s.

'Paskia, I'm sorry,' I say. 'Have I let you down?'

'No,' she replies, easing herself off the bed and looking at me like I'm mad. She did that when I tried to sit her down and talk to her about periods. 'Anyway, I told that Simon bloke that you were in bed and that Dad was off to play football and he asked me whether he could come round.'

'What did you say?' I ask in alarm.

'I said "whatever".'

As if there could be any other answer to any question. She may not be like other eleven-year-old girls in some respects but in others she's a tweenie down to the core.

Midday

The doorbell chimes its *Match of the Day* tune and I know straightaway that it's going to be Simon. By some happy coincidence I have spent every second since Paskia implied that he was on his way round here grooming, brushing, lotioning, perfuming, powdering and painting.

A rather flamboyant negligee is about my person and I am ready to receive male visitors.

There's a tentative knock at the door and I sense that Simon would rather meet me anywhere in the world than in my bedroom.

'Come,' I say, gently easing the front of my frilly garment down to reveal large, uplifted, tanned and shimmery breasts.

Simon stands in the doorway. He looks like a small boy, clutching a rather pathetic-looking bunch of weeds, and smiling, looking around the room rather than straight at me. 'Are you okay?' he says to the walk-in wardrobe.

'I'm fine,' I say. 'Have a seat.' I indicate the edge of the bed and he looks at me as if I must be entirely insane and continues to stand.

'For you,' he says, pushing forward the clump of weeds. 'There were more of them when I set out but I couldn't quite hold on to them when I was cycling.'

'Thanks,' I say. There's something quite empowering about this situation, with me being in bed and him standing there, but him being the one who is so incredibly nervous. Normally I'm the nervous one around him as we're talking about work stuff and writing books. The thing is, though, I don't want to make lovely Simon feel uncomfortable.

'Do you want to wait in the drawing room?' I ask. 'I'll get up, get dressed and join you down there.'

He looks like a man whose dying child has just been offered an unexpected heart transplant.

2 p.m. (Sorry, I know I've kept him waiting ages, and you must think me appallingly rude, but it takes me a long time to get ready – there's nothing I can do about it, it's just the way I am. Okay?)

I float into the room – a sea of silky aquamarine shimmering about me, tight white trousers clinging to me, and high-heeled boots elevating me. I've had to redo all my eye make-up because it was smoky and bedtimeish, which would have looked *mad* with the blue top!

'Coffee?' I ask, but he indicates the three cups, the plate on which he's obviously been served lunch, two wine glasses and a water glass.

'Oh, yes, sorry it took me so long.'

He shrugs.

'Did you come to see how I am, or have you got something to show me for the book?'

Simon looks uncomfortable. He tells me to sit down.

'I've found something out that you're not going to like,' he says.

'I don't think anything would surprise me any more,' I reply, and mean it. The world has just got barking lately.

'This might.'

Simon unrolls a large piece of paper that he had tucked down the back of his trousers. 'Because I was cycling,' he explains. He lays the paper flat out and I can see it is a mock-up of an article for that gutter-press horror the *Daily Journal*.

'Sorry,' Simon says while he begins some unwieldy and complex explanation of the sheet he's just laid in front of me. His mutterings seem to amount to the fact that his friend Yvonne is the features editor of the *Daily Journal* and used to be a brilliant investigative reporter on the *Sunday Times*. He had called her and asked her how he should best go about researching this story on my dad, and this Yvonne woman stopped in her tracks and said, 'Tracie Martin? How do you know her?' Simon had explained then Yvonne told him that there was a big inter-view being planned with Mum, who had contacted the paper to say that she would like to tell the world all about what her daughter's *really* like.

'What?' I ask. 'My mum's going to write an article about how horrible I am? That's insane. It's not even as if I'm famous or anything. I'm just a normal girl, married to a footballer.'

' . . . And doing a column for their big rival.'

'So the *Daily Journal* will write a piece about me because I write a column for the *Daily Mail*? How weird is that?'

'No, it doesn't quite work like that – it's just that the *Daily Journal* will be far more inclined to stitch you up because you're a *Daily Mail* columnist, but the fact is that your glamorous mother is having a go at you, a rising star married to a former England footballer. It makes quite a nice page-seven piece.'

'Fuck!' I say, because it seems appropriate and I can't think of anything that seems more so.

'Indeed,' Simon replies.

I read through the piece and it's *horrible*. My opinion of my mother, while revised drastically since the revelation that my father always wanted to meet me and she wouldn't let me, is sinking further.

'I think she must realise that you went through her things and have found out about your father,' says Simon. 'Have you talked to her at all?'

'I haven't talked to anyone,' I say. 'I have been in bed feeling like death ever since. I haven't even told Pask and Dean. There are tons of messages on my phone but I can't summon up the energy to answer them.'

'Bring it here.'

So Simon goes through my messages. 'Twenty-seven of them!' he announces. 'Eleven from me, three from your mother. The rest are from the *Daily Mail* and the publishers and six odd ones from someone called Michaela. I would talk to the *Daily Mail* as soon as you can – they want to know all about your column for Monday. Just give them a quick call and they'll be off your back.

'Now, your mother . . . let me play them. Here we go . . . blah, blah, blah . . . Okay, well, it seems she doesn't realise you know about your father, but she's muttering away about how she knows that you have the phone and that you're evil for going through her things. The Michaela girl is also going on about the phone you've given her and how it all makes sense.'

I try to provide Simon with a simple explanation, which, from the look of confusion on his face, I don't manage. I apologise for not mentioning the phone to him, but it was kind of a private thing for Michaela. He just smiles and nods and shrugs like a man who is thrilled to be out of a conversation that he has no understanding of and little interest in.

'Well, good. Glad that sorted itself out then,' he says. 'You're going to need to talk to your mother this weekend and tell her not to write this article. The *Daily Journal* are due to run it a week today.'

'I'll do it now,' I say, lifting the receiver and dialling Mum's number. I realise that she will probably be at the match – supporting either Ludo or Andre or whichever teenage footballing sensation she's currently got the hots for, so I ring the mobile, putting it onto loudspeaker so Simon can hear.

'What do you want?' she says. 'I'm amazed you have the cheek to call me after what you've done – going through all my things and telling lies about me.'

'I haven't told any lies about you,' I say.

'Explain why I've had Michaela here – screaming and shouting at me, accusing me of having an affair with her stupid boyfriend? That's because you interfered, isn't it? You had to get involved.'

'Angie, I had no choice. I had to give the phone to her. It was the only honest thing to do – the poor girl was going out of her mind.'

There's silence on the other end of the phone.

'Anyway, I didn't call to talk about that – I wanted to talk to you about this article in the *Daily Journal*.'

'How do you know about that?'

'My friend Simon told me,' I say.

Simon is right next to me, madly waving his arms around to

indicate that he really doesn't want to be involved. 'Wimp' I mouth to him.

'Well – I thought the article for the *Daily Journal* was the only honest thing to do.'

'You bitch,' shouts Simon in an outburst that seems totally out of character. 'How dare you treat your daughter like this. How dare you. I'll stop you, you know. I have contacts. I'll stop them running this next week.'

'Angie,' I say. 'Mum.'

But the line is dead. When I phone back, it's engaged.

Simon looks devastated.

'Well, that went well,' I say.

'Mmmm,' mutters Simon. 'I'm glad I managed to keep my composure . . . sorry!'

I give him a massive hug.

'I will stop her,' he reiterates. 'Just you wait and see.'

Sunday, 18 November
7 a.m.

'Dean,' I say, snuggling up to him and putting my head on his chest. He moves to stroke my hair, cops one feel of the hair extensions and pulls his hand away quickly. If I were a scientist, when I wasn't inventing a pill to stop women getting wrinkles, I'd definitely be devising a way to make hair extensions that don't feel like you've got beetles in your hair when your man strokes it. I miss having Dean run his fingers through my hair, but not enough to take the extensions out . . . obviously!

'What is it, babes?' he asks, and I can't quite work out how to phrase this. I've decided to tell him about my discovery because if Mum ends up writing a piece in the *Daily Journal* next week he'll have the shock of his life.

'Listen, sweetie. I went to Mum's house last week and asked her whether she could help me with this book I'm going to write – you know, the one about me being a Wag. The one with the advice columns in it.'

'That's nice,' he says. 'I think she'd like that.'

'No. It turns out she doesn't. She said she doesn't want me to have anything to do with it. She got really cross. Started screaming and shouting and telling me there was no way she was getting involved.'

'That's a shame,' he says.

'Well, yes it is, because I went through all her stuff when she was out – looking for anything that might help with the book, and . . .'

'Trace,' he says, sitting up. 'You shouldn't go through your mum's things.'

He's got a look of such innocence on his face. He has no idea what she's like. I can't even bear the thought of telling him. It will destroy all his trust in mankind. He always does his best and expects the best from everyone. He couldn't ever conceive of anyone being so nasty.

'Okay . . .' I tell him everything – about the phone and Andre, about the article she's planning to write and about my dad being eager to meet me and sending all this money. He looks as devastated as I imagined he would.

'Oh, Trace,' he says, stroking my hair despite the extensions threatening to break his fingers. 'Oh, Trace.'

'What do you think I should do?' I ask.

'Have you talked to her?'

'I tried, but there's no point – she's just a liar, a thief and a cheat. Simon ended up screaming down the phone at her. She's evil, Dean. You know what she called me in one of the letters to my dad?'

'No,' he says.

'Live By Satellite.'

'Oh,' he says. 'What does that mean?'

'It means I'm slow.'

As Dean struggles to understand, I hear my phone ringing. Pask has changed it to Kylie Minogue's 'I Should Be So Lucky', one of my favourite songs in the world. My man leans over, picks it up and hands it to me. Simon's name has flashed up on the screen and Dean mutters something unintelligible and rolls over.

'Are you awake?' Simon asks.

'Er, yes,' I reply, thinking, Hello . . . who's live by satellite now?

'Meet me,' he says. 'It's urgent. Have you seen the papers?'

'It's seven a.m., Simon,' I say. 'I haven't seen anything outside the bedroom.'

'Well, good. Don't open any newspapers and don't switch on the television. Just come and meet me.'

'Can you come here?' I ask, and Dean rolls over and makes throat-slashing signals to indicate that he really doesn't want a bearded, left-leaning writer in his house before he's had breakfast. (That left-leaning bit, I should point out, is referring to Simon's politics. When Simon first said it, I was quite alarmed and always stood to the right of him in case he fell on me.)

Happily, Simon seems to have the same view as Dean about coming to our house.

'No!' he cries. 'Not at your house. Somewhere else.'

'Um . . .'

'Somewhere people aren't likely to find us.'

'What people?'

'The world's media.'

It's too early for this sort of conversation.

'Do you know the Sunnyside Sheltered Accommodation?' I ask. It's my bolt-hole. Nell won't mind.

'No, but I'll find it.'

I give him the directions and he issues a warning which has me, frankly, amazed.

'Don't be surprised if there are photographers and journalists hovering around your house. You may have to lose them.'

'Right.'

Simon's gone. Dean's looking at me with those confused eyes of his. He's only just got to grips with the fact that my mother's a vicious and nasty piece of work, and my father's alive and kicking and keen to meet me.

'Will you come with me to Nell's place?' I say. 'Simon wants to meet me. He says it's urgent and we need to lose the world's media on the way. I'd really like you to come.'

9 a.m.

Here we are then. Life's never simple, is it? We walked out the front door into a barrage of flashing lenses and questions about our relationship, and my mother's centrefold piece in the *Sunday Journal*. I shrugged, convincingly looking as if I had no idea what they were talking about, because I did, indeed, have no idea what they were talking about. The piece that Simon showed me was for the *Daily Journal* – so what's this one?

'Head for the old ladies' home and make it snappy. We'll need to lose the paparazzi en route,' I said to Doug. It's possibly the first time those two sentences have sat next to one another in the same instruction. Doug looked as if he'd died and gone to heaven as he broke every road-using law in the world (in other words, he drove like me) and arrived at the nursing home mere seconds after we left our house. Now Dean and I are on the floor in the back of the car, trying to call Nell on the mobile to check she's in. Dean is saying all sorts of 'wise after the event' things like, 'Wouldn't it have been a better idea to call Nell *before* we left the house?'

When Nell finally answers the phone, she announces that she woke up this Sunday morning to be greeted by Jesus himself standing at the door, and I realise that Simon has got there before us.

'Come on,' I instruct my husband, and the two of us run across the deserted car park and hurl ourselves into the lift up to Nell's flat. As we get out of the lift, we can hear the conversation taking place in Nell's home. The TV is obviously blaring out, so she and Simon are bellowing at one another above it. When I walk in, Simon looks utterly relieved. Then he sees Dean. 'What a pleasure,' he says in a most unconvincing way, and the two men shake hands. They are just too different ever to be mates, but it would be nice if they could at least pretend they liked each other.

'This is the problem,' says Simon, dramatically throwing open the *Sunday Journal* and revealing a topless, heavily airbrushed picture of my mother in which she is listing every conquest she ever made in Hollywood and telling the world that, in me, she spawned the devil.

'She was a vile and horrible child. That's why her father left. If I did not have such love in my heart, love only a mother understands, then I would have left her, too.'

'I thought you said they weren't going to run this until next Saturday?' I say, as Simon fidgets with his beard.

'The *Daily Journal* didn't. It was the *Sunday Journal.*'

'Why would she do this?' asks Dean quite aggressively, as if this is all Simon's fault.

'Jealousy, I guess,' says Simon. 'Perhaps she wants to ruin what you've got because she's jealous of you. I don't know. Perhaps I was responsible after I was so rude to her on the phone yesterday.'

'No, Simon, don't be silly. She's always been jealous of Tracie,' says Nell from the corner. 'As long as I've known you, she's envied your relationship with Dean and all the friends you make so easily. She tries to keep me out of your life as she kept your father out. She's jealous of your youth and beauty, too.'

'My beauty? Ha! She's the one who's beautiful. I'm nothing to look at!'

'Whaaaaat?' they all chorus. Then Dean says something that I know I'll remember for the rest of my life.

'You're stunning. Tracie, what is wrong with you? Can't you see how much more attractive you are than her? She's nothing next to you.'

'Oh.'

I must admit I'm shocked by the outburst. Growing up with Mum involved being told daily how many men she'd had, how popular she was, and how beautiful. It also involved me being told how dull, plain, ugly and pointless I was. I guess that sort of daily reinforcement makes a dent on you, psychomagically speaking, and affects your self-esteem. When I look at Mum, I see someone wholly beautiful, whereas when I look in the mirror I see someone trying desperately hard and failing miserably.

'What should I do about it?' I ask Nell.

'I think you should ignore it completely,' says Nell, and Simon is nodding his agreement. He tells me that the *Daily Mail* will be eager for me to address this in my column tomorrow, but that I should refuse, rise above it, show dignity in the face of such colossal pressure and continue to live my life, alongside my husband, my daughter, Nell, and those who love me.

'Okay,' I say. 'And what should I do about the book?'

'I think you should probably not do it at the moment,' says Simon, rather charitably considering that he's set to make lots of money from it. 'I think you should continue to do your handbook pieces, and when you're ready we'll take a look at how to structure the book, and whether you should go into much detail on your background, home life and childhood.'

'Cool,' says Dean, and I can see he's looking at Simon with a hint of admiration. Good. Perhaps he'll realise why Simon's become such a good friend to me.

'Right,' says Nell. 'So have you lot finished using my place for a meeting room?'

I give her a kiss on the cheek and thank her, telling her there's nowhere on earth I feel safer and happier. That makes her day, she tells me, and I stomp out of the flat, tripping over the edge of the rug, wishing that I hadn't worn these silver platform boots, but they're the only things that match my silver knickers, and I really wanted to wear the silver knickers with the white mini, because it's so short that you can see them straightaway. Now, though, the knickers are feeling so tight that I can feel my internal organs pushing up against one another. I'm sure if I were flexible enough to put my head on my stomach I'd hear them crying for mercy.

'Come on, Dean,' I say, gathering myself after the small stumble. 'Take me home. I need to get out of these knickers, and I may need your assistance.'

Monday, 19 November
10.45 p.m.

When I read the article I wrote in the *Daily Mail* this morning, I realised the sombre mood I was in yesterday rather reflected itself in the piece, despite my best efforts to be upbeat and full of vitality. In the end I had emailed it to Simon, who forwarded it to the *Daily Mail* for me, so saving me having to get in contact with them. Then Dean and I forwarded all our calls to Rupert Sebastian at the PR agency, who was delighted to hear from us again. I bet he is, now I'm famous. He said he'd handle everything and Dean and I went and had a nice romantic Jacuzzi together and went to bed early. Despite all the hassles of the day, I think it was the nicest night of my life.

FUNERALS

A tip – don't wear black! You'll just end up looking like everyone else. Honestly, funerals can be a real minefield for Wags – a real minefield! Unlike the wedding scenario, upstaging the principal character at a funeral is not part of the aim. If you can't look better than a dead person then you have some serious issues to contend with. The other thing about funerals is that it's all about grief, so turning up in sugar-pink glittery jackets and hurling champagne down your throat like there's no tomorrow is not considered de rigueur. Neither are dancing round your handbag and belting out the words to the latest Sugababes track, nor chanting 'bitch, bitch, bitch' when the girl who used to go out with your man enters the room. Tempting as it might be!

If it's the funeral of a former football great, or even a former football not-so-great (like the portly club chairman who meets his maker on the golf course or the funny little guy with the stick who, it turns out, was club secretary during the war and stopped the Germans from digging up the pitch), then the stakes are so much higher. Consider how many other Wags there will be at the funeral!!! My advice to you at funerals is to make like it's not a funeral. Think of all those sad old men, crying because old Alfie's gone.

Don't they need to look at someone pretty and delicious to cheer themselves up?

Ignore convention and reach for the stars. Break the rules and wear what you want. Some things are too important to change just because some old man got ill and died. Wear the pink hat with feathers if it makes you happy, ignore the screams of your husband when you come down the stairs covered in sparkly pink face dust, and sporting a tiny micro mini. Be yourself. Throw caution to the wind. Above all – avoid black!

Tuesday, 20 November
10 a.m.

Life's been really difficult since the article in the *Sunday Journal*. I expected to be hassled yesterday because Rupert Sebastian and everyone said I would be, but by today I really thought it would all have calmed down. When I changed the divert on my phone, though, I found I'd got loads of messages, including another one from Mindy saying that I was invited to a girls' night because her friends had all heard about me, but pleeeeaaassee don't tell Angie she called. The rest of the messages were from newspapers, journalists, radio stations and my friendly local paper – all wondering what my response to Mum's piece will be. There was one from Sally, too, asking whether I remembered her, and saying that she'd seen the piece in the paper. 'I am so sorry. I remember how difficult your mum was,' she says. It occurs to me that Sally is one of the few people in the world who genuinely does know how badly Mum treated me. I can't face calling her back right now, but I send a text through thanking her and promising to be in touch soon.

When I switch on the television they are debating it on the Matthew Wright show. I love him – I think he's great, but it's horrible when he's talking about you and he's never even met you. 'Should a mother ever turn on her daughter?' it says at the bottom of the screen, and I listen while a selection of callers ring up and say either no, a mother shouldn't ever do that, or yes, sometimes a child's behaviour warrants it.

'This is not a child we're talking about, though, is it?' says James from Dunstable. 'This woman – this Tracie Martin – is an adult. I bet she's a right troublemaker for her mother to do this in the papers. The mother's a bit of a looker, though, isn't she?'

'Can't deny that,' says Matthew, and off they go again, to another caller with views on my life. I switch the television off and sit back in my chair. I'm going to have to talk to Mum. This is just daft. I pick up my mobile and dial 141 before the number. I'm sure she won't take the call if my number flashes across the screen.

'Mum, it's me. Don't hang up. Please don't hang up,' I say.

There's silence.

'Why, Mum?'

'I had no choice,' she says. 'You drove me to it.'

'I did no such thing. What have I ever done to upset you so much?'

'You made me look a fool down the club with that phone thing, and I know you went through all the letters from your father. The next thing will be you and him all lovey-dovey and me locked out in the cold on my own.'

'If that happens, Angie, it will be all your own fault. Why didn't you tell me about Dad? I don't understand.'

There's silence. I do understand, of course. I know that it was about money. That, somehow, makes it all so much worse.

'We need to meet,' I say. 'Let's have a coffee later.'

'Darling, I urged you not to have such a ridiculously high profile. I tried to stop you because I never wanted him to be able to trace you easily or approach you, but you insisted,' Mum is saying. 'I did it for your own good. I couldn't have him contact you – he's evil, pure evil. That's why I did the article . . . to protect you. I thought that if I wrote bad things about you it would keep him away.'

Right. Of course, Mum – you're my hero, my saviour. It wouldn't be because the *Sunday Journal* paid you a fortune, would it? What scares me is that if I hadn't been through all her things, I might have believed this rubbish.

'I want you to come round now,' I say.

'Okay,' she replies, and suddenly I feel terrified.

Ten minutes later

Mum's not here yet, but I guess it takes ten minutes to drive here, and she'll want to get ready, so say forty minutes. I expect she'll be here in forty minutes.

Forty minutes later

No sign of her yet.

One hour later

I've tried calling but there's no answer.

197

A text has arrived. Mum's not coming. She says she can't face me and she wants to be left alone.

Fine. I'll leave her alone then. I'm going to pull my life back together without her, and the first thing a woman on a mission needs to pull her life together are some serious beauty treatments. I shout through to Alba to call the beautician's and get me an urgent appointment while I go upstairs to get ready.

I feel better when I come back down. False eyelashes and glittery blusher always do that for me. I shout over my shoulder to the staff that I will be back in around three hours, in time to see Dean for lunch before he goes off to watch Paskia play in a blessed football match this afternoon. 'Can you prepare a light lunch?' I shout gaily, before wrapping a scarf around my neck, donning a balaclava, and running out to the car with my sunglasses on. I feel a bit of a fool when I get to the car because there are no paparazzi anywhere. I'm sure Doug sniggers as I slide onto the back seat.

'Utterly Fabulous, please,' I instruct, and off he goes towards the beauty salon. When I get out I decide not to take any risks, and wrap the scarf back round my head and run inside. Doug says he plans to head back to the house, then will come and collect me later. I remind him that he needs to take Dean to the school later for the football and he shrugs. I'm sure he wishes bloody Dean would learn to drive as much as I do. He's a grown man, for god's sake, and not just any grown man – a footballer! Who ever heard of a footballer who couldn't drive? He should have eighteen cars – most of them costing more than a yacht. So much of a footballer's pride is tied up in his car. Think of dogging, for heaven's sake! Dean's just lucky he's not a pervert or he'd be really stuck without a car.

In I go, and luckily there is no one about except Lisa, the beautician, who is tending to someone's mangy-looking feet. I unravel myself from my absurd disguise and she seems surprised to see me. 'Gosh – it's you in there, is it?' she asks. 'Are you cold or something?'

Thank goodness the *Sunday Journal* isn't read by nineteen-year-old beauticians operating out of salons in Luton town centre.

'Hi, Lise,' I say, blowing her a kiss. 'Will you be long?'

'Long? What do you mean?' she asks, rubbing away at the woman's feet with the cheese-grater thing and staring incredulously at the calluses and dry skin. 'Has it been quite a while since you had a pedicure?' she asks the woman, as buckets of dead skin fall off the soles of the woman's feet and land on the pile of towels.

'Well, I've got an appointment for my nails and I desperately need to get a facial done after that, so I could do with getting going as soon as possible.'

'You haven't got an appointment today,' says Lisa, continuing with her work. If she scrubs any harder she's going to get right through to the bone.

'I have,' I protest. 'Alba called up and booked one.'

'Nope,' says Lisa. 'Not in the book.'

'Ow!' yells the woman being treated. 'That hurt.' She looks up at Lisa and sees me standing there. 'Oh. It's you!' says the woman, tending the now raw and bleeding stump. 'I've read your columns in the *Daily Mail*. I think they're great. But what about your mum on Sunday? My goodness, I couldn't believe that.'

Suddenly I feel all flustered and under pressure. Lisa's looking at me with renewed admiration as the bloody-footed woman explains about my newfound fame. Lisa's eyes are wide and bright. There's nothing she likes more than a bit of gossip, and this is soooo much more than a bit of gossip. Now she's muttering on about probably being able to fit me in after all, but all I can think about is getting home. I really don't want to sit around here for three hours with these women, chatting and oohing and ahhing about how hard-done-by I am and how awful Mum is, then no doubt have them saying 'no smoke without fire' as soon as my back is turned, and wondering what I was really like as a child that my father would have nothing to do with me and my mum would turn on me so suddenly like that.

'Bye, everyone,' I shout, moving out of the shop as I wrap my scarf around my face. I descend the small step as quickly as my ferociously high wedged shoes will allow, and remember with an almighty rush of disappointment that Doug has gone back to the house. Shit.

'Taxi!' What a result. I jump in and mumble directions that need repeating several times before the driver understands them, but I simply don't want to remove the scarf. I don't want anyone to see me now. I don't want any more sightings of the Distressed Wag of Luton. I just want to be at home where I'm safe, surrounded by my loved ones.

'Are you a terrorist?' asks the driver suspiciously. 'Only, the scarf and the fact that you're obviously not English. You're not one of them suicide bombers, are you?'

I shake my head and he feels happy with that. Presumably he knows instinctively that even suicide bombers would tell him the truth if asked directly about their occupation.

Back at the house, half an hour after leaving it

As I step out of the taxi, negotiating payment of the driver with the battle to stay upright when wearing wedge-heeled shoes on gravel, and struggling to prevent the scarf from falling in case there are paparazzi hidden in the bushes, I can sense straightaway that something is wrong. For starters, there's music blaring out of the house. It sounds very much like there's an enormous party going on but there can't be – I know Dean's at training all morning (or, more accurately, he's 'watching training' all morning). Similarly, I know that Paskia Rose is at school, preparing for her first bloody match for the school team this afternoon. She's talked of nothing else for weeks. There's no way she's at home. The only way she's not at school is if she's been struck down by some dreadful illness or injury, in which case I'm assuming the chances of her being in the house playing 'Papa Don't Preach' at full volume are considerably less than the chances of her being in hospital.

'Hello?'

There's the sound of footsteps racing, loud foreign voices shouting, and in the air hangs the scent of people in considerable panic. I follow the sounds and see my entire staff, dressed in my clothes, leaping around and dancing like fools, drinking expensive wine from the bottle and WEARING MY MAKE-UP!! Be still my heart.

'What's going on?' I ask.

'Nossing,' says Alba, batting her heavily made-up eyes. Suddenly her accent doesn't seem so sweet any more.

'No*thing*, Alba,' I say coldly. 'The word is "no*thing*". But clearly that is not the right word because there is no question that you are doing something. What are you doing?'

'Party,' says Doug, emerging from the kitchen. Happily he's not wearing any of my clothes, but he does have Dean's aftershave on, which annoys me, and he's drinking out of Dean's favourite Arsenal tankard – the one Dean never drinks out of because he wants to keep it all nice and special in honour of his brief spell in the Premiership.

They're all looking at me as if I'm somehow to blame here. In their various foreign tongues I can hear them whisper to one another. Angie's name is mentioned. Has she put them up to this? Or is this their way of paying me back for my perceived behaviour towards Mum when I was a child – the same behaviour that alienated my father and led my poor mother to spend years alone? There's only so much a girl can take – even a meek and mild Wag like me. I'm looking around at them and it's as if they can sense the change in me like dogs can sense the oncoming of thunder.

'Sorry,' says Doug, but it's way too late. I've spent months wondering where my clothes and jewellery have got to. I remember my lovely new white Gucci handbag that Dean gave me. It was perfect. Then, before I used it, I found a scuffmark on it and had to throw it away – not even Oxfam would want it in that condition. I remember all my things forever being out of place in the wardrobe, and wondering on occasions whether Dean has been cross-dressing or something. Thinking perhaps that's why the football is going pear-shaped . . . because he's about to have a sex-change. In his heart he's a woman!

Now I know. My husband is not cross-dressing, instead my staff are thieves who exploit me at the drop of a hat. Christ, I was out for less than an hour – imagine what they get up to when we go to Marbella on holiday . . . it really doesn't bear thinking about.

'YOU ARE ALL SACKED!!!' I scream at the top of my voice. 'All of you.'

The shouting has made me feel quite light-headed. I hate shouting at people. Just hate conflict of any kind. I hate the thought of people not liking me, but I know I have to get these people out of my house.

'We have rights,' says Doug.

'And so do I,' I declare pompously. 'I have the right to live in a home that is not being attacked from within. I have rights, too.'

Quite a Churchillian moment, that, but rather undone in its intensity by the fact that I burst into tears seconds afterwards, and then cannot stop sobbing. I feel let down by everyone. The staff look around, glancing from one to the other, knowing what they've done is bad, but feeling, I guess, that they've got away with it for so long, and I've never raised my voice in all the time they've been here, that it feels almost unfair they've been caught now.

I end up doing something ridiculous – writing them all huge cheques for their next three months' wages and booking them into a hotel for a week. It costs me tens of thousands of pounds (well, technically, I suppose, it cost Dean the money, but I wrote the cheques so I felt the pain, too). They all troop out, looking at me as if I'm the most evil person alive. I feel it, too. Though why I should is beyond me. Once they're gone I realise that they have all left wearing my clothes and thousands upon thousands of pounds' worth of jewellery. I also realise that the house is a complete mess and I have no staff, no one to sort my clothes out, and we don't have a driver. Shit.

For some reason I can't explain, I pick up the phone and ring Sally. She's so thrilled to hear from me, that I'm immediately cheered up.

'Oh my god – is that really you?' she says.

'Of course,' I reply. 'Look, thanks for the message you left. It was very kind of you to call.'

'Gosh, that's all right,' says Sally, nervously. 'I know you must have millions of friends rallying round you right now, and I'm just sure those Wags are looking after you, but I just wanted to call because – you know – I remember how tough it was for you growing up. Are you okay?'

'I'm fine,' I say. 'Having a few problems at the moment but I'm sure everything will be just great in the end. How about you?'

'Oh, not bad. I've just passed my level one, football coaching award.'

'Wow,' I say, guessing that's a good thing. 'Pask plays football, you know. Apparently, she's very good.'

'I'd really love to come and see her play some time,' says Sally.

'Of course,' I say, thinking how dull life as a butcher must be if she'd love to spend the afternoon watching a teenager she's never met kicking a ball around.

'That would be brilliant. When's she playing?'

I explain that Paskia has a match that very afternoon.

'I'll close the shop early,' says Sally.

'Okay.' I give her directions and put the phone down. It's only then that the true horror of what I've done hits me. I've invited Sally to a football match and the woman is simply clueless when it comes to clothes.

1 p.m.

Dean walks in and nearly falls over the hoover. 'What the hell are you doing?' he says, as I rush around the place in hot-pants and a crop top, dusting and cleaning. I wouldn't say I was a natural at this – I've broken a vase and three glasses – but blimey it's good for the soul. I feel rejuvenated and refreshed. My frustration and anger are things of the past.

'Where is everyone?' he asks.

'I sacked them,' I reply simply. 'It's just you and me now, dear. Back to basics. We'll have to manage on our own.'

'What???? Without staff? What will we eat?'

'I admit, it's not going to be easy, and I think we'll be eating lots of takeaways until I get the hang of the toaster, but it could be good for us.'

'Er . . . no,' he says. 'Are you mad? Has all this stuff with your mother finally tipped you completely over the edge?'

I smile, sit him down, offer him a coffee, realise I don't know where the kettle is, so withdraw the offer of coffee and sit next to him. I explain about Mum not coming to see me when she said she would, the beautician messing up my appointment, and how I had to sack all the staff.

'That's not like you, love,' he says. 'And legally, aren't we supposed to give them warnings and stuff?'

'That's what I thought,' I confess. 'So I ended up paying them off by nearly twenty thousand pounds. I know it sounds a lot, but it was all I could think of to do.'

'Whaaaaaat?' he asks. 'What have you done that for? You've spent an absolute fortune and we still have no staff at all. Tracie, honey, I know you've been through a tough time, but that was simply ridiculous. Why didn't you call me?'

'I don't know.'

'What am I going to do now? How will I get to Paskia's school to watch her play?'

'I'll drive you,' I offer, largely because I want to do something good and nice for Dean. I couldn't bear it if he turned on me as well – it's like my whole entire life is falling apart here with everyone suddenly hating me. 'I'd like to watch Pask play football in any case.'

'Oh,' says Dean, flummoxed that I am prepared to utter the words Paskia Rose and football in the same sentence, let alone announce that I wish to watch her play. I tell him that I've invited Sally to come and watch and he smiles.

'Good,' he says. 'Come on then. We'll get some chips on the way.'

It's only then that I realise what I've done. Dean is bound to notice that the hire car hidden in the garage is not the same as the one he bought me which is currently still on vacation in Croydon. Happily, being Dean, he does no such thing. Indeed, so little notice does he take of cars that he chats all the way to the chip shop about what a good car it is and how pleased he is that he bought it for me.

We pull up at the school and I find I've had a rather sudden change of mind. I can't face this football after all. I can't face the people here, nor the cold muddiness of it all. I'll just go over, say hello to Paskia, then I need to go and hide somewhere. Maybe if I lie in the back of the car no one will see me? Although this will not be a pleasant experience, what with the awful vinegary smell now pervading the car from our lunch-on-the-run (I didn't eat any, you'll be pleased to hear, but Dean ate loads).

'Okay, love, let's go and support our superstar daughter,' says Dean, eating the last of the chips, scrunching up the paper and rubbing the back of his hand across his greasy lips. 'Let's see if she's gonna have the same style and sophistication as her old man.'

Dean leaps out of the car and I begin to clamber out, hoping no one can see me because the red micro-skirt has to be hitched right up to my waist before I can conduct this manoeuvre with any degree of effectiveness.

'Why, Tracie,' bellows Tarquin, one of the fathers – I've no idea which one is his daughter, but whoever she is, she came to play at ours one day and I recall him picking her up. He wasn't quite so friendly on that occasion, and Pask told me later that her friend said Tarquin had called us 'common'. He reaches out his hand to assist me in my clambering, in what is a rather gallant move, but the gentlemanly gesture loses some of its gloss when I catch him staring openly at my thighs. He's terribly upper-class, too much so to say anything smutty, but I know from the look in his piggy little eyes that he's thinking, 'Woof!'

'Darling, you're our local celebrity,' says a woman in a Barbour. (His wife? Do people still wear Barbour?) She looks inordinately pleased to see me. She's beaming and so is he, though his rosy-cheeked beam is more lascivious than welcoming. I just smile back and shrug as other parents come over and warmly shake my hand. I'm suddenly the one who everyone wants to meet. I don't think these parents have looked twice at me in the past, except, perhaps, to smirk at my attire. Now I'm the pretty girl at the party! I feel my black mood lifting – this is really quite nice.

'You're just a joy to read,' says a portly woman. Her voice is terribly shrill and quite annoying. 'So hysterical, my dear. A delight! I never take the *Daily Mail* but I have been doing so expressly to read your adorable words.'

I'm not very good at taking all this praise. Until I started doing the handbook I don't think anyone had praised me for anything . . . not since I drew that bunch of bananas in art when I was about eight and Mr Dagley told me they looked realistic. See – I can't have been praised too much over the intervening years if I remember that comment so vividly. I just don't know what to say when someone who's so much more intelligent than me and bound to be a better writer than me starts saying my columns are good. Do you say, 'Yes, they are, aren't they?', or do you tell the truth, which is, 'Gosh, thanks so much for saying that but I'm sure you're all just taking the mickey out of me. I'm sure you don't really read them, and if you did you'd probably think it was complete rubbish'? I don't know. That's why I find it hard. I just give a pinched smile and look around for Dean.

The woman is asking the growing crowd of people around us whether they have seen my articles.

'Yes,' they declare. 'Of course we have. Paskia Rose brings them into school and all the girls photocopy them. There's quite a flurry of activity around the secretary's office on a Monday morning, and the school are more than happy for the girls to photocopy them because your writing is so funny and adorable. We're really all proud of you.'

A warmth spreads right through me, despite the freezing temperatures. How lovely of Pask to take them into school. I never realised how proud she was of what I was doing. It strikes me that I've never really talked to her properly about it all. I think I'll take Pask out for the day – a Waggy day – maybe the spa or something. Just to give her a real insight into what it is to be a Wag, and where my inspiration for the columns comes from. For now, though, I need to find Dean, and there's no sign of him at all.

He must have run off while my fan club was assembling itself. What must all this be like for him? I feel quite sorry for him. One minute he's the main man, with the world at his boots, and everyone wanting to meet him. I was his little blonde – the essential accessory for the perfect footballer. Now, suddenly, without me really meaning it to, it's all changing. These people all want to meet me; I'm being offered hundreds of thousands of pounds to write a book; the TV shows keep calling; and I have to go out with scarves round my face in case the paparazzi are hovering. Meanwhile, poor Dean's stuck at a club he hates, and struggling to keep up with the training let alone work his way into the team. He must feel awful. I suppose I've never thought about how all this must be for him. Poor thing. It must be just terrible.

'Dean,' I shout. 'Dean. Where are you?'

The others watch as I stagger off across the grass in search of my husband, long pointy heels digging into the mud as I go.

'Isn't she a marvel?' they're all saying. 'Truly, she has the heart of a poet. The Chaucer of our times.'

'Deany?'

I find him on the far side of the pitch, of course, by which time my legs are coated in mud splatters and my shoes are ruined. He's standing next to Sally who, as I feared, has come dressed like a boy – wrapped in a big, shapeless jacket and with jeans and boots on. She and Dean are deep in conversation about tactics and field positions.

'This is the goal that Pask will be scoring in,' he says all enthusiastically. 'I've shown her some moves. I think she's gonna be great.'

'Hi Sally,' I say, and she gives me a big hug. Then I turn to my husband. 'Listen, Dean, I think you should be Pask's coach, and I think you should buy that pub you were talking about – the one with the dogs behind the bar, or whatever it was. I think you should do what makes you happy.'

'No, not dogs behind the bar,' he says with a chuckle. 'Dogs in the pub, you know – with their owners – great big black dogs lying by the fire while the men talk about the good old days and fart a lot.'

'Well, whatever,' I say, quite relieved that this pub appears to be being filled with men, in his head at least. It means that I won't be expected to go in there, and it means there'll be no lovely ladies in there to turn his gorgeous Brylcreemed head. 'You should do what you really want to do. I want you to be happy.'

'Whooooaaahhhh . . . here they come,' he says, pulling something out from his pocket. It's a rattle. Oh god, no. We're back in the 1970s all of a sudden. 'Here come the superstars! Hooray! Hooray! Hooray! Rattle! Rattle! Rattle!'

'Listen, I'm going to wait in the car. I'm a bit cold,' I say.

Dean moves to take off his jacket. I appreciate the thought, but it's a big, fat, puffed-up thing that would make me look about twenty stone, so I wouldn't wear it if the Ice Age suddenly kicked in and we all started freezing to death. 'No thanks,' I say, and blow him a kiss. 'I'll be in the car. See you later, Sal.'

10 minutes later

The strangest things can happen to a woman as she lurches through the mud on her way to the car. For example, she could fall in love. That's what just happened to me. Can you believe it? I don't mean in love like a man loves a woman, but in love in terms of discovering I love something. And you know what that something is? Watching my daughter play football. I'm sheltering between two large trees right now, mainly so I don't have to talk to a whole bunch of posh parents who keep telling me 'dahrling, you're insanely good', but also because I don't want anyone to see me in this state – with mud splattered all the way up my legs and tears running down my face.

That's right – tears. And I know what you're thinking – why are you crying, Trace? What is it with you at the moment, you daft moo? You always seem to be in tears! Well, the truth is that these are tears of joy and happiness. Seriously! It's not the fact that my mum is selling stories on me or that my entire staff have been taking the piss out of me that's reduced me to tears, it's the fact that Paskia is so good at football. I mean not just good, she's really good. She's scored three goals so far and ALL IN THE RIGHT NET. Every time she gets the ball, everyone cheers and shouts and the opposition parents mutter things like, 'Oh no, not her again.' More staggering than all this is the fact that I feel so incredibly proud of her. Seriously. So she's not like me, she doesn't like the things that I like – but that's okay, isn't it? In fact, it's great that she's gone off and built her own life and done what she wants to do, and it's doubly great that she's so bloody brilliant at it. I don't know the first thing about football, but three goals in twenty minutes? Come on . . . there's only twenty minutes in each half, so she's doing pretty well. Let's face it – we're talking Madonna here, aren't we? Madonna? Is that right? You know who I mean – the fat guy who uses his hands to score sometimes. Or is it Madaronna? Something like that.

Now they're standing around eating bits of orange for some reason, and the head teacher has come out to personally congratulate Pask. I'm right near where they're standing. It's funny to be here, unseen, watching my wonderfully talented daughter. 'Marvellous,' he is saying. He's just a foot away from me. 'Did your mother come to watch today? We're all dying to meet her.'

What? How embarrassing. How can they be dying to meet me?

'She's in the trees,' says Pask.

Fuck! How did she know I was here?

'Oh my god! It's Tracie Martin!' shout the girls, and they race over to me, excitement burning on their fresh young faces.

'I, like, read everything you ever write,' says one.

'It's so, like, cool. You're the best, man.'

Oh god. What to say?

'Mrs Martin, do come out of there,' says Mr Mallam, the sprightly head teacher, leaning over, shaking my hand and pulling me out of my little tree camp. 'Ladies and gentlemen, we have a celebrity in our midst,' he announces. 'May I introduce the leading newspaper columnist Tracie Martin?'

There are 'ooohhs' and 'aaahhhs' and a few bemused 'What was she doing in the trees?' Then a small clap starts, mounting into a full-scale and terribly unexpected round of applause.

I'm standing there – legs covered in mud, make-up all over my face from the crying, and my hair a tangled mess from the branches. 'Thank you, thank you,' I mutter, unsure what else to say.

'Would you like to say a few words?' asks Mr Mallam. 'It would be lovely if you would.'

No, of course I wouldn't. I can't think of anything in the world that I'd like to do less, to be honest. I'd rather sit down and eat all my own hair, or have my bikini line waxed in front of them all. I'd rather dance topless around the pitch than make a small speech – I can't think of anything, anything, anything worse. The trouble is – he's done what posh people do – he's asked me in front of people, thereby taking away my option to decline.

'Go on,' those nearest are saying. 'Go on, Tracie.'

I feel like the world's closing in on me. Not only do I not want to give the speech, I don't want to be even standing here in front of everyone with my muddy legs and my messy make-up. Then, suddenly, a moment of pure genius – the referee blows the whistle and announces that it's time for the second half.

'Oh no, oh, what a shame. Oh damn. Never mind,' I say. 'Maybe some other time?'

'Yes, of course, Mrs Martin,' Mr Mallam says. 'In fact, why don't you present the MVP award at the end?'

'Yes, sure,' I say, thinking how appropriate it is to be asked to present an award for Most Visible Pantyline, and how lovely that they should have such an award. Too many people fail to appreciate the beauty of a big, visible pantyline beneath tight clothing. I think larger ladies, in particular, suit this look.

'Am I looking for big knickers or just the line itself?' I ask.

'Sorry?' he says quizzically, as if my comment is entirely inappropriate. It was him who brought up the talk of most visible pantylines, not me.

'Knickers?' I shout. He walks away at quite a speed so I head back to my little tree camp. Funny man.

Sunday, 25 November
Midday

I went to the gym with Michaela this morning. No, don't drop this in horror and look away in anger thinking, That Tracie Martin has really sold out. I didn't *do* anything in there, like exercising, and I was reeking of alcohol from the night before. In fact it's not so much that I went to the gym as passed through it . . . on the way to the spa. It turns out that gyms are ridiculous places, with all these people running on the spot and cycling to get nowhere.

I'd planned to have a day at the spa with Pask, but she said, 'Mum, I can't face it,' and point-blank refused, so I've come with Mich instead, to catch up on everything that's happened.

We walked past all these people in trainers (the only trainers I possess have four-inch heels, like the ones Posh wore to throw that ball to the LA Dodgers cricket team or whatever they were). Then it was time for the most vigorous part of the day – getting changed. I chose to wear my new gold cut-away one-piece (it demands a serious bikini wax to get away with it – happily I'm a serious bikini wax sort of a girl). The swimming costume is halter-neck, with a large gold chain holding it in place, and it also has gold studs up the sides and diamantés round the neckline. I wore it with lovely high, strappy sandals and three ankle chains on each leg.

I was all set to have a lovely relaxing time, but unfortunately that wasn't to be, as Mich spent the entire time muttering on and on about Andre and how she really liked him. I don't mind at all being a sounding board for friends in distress, and obviously I expected the subject of Andre to crop up once or twice, but – honestly – she didn't stop talking about him. I find it really hard now because my mother's at the centre of the whole bloody thing, even though – apparently – she has denied it constantly. My mother left a message on Mich's answer-phone, saying that Andre's mobile had never been in her house, and that I had clearly planted it there. Hello? The thing is, I found the phone in the flat and didn't show anyone – not even Simon – so it's my word against hers. Mich believes me, but my mother can be very convincing and I'm sure Mich has moments when she wonders whether it's actually me who's having an affair with Andre. Oh god. It's such a mess.

'Have you heard anything from your mum? Or anything at all from Andre?' she asks. 'I just need to know what's going on.'

When I tell her that I honestly don't know anything she sinks into three and a half minutes of deep depression. She ends up storming out of the sauna twice during that period, much to the distress of those crowded in there hoping to do some sweating if only someone wouldn't keep opening the door and letting all the cold air in.

'Come on, love,' says some guy. 'Are you in or out?'

'Ask her,' screams Mich, pointing aggressively towards me. 'She's the one whose slag of a mother slept with my boyfriend, stole his phone and abused me.'

'Ooooooaaaaahhhhh,' says the entire sauna crowd. Bet they've never seen anything like this in here before.

They turn to me, awaiting my reply, but I'm not all that talented in the quick-comeback department, so I just smile in an embarrassed fashion, and I can tell they're very disappointed in me. They feel I've really let them down. The thought of doing so pains me momentarily, until I get a grip on myself and remember that it's just a bunch of sweaty blokes and I really shouldn't be bothering myself over them.

I sit and look down at my hands, away from their faces, and they're soon all chatting again, so I can go back to my original worry – before the worry over Mich's depression followed by my fears at having upset the sauna men. My original and enduring worry concerns saunas themselves. I'm always convinced that the glue holding my extensions in place will melt in the heat, and the extensions will fall out in the shower. You see, there was a guy in the sauna once who was reading a book, and he said the pages kept falling out.

'Why?' I'd asked brightly.

'Because the glue melts,' he'd replied with a smile.

'Aaarghhhhhh . . . my hair!' I'd responded, which, I have to accept, is not a logical or predictable response. He certainly didn't seem to think so.

'You what?' he'd said. But it was all over for me – I went running out of there, clutching my roots and praying that my hair wouldn't all come out. I'd rung my hairdresser straightaway. 'Don't worry,' she'd said, explaining that the extensions-falling-out-in-the-sauna rumour was a bit of an urban myth, like fake boobs exploding in aeroplanes.

'Really?' I said, with considerable delight. 'So I can go on aeroplanes, too.' Normally it takes us days to drive across Europe. Thank god Luton have never made the Champions Cup.

HOW TO BEHAVE IN THE GYM –
IMPORTANT POINTS OF ETIQUETTE

Ooooh, be careful my lovely Wag friends. The gym can be a terribly masculine place. If you go there and breathe in too much testosterone, or use the weights too much, you'll grow a moustache, or a deep voice, or even muscles like Madonna, perish the thought. You need to avoid any piece of machinery that looks as if it would attack you, given half a chance. Any Wag worth her pierced navel would, as a rule, be best off in life avoiding interaction with any kind of machinery at all – washing machine, dishwashing machine – if the title of an appliance has 'machine' at the end, you should be contemplating the number of staff you need to employ to operate it.

So, back to the gym . . . Clearly you should wear pink Lycra in the gym at all times (leggings and crop tops, or a natty cat-suit). Go for a hair band and those little socks with pom-poms on the back if you can (pink pom-poms, of course). Trainers need to look permanently brand-new, so if you find yourself using them for more than walking around and flirting with the personal trainers, then you need to buy new ones after every visit. I would, though, suggest that walking around and flirting with the personal trainers (if done properly) will be more than enough exercise for you.

If you want to get slimmer, you are in completely the wrong place – you need to be visiting a cosmetic surgeon, not a gym. The other thing you can do is to leave your gym bag lying around, because I was once told that if your gym bag is stolen with your trainers and your gym clothing in it, when the thief wears the kit to exercise it is you who will get the benefit. You take the risk, of course, that the thief, or the person to whom the thief hands the kit, will build you a body that you're simply not happy with. But if you currently have a body that you don't like one bit, you may choose to take that risk.

Saturday, 1 December
3 p.m.

Dean is now so completely fed up of things at the club that he hasn't gone to watch the match today. He's sitting here, counting on his fingers how many years it's been since he didn't go to watch a match on a Saturday. He's run out of fingers and toes, so now he's using mine, and we're halfway through my second hand before he begins to feel he's at the right number.

'I should just leave,' he's saying. 'What I'm really enjoying is helping out with Paskia's team. I don't like Luton Town. I'm just fed up there.'

I understand where he's coming from, but I really can't encourage him to give up his football, as where would that leave me? From a selfish point of view, it's really nice having him at home, though – I do like that bit. It's a shame I can't be a Wag without him having to play football. That would be ideal. This morning it's been just the two of us, sitting on the sofa with *MTV* on in the background. *Footballers' Cribs* was on, so you get to see all these fab houses – beautifully done out. It's all making me wish we had a gym and a swimming pool at home . . . which makes me think of Mum and what she's got in her house. She's not even called, or attempted to see me since she failed to come round for coffee. Mindy's called a few times – leaving messages inviting me out on girls' nights because her friends will be impressed that she knows someone in the papers, but she always says 'Don't mention it to anyone down the club' so I never return the calls.

Paskia's gone to football, and the new squadron of cleaning staff don't start until the beginning of January. We've had takeaways galore over the past few weeks, because I remembered how hard cooking was as soon as I started. I have a cleaning company that comes in three times a week and a lady who does ironing and washing, but the rest of the time I'm all on my own doing everything for the family.

I'm quite enjoying the peace and quiet until the live-in staff start, though. I feel like Dean and I have been through a lot, and now things are great. Paskia is our pride and joy, she's even forgiven me for presenting her with the Most Visible Pantyline Award – not realising it should have been Most Valuable Player. Dean and I have talked at length about the future and, as he says, though he's still in love with football, it seems football's not in love with him. He's going to buy himself a pub. And do you know what? I don't even mind.

Friday, 14 December
2 p.m.

I hate this. I don't mean that I hate coming to the football – I like that a lot, I'm starting to discover – I just hate watching the football outside, standing up. I like supporting Paskia Rose, but god, it's so awful standing around on these cold pitches. I'm thrilled that Dean seems happy again, but I just don't like standing in the mud – but is that too odd? If I liked standing in the mud I would have become a farmer or something.

In the past, my role at football was always sitting in the posh seats with the other Wags, talking about hair, make-up and handbags. Now I'm down and dirty with the mums and dads at the school and none of them has a decent handbag or a pair of shoes worth talking about. They're simply not the sort of people you can rush up to and announce, 'I had a fabulous bikini wax today.' Trust me – I've tried!

'Dahling,' comes a voice. 'Remember me? Petunia Smethers-Kingston. My daughter Augutini is in the team. She's great friends with Paskia Rose.'

'Hi,' I say, feeling more uncomfortable than ever. I have no idea who Augutini is. The name sounds like a cocktail. The woman starts withering on about my pieces in the *Daily Mail* and she's heard that I'm writing a book and how there's a book in all of us, and she's sure mine will be just great.

'Where are you with it at the moment?' she asks, and I tell her.

'Literally nowhere.'

She laughs, so I laugh too, and what a jolly sight this must be – two mothers laughing gaily as their girls run around on the football pitch. The hero status I seem to have here because of my columns is terribly baffling. I'm definitely getting more accustomed to it, and I'm not quite so embarrassed when complete strangers rush up to me, but I don't think I'll ever get used to it completely.

It's working out really well for Dean as Paskia's football coach. He says that she could be very good, and that she has a lot of natural talent. He's very keen to be the one to nurture it, and, boy, has he thrown himself into it with unparalleled commitment. He's even got the sponsorship and marketing people at the club to help him find a sponsor for the school team, and he's organising for an American team to come over at the end of February on tour, to show the girls how good they could become. I have to say this whole thing about American girls playing football has thrown me completely. I had no idea the girls over there behaved like that. I thought they were too busy with their beauty pageants and cheerleading.

Luton Town club has been astonishingly helpful – mainly, I think, because they genuinely really like Dean and want to help him – but I know that some of the guys there are relieved to have got Dean off their backs and that he has something to occupy his time. He used to be hanging around at training sessions, unsure what to do with himself. Now it's like he has a mission, a purpose. Having links between the club and America for future transfer possibilities also appeals to the club. So, Dean's gone from being something of a pain to a coach with real potential, offering a link to America. The girls that are coming over are a junior side with the LA Raiders and they're linked to a school side in Los Angeles.

The tour has become Dean's reason for living. Now he's desperate to get his girls up to standard so they're not embarrassed when the American hotshots descend.

'What's that?' asks Rupert Smethers-Kingston, wandering along beside me. The two of us look over to the bushes.

'It sounds like there's someone in there,' I say.

'Leave it to me,' says Rupert in his terribly assertive way, and he moves over to investigate. It turns out his investigation techniques involve bashing the tree rather viciously with an umbrella.

'Everything awright?' Dean has come to join us and I realise that the match must have finished.

'Yes, fine,' says Rupert, moving away from the tree and shaking Dean's hand. He points at the tree with his stripy umbrella. 'That's sorted the little rodent out. Now, how did our girls do?'

Saturday, 15 December
Another morning, another early call from a man I used to call my friend.

'Simon, it's six a.m.,' I shout into the wrong side of the phone. I have my eye mask on and can't see a thing. 'If you cared for me you would not ring before midday.'

'It's not six a.m.,' he says defensively, sounding slightly offended. 'It's eight thirty a.m. I've been waiting since six a.m. to call you. I've been sitting here like an idiot waiting for the right time to ring, so don't have a go at me.'

I remove my eye mask and glance at the clock. He's right. It's 8.30 a.m. I lose all track of time when Dean doesn't get up in the mornings. He used to be jumping out of bed by 7 a.m. on a Saturday, so I'd know roughly what time it was. Now the only time he bounds out of bed is when he's coaching Paskia's team or planning their tactical strategies, and that doesn't involve much Saturday work, thank goodness.

'Sorry,' I say to Simon. 'I had no idea what time it was.'

'It doesn't matter. Can you talk?'

Dean has his eyes closed but I can sense he's awake.

'Hang on. I'll get out of bed.'

'No, I mean, can we meet to talk?'

'Why, what's happened?' I ask tentatively. 'Nothing bad, is it?'

I really don't need anything else that's bad to happen in my life right now. I feel like I've been through so much and have come through it all.

Mum and I simply aren't talking, but that's fine. It seems like the only sensible thing to happen after all she said about me in that article. Having her out of the way has been far less painful than I ever imagined it would be. I guess I have finally discovered what is really important. Dean's realised what a horror she is too, which I'm quite pleased about. I hated the way he bowed and scraped and fell to his knees whenever she was in the room.

I heard from Suzzi that Mum is furious with Dean for not returning her calls, but neither of us cares. He just deletes all her messages, which must make her madder than ever. I can't go down the club any more because I get mobbed by fans of my column, so Suzzi reports back and updates me. She's been taking her baby daughter, Beauty Blossom Bouquet, down there, and dressing her all in pink. She's going to get the little girl's ears pierced next week, which is really sweet.

I'm happy not to be going down the club for the time being. I'm still a Wag, I'm just a virtual, remote sort of a Wag. Very twenty-first century of me, I think.

Anyway, Dean and I are really close these days and spend loads of time together, which is great. In fact, the only person I feel I need to make amends with, after everything that's happened, is Nell.

I've talked to Dean about it all, and how on a whim I invited her to come and stay at Christmas, then Mum made me cancel it. I know that Nell bears me no malice for the whole thing because she's told me, but I really would like to make it clear to her that I did and do want her to come for Christmas. Mum made me change things, but I genuinely want her and the two other mad witches to come and brighten up our Christmas Day. Dean thinks that's a great idea and we're planning to pay a surprise visit to her tomorrow – me, Dean and Pask. We're going to take the three of them out for Sunday lunch, buy them lots of sweet sherry, and tell them it's open house this Christmas. See what I mean – things are really looking up for me right now. I feel like I've rediscovered my family. So, that's why the thought of Simon charging in with bad news is particularly unwelcome.

'I'd rather talk you through it all,' he repeats.

'Oh god,' I reply.

'Look. Where can we meet?'

I would suggest Sunnyside but I want to save that for tomorrow when we turn up for our surprise visit. It will take some of the gloss off it if I arrive today with Simon in tow.

'Nell said we could meet at Sunnyside any time we wanted,' says Simon.

'I'd rather not,' I reply. 'Anyway, when did she say that? Have you seen her?'

'Yes, I've been going round there to help mend the heater,' he replies.

'What?'

'She asked me . . . that time I met you there before. She said did I think I could make the heater give out any more warmth . . . Poor woman – she's freezing in there.'

'She's not,' I say. 'Have you felt how warm it is? It's not possible for a room to be any warmer.'

'Well, it is now,' says Simon. 'I removed the temperature gauge so now it's always boiling hot. She loves it. She's much happier when it's scorching. Ethel and Gladys have asked if I can do theirs.'

'Right.'

'Anyway, we could meet there.'

'No,' I insist. 'Come here.'

He's found my dad. That's what Simon was so keen to talk to me about. My father has been traced and he's living in America.

'Fuck!' I say. And I realise that 'fuck' seems to be my new favourite word. I've had a lot of cause to utter it recently.

Simon nods his agreement.

'How did you find him?'

'I know people,' says Simon, before being less evasive and confessing that the letters we found at Mum's had old addresses on them, and his new job on the *Guardian* has introduced him to a load of people who helped him, therefore tracking down my father wasn't too difficult.

'What's he like?' I ask.

Simon shrugs. He says he doesn't know much about him except that his name is Nigel Harris and he seems to be running a successful IT company with offices dotted across the west coast of America. He has no criminal record. He's fifty-eight years old, is married and has three children and six grandchildren.

'Half brothers and sisters . . .' I declare. The thought is so appealing. The idea that Paskia has aunts and uncles and cousins. It's unbelievable.

'Does he know you've been asking questions?' I say.

Simon says that no, he doesn't, but he wonders whether, armed with the precise information about him, I should consider going through an agency that will contact him on my behalf.

'But . . . he's in America.'

'Well, yes. But you could talk – email or whatever – just get the contact started up between the two of you, then it may be that one of you will be willing to make the journey. I think he must be desperate to see you. Remember, he's been sending letters, cards and financial support to you for thirty years. He's probably wondering why you've made no effort to get in touch. He'll have no idea that you didn't know of his existence.'

Simon's so wise.

'Can you come with me to see the people who help you to locate missing parents?'

'Of course I can,' says Simon, and we hug – a big friendly hug that seems to go on and on until Dean's footsteps can be heard tip-tapping down the hallway, and Simon pulls away from me as if he has been stung by a wasp.

'Right, must be off,' he announces as Dean walks in. The two men shake hands very formally and Simon heads for the door. 'We'll talk soon,' he says.

'Shame he had to leave,' Dean says when the front door has closed. 'He seems like a nice bloke. I didn't think so at first – what with the hair and that – but he's all right.'

'He is,' I agree.

'But now it's just the two of us,' says Dean, taking my hand, and I decide that the news about my father can wait. 'Shall we switch off our phones and go back to bed . . . for the day?'

This is *definitely* one of the benefits of Dean not playing football.

Sunday, 16 December

I think I may have to take the phone out of the bedroom. Simon seems utterly obsessed with calling me at dawn.

'Mmmmmwhatsitnow?' I say.

'Oh god,' he replies.

I pull off the eye shade and see that it says 8.50 a.m. on the clock.

'Oh god is right,' I say. 'Why would you ring me at eight-fifty a.m. on a Sunday morning? Why would anyone do that to another human being?'

'Oh god,' he says again, and I realise that something's happened.

'My father!' I declare.

'No,' he replies.

'My mother!' I declare.

'No,' he replies.

'Paskia Rose?'

'No,' he replies.

'Give me a fucking clue,' I hear myself cry.

'The *Sunday Journal*,' he says. 'They're saying that Dean is having an affair with a schoolgirl. It's your mum again. They've got pictures and everything – I'm so sorry, mate. Angie is talking about an affair she had with Burt Reynolds and about her disappointment with the way Dean treats you. She can't believe that he's sleeping with girls practically the same age as his daughter. Sorry, Tracie. I'm just telling you what it says in the paper.'

'Burt Reynolds? What are you talking about – Burt Reynolds?'

'Never mind that – Dean is having an affair – that's the most important thing. They've got pictures.'

I slide out of bed, trying desperately not to wake Dean. If he opens his stupid eyes right now there's every chance I'll poke pins into them. He's messed everything up. Stupid idiot. Dean, of all people. I thought he was different to other footballers. I should have known it wouldn't last – infidelity and footballers go together like pink lipstick and orange foundation.

'Didn't they call you and ask for a comment?' says Simon, and I explain that our phones were off all day.

'What about Rupert Sebastian?'

'Rupert Sebastian doesn't have our home number. Simon, you're the only person who's got it. Rupert always calls the mobile, and that's off.'

'Oh, gosh,' he says, sounding inordinately flattered. Then he pulls himself together. 'Do you want to meet?'

I tell him that I do. I think I need Simon to make sense of all this.

'Why would he?' I ask, the tears filling my eyes as I contemplate a future without Dean – nothing but emptiness, Waglessness and solitude. A single mother, like Mum was. A poor former Wag whose husband has been unfaithful, whose mother has been disloyal, and whose father is on the other side of the world.

'I don't know, sweetheart,' says Simon softly. It's unusual to hear him use such terms of endearment. 'He must be mad. Where shall we meet? Shall I come there?'

'No!' I cry. It seems that the Sunnyside Sheltered Accommodation for the Elderly is the obvious place for a rendezvous, but first I want to see the paper for myself. I tell Simon that I'll see him there at 11 a.m.

'Why eleven?' he asks. 'Don't you want to meet sooner?'

'I'm not dressed,' I say. 'In fact, I haven't even worked out what I'm going to wear yet. Eleven will be cutting it fine.'

12.30 p.m. (Yes, I do know that I'm an hour and a half late – it took me longer than I expected to choose what to wear because I had to get my outfit just right. I searched for the picture of Princess Di when she appeared before the world's media for the first time after hearing about Prince Charles's relationship with Camilla Parker-Bowles. I have to say that I do look very good in my tight velvet cocktail dress and regal-looking choker. It might not be entirely appropriate for where I'm going and the time of day, but you need to get revenge outfits spot-on for them to work. Not that it worked for Di because she never got Charles back. Oh god. Was this outfit a mistake? Do I have time to go home and change?)

I'm in a taxi heading for Sunnyside. This might be the worst day of my life. It's enough that my mother has turned on me so dramatically, but another thing entirely to discover that Dean has betrayed me. That's something I could never have predicted. It's something I've never even considered. Even in my worst nightmares I just always felt that whatever else happened in life – if there was a nuclear disaster, a world war – or worse, if I lost all my hair or something – one thing could always be guaranteed: there'd always be Dean by my side. He's my saviour, my rock.

I'm too sad for tears, and this is nothing to do with worrying about eye make-up smudges or anything. This is because I have a feeling right down deep in my stomach, extending down into my soul . . . a feeling that my life is simply not going to be worth living any more.

The thing is – the paper has pictures. Dean has his arms round a young girl, then he's kissing another girl (slightly older, I'm relieved to see, but she's still young). He takes her overnight bag from her at some hotel and leads her to the lifts to take her up to his room. It's awful. Mum's quoted in the piece and it says that neither me nor Dean were available for comment. They didn't try too hard, did they? They obviously didn't want to let anything we might have said ruin their story.

The thing is, it's not even all that comforting for me to blame the newspaper, because they're reporting the facts and, unfortunately, there can be no question about this. I've tried to rationalise it, think it through and explain it. But they have photos. They have proof. He did it. It's devastating but there's no question. My husband is a cheat. The horrible thing is the age of the girl. She must be about eleven. About Paskia Rose's age. Have you ever heard of anything more disgusting? I really don't think I have. Not ever.

12.45 p.m.

I arrive at Sunnyside to find Simon standing outside, looking bereft.

'Sorry,' I say. 'I just wasn't in the mood for rushing.'

'Where's Dean?' he asks.

'Still sleeping. He has no idea about the piece. Why didn't you go in?'

'I've been ringing the bell but there's no answer,' he tells me.

'I'll call her,' I say, and I switch my phone on. That's a mistake. 'You have 806,894,568,590,860,456,890 million messages,' it says. All of them, I'm sure, from the *Sunday Journal*.

I call Nell's number but there's no answer.

'We'll wait,' I suggest, moving to get out of the taxi.

'No!' says Simon. 'There are photographers on the other side. Stay in the taxi.'

'I'll have to charge you,' says the driver, so I agree that he will be paid per hour to stay with us for the day.

Simon gets in and we slouch down and I start to tell Simon all about my love for Dean and how life simply wouldn't be worth living without him.

'I always thought that if Dean had an affair, I'd use the opportunity to get myself photographed looking wronged and mournful, but I can't even face ringing *Heat* – that's how depressed I am.

'You know, Simon – this is about my love for Dean, not about my love of being a Wag. I feel strangely disloyal saying that, as if the Holy Saint of Wags might hear me and banish me from the Order, and subject me to a life free of miniskirts, boots, tans and crop tops. But it's true. Right now, in this moment, I don't care if Dean never plays football again – I still want to be with him. My love for him is greater than my love for Cricket. There – I've said it. There is no greater love than that.'

Simon has a strange look on his face – I'm unsure as to whether it's utter bemusement or the fact that he's entranced and quite moved by my declarations of love. Whichever it is, there's no question that the constant bleeping from my phone – informing me of the barrage of messages on it, just waiting to be picked up – is ruining the moment a little.

'Just play them,' he says. 'Or I will, if you want.'

I decide that 'I will, if you want' is the way forward and I hand him the phone. There's much shoulder-lifting, screwing up of his face and raising of eyebrows. A few 'Oooohhhhhs' at the pressure techniques being employed by the reporter, whose voice he's listening to, then an 'Oh no.'

'What?'

'Tracie, Nell's been taken ill,' he says. 'One of these messages last night is urging you to call Sunnyside.'

'Oh no. God no. I couldn't bear it if anything happened to Nell.'

Simon scribbles down the number for the warden and calls her from my phone.

'Nell's in hospital,' he says. He's quite ashen. 'We need to call Dean.'

It's Simon who ends up ringing my wayward husband and telling him that he needs to head for Luton General as quickly as he can. 'The Roses Ward,' says Simon. Then, as an afterthought, he says, 'Have you seen the *Sunday Journal*? If not, I'd get yourself a copy.'

We zoom round the outside of the nursing home and off towards the hospital. The men with the cameras slung unsubtly round their necks see us and make to follow us. You know what – I don't care. Let them photograph all they want and write all they want about me and my family. All I want right now is for Nell to be okay. I sit there, saying silent prayers to a god in whom I do not believe. I make promises to the sky, telling someone, anyone, that I'll always be good, always look after people, never be selfish, and always be kind if they would just, just make Nell be okay. I'll even forsake nail extensions, dye my hair brown and go for days without make-up, if only she'll get better. Ooooo . . . hang on. I'm not sure about that last one.

'We're here,' says the driver, and I clamber out, running into the hospital and rushing for the ward. Simon is in hot pursuit as we chase along the corridors, shouting to the nurse to tell us where she is. We were told bed four on the phone, but there's no bed four. 'Bed four!' I scream. 'Where's bed four?'

Two nurses come up to us and a doctor walks slowly down the corridor towards us.

'Where's bed four?'

'Calm down, madam,' says the nurse.

'Bed four,' I scream with all my might. The morning's horrors are combining within me. This is the physical manifestation of the pain I'm suffering. Dean and Nell. Not Dean and Nell. Why those two?

'BED FOUR!!!' I'm crying, screaming and sobbing hysterically now.

'Bed four is round the corner,' says the doctor. He takes my arm and leads me to sit down but that's the last thing I want to do.

'I need to see her,' I say. 'Let me see her. Take me to her.'

'Listen to me,' says the doctor. 'She's gone into intensive care. She has a small hole in her heart. She's very weak. We're trying to see what we can do.'

'Sew it up,' I announce, all my thorough knowledge of intricate cardio-surgery displaying itself before the world. I love *Casualty*. 'Just sew it up.'

'We can't do that,' he is saying patiently, as if he's thought about the option I presented but has to dismiss it. 'She's far too weak to operate on. She needs to be more stable.'

I look round and see that Simon has disappeared.

'I'm all alone,' I say to this kindly man. 'If Nell goes, that's it.'

'We're doing all we can,' he says, desperate not to commit himself to a prognosis or a stab at what sort of recovery she might make. 'I promise you, there is nothing more that I can do.'

Then, the sound of footsteps. Simon is running up the corridor with Dean next to him.

'I've told them on reception not to let the paparazzi in,' says Simon, as the doctor looks on in alarm, wondering, I'm sure, who the little old lady in the bright green tracksuit is that the tabloids are chasing her.

'You two need to talk,' says Simon.

'Do we?' asks the doctor.

'Not you – these two,' says Simon, motioning between Dean and me. Dean is as white as a sheet. Tough. He deserves everything he gets.

'This way to the waiting room,' says the doctor, pointing to the right. 'I will come and tell you as soon as I have further news.'

This is not the way I would have pictured it happening, but I am forced to confront my husband about his very public two-timing of me in a very small and very hot waiting room at Luton General Hospital in front of two old ladies in pea-green tracksuits and a bearded writer on his hands and knees as he attempts to crank up the heating to terrifying levels.

Ethel and Gladys have been here all night. Dean is relieved to hear they were given beds, but he's still destroyed that he could not be here with Nell. I'd feel sorry for him if he weren't a child-abusing, two-timing pervert.

'This is all lies,' he says, sweeping his hand across the *Sunday Journal*. 'You know who this is, don't you?' He indicates the pretty girl who's smiling up at him as he wraps his arm around her. 'It's Emily. She's in the football team. These pictures must have been taken at a training session. Someone must have been hiding in the bushes and taken them.'

I snatch the paper off him and look more closely. The girl is wearing a white top very similar to the school's one.

'But what about this?' I indicate the older girl – she must be about sixteen – and the way he is carrying her bag for her and leading her to the lifts at the hotel in Luton Town Centre. 'Talk me through that one, Mr Clever Trousers.'

'Yes,' says Ethel, rather unhelpfully. 'Talk us all through that one.'

Dean looks around the room and shakes his head. Simon looks up and as he catches sight of the anger on Dean's face he knocks the radiator with the spanner and water begins to spurt upwards in an almighty whoosh. Simon screams and jumps back and the two old ladies laugh uproariously.

'This is Sandra,' Dean says.

'Oh, well, that's okay then,' I say sarcastically, while throwing cushions in the direction of Simon's small water fountain.

'Thanks,' says Simon, desperately trying to replace the valve while mopping up the worst of the spillage with the cushions.

'Sandra,' says Dean, raising his voice to be heard properly over the commotion, 'is the student teacher who is acting as liaison officer for the American trip. I met her at the hotel so we could check it was all right for the girls to stay in when they come over. She brought a bag of shirts for me to take down the club and get them signed so we can auction them off. The shirts were in the bag. I took it off her, that's all. Then we went through to the coffee bar just the other side of the lifts. I don't understand what the problem is?'

'So you didn't have an affair?'

'No,' shouts Dean. 'No, I didn't. I never would, never could. I love you, you silly cow. I'd never do anything to hurt you.'

'Ahhhh . . . .' say the old ladies, and they break into a round of applause.

Neither Dean nor I are sure what to do at this point. Dean appears to kind of bow, whereas I feel myself go bright red and look back down at the picture. The more I look at it, the more I can see that it was taken at training. I can even picture where it was – just near the trees where I hid that time before Mr Mallam dragged me out to present that Most Visible Pantyline Award.

'I don't believe this,' I say to Dean. 'I thought my life was over.'

'You nutter,' he says, wrapping his arms around me and prompting another outburst of spontaneous applause. 'I'm gonna be here forever.'

Suddenly, the clouds have lifted. All we need now is the chance to see Nell and tell her that we love her, everything is fine, and we want her and the others to come for Christmas.

'I can't wait until we can talk to Nell and tell her to come for Christmas,' I say to Dean.

'I've got a better idea,' says Dean. 'Let's ask her if she wants to come and live with us.'

'Oh yes, oh yes,' I cry. 'Can we? That would be so great.'

'Of course,' says Dean, and I know that everything's going to be okay.

3 p.m.

We're still waiting for word on Nell. The photographers are still outside, and the two old ladies are still sitting here, slowly driving us all nuts. Gladys is threatening to do a moony for the waiting paparazzi, the thought of which has made Dean go a rather horrible green colour that almost matches Nell's tracksuit.

'Na, don't do that, love. Please don't,' he says beseechingly.

She looks rather put out. 'You wouldn't be saying that if I was seventy-five years younger. The men used to adore me when I was a young thing.'

'Christ,' I say, before I can stop myself. The idea that Gladys is coping with being seventy-five years past her best is quite a horrific one. Imagine looking in the mirror every morning knowing that you were once a looker who had the boys all chasing after you, and being greeted by the sight of endless wrinkles and leathery skin.

I tend to think of myself as being young(ish!) and of them as being old. I don't think that once they were young and pretty with the world at their feet, in the same way that I don't concede I'm ever going to be their age. No matter how many times people say to me that life is a journey, I, like everyone else, am stuck in the present and slightly looking to the past for inspiration, advice and lessons learned. Really, I suppose, it's the future that's important, and I'm going to have to learn to accept that if I'm lucky enough to have a future it's sure as hell going to be full of wrinkles, leathery skin, dodgy hips and clickerty-clackerty false teeth.

'Everything all right in here?' asks a kindly nurse, as Simon throws himself upon the evidence of his makeshift plumbing efforts and Gladys takes her seat again, having failed to carry out the threatened moony.

'How's Nell?' asks Dean.

'She's comfortable,' says the nurse. 'But not out of danger.'

As a catch-all description, covering all possible outcomes, I have to say this is pretty good.

'Can I see her?' asks Dean.

'Soon, I'm sure,' says the nurse.

Outside the window there's quite a circus of photographers and journalists. At the door to the waiting room a small crowd of elderly and sickly patients has gathered, intrigued to discover who in the hospital has caused all this fuss.

'We've seen the television,' shouts one rather deranged-looking patient, before she's led away back down the ward. Dean jumps up and switches on the television set, which is sitting high up in the corner of the room. It's a surreal moment when the anchorman goes over to Susan Walker live outside Luton Hospital.

'The information we have is that Tracie Martin, the columnist and TV personality, has beaten up her husband who was exposed as a love rat in this morning's *Sunday Journal*. He's been so badly beaten that he is now in a critical condition. He's described by hospital officials as being "comfortable, but not out of danger". We'll bring you more information as soon as we have it.'

There's something surreal about sitting in a waiting room with two little old ladies as the woman you love most in the world lays on a hospital bed, critically ill, while every minute is inaccurately broadcast to the nation. It's utterly and madly surreal. We need a new word for surreal.

'Hello. Is Dean Martin here?' asks the kindly doctor, the one who spoke to me when I first arrived.

'That's me,' says Dean.

'Can I have a word?' he says. He looks very serious; I wonder whether they're planning to operate. I hope, if they are, that I can go in and see Nell first. I just desperately want to tell her that she can pack her things and leave the Sunnyside Sheltered Accommodation for good. I'm dying to tell her that her future is with us. We'll prepare her a nice room in the house and she can be part of our lovely, warm and happy family.

'You come too, Trace,' says Dean as the doctor leads us off to a small anteroom. As he walks in, the two nurses in there look up, see us and leave. I think that's when I first realise something might be seriously wrong.

'I'm sorry,' says the doctor. 'Really. I'm dreadfully sorry. We did all we could to save her, but we lost her. She slipped away peacefully and quietly. I was holding her hand. It was quick and it was painless. I'm so dreadfully sorry.'

Monday, 17 December

HOW TO BE THE GRANDMOTHER OF A WAG

It's vitally important for every Wag to have family who reflect her social position. It is difficult enough creating the right Wag image. The last thing you need is some grandmother coming along in a neat little caramel-coloured cardigan with clip-on earrings and a powder-puffed face to mess it all up. Grandmothers have a tendency to wear brown and dark cream. When they go out somewhere more formal, they may wear navy. Clearly, these sorts of fashion crimes need to be stamped out urgently if you are to avoid being made a fool of. Navy is only suitable for sailors and police officers, and then it doesn't look good, just 'suitable'. Grandmothers should be encouraged to break with tradition, throw caution to the wind and adopt ridiculous Tammy Wynette-style hair. They should wear ridiculous velour pea-green tracksuits, preferably ones they got free from the bingo, and they should appear everywhere with their mates, as though they are fourteen-year-old girls out on the pull, because that's what they need to be, in their heart-of-hearts – teenage girls hoping to have some fun, not wanting to hurt anyone, and looking utterly ridiculous in the process. The more ridiculous your grandmother looks, the more she will confirm your ultimate status as a Wag of discernment and stature. Grandmothers are an important accessory. They should be cherished, valued and protected.

Thursday, 20 December
10 a.m.

This was not how I had planned the run-up to Christmas. I'd hoped to be sitting at home this morning, watching Nell have her first couple of sherries and telling me about the war.

'You don't know you're born, you don't . . .'

It takes two drinks before the war stories start, so we always have a bit of a joke about whether to give her a second sherry.

'You can have it,' we say, 'as long as the bloody stories don't start.'

She promises faithfully not to take us all on a guided tour through wartime Luton, but in the end she takes just one sip of that second glass and she's away.

'You lot. You're so lucky . . .'

'Uh-oh, here we go,' we say.

Or should I say 'said' – it's all past tense now, isn't it?

'She felt no pain,' Dean keeps saying, and I feel like shaking him.

'No, but I do. I feel more pain than I've ever felt in my life before. I feel pain that she had no idea what future she would have had. She had no idea that we were going to invite her to live with us. She had no idea how loved she was.'

'She knew,' Dean says, but it doesn't feel enough for me.

'How do you know?' I ask him, praying with every fibre in my being that she made a phone call that I didn't know about, or that he found a letter, that the doctor said something . . . anything. I just wish there was something that could let me know beyond a question of a doubt that she knew how loved she was.

'You know,' I say to Dean, and I know I'm making things worse with my morbid harping-on about things that can't be changed, but I just have to talk about it, I have to excise my guilt by making sure everyone knows how evil I am. 'I hadn't talked to her properly or seen her for ages. I just kept out of the way because I wanted to make a big splash when I went to see her with you and Pask. I just hadn't communicated or anything because you know what I'm like – I would have given away the fact that we were going to ask her to come for Christmas, and I didn't want to do that.'

'Listen,' says Dean. 'You did nothing wrong. She adored you, she knew how you felt about her, and Gladys and Ethel know, too. Stop beating yourself up.'

'Okay,' I say.

12.30 p.m.

The church is full. Full of elderly women come to pay their respects. 'She was so young to leave us like that,' they're saying. I guess I agree with them. On paper she was an octogenarian, but not in spirit. I remember her running around the crematorium, placing flowers on all the friends and relations she'd lost. I remember the fun and the sadness. I remember this real and vibrant person, and even as the coffin sits there, just feet away from me, I can't believe she's gone. I remember what she said once about being glad she knew so many dead people. I remember how she would say that she was eternally grateful to have known them. I don't think I ever understood that. Until now.

Despite the emotional way I feel, I'm driven to make some sort of speech. There have been poems, little eulogies, and the words of a vicar who did not know Nell. I decide to tell them about the Nell I knew, for better or for worse. I stand up and walk to the front, revealing to everyone gathered in the small church that I am wearing a black boob tube, long black boots and piles of jewellery. On my legs I am wearing bright green tracksuit bottoms.

'I have a confession to make,' I announce to the assembled black-clad guests, and I can see Dean looking worried and Ethel and Gladys smiling at me. 'Nell had a cat,' I say. There's a silence. 'She kept it at Sunnyside.'

There are sniggers from Sally and Michaela sitting next to Dean. Mich is in a strapless gold and black evening dress, and Sally is wearing a plain black polo neck and awful grey trousers.

'She's had the cat for years – Coleen, it's called. I thought of that name. When she moved into sheltered accommodation, she was told she couldn't take Coleen with her. The trouble is, Nell couldn't bear to be parted from her, so she smuggled her in. Coleen has been living under the sink for three years.'

'Coleen?' says the vicar, who's standing right next to me.

'Coleen the Cat,' I explain slowly. 'She meant everything to Nell.

'The thing is that, at night, Nell secretly let her out, then hid her in the cupboard during the day. There were a few unfortunate incidents with litter trays and the furtive disposal of soiled litter, and that time when the warden saw all the cans of Whiskas and Nell had to pretend that she ate cat food. She ended up spinning this elaborate lie in which she claimed that during the war she was reduced to eating cat food in order to survive. She'd developed quite a thing for it, she said. The warden left her sobbing into her handkerchief, and promised to donate ten pounds a month to the war-widows fund.'

I look around and only Gladys and Ethel are laughing, but they're laughing so much that I'm glad I told the tale.

'She was nuts,' I say. 'And she loved a good party. More than anything, she loved a good funeral party, so let's not let her down, eh? Let's give her a good send-off. Everyone back to ours after, for as many sherries and Black Russians as you can drink.'

I'm not sure whether the applause was appropriate but it was definitely heartfelt.

Friday, 4 January
12.05 p.m.

I don't know why I do it, I really don't. But, in an effort to be 'one of the people', and to be a normal person like my readers, I have come into London today and am travelling around this beautiful city of ours by Tube. I know, I know . . . what was I thinking of? This is not a course of action that I would advise in any way, nor is it a course of action that I will ever be taking again. It's halfway through the day now and it's been the biggest disaster ever. Let me take you back and talk you through it . . .

Flashback to 8 a.m.

I made two principal mistakes at the beginning of the day when I decided to take Ethel and Gladys into London on the train. There we go – my two major errors are outlined in that very sentence: old people and trains. Let me spell this out: you don't ever want me on a train, you don't ever want old people on a train, and you especially don't ever want me taking old people onto a train.

Taking old ladies into London is never going to be an idea that you should allow to wallow in your head for any length of time, let alone take seriously and act upon. As soon as the taxi picked the two women up, I sensed that this was not going to go well. They'd both insisted on bringing their pull-along shopping trolleys with them, which I knew would cause mayhem on the Tube. I also knew that they would lead to security guards following us around everywhere because, as I read in *Heat*, more things are stolen with those things than with any other type of bag.

Pulling into Sunnyside had been weird. I kept thinking of the number of times I'd come there to see Nell and had been forced to go through the ritual of sharing out shopping. 'One sprout for you, Ethel; one sprout for you, Gladys . . .'

'Just here,' I told the driver, and I stepped out and hobbled over the cobbles to the door. Ethel and Gladys emerged wearing their lurid-green tracksuits, of course, and I knew immediately what a horrible mistake this was all going to be.

'Are you going to be comfortable in those?' asked Ethel, pointing to my shoes. 'You know – with having to walk around the shops all day. They seem very high.'

Thanks for the fashion advice, Kermit. I'm sorry, I really don't mean to be nasty, but honestly – she's not really in the best position to start dispensing words of wisdom about clothing, style and shoes.

'I think Ethel's right, dear,' said Gladys. 'Your feet will be hurting you.'

'They're Versace mules!' I inform them. Honestly, old people. What can you do with them?

We got on a train to King's Cross, then ambled over to Waterloo so Gladys could look at the clock, and bore us with her stories about how she met her sweetheart under there.

'Ahhh . . . them was the days . . .' she said. 'They were the days when men were romantic and knew how to treat a lady.'

'My Dean knows how to treat me,' I say, and to my surprise my two elderly travelling companions nod.

'He's a real gent,' says Ethel, as I drag them back towards the underground. It turns out it's quite a long walk across the concourse, and by the time we're at the escalators, I am deeply regretting my decision to wear high heels. These are taxi shoes. You can't walk anywhere in them. It turns out tweedledum and tweedledee are right about the mules being inappropriate for a shopping trip to town, but having shrugged off Ethel's earlier concern I can't now admit that – yes, old and senile as she is – she does have a point about the mules.

'You okay, love?' says Gladys. Presumably because I'm limping a bit now. It occurs to me that while I wear high-heeled shoes all the time, I never really do any walking in them.

'I'm just fine.'

They both look down at my feet. They can smell weakness at about ten miles, and they know I'm struggling.

'Want to get in the bag?' asks Gladys with a horrible raucous laugh.

Ethel points to her own sensible, supportive, old-lady shoes and suggests I buy similar ones. I nod at her while thinking that I would rather cut my feet off than wear shoes like that. Down the steps we go to catch the Tube, and that's when I have the flashback . . . I haven't been on a Tube train for years but I remember with stunning clarity what always happens – just as I'm about to hit the platform I hear 'stand back from the doors, stand back from the doors'.

That's what I hear now . . . with two elderly ladies in tow. Oh hell. It's like they know I'm coming and think it would be really funny to watch me lurch and hurl myself through the closing doors and into the carriage.

'Come on!' I yell to the wrinklies, and I grab hold of Ethel's hand, assuming that she has grabbed Gladys's, then I hurl myself at the train in a rather unseemly and undignified way, squeezing through the closing door and making sure it doesn't close shut on Ethel. Every carriage is packed, including the one I'm aiming for. It's obvious that the sensible thing to do would be to sit calmly on a bench and wait for the next train. After all, we're in no rush. To be honest, we've got hours to kill before lunch, so sitting down for five minutes would be nice. But no! I push through the closing doors into the packed carriage, pulling Ethel behind me. All the time, I'm assuming that Ethel is pulling Gladys, though I accept that, with hindsight, such an assumption may be considered obtuse and slightly reckless. Off goes the train, leaving a distraught-looking ninety-two-year-old pitifully watching us go. All I can see is the pea-green tracksuit blurring across the windows as I frantically attempt to open them and to shout to Gladys.

'Wait there. We'll come back for you.' She has both shopping trolleys lying around by her feet. Ethel looks as if she might start crying. I think I might join her.

We get to Embankment, get off the train, run along the platform down the stairs and get onto a train to take us back to Waterloo. Ethel is almost hysterical with fear about what might happen to Gladys.

'She might be raped!' she says.

I'm worried about what might happen, too, but I would have thought that would be the least likely outcome.

'My shopping trolley might be stolen.'

Yes, a much more realistic assessment of the risks, I would have thought.

Back to Waterloo, and my lack of any sort of sense of direction throws me momentarily, then I realise that if I just go to the platform, as I did before, as if I'm off towards Embankment, then Gladys will be there, waiting for us in all her green glory.

There are lots of people on the platform but none of them is Gladys. Not one of the people is over ninety and certainly no one is wearing a green tracksuit.

'Didn't she hear us telling her to wait?' I say to Ethel.

'I wouldn't have thought so,' says Ethel. 'I don't think she's wearing her hearing aid.'

Oh, for god's sake. What do we do now?

I slip my shoes off and push them into the top of my handbag.

'I told y—' begins Ethel, but I look at her in such a threatening way that she stops mid-sentence.

12.10 p.m.

We're all sitting in a fish and chip restaurant now, and the two oldies are telling me that they want 'just a couple of chips' and are hoovering up large portions of fried potatoes, fried fish, bread and butter, mushy peas and endless cups of sugary tea. Isn't it amazing how much old people can eat?

'Do you want any more, Gladys?' I ask.

'Go on then,' she says, as if she's doing me the most enormous favour.

They've already decided they want apple tart and cream afterwards. They'll eat more calories this lunchtime than I eat all season.

We eventually found Gladys at Westminster station. What a palaver. She got confused between Waterloo and Westminster after following us to Embankment. She says she asked a man on the platform what she should do, since her friends had gone to Embankment without her by mistake. 'Follow them,' he suggested. So she did.

I think there was probably a comedy moment going on as we rushed to get back on the train to Waterloo, because I bet our train passed her train going to Embankment. Then, with no sight of Gladys at Waterloo, we travelled back to Embankment, while the deaf ninety-two-year-old heaved two shopping trolleys onto a Tube train and went off to Westminster by mistake.

In the end, I had to report to the guard that we had lost her. I described her lurid-green tracksuit and an announcement went out across London. A guard from Westminster reported back immediately that she was causing mayhem by blocking the entire platform with her bags. He took her into his hut and gave her a cup of tea. By the time we got there she was telling him all about Coleen the cat, and how Nell used to keep her in the cupboard under the sink.

I think the station manager thought the loonies had arrived when another old lady, dressed identically to the first, strode down the platform with a heavily made-up woman wearing a very short skirt and no shoes.

Monday, 7 January

WHAT SORT OF UNDERWEAR SHOULD I WEAR AS A DEVOTED WAG?

I'm going to make this nice and quick because I believe there's only one answer. Okay, so you may see some nice frilly lingerie in the shops and think that would be appropriate, or like the idea of simple elegance. Stop! There is no more lovely a sight to a red-blooded male than to tear the clothes from the body of his beloved to discover she's wearing logo-ed knickers from the club shop. They really are the only things you should be wearing. Be they Aston Villa pants, nippleless bras with 'Liverpool FC Rule' across the chest, 'Up The Blues' across the bum or 'Manchester United for the Title' across the groin – they're all perfect! Just make sure you get the right team or you won't stand a chance of scoring.

Tuesday, 15 January
7.30 p.m.

God, it's too cold to be standing outside a restaurant in London's West End.

I hate this time of year. It's kind of no-man's-land time, with Christmas so far behind us that it's forgotten – the toys are broken, the clothes have been worn and everyone's eighteen stone overweight. Any joy at the memory of Christmas morning (and, to be honest, there wasn't much for me this year because of losing Nell) has faded away. In fact it was a completely bloody miserable time all round. I tried not to think about Nell but then I kept thinking about the year I've been through, and all the horrible things that have happened. I found that the misery of losing Nell had thrown me into an introspective cycle in which I thought properly for the first time about Mum and how she'd treated me, and about my father and whether I should contact him and try to meet him.

The apology appeared in the *Sunday Journal*, of course. They were mortified at what they'd done, and claims for libel have flown in from the girls themselves. Mum, according to the rumours I've heard, has disappeared off to Spain to live with Ludo, who's been signed by some godforsaken team in the January transfer window.

Simon came round on Christmas morning to say hi and ended up staying all day, which was nice. We talked a lot about everything that had happened and Simon said that he thought I should contact my dad. I suppose he's right – America's such a long way away that there really can't be any harm in getting in touch – it's not as if I'm going to start communication, decide it's a bad idea, then keep bumping into him in the food section of Marks and Spencer's, is it? He's not going to be turning up at my house, or following me down Luton High Street, is he? I could start emailing him and just see what happens . . . if he seems nice then maybe – one day – I could go out there or he could come here. Who knows?

The other slight diversion I have managed to find for myself this long winter month is planning to shadow the Beckhams for an evening. I know I shouldn't have after the curious incident with the dog and the bacon, but I can't resist it . . . especially after the soul-searching letter I sent them on Christmas morning in which I laid my feelings for them bare. I told them all about Nell and how upsetting that all was and asked Victoria if she'd ever lost anyone really close to her and how she coped. I told them how much they meant to me. Did they care? Did they buggery! I had the letter, tucked inside a Christmas card, biked over to them, but it was no good. A bloody eight-page letter!!! I sent them a Christmas hamper too, as I do every year, but it made no difference. There just doesn't seem to be any interest on their part in making friends with me. I can't see why. I don't know what is happening in their minds to make them think that it's a bad idea to at least acknowledge me and my efforts to make amends after what happened that time. It's not like it was Victoria's dog! It's not like it was a very nice dog . . .

After the disappointment of the Beckhams not getting in touch, I read in *Heat* that they were going to The Ivy on 15 January for a special birthday dinner for one of David's friends. I read it, put the magazine down, read it again and wandered around the house. Now then, Tracie, I thought to myself. What are the chances of you being able to get yourself a table at The Ivy on 15 January? I knew I could. If you've got money you can get yourself a table; the trouble was that I feared the table would be nowhere near theirs. Still – worth a shot.

So here I am! Outside The Ivy, having left Dean and Paskia Rose watching *World Cup Howlers* – one of those Channel Five offerings that you think's going to be awful, then when you start watching it you can't stop and you end up waiting till 1 a.m. to find out which is the worst howler of all time, even though you really don't care a jot. They're also working their way through a box set of football DVDs that Dean bought Pask for Christmas.

When I think of them cuddled up on the sofa in the warm, I feel a pang of jealousy. It's cold standing here outside The Ivy in tiny white shorts in the middle of winter. I'm not completely sure what to do now that I'm here. Eating on my own is not going to be much fun – especially as I can't eat anything anyway – and the happy shiny couple have gone in under what looked like armed guard. 'Vic!' I shouted. She turned round, saw me, looked very scared, then was crowded and eased into the restaurant before I could get anywhere near her.

'If I pay you a lot of money, could I get a table near the Beckhams'?' I ask the bloke on the door.

'No,' says the bouncer.

'I have a table already – I just need to get a guarantee that it's right near theirs. I'll pay a lot of money,' I reiterate.

'No,' says the bouncer.

'Okay,' I say.

Now the question is whether it's worth going into the restaurant just to be in the same space and breathing the same air as Victoria, or whether I should head home. At least I saw her.

The thought of Dean and Pask propels me towards the car, and I leap in and tell Ronald to drive me home. He's so much nicer than Doug. More respectful. He's altogether more sophisticated and much better-looking. He used to drive opera singers around (i.e. he's dead posh). He knows the names of all sorts of operas and keeps bursting into song. His voice is terrible and I really want to laugh, but it's interesting hearing about all the fat opera singers and how much chocolate they eat. At times like this I really wish Nell was here. I miss her so much.

Monday, 4 February

HAIR REMOVAL

It goes without saying that hair on your body anywhere other than on your head, your eyebrows or eyelashes is a thoroughly bad thing. Get rid of it. If you have a facial hair problem of any description, this has to be your priority. Head for the salon and get it lasered off at top speed. You could use hair-removing cream or wax or pluck it out, but hair on the face is such an incredibly bad thing altogether that I think nuclear radars blasting through it (I think that's what the lasers are) is the only thing to do. Elsewhere on the body, hair is undesirable, too. You could go for the laser treatment all over, like I do, and like most women I know who are serious about being Wags, but if this makes you feel uncomfortable, or you have reservations about paying the ten thousand pounds that it will cost and would rather use the money to put down a deposit on a house, then you need to head for the waxing salon. You also need to stop and think about how seriously you are taking the process of becoming a Wag if you would honestly prefer to provide a home for your family than to have the hairs on your legs nuked.

Anyway, waxing – no pain without gain. First off, lose all the hair on your legs and bikini line. Don't mess around with the Hollywood, Bollywood or whatever. Just get them to rip it all off. The only exception to this is if you are interested in getting them to do some topiary down there for you. You know – marking out a Cross of St George, an initial or a football shape as they go. This can look great if done well, but if not – just stick to the 'all off' approach.

Next come underarms – mmmm . . . wax it away. You don't want to look like a chimpanzee when you raise your arms in the air. It's astonishing to me that women have this hair there. Why would we? Scientists bleat on about the hair catching the hormones that are secreted, making you irresistible to men, but – hello? –

what man is going to come near you to smell it if you've got a great big bush growing under your arms . . . No, no, no. All hair on the body needs to be removed. End of story, end of discussion. Waste no more time – just get on with it.

Tuesday, 5 February

Dean came skipping back from training today like a schoolgirl who'd been given her first cigarette.

'Guess what?' he asked.

I couldn't guess.

'No, guess. It's brilliant news!'

'Ummm . . . you've been called up for England?'

'No,' he says sulkily. 'It's not that good. Try again.'

'Luton want to sell you to Chelsea?'

'No. It's not that good. Try again.'

'I don't know.'

'Keep trying.'

'You're back in as captain?'

'No. It's not that good. Try again.'

'You're back in the team?'

'No. It's not that good. Try again.'

'You're on the bench?'

'No. It's not that good. Try again.'

'You're in the second team?'

'Oh, Trace, you've ruined everything. Now my news isn't going to sound very exciting – why did you have to say all them things?'

'Well, I don't know. I'm not very good at guessing games. What is the news?'

'Luton are going to make me deputy assistant coach.'

'Well, that's good.'

'Yes, but not yet. I've got a two-month trial in which I have to help the other coaches – you know – picking the water bottles up from the side of the pitch, making sure the cones are laid out properly. That sort of thing.'

'Great,' I say, but I'm thinking, This is the man who once played for England and now he's laying out cones for a living? 'You must be really proud of yourself.'

'Yeah,' he says, scratching himself furiously. 'Dead proud.'

Friday, 8 February
2 p.m.

He's been doing this great new coaching job for about three days and already he's bored to tears with it. I know this for a few reasons: because he keeps saying 'If I have to pick up another f***ing water bottle I'll scream', and – more significantly than that – because he keeps mumbling on and on and on again about the pub he wants to buy.

He put out 'feelers' a while back, and information has come in about a little place called the Black Bull. It's in Stockwood, just outside Luton, and Dean has asked me to come and see it with him.

We're sitting in the car outside it now, and, if I'm honest, it looks like every other pub I've ever seen, but scruffier.

'This could be our future,' he says brightly, and I feel a tight burning sensation in my chest and the words 'not on your life' flash through my mind.

'Come on, love,' he says, helping me out of the car. My white stilettos sink straight into the mud. 'It's a bikers' pub,' he says, as if this is a good thing.

'Oh,' I reply, wading through the mud and over the pebbles. This might be the scruffiest pub in the world. 'Does that make it good?' I ask.

'They tend to drink a lot, and at least you've got a regular clientele,' he explains.

I'm just nodding now, because as we get closer to this place it looks more and more awful.

I push the door and walk in. Then I see the dartboard and the large-bellied men. I smell the beer, pork scratchings and dogs and walk straight out of the next door without stopping.

'Nice, isn't it?' says Dean with a smile, when he emerges twenty minutes later to find me coating myself in perfume.

'Er, no,' I say. 'I think you should stick with coaching.'

'Okay, you're probably right,' he shrugs. 'But I thought it was great.'

Saturday, 9 February
10.30 a.m.

Dean's just left. He's going to be gone all weekend, sorting out the visit from the LA team. He seems to think it's going to be the most exciting thing to happen to Luton. I have to disagree. The most exciting thing to happen to Luton was when they opened the shopping centre with tanning beds and everything. I was only twelve, and I think I cried with happiness that night. I'm not sure I've ever been quite as happy since.

Sunday, 10 February
3 p.m.

It's so funny being at home without Dean. I suppose I got used to it through his playing career, but now it feels odd not having him around. He's been phoning every five minutes, of course, but that's not the same as being able to look over and see his tattooed torso and reach out and touch him, running my hands across his heavy gold jewellery and his hairless chest. He said this morning that all the planning has gone brilliantly, Paskia's team are looking really good. (I had to get him to qualify that – after the *Sunday Journal* piece I'm a bit nervous when he makes comments that could be misconstrued – but it turns out he means that their footballing skills are really good.) The girls have worked hard and they've got a real chance to impress this bunch of Americans.

Monday, 11 February
11.30 a.m.

Simon . . . bless him! Is he the nicest man in the world or what? He's only gone and had a meeting with the publishers this morning. He thought I had too much on my plate, so he went on his own, just to make sure we don't lose the deal. He explained about everything I've been through and asked them whether, in light of that, we could do a book that is just my advice, without any of the details about my childhood.

'They said okay,' squeals Simon. 'We can still do the book – we should dedicate it to Nell.'

There's good news and bad news, as it turns out. The publishers need the manuscript by the end of May in order for it to be published in August to coincide with the beginning of the new season (that's the bad news – will have to get cracking, no time to waste). The good news is that it only has to be fifty thousand words of advice for would-be Wags. There will be line drawings in it that will take up the rest of the room, as well as quizzes and fantastic advice on Wag wardrobes (all modelled by me!!!) and Wag hair and make-up (me again!!).

BOOKS

The truth is that Wags shouldn't read – not really. But such is the process of evolution and the amount of wording on packaging in today's society that Wags have had to start learning to read in order to know how to operate their straighteners. What is very clear, though, is that Wags should not read books. If you're caught flicking through anything over 300 words (I make sure that my columns are never any longer) then you need to think clearly about whether you are operating within the spirit of Wag law. Now, I have a confession to make at this stage, because I, Tracie Martin (heart over the 'i' if you're writing it down, remember), am going to be writing a book. Don't worry, though – I haven't become a lesbian or a communist or anything. The book will be easy to read, full of pictures, and each little piece of advice I give will not in any way break the 300-word rule, nor contain words likely to cause offence (i.e. difficult ones). I am hoping that, come August when my book is out, it will be the only book you will ever need to read.

Okay, so my little literary offering may not trouble the Booker Prize judges, but anything that troubles them would be as welcome in my handbag as an expired credit card. Most books are overrated and don't have pictures. This one will. It will be easy to follow and fun to read.

SUITABLE JOBS FOR A WANNABE WAG

If you are a Wag then I don't expect you to be working, so this advice is really for women and girls with their hearts set on becoming a Wag. From the outset I would like to make it very clear that to become a Wag you shouldn't get a job in football. Don't take a job as club secretary or working in the club shop thinking you're going to meet lots of players. The simple fact is that no woman working in the football world has ever made it to the top rung of the Wag ladder. Indeed, the industry that produces 107 per cent of all Wags (roughly – I haven't checked it) is the beauty industry. I would urge you most strongly to remember this simple motto: if you want a man who plays the beautiful game, then you need to get a job making people beautiful (© Tracie Martin 2007). Whether you're a nail technician, a tanning specialist, a facialist, a make-up artist or a hairdresser, your chances of ending up with the man of your dreams are greatly improved simply by this choice of profession. There are just a couple of other things that you must ensure. First, the salon should be within half a mile of a football ground. Second, every time a football player walks past the salon, you should either flash your boobs or peer out at him seductively through streaks of plastic hair extensions, chewing (open-mouthed) on a mouthful of bubble gum. It's worth bearing in mind that bubble gum is a better flirting tool than chewing gum because you can blow bubbles in a teasing manner – just make sure the bubbles don't burst all over your face!

Saturday, 16 February
4 p.m.

I want to get Paskia Rose and Dean 'good luck' cards for when the Los Angeles girls come, but I've found myself distracted and I'm in Gucci, surrounded by bags from Dolce and Gabbana, Versace and Selfridges. I love it! The only problem with being such an avid shopper are the USIs (Unidentifiable Shopping Injuries). I end up with bangs all over my shins from the bags, blisters on my feet, and always odd bruises that I can't account for. It's a treacherous business, shopping. I need one of those blokes with the buckets and sponges like they have down at Luton.

I lay my garments out on the counter and look up at the assistant. Behind her there's a large ornate mirror. In the mirror I see Mindy, Julie and Debs enter the shop. They wander around a bit, pick up some items and all three head for the changing rooms. I pay for my handbag and matching shoes, and a lovely pink top, and walk after them into the changing room.

'Hello,' I say, pulling back the curtains of the three cubicles.

'Ahhh,' cries Mindy, then she sees me. 'Tracie, what are you doing here?'

She's bright red and her hands have flown down to cover herself. I look more closely and see why.

'Mindy, how interesting,' I remark. 'Your underwear doesn't match.'

There's a cry of horror from the other dressing rooms, and Julie and Debs walk out (in matching lingerie, I'm pleased to report).

'It's true!' says Julie in dismay.

'Oh my god!' says Debs.

'There's something else you don't know about Mindy,' I say. 'She's been calling me up and inviting me out.'

'Ahhhhh,' say the Slag Wags in perfect harmony.

'She's invited me to parties and drinks evenings and said all her friends are big fans of my column. The thing is – I don't return the calls, because you're not worth the effort. Look at you – you may look perfect on the outside but underneath you're all bad, all wrong. Underneath, Mindy, you're nothing but mismatched lingerie.'

With that, I spin on my heels and charge out of the shop, swinging my bag recklessly as I charge down New Bond Street.

Ah. Revenge. So, so sweet.

Sunday, 24 February
9 a.m.

Today's the day. After months of preparation and hours upon hours of tactical discussions with Paskia Rose, this is the day when the LA players arrive in town. They're due to arrive at 2 p.m., but Dean has been up, shaved, dressed and pacing around since shortly after midnight. He's far more nervous about the performances of these girls than he has ever been about the performances of Luton Town.

'But the girls – they're all me,' he says, rather alarmingly, when I ask.

'What I mean is, everything that the girls have become, all the skills they have learned, I taught them. Sally helped, of course. In fact, she's been a great help and she'll make a brilliant coach one day, but I was in charge. I was the one organising things and making them happen. I liked that. It was my hard work and now it's paying off. It's different with Luton Town because there's a whole team of coaches there – it would be hard to say which of the coaches is responsible if a team does well. But these girls – they came to me like starlings with broken wings and I've nursed them, tended to them, I've built them up and made them strong, and now I'm ready to release them out onto the international football stage.'

I'm just looking at him now, but not in a bad way. It's just that I'm not used to Dean talking in this kind of romantic way. It's nice.

'I've never heard you be so enthusiastic before,' I say.

'I've never felt so enthusiastic before,' he replies. 'I love coaching these girls because they want to learn, and I'm full of confidence that they will win hands-down against these American impostors.'

I give him a big kiss, one which he heartily deserves. 'And I'll be supporting you all the way,' I say. And I will. I've bought some new clothes especially for it.

Monday, 25 February
9 a.m.

They have arrived. Dean is in a deep depression. It turns out the girls are very big. Their smallest is bigger than our tallest.

Tuesday, 26 February
11 a.m.

Dean is both relieved and angry today. He's found out why the players from LA are so much bigger than our players – it's because they are two years older. Some sort of muddle-up has meant that the thirteen- and fourteen-year-olds are over here. What should he do? He shouldn't play eleven-year-olds against them, but these girls have been training for months for this moment.

'Sod it,' is his verdict on the morality and safety of playing the two sides against each other. 'Let 'em play.'

It's going to be like that Russell Crowe film where they wear the sacks and the dreadful sandals.

Wednesday, 5 March
10.30 a.m.

The day of the match, and I'm told that I'd be mad to miss it. Yeah, sure – every mother wants to go along and watch her daughter being bashed around and chopped down by someone twice her size. I'm going along to watch, but only under duress. It's clear from what Dean said that our only chance of success is if Paskia Rose has a good game. She's the best player by a mile and only she can help the team to victory. It seems an inordinate amount of pressure on her shoulders, but Dean keeps convincing me that champions thrive on pressure, and that our dear daughter is nothing less than a champion in waiting. 'You'll see,' he says, and I'm starting to believe that I will.

5 p.m.

That was unbelievable. It was Paskia Rose against the whole of Los Angeles! You should have heard those LA parents! Blimey, they can shout! Pask scored a goal; LA scored a goal; Pask scored a goal; LA scored a goal. It was 3–3 at half-time and 6–6 at full-time. In extra time Pask scored twice. The coach on the opposition's side couldn't believe what he was seeing. He asked Dean how he got the girls so fit and tactically astute, and the way Dean explained the training regime it sounded like something from East Germany. I'm sure he'll get arrested if anyone hears him talking like that.

'You're a star coach, and she's a star player,' the guy is saying, and I know instinctively that we'll have another couple of those Visible Pantyline trophies to take home with us.

20 March – my birthday (sshhhhhhhhh . . .)

'Surprise!' she says, and I open my eyes to see a freckly, plain-looking girl, clutching a flamboyantly decorated pink cake. I know I should be flattered, I know I should be thrilled that she remembered but . . . 'For God's sake, Pask. Don't you know by now that I NEVER celebrate my birthday?!'

Paskia Rose takes a step back and almost trips over my pink mules. She steadies herself and looks at me. 'But why, Mum?' she says. 'Why don't you celebrate it?'

My daughter is more stupid than I ever imagined possible. Does she know nothing?

'Because I don't want to get any older. I'm quite old enough!'

'But just because you don't celebrate your birthday doesn't mean you won't get old,' she says.

'This sort of perverse logic isn't getting us anywhere,' I respond, rather too aggressively, if I'm honest.

'Oh,' says Paskia, clearly hurt.

I decide I ought to try and act like other mothers, not something I can usually be found guilty of, so I prepare to make like I'm interested in the culinary creation before me. I sit up to look more closely at the cake. Is that Barbie on it? Actually, it's quite sweet.

'A real tour de France,' I declare.

Unfortunately, the sudden sound of my voice prompts Paskia to take a step back again, but this time she fails to steady herself as she tumbles over my mules. She pitches forward, still holding the cake, and suddenly all I can see is pink and white heading straight for me. A fraction of a second later and it's hit me full in the face. I can taste the creamy icing and just the sensation of it on my lips makes me feel like I'm putting on weight. I'm digging Jelly Tots out of my eyes and nose.

'You like Jelly Tots,' Paskia is saying, defensively. 'I put them on especially.'

'I like eating them,' I respond. 'Not wearing them in my eye sockets.'

'Oh,' says Pask, looking at me.

Then we both burst out laughing. It's just giggling at first, but before long, I'm crying and choking on Victoria sponge, jam and lumps of fondant icing. There's cake all over the bed, in my hair and in my ears. Still we laugh, howling and wiping the tears from our eyes.

'Happy birthday, Mum,' she says, and for some reason I can't explain, I'm suddenly really pleased she chucked cake all over me.

'Come and give me a big hug,' I say, reaching for my daughter as she screams and squirms away from me. 'Come here,' I demand, getting out of the bed and walking up the corridor, Dalek-like, with my hands outstretched and covered in cake.

'No,' she screams again, running downstairs away from the cake-covered monster pursuing her. She reaches the bottom of the stairs and looks up at me.

'Mum,' she says.

'Yes.'

'I think you're great. Have I ever told you that before?'

'No,' I say, startled, touched and utterly thrilled. 'No, you haven't.'

'Well, I do,' she says. I think this might be the best birthday ever.

HOW SHOULD A WAG THINK OF NAMES FOR HER CHILDREN?

One thing that can really help you to stand out in a crowd, and ensure that you are clearly identified as a Wag, is to give your children utterly ridiculous names. If it's a girl, it should always be double-barrelled and of almost sick-inducing girliness. Ideally it should be the sort of name that you'd give to a perfume. My daughter is called Paskia Rose – that should give you some idea of the level you're aspiring to. If I ever had another girl, I'd call her Fifi Fluff-Fluff Daffodil or Sweetpea-Precious or something like that. Any names with Princess, Lady or Femme in them are also very good.

When it comes to boys' names, you obviously need to lose the femininity but be no less absurd. The Beckhams have set a ludicrously high standard in this area, with Brooklyn, Romeo and Cruz. Names like Wolf, Spear and Hunter are also good. If you think of the sort of names that all-in wrestlers might call themselves, you won't go far wrong. If you want double-barrelled, try names like Lightning-Wolf or Mountain-Spear. Be aware, though, that your child will amount to nothing with a name like this, and that most boys who play for England are called names like David, Wayne, Terry and Frank. And Dean.

HOW SHOULD A WAG PLAN HER WEDDING?

He's finally proposed and has shown just how much he loves you by presenting you with a ring so massive that your finger keeps dislocating under the weight of it. You are going to make that crucial transformation from girlfriend to wife. You are also going to be able to indulge in every Wag's fantasy ... a wedding. You may even discover, if he gives you enough money to plan the event properly, that you are starting to fall in love with him.

There is much you need to bear in mind when you're planning the ideal Wag wedding, but these three instructions must ALWAYS be borne in mind:

1. There must be a fairytale theme.

So, think pretty, pink palomino horses, carriages, huge dresses, thrones, crowns, winged angels, fairies, glitter, bunny rabbits. Make sure you look like Cinderella. Think of yourself as a fairytale heroine – a small, delicate creature being swept right off her feet by a handsome prince. All the usual Wag rules still apply – loads of make-up, very long hair, plenty of jewellery, very high shoes and a terrifyingly expensive dress. Make sure the venue looks like a castle and that the cake is bigger than the groom.

2. You must spend as much money as humanly possible, and be clear and overt about how expensive and extravagant everything is.

3. You must sell out at every opportunity.

So – Hello! *magazine want a picture spread?* – Yes!

The local paper *want pictures of all the guests?* – Yes!

The Sun *wants to sell your garter on line?* – Yes!

The Sunday Sport *wants pictures of the consummation?* – Yes!

WHERE SHOULD A WAG GO ON HOLIDAY?

It's come to that time of year when a Wag's thoughts may drift from shopping and beautifying, to the planning of a holiday. Where should she go? What places are Wagerific and which should be avoided?

Well, when it comes to holidays, as when it comes to anything, how you look is obviously the most important thing to consider. What will look good in the photographs? What will impress the other Wags?

Somewhere hot is vital – you want sun in the photographs and you want to be able to wear very few clothes. But remember, as you're hunting for the sun, that you need to find somewhere with as few locals as possible. So, while it may be hot in India, this is clearly not a great destination unless you head for somewhere more touristy like Goa, because the cities are just teeming with locals and many of them are poor. You're much better off in the Caribbean, or in the more popular areas of France and Spain. Clearly, the Canary Islands are ideal – Lanzarote and Tenerife. How could you go wrong? Hire a yacht and pose on it all day, then get completely trousered in the nightclubs of an evening. Cover yourself in baby oil by day and night and head for an early evening drink at the sort of bars that encourage wet T-shirt competitions. You'll be able to get egg and chips for your man and there'll be plenty of shops selling big gold jewellery. Book it NOW.

WHAT SORT OF MUSIC SHOULD A WAG LISTEN TO?

Well not that classical shit for a start! If it hasn't got words, switch it off. Music sung by women is usually the best. The Pussycat Dolls are exceptional, as are Sugababes and (obviously!!) Girls Aloud and The Spice Girls.

There are a couple of others worth looking out for – 'Barbie Girl' by Aqua is brilliant, as is 'Saturday Night' by Whigfield. Anything entered into the Eurovision Song Contest is pure Wag territory, as are the sorts of songs played at weddings, for example 'Power Of Love' by Jennifer Rush.

If you want to listen to male singers, stick to ballads, nothing too heavy. Go for 'Love Is All Around' by Wet, Wet, Wet, or 'Back for Good' by Take That.

It goes without saying that if you and fellow Wags are asked to sing karaoke, ALWAYS go for 'I Will Survive' by Gloria Gaynor.

Monday, 14 April
2 p.m.

I have never worked so hard in my entire life. I've spent the past month furiously bashing away on the computer trying to get as many interesting tips and articles written for the book. I'm sending them through by email to Simon and he's checking them and liaising with the artist who's doing the line drawings to go with them. They're sending through cover ideas soon, which will be amazing. I'm sure they will want my creative advice, the best of which is pink – it has to be pink!

Tuesday, 15 April
4.30 p.m.

Paskia Rose came home from school today, kicked off her shoes, stuck on her football boots and went out into the garden as usual. Once there, she belted the ball with unusual vigour at the poor trees, shaking them from their roots to the tips of their leaves. Her aim was perfect, the swing of her leg looked ideal, and I could see what so many have seen – my daughter is a truly talented football player. And yet, even through the lovely French doors looking down into the topiaried garden, I could tell something was wrong.

She saw me looking and walked back up to the house.

'You know,' she said. 'The most exciting thing in the whole wide world happened today, but I'm scared to tell you.'

'Scared?'

'Yes. Because if you say no all my dreams will be over.'

'Pask!' I say, alarmed that she would think me capable, let alone willing, to end all her dreams at a stroke. 'Tell me.'

'I've got to wait until Dad comes home.'

'Why?'

'Because it's his dream too,' says my daughter.

Now she can see my look of general bafflement changing to a look of concern, and she realises she'll have to tell me before Dean comes back.

'Okay, but pretend I didn't tell you,' says Paskia Rose, and I am forced to make a deal with an eleven-year-old.

'The guys from Los Angeles want me to go out there. They are prepared to offer me a scholarship in an American school, and I can start in September.'

'You're not going over there on your own. Are they insane?' I say. It's like those Russian tennis players and Romanian gymnasts, taken away from their families as soon as they can walk and forced to train twenty-five hours a day.

'No, not by myself, they want to make Dad the President of Football Coaching and Operations at the club.'

My god! They've asked Dean to be a President in America! I can picture myself as the First Lady. But much better dressed than that Hillary.

'Dad says that if he takes the job he might be able to offer Sally a job over there as a coach.'

'And when did all this happen?'

'Today,' says Paskia Rose. 'Can we go, Mum, please? The Beckhams are out there so you could be friends with them.'

Oooo . . . now that's true. And that *would* be fun.

'And Tom Cruise would pop round and say hello, and all these film stars.'

Mmmmm . . .

'I'll have to think about it,' I say. 'Let's wait till your father comes home and we'll all talk it through.'

Wednesday, 16 April
2 a.m.

We've been talking through the whole thing all night, and there's no getting away from it – going to LA would suit us all incredibly well. Since the bust-up with Mum, I have nothing to tie me to Luton. With the difficult situation with Dean at the club, where they want him to do nothing more than clear away the tracksuits, even though he's shown himself capable of being an outstanding coach already, it's only a matter of time before that relationship comes to an end, which means he has nothing to tie him to Luton either. Nell's death and Paskia Rose's eagerness to go combine to produce an irresistible cocktail. Almost as irresistible as a Cosmopolitan. We sit up doing that thing where you write down pros and cons. The pros list is about eighty-five times as long as the cons list, which only has the house, Suzzi, Mich and Simon on it. When I called Simon earlier today he was horrified when I said I was planning to move to LA. 'I love you,' he blurted out. That was a bit alarming but when he got no response from me, he said he'd come out to stay and we could write a follow-up book about a Wag in LA. There's no reason, in other words, why we shouldn't go. The really great thing, of course, is that I'd still be a Wag – more Nancy than Posh, but hell! Who cares! Vic will be my new best friend.

This morning I pressed the button on my computer twice. First to send my book to the publishers', then to book our tickets to LA. We're going! I can hardly believe it, but after the year I've had here I can't wait to get away. There's been quite a lot of negotiating, stalling, rethinking and changing plans on the deal and the payment for Dean when he gets there. The money is not as good as it would be if he were playing, but there are huge success bonuses which mean that if he manages to notch up a few victories, which we all know he can, then he'll be making a fortune.

I've been talking to some media people in LA, too – the publisher put me on to them and they're keen to promote the book over there and make a big hit of it. They think they should be able to get Posh to help promote it because she's signed up to the same publisher. Imagine that!!!! We really will end up being great mates then. The Slag Wags will be reading all about me in *Heat* and the newspapers. Ha! I hope Mum sees it too.

'All done?' asks Dean, as he stumbles through the door with piles of carrier bags.

'All booked,' I confirm.

'What are they?' he asks, indicating the pile of envelopes on the edge of my desk, all addressed, stamped and ready to go.

'Just a few goodbye letters,' I explain, and in many ways that's true. They are letters to be sent as I leave the country. The letters are addressed to every player and every Wag at Luton Town football club. They contain photocopies of Mum's birth certificate as well as photocopies of the before and after pictures that Simon found when we went round to Mum's house that fateful day.

'Any regrets?' asks Dean.

'Only that Nell won't be coming with us.'

'Now that', says Dean, 'would have been worth seeing. Nell in LA! Bloody brilliant.'

Dean smiles, and wraps his arms around me, and I know we've done the right thing. I just hope they understand Wagdom in LA. I hope they have proper hair-extensions places and proper fake-tanning booths. I really don't want to go a stunning shade of Californian tan. I want to be orange. I don't want natural sunlit streaks through my hair – I want it to be artificial in every way. I'm terrified that they don't seem to like dressing up there, and that they mince around the place in flip-flops instead of taking their chances on mountainous heels. Most of all, though, I find myself in the uncommon position of hoping that my little family will be happy. How quaint is that? Don't tell anyone. If they ask, tell them that Tracie Martin (small heart above the 'i' in Tracie, don't forget!) spun on her high heels and headed for the airport in the tiniest skirt imaginable. Tell them I shouted 'Whooah' as I left, and flashed my marabou-fringed knickers before downing three bottles of Cristal. I can't imagine what they're going to make of me in Los Angeles . . .

Acknowledgements

Many thanks to everyone who helped with the book. To Sheila Crowley, my glamorous and increasingly young-looking agent (it's Pilates, apparently, though I'm inclined to think that it's the late night singing that keeps her so young); and to the fantastic Maxine Hitchcock – my sympathetic, intelligent and hard-working editor. As a writer, one is trained to dislike editors and publishers, but I find myself in the unfamiliar and uncomfortable position of having found all at AVON great to work with – fun, professional and understanding. So to all the team there – an enormous, heart-felt thank you for all your support, encouragement and hard work – specifically Keshini Naidoo, though I wish she hadn't introduced me to Facebook, and Caroline Ridding for her backing and enthusiasm from start to finish. To the rest of the team there, too, working behind the scenes to get books onto shelves and into people's hands – from sales, to design, proof-reading and marketing – thank you. Thanks to the promotions team at Midas, especially Katrina Power whose creative thinking sometimes left me terrified, but never failed to impress!

Thanks to Louise Voss for reading it at the last minute and reassuring me by laughing a lot, and to George Kervin-Evans who was my sounding board all the way through – if he didn't laugh, it didn't go in the book.

Thanks, finally, to the Wags themselves for inspiring this character and this story. The book is a spoof, of course – it's a lighthearted, silly and funny bound through Wag territory. But Tracie Martin herself is a huge success – she's warm, bright, engaging and more knowing than many of those who seek to denigrate her. Here's hoping that Victoria, Coleen and the one who always wears crop-tops get the joke!

Inside the mind of Tracie Martin

1. Tracie, you're obviously a style icon in your own right, but who you would say has been the biggest influence on your look?

    I'm most inspired by women who have class and sophistication – like Jodie Marsh, Jordan and Chantelle from *Big Brother*. But my number one style icon is Victoria Beckham . . . the queen of class, sophistication and matching shoes and handbags. She is the woman I most admire . . . I am impressed with everything about her – from her ability to breathe in those tight corset dresses to her ability to walk in those crippling, stilt-like shoes.

2. As well as being Luton Town's most famous WAG, you are now part of the literary scene and can add 'author' to your list of achievements. Can you name any books that have inspired your unique writing style?

    Coleen's book has influenced me most because of its lovely pink cover. It's probably nice inside too, but I haven't looked. Victoria Beckham's book is great because everything about her is perfect, and I really like *Heat* magazine, *Hello!* and *OK*.

3. What do you say about the controversy by certain managers saying that footballers are too influenced by their wives when it comes to choosing a team, with wives insisting on being near designer shops, meaning that 'less glamorous' clubs lose out on new players?

    How can any manager say that WAGs are too influential? If WAGs were influential, there would be fluffy pink covers on all the seats in the stands, there would be champagne and Bacardi Breezers served instead of lager, and the teams would play football inside where it's nice and warm. There would be shops like Cricket dotted around the stadium and make-up artists and hairdressers on hand at all times.

4. **Which five guests would you have at your dream dinner party (or private booth at Chinawhites!)?**

Obviously, Sexy Becksy will be there (sorry, that's Lady Victoria Beckham to you), Jordan and Jodie can come because they like a party. Then Coleen and Alex Curran. Then I'd like Kerry Katona, Daniella Westbrook and Cheryl Cole. There – that's five, isn't it? The party would be interesting. Not much would be eaten so there'd be plenty of food left for Posh and Jordan to hurl at one another. What fun!

Available at
ASDA
~~£6.99~~ £3.86
there's no place like ASDA
A WAG ABROAD
Watch out LA:
here she comes!
Tracie Martin is back! Can she survive LA with her pride, bank balance and marriage – not to mention her fake tan – intact?
OUT
JULY 24TH!
ALISON KERVIN